# A Trashy Affair

## by

## Lynn Shurr

**A Trashy Affair**

Cover Art by *Cover Artist*

The Wild Rose Press, Inc.
PO Box 708
Adams Basin, NY 14410-0708
Visit us at www.thewildrosepress.com

Publishing History
First Champagne Rose Edition, 2014
Print ISBN 978-1-62830-050-5
Digital ISBN 978-1-62830-051-2

Published in the United States of America

**As Jane approached, the man stood up and up,** a six-footer at the very least. At five-four, five-six in heels, she wasn't that short, but still he loomed over her in a threatening way. His big jaw with its blue-black shadow added to the effect. Turned up on his broad shoulders and tucked behind his ears, his dark hair needed trimming. His cheeks were gaunt and his nose a sharp blade. Under black brows, a pair of eyes that sparkling shade of electric blue she usually found attractive stared directly at her.

Jane released the beer cans to clatter at his feet. "I'm not afraid of you no matter how tall and big you are."

"I hope not." He unleashed a huge, white grin, the same kind of smile the Big Bad Wolf must have given Little Red Riding Hood before devouring her, but he immediately subdued it. "My granny always told me to stand up when a lady enters the room."

"This is not a room." She bit off each word and spit them at him.

"No. We could go inside, but I don't have much furniture, only a king-sized bed right now."

The pig! "I have no desire to see your bed no matter what the size. I came about these cans you continue to toss into my ditch." Jane gestured dramatically toward the small heap of bright aluminum.

"My mama says we should throw our cans by the road for the homeless guy on the bicycle to find because he need the money. Helping the poor, you know."

"Helping the poor, my ass! You are littering."

He looked over her head at her ass and nodded with approval. "My mama isn't right."

## Dedication

For Lois Grant,
a great storyteller,
and Julie Williams Champagne Vidos,
a wonderful librarian,
both of whom said they would love to have
a book entitled *A Trashy Affair* dedicated to them.

~

And also for all those
who care enough about the earth to recycle.

Chapter One

Sunset, her favorite time of day. Jane Marshall leaned back in the porch swing, took a sip of red wine, and prepared to enjoy the show of a blazing yellow sun embedded in sheets of orange and pink clouds sinking behind the row of longleaf pines across the way. The open oval in the lattice on the far side of the porch where she'd trained the wisteria vine provided a perfect frame for the spectacle, always outstanding this time of year, when the farmers burnt off the cane fields. She loved Louisiana where even in November she could sit outside wearing a light skirt and blouse at five p.m., the temperature being about seventy-five today. Better yet, a morning frost earlier in the week kept the mosquito population down.

A glint of silver caught her eye—not a meteor, not a speeding bullet—but a flattened beer can sailing over the wrought iron fence surrounding the newly built townhouses across the two-lane road running in front of her house. It landed in her drainage ditch, the one she constantly had to clean of other people's rubbish simply because she lived near the new stoplight. Drivers felt free to toss their soft drink cups and fried chicken boxes there while waiting for the light to change. She glared at the man who sat on the front stoop of one of the identical houses along with a six-pack of tall aluminum cans minus one.

This aspect of Louisiana she did not love.

He probably could not see her. The wisteria had gotten a little out of hand, and the large azaleas across the front of the house were badly overgrown and needed cutting back. But last weekend she'd helped the local humane society with pet adoptions in Chapelle's town square. The weekend before that, she ran the 10K race in support of breast cancer survivors—and finished despite not making a very good time. At the end of the next week, she'd signed on to serve a holiday meal to the poor, and right after Thanksgiving would be wrapping presents in the mall to benefit a diabetes association. The yard work must wait a little longer.

A second crushed can from the same source tumbled into her ditch like a piece of a falling satellite. Not too long ago, she could look north and see rows of sugarcane bending like green waves in the wind. Now, she had a view of the townhouses, all the same except for different colored shutters. At least, the builder had sprung for a couple of live oak saplings on either end of the row.

Jane did not entirely place the blame on the beer-swilling guy, big lout that he was. Ste. Jeanne d'Arc Parish no longer had a recycling program thanks to her. Armed with all the knowledge supplied by her degree in Renewable and Sustainable Resources, she could not convince the parish council members to continue the project. Of course, they ignored her recommendations on the new garbage collection contract, too, and what a disaster that turned out to be. Despite writing the specifications herself, despite telling the all-male governing body that Burl Oubre Waste Hauling did not meet those specifications, they'd signed on with this local man anyhow, cutting out black-owned, always reliable Senegal Trash Services.

Jane closed her eyes and saw red behind her lids. Again in her memory, her arch-nemesis on the council, Bernard Freeman, rose to make his point, or more likely to intimidate her with his height and bulk and five o'clock shadow. "Look, little lady, my constituents expect us to make the best use of their tax dollars and create jobs. Mr. Oubre, here, is one of our own and will hire more workers once he gets this contract. He submitted the low bid. We have to go with the lowest bid. It's the law."

Forced to look up at the councilman, she stared directly into his hard blue eyes and replied, "My name is Ms. Marshall. We do not have to give this company the contract if it cannot meet our specifications. I personally visited Mr. Oubre's landfill. His equipment is too old and inadequate to serve an entire parish. I strongly suspect the landfill itself is in violation of several environmental laws. What will you do if it is shut down?"

Burl Oubre, better known as Bubba to his cronies, stood up in the audience. Fond of saying, "My name is pronounced oob which rhymes with boob," he'd put on an LSU tie, though he'd never attended any college, and an ill-fitting mustard-yellow sports coat left unbuttoned to accommodate his paunch. He rubbed the gray stubble on his chin. "I plan to fix all that once I get the money from the contract, honey."

"By his own admission, Mr. Oubre's company does not meet our standards. Nor is he able to provide recycling services. As parish environmental project manager, I ask you to decline his bid." At that moment, she'd felt like the wholesome filling sandwiched between a moldy crust and a piece of processed white bread—the garbage collector and the slick real estate developer/councilman.

"Mizzz Marshall." Freeman drew out the honorific and earned a chuckle from Bubba Oubre. "Only twelve hundred out of twenty-two thousand parish residents bother to recycle. The program costs three hundred thousand dollars per year. Our people want lower taxes, more jobs. We cannot afford to recycle at such a high cost." Showing off his best side, his beautifully cut silver hair, and his finely tailored navy blue suit, he played to a single news camera taping the meeting, not to Jane.

"It's a matter of educating the public, Mr. Freeman. I go to schools and civic organizations every month encouraging people to save our environment, to—"

The parish president, dumpy, bald, tired in the eyes, and usually one of her supporters, banged his gavel. "We need to move on with the agenda. Can I have a motion to take the bid under advisement?"

Freeman so moved. Seconded. And she knew that Oubre would get the contract and recycling would be suspended.

Jane opened her eyes just in time to see another beer can—this one simply squeezed in the middle and not flattened—wing its way into her ditch, an ugly bird settling in the weeds. Well, she'd had it. She might not have any power with the parish council, but by damn, she could take down one obnoxious jerk. Setting down her wine glass before she broke the stem in her rage, she stomped to the steep-sided trench that kept her yard from flooding in the frequent heavy rains. Heedless of lurking snakes or broken bottles, snagging her hosiery or muddying her pumps, she descended to its bottom and found all three of the cans. Charging up and out onto the verge of the roadway, she crossed the street and entered the gates of Cane View Chateaus. Yeah, this guy still had a view from his upstairs rear bedroom and most likely did not appreciate it one bit.

As she approached, the man stood up and up, a six-footer and then some. At five-four, five-six in heels, she was not *that* short, but still he loomed over her in a threatening way. His big jaw with its blue-black shadow added to the effect. Turned up on his broad shoulders and tucked behind his ears, his dark hair needed trimming. His cheeks were gaunt and his nose a sharp blade. Under black brows, a pair of eyes that sparkling shade of electric blue she usually found attractive stared directly at her.

Jane released the beer cans to clatter at his feet. "I'm not afraid of you no matter how tall and big you are."

"I hope not." He unleashed a huge, white grin, the same kind of smile the Big Bad Wolf must have given Little Red Riding Hood before devouring her, but he immediately subdued it. "My granny always told me to stand up when a lady enters the room."

He probably ate that granny right after she taught him some manners. "This is not a room." She bit off each word and spit them at him.

"No. We could go inside, but I don't have much furniture, only a king-size bed right now."

The pig! "I have no desire to see your bed no matter what the size. I came about these cans you continue to toss into my ditch." Jane gestured dramatically toward the small heap of bright aluminum.

"My mama told me we should always throw our cans by the road for the homeless guy on the bicycle to find because he needs the money. Helping the poor, you know. She heard someone say that once and believed it strongly."

"Helping the poor, my ass! You are littering."

He looked over her head at her ass and nodded with approval. "My mama isn't right."

"Damn straight she isn't right. Our parish might not have a recycling program right now, but you could at least save these cans in a garbage bag until we get one started again."

"I mean Mama isn't right in the head."

"Oh! I'm so sorry. Is she bipolar, depressed?" Groping for more mental illnesses, Jane knew her face turned the same color as her bright red blouse.

"Nope. Just simple. She was born a twin. Stayed in the birth canal too long waiting for the other one to be born. Oxygen starved, but she did better than her brother. He died premature."

Jane stooped to retrieve the cans and hide her embarrassed face with the two wings of her chin-length bob. Right now, she wished she had hair as long as Rapunzel. She handed the fellow the squashed aluminum. "Would you save them for a while, please?"

"Sure. Why don't you sit down and have a beer? Still three left. I like to watch the sun go down." He gestured with one large hand toward his stoop. The other held all three smashed cans.

After her rudeness, Jane felt obligated to take a seat on the cool cement step and try to explain herself. "No thanks on the beer."

He sprawled beside her, his long, jeans-clad legs stretched down the length of the short flight of stairs. After forming a pyramid of the crushed cans, he freed another beer from the six-pack ring, popped the top, and took a gulp. Setting his drink aside, he held out a hand sprinkled across the back and knuckles with short, black hairs.

"Merlin Tauzin. Don't call me Mer, Lin, or Merry. Merlin is okay, but most folks call me Blackie."

Thinking he did resemble the villain in an old western movie, Jane placed her hand in his, fully expecting him to prove his masculinity by crushing her small bones. "Jane Marshall, parish environmental project manager. Sorry I went off on you. Recycling has been discontinued, and I can't seem to convince the council to bring it back. My fault. I mistook you for the kind of guy who throws his cigarette butts down in parking lots and walks away."

Surprisingly, he clasped both of his hands, chilly from the sweating aluminum, around hers and gave a gentle shake. "They're a bunch of dumb-asses, the council. And I don't smoke. I chew." He turned his head and hawked a gob of spit into the mulch surrounding a decorative crepe myrtle planted between the townhouse stoops.

Jane ripped her hand away, intending to leave at once. His big white, unstained teeth showed again briefly. She regarded the clear sputum sinking into the earth and settled down again. "You don't chew either."

"Just having some fun with you. Can't chew and drink beer at the same time, though I might know some dudes offshore who can." He took another swig.

"You work offshore?"

"Yep, seven days on, seven days off. I fly work crews out to the oil rigs."

"You seem to drink a lot for a helicopter pilot."

"Not at all when I'm on, much as I want when I'm off. Twelve hours between bottle and throttle." He cocked his beer can at her. "Next time you come to visit, I'll have some wine to offer."

"How do you know I drink wine?"

"I see you sitting over there on my granny's porch having your evening libation."

Jane moved a few inches away from the heat of his body and crossed her arms over her chest. "You've been watching me?"

"You favor red clothes. Even with the bushes all grown out of control, you stand out like a cardinal perched in a yaupon tree. Granny would be upset about the state of her yard."

"I'm not trying to attract attention. Red is a power color. I deal mostly with men, so…"

"The dumb-asses you work for."

"My employers. I had no idea that dear old lady I bought the house from was your granny. After finishing all the renovations, and it needed a bunch, I don't have money for a yard service. I'm often busy on weekends."

"Yeah, I wanted that old place, but I was away at the time she sold it. I had all that flight and dangerous duty pay saved up from the service, so I got a townhouse instead. Granny likes the way you put a red metal roof on the old place and a red door, the bright green shutters, too, but let the weathered, gray cypress alone. Says that red lamppost you planted by the driveway is cute, but if you let the wisteria keep growing, it's gonna strangle the azaleas and crawl right into the attic. That's where I used to sleep, me and my half-brother, in the attic. The *garçonniere*, she called it." Merlin rolled the tall beer can between his palms as he reminisced.

"I thought Olive Tauzin went into assisted living."

"She's still there. I take her out for church, Sunday dinner, and a drive when I'm not working. Like I said, she's upset about her yard."

"She's not the only one. My neighbor across the fence is after me, too. I swear I'll get to it even if I have to take a day off from work. I need to go. Nice meeting you, Mr. Tauzin."

"Merlin or Blackie," he corrected and stood like a gentleman to see her off.

****

Jane rose, moved across the parking area and out the gate into the blue twilight. Merlin watched the easy roll of her rounded hips under the snug gray skirt. He liked the smooth, straight sweep of her dark brown hair down to her pointed chin, the cute bangs, her full breasts all wrapped in red. She had green eyes like—not emeralds, not olives, not jade. Shit, he wasn't a poet. The shade of her eyes reminded him of nature, trees and ferns and such. Best of all, she made him smile. When did that last happen?

Jane Marshall had come at him like that plucky little chicken hawk in the cartoons, the one always trying to carry off the big, white rooster. Well, Jane could carry him back to her nest any day, any time. She had no way of knowing he was a falcon, too, and not poultry. It had been a long time since he had any appetite for a woman, but he truly did now.

Merlin chugged the last of his beer, stamped the

can flat and sent it soaring toward her ditch. She noticed, turned, and threw a "What the hell!" gesture his way. Merlin cupped his mouth with his hands.

"I'll be over to pick it up tomorrow, Jane! That's a promise."

Chapter Two

Clang, clank, chug. The sound repeated and grew louder. CLANG, CLANK, CHUG. About to slip into the jacket of her dark green suit, Jane realized she hadn't put out her trash last night after the major Merlin Tauzin distraction. Not that she had a trashcan to drag to the curb. B.O. Trash Hauling never delivered her new one after the parish hauled the old receptacles away. She suspected, but could not prove, an intentional slight.

When B.O. took over the service the first week in October, she called their number politely requesting they bring her a new can as she had not received one. Sure, sure, by next week. Just set your trash bag on the curb. Full of doubt, she'd done so. Before midnight, wild animals, dogs, cats, raccoons, coyotes, and who knew what else, tore the plastic bag to shreds and spread some pretty intimate items the length of the street. Picking up used tampon holders with rubber gloves by the light of the moon, not her idea of fun.

Week two, Jane called again. Still no container. The woman on the other end of the line solemnly informed her that someone at the parish council had given B.O. Trash Hauling an incorrect figure in the specifications on the number of receptacles needed. What a lie! Jane had provided those figures. More had to be ordered from China, the woman claimed.

Obviously, these were coming on a slow boat because Jane still had no trashcan by the end of October. Meanwhile at her office in the parish courthouse, her phone rang incessantly with complaints from others in the same predicament. Final count of the unserved—twelve hundred, the same as the number of those who once recycled. Coincidence, she thought not.

Jane could only suggest the solution she now relied on. Ask a neighbor with a can if they would share. She buddied with Lloyd Babin, a widowed retiree, her neighbor across the fence who had a light trash load each week. Lloyd kept an immaculately mowed and edged lawn lined with marigolds in the summer. He nurtured a bountiful garden at the rear of his house and brought her autumn tomatoes in a basket as well as sacks of grapefruits and sweet Satsuma oranges. He'd offered her space in his trashcan and only asked one thing in return: would she please trim her bushes and get her yard in shape before the trumpet creeper sprawling all over her ramshackle garage took over the neighborhood? She made her promise and so far had not kept it.

Jane dashed around her house emptying wastebaskets. With the addition of the tall kitchen bag under the sink, she collected two full, biodegradable plastic bags and sprinted for Lloyd's receptacle. Too late. The garbage truck chugged away from the Babin home and headed past her house to the main road.

"Wait! Wait! I have trash!"

Following the line of ooze from a leak in its bottom, Jane pursued the dark blue vehicle with the peeling orange lettering to the stop sign on the corner. Two plastic grocery bags from its open rear caught the breeze and wafted toward her. One attached itself to her face. The other sailed down the street to the bayou. Quickly, she stuffed the bag threatening to suffocate her into one of her sacks. The garbagemen snickered, but she marched right up to them and held up her burden. A corner of the bag holding decomposing lettuce and a moldy tomato leaked and dribbled on her burgundy-colored blouse.

"You missed these."

"Sorry, ma'am. All trash must be placed in a can, boss says." A big grin spread across the B.O. employee's dark brown face.

"What! Just a few weeks ago I was told to leave bags on the curb."

"That Ethel, she don't know nothing. Only an idjit would put bags on the curb. We gots coyotes round here."

"I know. Please take my bags."

"Can't." Suddenly, his grin vanished along with the early morning light.

A cloud must have obscured the rising sun. Jane shivered in the long shadow cast from the east.

"Take the little lady's garbage."

His approach disguised by the noisy heaving of the truck, Jane turned to find Merlin Tauzin, the source of the long shadow, looming behind her. Like the Grim Reaper, he held a long-handled pruning hook with a lethal-looking blade in one hand and a chainsaw worthy of a mass murderer in his other big paw.

"Here, let me show you how easy it is." He handed Jane the pruning hook and set down the chainsaw. Divesting her of the garbage sacks, Merlin tossed them over the head of the man giving her a hard time and into the back of the truck. Then, he skirted around the fellow and pulled the lever to rotate the trash. "See, no-brainer. Now, I want a shiny new trashcan delivered to Miss Jane before next week."

"No can do, boss. We outta them. She could go by the parish barn and get an old one. Gotta be green, not a black container. That will fix her up right fine."

"Good, we'll do that. Here, I forgot this." Tauzin dug a round of flat aluminum from the hip pocket of his worn jeans and offered it to the guy like a tip.

Jane snatched it away. "We recycle these, Merlin."

"Right. Drive on. Your truck is leaking into the ditch."

For a garbage truck, the vehicle peeled out fairly fast with the garbageman barely hanging on in the back. It pulled into the safety of the Cane View Chateaus parking lot and disappeared around the back of the townhouses.

"I could have handled that, you know. You did not have to come to my rescue." Jane returned the pruning hook. "What are you doing here with that so early in the morning anyhow?"

"Yeah, I could see how well you were doing." He eyed the stains on the front of her blouse. Two days growth of very black beard hid a hint of a smile on his face.

"Another thing. Do not refer to me as little lady. One of the councilmen always uses little lady when referring to me. I dislike it intensely. You hate being called Lin and Merry, and I respect that. It's Jane, just plain Jane." She looked straight up at him to make her point.

"Hardly. You have pretty green eyes, sugarplum."

"Aren't sugarplums made from prunes? So not a great compliment. That term could be considered sexual harassment."

The hint of a smile emerged from his dark beard and spread across that big jaw. "I guess it might be if you worked for me or I worked for you, but since I'm here to clear your yard for free, I don't think so. Still, I won't use it again. I'll think of something else, Green Eyes."

"Look, I can't take time off to help you with the yard today. I have to change my blouse and get to work by seven-thirty—Blue Eyes."

"I took care of this yard for years and have time to spare, so you just trot along to the courthouse and let me get to it. Blue Eyes, I kinda like that."

Jane offered the crushed beer can. "Fine, go crazy with that chainsaw. While you're at it, put this in the barrel inside my creepy garage."

"Sure. My hands are full. Can you just slip it into my back pocket?" Those blue eyes gleamed with wickedness.

"No. I cannot." She forced the disk into the front pocket on his already grubby T-shirt.

"That's good, too."

Frowning, Jane changed the subject. "You have a lot of yard equipment for a man who lives in a townhouse."

"I found all this in your 'creepy garage' right where I left it when I went into the service. Used to be a cowshed. My grandpa converted it to a garage when he got his first truck. Sorry you don't like it."

"It's not the building itself. Every time I go in there, I stir up long-legged spiders and step on a few of those crunchy stick insects. You know those creatures can blind you with their spray."

"The daddy-long-legs are harmless, and I doubt if the walking sticks will blind the bottom of your sneakers."

"Once, I thought I saw a snake."

"Possible," he admitted. "When I'm done with the yard, I'll clean out the garage."

"I need to pay you for all this."

"Nope, I'm doing it for my granny. She could have a heart attack if the place gets anymore overgrown."

Jane checked her watch. "No time to argue. We'll settle this at lunchtime, Merlin."

"Say, if you bring me a fried shrimp po-boy from Tujacque's, I'll consider us even, Jane."

Nodding, she ran back to the house to make a quick change and a fast trip to work.

****

With her arms folded across her stocky body, Nadia Nixon stood by the time clock and watched Jane's frantic approach with an expression like a feral cat about to pounce on a dove pecking at birdseed in the grass. She wore her blonde hair pulled back so tightly into a stubby, under-turned ponytail that her glittering eyes actually slanted. Nadia liked nothing better than catching a person who clocked in late. It highlighted her morning, and she relished such an event like a rich dessert or a fine wine throughout the day.

"I know I'm late. I got garbage juice on my blouse and had to change," Jane blurted.

"Your reason for cheating the parish of fifteen minutes of work time does not matter. I will expect you to clock out at four-forty-five rather than your usual four-thirty," the Chief Administrative Officer for the parish said.

There went her peaceful half hour of sunset watching and wine drinking before dinner, but she would never give more pleasure to Nadia by saying so. "Of course," Jane replied.

She could have said, "What about all those unpaid hours I spend at council meetings or speaking to civic groups in the evening?" but Nadia would simply sneer and tell her she was a salaried worker and that was her job.

When Ste. Jeanne d'Arc Parish decided to convert from the old police jury system of government to a parish council with an elected president, the vote for a new leader swept Wofford "Woof" Langlois into office. He'd been sitting in the president's chair for forty years because the new constitution had no term limits, a fine old southern tradition. Woof's mellow blue eyes grew watery, his bottom spread, and his dark hair grayed and receded until it formed a ring around his bald noggin, but still he served his county in the same capacity year after year.

Some of the parish councilmen, restless to take over that office, finally decided that Langlois gave away parish services too freely and hired far too many friends and relatives who felt obligated to vote for him. They demanded he take on an administrative officer to cull the flock of his devotees in the name of efficiency and better government, to make certain parish resources were not squandered on people who felt grateful after having their shell road graded or riprap dumped on the eroding edge of their coulee for free. In other words, they wanted a hatchet man and found that person in

Nadia Nixon. She might have been called a hatchet woman, but her sexuality was often questioned. The councilmen said she had a big pair of balls or sometimes flip-flopped and referred to her as a ball-buster. Whatever, she did love her job.

"Nice blouse, Marshall," Nadia sneered in her deep voice. "You get it at the thrift shop?"

"Thank you, a gift from my grandmother." Because I have a grandmother, you spawn of Satan. But, Jane smiled sweetly. She hated the white nylon blouse with the ruffle down the front, and probably her grandmother *had* gotten it at a church sale to benefit the missionary fund. Gran did love ruffles and could never understand they were out of style along with nylon. The frill made her chest look huge, and being semi-transparent, the blouse showed her bra straps. At least, her jacket covered most of it, and if she spilled on herself at lunch, it repelled every substance known to man.

"I'll be here waiting when you clock out, Marshall. Oh, pathetic performance in that 10K race the other week. You know I can run a half-marathon without breaking a sweat."

"Impressive, Nadia. I did the best I could for charity. All my sponsors had to pay up because I finished the course. Now, I'd better get to my desk."

"Yeah, complaints about the new trash haulers are piling up like—garbage."

"Witty, very witty." Jane strode away. Ever since that race, the henchwoman had been particularly vile to her. While Nadia finished first, boasting about shaving seconds off her personal best, she'd had only six sponsors, poor old Woof and a few councilmen. Jane, much more popular with the employees, had dozens sign her sheet and raised far more funds simply for finishing. "So there," Jane mumbled under her breath. She must be careful.

Nadia had no friends, but she did have toadies who tattled to her on a regular basis. Mostly young women with limited skills and experience, they waited for Fridays when the axe woman would fire someone late in the day for a minor infraction and possibly open up a better position for them. While some were rewarded for turning in a co-worker over checking their personal e-mail or doing online shopping, most only got their workload doubled with no increase in pay. Cutting the payroll by attrition, Nadia called it.

Much as she wanted to, Jane could not afford to cross Ms. Nixon. She had a house note, renovation and car loans to repay. Employment opportunities for environmental project managers did not abound. The tighter the economy got, the less the public seemed to care about protecting the land and waterways. At her desk, Jane set to work trying to obtain a federal Super Fund grant to clean up an abandoned oil well site with a wastewater pond leaking into the bayou and fending off complaints about B.O. Waste Hauling. The morning slipped by as rapidly as spilled petroleum spread across the Gulf of Mexico.

On the stroke of twelve, Jane sprinted to the time clock. May Robin, the office receptionist and unofficial MawMaw of everyone, asked, "Not eating with us today?" The woman, a fixture since Langlois first took office, removed her own adorable insulated and reusable patchwork sack from a desk drawer. Jane encouraged everyone to use similar lunch bags rather than paper or plastic, and May had converted. The receptionist also sold the bags made by her sister-in-law to the other workers. Naturally, Jane bought one, but had left it at home this morning.

"No, I need to feed the guy who volunteered to do my yard work and then run out to the parish barn to see if I can get one of the old trashcans."

"You still don't have a trashcan? When I didn't get mine I asked Bernard Freeman for help, and they delivered one right away." May patted her bright red hair to make sure every strand remained lacquered into place. Believing no one knew her age to be seventy-three, she took personal leave time every two weeks to have her now white roots retouched.

"Evidently, B.O. is out of cans." And she would not ask Bernard Freeman for a favor if he were the last political striver on earth. For sure, he wanted Langlois' job.

"A guy is doing your lawn for free," May continued, oblivious to Jane's need to hurry. "A man in your life at last, *cher* heart."

"No, only a friendly neighbor. I really have to leave." She crossed the small lobby and pushed the elevator button. On most days, she would take the stairs from the fourth floor, but not now.

"I can still fix you up with my nephew. He's an undertaker. They make great money."

"Thanks, May, but you know I'm a career girl."

The offered fix-up, Waldo Robin, age fifty-three, had been divorced recently by his second wife. Wife Number Two gave as her reasons for leaving Waldo that his hands were too cold and living over the mortuary freaked her out. In a town like Chapelle, Louisiana, where most people still married young or at least by the age of twenty-one, pickings remained pretty slim, but Jane had no time to hit the bars and bistros of the nearby city of Lafayette in search of love.

"Until the right man comes along," May called after Jane as the elevator doors shut.

Now, to swing by the drive-up window at Tujacque's, grab the pre-ordered po-boy, deliver it to Merlin, and then hit the long road to the parish barn to retrieve a trashcan. She left the elevator on the main floor, sprinted across the lofty main lobby, and exited between the huge Ionic columns of the antebellum courthouse. Doing a reverse Rocky move down the long flight of handicapped inaccessible marble steps, Jane dashed past the spot where Jefferson Davis once tried to recruit the French settlers to the Confederate cause, largely failing. She slipped on the bronze plaque inserted in the stone on a landing that noted Huey Long once stood here and won the local vote with great success, but regained her balance in time. Tourists liked to pose there, but not Jane. Finally, she reached the parking lot and raced for Tujacque's.

The parking lot of the modest cement block building painted with a figure of a giant crawfish overflowed with trucks and SUVs. She swerved into the long line inching past the drive-up window before she realized she would have been better off going inside. By that time, a tractor pulled in behind her and cut off the possibility.

"Come on, come on." Jane drummed her fingers on the steering wheel of her little Honda hybrid. Finally reaching the window where an old woman in a greasy apron sorted through the white paper bags one by one until she came to Jane's order, Jane thrust a twenty-dollar bill at her.

"I'll have to go up front for change, dear."

"Keep it!" She peeled out for home only a mile away just across the city line. From the road, her yard looked much better already. No sign of Merlin, but a huge pile of leafy severed limbs sat on the curb. Jane drove to the back of the house and parked her car by the dilapidated garage still overwhelmed by trumpet creeper. Still no Merlin. Sack and keys clutched in her hands, she mounted the steps to the backdoor.

"It's not locked," a deep voice said from inside the kitchen.

Holding her keys in the defense position, she bumped the door open with her hip. Hunkered unhappily over a glass of her unsweetened iced tea, Merlin sat at the kitchen table. Sweat plastered his white T-shirt to his body. She could see his black chest hair and relaxed nipples through the fabric. Strangely, he didn't stink but filled the room with a sort of manly aroma, not unpleasant at all.

"You got any real sugar for this? All I can find is the artificial stuff that gives you cancer," he complained.

"Here...to go with your heart disease." Jane thrust the grease-spotted bag at him. "How did you get inside?"

"I could have gotten in here any number of ways, broken a window, knocked down a door, but I used the key Granny always kept in the back of the garage under the old milking pail." His black-whiskered face lit when he unloaded the sack onto her pretty, lemon-yellow tablecloth. "Their fresh steak-cut fries, too! I do love a woman who anticipates my desires. Wanna share?

22

There's plenty here for both of us."

Merlin unraveled the sandwich from its white paper wrapping. Fried shrimp burst from the overstuffed walls of a small loaf of French bread. Sliced tomato, shredded lettuce, and thin-sliced onions spilled over the sides. Mayonnaise oozed from its bottom. "Fully dressed! Exactly the way I like my po-boys, but not my women."

Jane considered lobbing the energy bar she rooted from among the apples in the fruit bowl on the table directly into his face. No time. She took her stainless steel water bottle from the refrigerator. "Enjoy your coronary and remind me to get the locks changed. I need to get to the parish barn to pick up a trashcan."

"Hey, I'm harmless to women, children, and small, furry animals. Sugar?"

"What did you call me?" She turned to glare at him from halfway to the door.

"I asked for sugar for my tea. The only other drinks you have are diet sodas."

Relenting, Jane set down her own lunch and returned to the cupboards. After moving some cereal boxes and packages of whole-wheat pasta around, she unearthed a sugar bowl painted with plump lemons. She took a spoon from a drawer, broke up the lumps inside the container, and handed it to Merlin. He shoveled sugar into his tea.

"You sure like lemons. Lemons on the dishware, lemons on the tiles over the sink, lemon border on the wallpaper. And some real nice lemons…" He ogled the absurd white ruffle on her blouse.

"So what!" Defiantly, she thrust her breasts out even farther.

"Coming along in the garden. My grandpa planted that tree." He watched her chest deflate. "Yep, sour but sunny. We could make some real good lemonade in here."

If his lips weren't smiling, his blue eyes did. "Why don't you sit down and eat a real meal. Plenty for both of us."

"If I start eating Tujacques' po-boys, I won't fit on the kitchen chairs anymore. Gotta go. Trashcan. And by the way, the yard is really shaping up. You could do this kind of work for a living."

"I did once when I was in high school. Dug holes, spread mulch, and worked my way up to pruning. Eat with me. Then, I'll go along to the parish barn and help you get a can."

"I can handle it."

"Really. What kind of car do you drive?"

He looked out the window at her small, black Honda. She suspected he already knew.

"A Honda hybrid hatchback. It has plenty of room and gets fifty miles to the gallon, unlike the big-ass trucks most people drive around here. What do you drive?"

"A big-ass truck. Sure you don't want my help?"

"I said no. Lock up when you finish, please. And help yourself to an apple for dessert."

"Tempting."

He didn't show it, but she knew Merlin Tauzin smiled on the inside of that big body overwhelming her cozy kitchen. She was going, going, gone to the parish barn.

\*\*\*\*

Merlin found some catsup in the refrigerator and

baptized the fries with it before settling in to eat. Would have been nice to have her company for lunch right here in his granny's kitchen, even though it looked a whole lot different now, better in fact. He suspected Jane had the ability to make lots of things better, maybe even him.

Chapter Three

The place might as well have been a ghost town in the southwest desert. Apparently, everyone at the parish barn had gone out to lunch except for a lone woman in the office who, using her ham sandwich as a pointer, gestured to the cache of used trashcans at the bottom of the small hill. "Help yourself, hon. With the shortage, they're going fast."

Jane threaded her way through a maze of heavy equipment dwarfing her small vehicle. Several of the machines looked as if they fed on subcompacts for snacks. She parked and began her search for the perfect receptacle. After a few minutes, she returned to the car to shuck off her jacket.

In the usual way of Louisiana weather, the pleasant autumn temperatures had given way to summertime again. Must be well over eighty degrees, she estimated. The nylon blouse stuck to her arms and back, pasted there by perspiration. Not a shade tree within a mile, but a few black vultures picked at an armadillo carcass near an earthmover and perched on its cab. They regarded Jane fearlessly as a possible next meal.

Keeping an eye on the birds, she ventured into the rows of abandoned trashcans, raising lids and slamming them as foul odors wafted into the air and maggots squirmed in their bottoms. Flies attracted to her sweat lit on her shoulders and buzzed her lips. She flailed them away. Finally at the end of the third row, she found a green container that appeared to have been washed and rinsed by some responsible citizen before they turned it in for the new B.O. model.

Joyously, she tried to drag it back to her car. Its wheels sunk into the sand pile where it had come to rest. Straining and cursing under her breath, she finally gave a good tug and got the can rolling across the lot. At her car where she'd already folded down the backseat to receive her prize, Jane popped the hatchback and prepared to lift her treasure for transport. Heavier than it looked, much, much heavier. After three tries and balancing it on her knees, she had the container at bumper level. Now to get the wheel end up and inside. The damned thing crashed to the ground again. But, she did know how to raise it again after those few abortive tries. Up and in! Not quite. No matter how hard she shoved, the wide mouth of the container refused to fit inside the hatchback. Its lid hung open over the bumper like a huge, laughing mouth. Cops were sure to stop her if she attempted to drive home this way. If she had rope, she could tie it on top of the Honda like a Christmas tree—if she could get it up there. Maybe when the men came back to work someone would help her out. One o'clock! She should have been at her office by now.

An electric blue, high-rise, double cab truck with a four by four bed and a full rack of spotlights splayed across its roof like glass antlers turned in at the gate of the razor wire-fenced compound, the first of the returning workers no doubt.

"Over here, over here!" she shouted and waved.

The truck roared like a lion about to devour a

Christian in the arena and charged her way. The vultures ran awkwardly along the ground and took off for a safer realm. In a cloud of dust, the big rig came to a stop beside her hybrid, and out of that dust climbed Merlin Tauzin.

"Sure you don't want any help with that?" he said.

"I will admit when I'm wrong. Yes, I would appreciate your help." Better than relying on the kindness of strangers, she supposed.

With one good heave, Merlin uncorked the can from the hatchback and tossed it into the back of his Ford F-150 Platinum with its tinted windows and custom paint job. "Big Blue and me will take this home for you."

"You named your truck?"

"Yep."

"Shouldn't it be called something more dynamic like Blue Lightning?"

"Big Blue is strong and tough but not especially fast. You'd name a stockcar Blue Lightning."

"I see. Well, thanks. I'm late for work. I owe you another po-boy."

"Nope. You owe me a whole dinner. A big-ass truck guzzles a whole lot of gas, you know. It's a long drive out here." A smile tugged at his lips but failed to escape.

"I can accept that. We'll discuss the details later. I have to run."

"Seems you're always running, Jane."

"If you knew Nadia Nixon, you'd understand."

"Can't say that I do. Go on wit' you, but don't go over fifty. I wouldn't want you to ruin your ecology rating." Again, one of those suppressed smiles.

"I won't. Thanks for coming to the rescue."

"Anytime." He waved her off with one big paw.

Jane pulled out raising her own dust, but it hardly amounted to anything.

\*\*\*\*

Sweating like a marathon runner on a hundred degree day and fifteen minutes late, Jane clocked in under the scrutiny of Nadia Nixon. She swore the woman never ate lunch, just plugged herself into a wall socket and recharged.

"Another fifteen minutes late, Marshall. I expect you to stay until five and don't care if you have Friday night plans, a heavy date, or dinner with your grandma scheduled." Nadia in her perfectly pressed, prison warden gray suit wrinkled her broad nose. "You stink. I'm writing you up for improper hygiene. I might also mention inappropriate attire. A person can see right through that blouse."

Jane hunched her shoulders. People were unsure about Nadia's sexual orientation, and she certainly didn't want to allow the woman any extra thrills. "Give me a break! I spent my lunch hour at the parish barn trying to get a trashcan. Look, I'll just put my jacket on again and stay in my office the rest of the afternoon so I don't offend, okay?"

The padding in her suit coat barely moved as Nadia shrugged. "You wrote the garbage contract, so don't expect me to feel sorry for you. I'll be watching to make sure you don't move out of that room. Now get to work."

"I advised against accepting the low bid, and I don't want your pity!"

Jane went to her glass-walled office and sifted

through her messages. Most were complaints about the trash hauling service. She passed them along to Ethel at B.O., getting a noncommittal uh-huh from the woman. The rest of the afternoon, she worked on the Super Fund proposal forms, even skipping her break and denying her need to pee. Fortunately, that foray to the dump had dehydrated her a little.

She stayed put when everyone else went home at four-thirty. She remained where she was past five when the cleaning crew arrived to do the office. At five-fifteen, Jane sauntered over to the time clock where Nadia lurked and inserted her card with a sharp ping. As she withdrew it, the president's assistant snatched it from her hand and made a notation on the side.

"No unauthorized overtime! Don't begin to think we'll pay you for those extra fifteen minutes."

"I would never expect that. Nor to be paid for all the evening meetings I attend or charity events I go to in the name of the parish. Have a nice weekend, Nadia."

Thinking the woman probably lived in the dark basement of the courthouse like an evil troll and never left the building, Jane wended her way home.

Chapter Four

At least, Chapelle's rush hour, which usually lasted only fifteen minutes, had ended, one nice break in a horrible day. Nearly missing the entry to her gravel driveway because of all the yard waste heaped on either side, Jane parked by her dilapidated garage. With darkness falling swiftly, she appreciated the light from her little lamppost. Still, the big pecan tree in her yard cast a deep shadow across her path to the backdoor.

Something huge and threatening separated itself from the darkness—maybe a black bear ousted from the cane fields being cut in the area. Should she retreat with caution to her car or roll into a ball and play dead? She could never remember which applied to black bears. Jane took a slow step back.

"Going somewhere?" Blackie Tauzin said. "You just got home. Missed a pretty sunset tonight. I've been sitting here watching it."

"Oh, Merlin! You frightened me." Her hand rested over her pounding heart.

"Didn't mean to. I finished with the bushes and got the trumpet creeper off the fence but left it on the garage. I know it's a noxious vine, but the orange flowers are nice."

"Yes, I like them, too. Besides, I think the garage might fall down if you pull it off. That vine is sturdier than the walls."

"Is that why you never park inside—besides the critters, I mean?"

"I still have two years of car payments to make and can't afford to have a building fall on my Honda." Jane advanced into the spill of light coming from her kitchen window.

"It's sturdier than it looks, and nothing in that garage will hurt you. Even snakes run away given some space. The sun may be gone, but you look like you can still use some wine."

He held open her unlocked door. Jane entered and immediately became engulfed by the rich aroma of a pot of gumbo on the stove.

"My mom came by and saw me working over here. Her husband went hunting last week, and she brought me duck and andouille gumbo for my supper. You like that kind?"

"I love all kinds of gumbo."

"Couldn't find your rice cooker, so we'll have to settle for that brown Minute Rice you got in the cupboard." Merlin went to the stove and checked on a smaller pot. He shook his head over her pitiful rice. "Yeah, it's ready. You want to eat now?"

"Thanks, but I need to wash up. Nadia Nixon informed me I had body odor after my foray to the parish barn. I wouldn't come too close right now."

Disregarding her comment, Merlin came close, very close, and sniffed. "I've smelled lots worse things, but go ahead if you want to shower. The food will keep."

Jane backed away slowly as if he really were a black bear invading her house. "Okay. By the way, I don't have a rice cooker. My family moved here from

Montana. We're more meat and potato people, gumbo eaters, not gumbo makers."

"Then you are in for a treat. My mom makes the best duck and andouille gumbo."

"I thought she was simple-minded."

"Even the simple can learn to cook with a little patience. Granny has lots of patience, only she was about out of it with the state of the yard. All I could do to keep her from marching right over here on her walker and taking you to task about it."

"Again, sorry. I do keep the grass mowed."

"After I get the pansies and ornamental cabbage planted in the flowerbeds for winter color, you'll be square with her."

"I have flowerbeds?"

"Sure. What did you think those circles of angled bricks in front of the house were?"

"Obstacles to mowing? The tops of old cisterns?"

"Flowerbeds. Get on wit' you. I'll set the table."

As soon as Merlin turned toward the cupboards, Jane retreated and ran for the safety of her bathroom. She locked the door and dragged the clothes hamper under the knob, pretty flimsy defenses considering Merlin's size. But what had he done except offer her his mama's gumbo and clean her yard all day? Feeling foolish but not removing the obstacles, she stripped down and showered quickly giving her hair only a once-over with citrus-scented shampoo.

Toweling off, she realized she hadn't brought fresh clothes into the bathroom. She could try to streak to her bedroom and hope Merlin wouldn't notice or simply put on the pink sweat suit hanging on the back of the door. She used it to exercise at the all-ladies gym, but hadn't had the time lately. Good thing because the baggy top and pants were still freshly laundered. Jane took a whiff of her underwear and decided going commando might be better. After all, sweat suits, even pink ones, did not scream, "Take me right now on the kitchen table, you big, hunky male." She combed out her hair and added pink bunny slippers to her ensemble hoping she projected the message, "No sex tonight."

Makeup free, she padded to the kitchen where Merlin scooped rice into two of her lemon-patterned earthenware bowls. He took in every inch of her outfit, then turned to ladle the gumbo over the rice.

"I like a woman who looks as good without makeup as with. I can't abide waking up to raccoon eyes and lipstick all over the pillows. You look as soft and sweet as those bunny slippers."

"I'm not soft and sweet! I'm tough and—and lemony."

"Sure you are, sweetheart." He brought the bowls to the table and held a chair for her. When was the last time that had ever happened on a date? This isn't a date. Remember that, Jane, remember. She took her seat, but Merlin lingered with his big hands on the bentwood back of her chair. He lowered his face very close to hers and inhaled. "Lemons, a nice, fresh scent."

"Would you mind getting the wine from the fridge?" Anything, anything to make him move away before she blurted out that he smelled good, too. He wore a clean, white shirt open at the neck, no undershirt, a little black chest hair showing. His jeans, a pale stone-washed blue, were new. Though he hadn't shaved, he'd showered, probably at his own house since her bathroom remained immaculate. The dark hair she assumed to be would sweaty, he'd slicked back still damp. He exuded the scent of some spicy, masculine body wash when she would have figured him as a plain soap man. Merlin cleaned up nice after doing her yard. After doing her....

Jane stood up so suddenly, she nearly knocked the two half-filled wineglasses from his hands. Good thing he hadn't topped them off or she'd be wearing pink and red, not a good color combination for her. "Whatever is wrong with me? I am such a poor hostess. We should have salad with this and some dessert."

Jane bolted for the cupboards and grabbed a pair of wooden bowls. She dumped ready-made salad from a bag into them and placed one by Merlin's gumbo. He still stood there holding the wine while she rabbited around the kitchen and took a pound cake from the freezer.

"We can have this with ice cream and chocolate syrup. Lo-cal ranch dressing or fat-free Italian?" she asked as she seized the two bottles from the refrigerator rack and brought them to the table.

"Ranch, I guess. I knew I should have picked up some potato salad and French bread."

"No, no. This is fine. Great. Sit and eat before the gumbo gets cold."

He set the wineglasses on the table and held her chair again. This time, he guided her with his hands on her shoulders. His heat and strength shot down the length of her body all the way to her bunny slippers. No, no, no. She preferred college-educated men who wore suits and shaved daily. Metrosexuals, yes, that's what she liked. They had some of those in Lafayette, but not really in Chapelle. She needed to get out more.

That was all. Jane took a gulp of wine. An awkward silence set in while she sampled the gumbo and Merlin prodded his salad with a fork as if the vegetables might not be entirely dead.

"Really great gumbo. Thank you for sharing, Merlin."

"No problem."

"So, tell me all about yourself." An old chestnut, but a good one. Everyone liked to talk about themselves.

"Not much to tell. I was born in this parish, raised in this house. I never knew we had red pine floors under all that green linoleum. Nice." He gestured with his spoon at Jane's pride and joy, her lovely hardwood floors liberated from several layers of ugly coverings.

"Thank you. You went to school here as well?"

"Yep. The public high school, not the Catholic or fancy private one. Did a couple of years of college at the university in Lafayette before I quit."

"Too much partying?" Jane said that with a smile, but he did seem the type to flunk out from excessive drinking. Probably excessive women, too.

"I didn't take to it much. I never could understand why I needed courses in English and a foreign language in order to study petroleum engineering. I mean, I already speak English and people who move here should do the same."

So, he was one of those guys. Figured. "Both my older brother and my dad are petroleum engineers. My brother is working in Helena now, and my father is teaching some courses at Montana State University in Bozeman since he retired."

"Good for them. They stayed the course. I didn't."

He finished his wine and poured another glass full to the brim this time.

"But, you must have gone on to get helicopter flight training."

"Courtesy to the U.S. Army. When college seemed a waste of time and money, I enlisted. Four years in the service, two of those in Afghanistan."

"That must have been an interesting experience."

"If you like grit in your food in summer, freezing your ass off in winter, and praying the Russkis haven't sold the war lords any rocket propelled grenades lately. I don't really like to talk about it."

Jane grasped another straw of conversation. "Your family. I met your grandmother at the closing on the house. She's still very sharp for all her physical infirmities. You told me about your mother, and you have a step-father who shoots ducks." She took another appreciative spoonful of gumbo. "Brothers? Sisters?"

"Half-sister, half-brother. Brittney is a waitress out at Broussard's Barn same as my mom. Doyle, he wanted to follow in my footsteps and signed up for the service when he should have stayed in trade school. Only he didn't have the brains to get into flight training. He takes after my step-dad, not the brightest bulb in the bin but a good kid. Doyle thinks it's great the army taught him to drive a truck so he can have a career like me when he gets out—if he comes out alive. I keep telling him always stay in the middle of the convoy, don't take point or drag. If he gets blown up by an IED, it will be my fault for not being around to talk him out of it, but I was doing my second stretch in Afghanistan at the time and me getting that medal didn't help discourage him. Now he's over there, and I'm home safe and sound." Merlin wiped his hand over his mouth as if he tried to stop the rush of words.

Jane wanted to take that hand and have it lie quietly in hers. "People make their own decisions for better or worse. You can't blame yourself for that. What did you do to win a medal?"

He stood as abruptly as she had earlier in the evening. His gumbo bowl sat empty, his salad barely touched, and his wineglass down to the dregs again. "I didn't deserve to be decorated. Look, I'm tired from doing your yard work. I need to leave."

"Won't you stay for dessert?"

That tight, suppressed smile appeared on his shadowed face again. "Ask me that another time and I just might, sweet cheeks. Keep the rest of the gumbo. Good night."

\*\*\*\*

Merlin closed the door behind him and escaped from the light of the kitchen. He paused under the old pecan tree and gazed at the moon dressed in blood red by the haze of the low-burning fires cane farmers set to burn the stubble. The warm air remaining after the day's heat coaxed a few cricket frogs to come forth from their crannies and start a chorus of song.

He breathed deep, the way he was supposed to when agitated. Anti-social behavior, a symptom of Post Traumatic Stress Disorder, according to the army psychiatrist. Jesus, he'd spilled more to Jane in a half hour than to the shrink in the past year. Now, he'd blown it with her. His plan to practice living a normal life with a night out dining and dancing with a pretty woman had gone up in smoke quicker than gasoline poured on the chaff.

Good thing the owner of the helicopter company had served in 'Nam and understood, knew that when Blackie Tauzin said he'd die before letting anyone in his care come to harm, he meant it. Sure Braxton Rice had written him up a couple of times, once for not shaving, and another for being surly to customers. Shaving more often, not a problem. Playing nice when all he wanted to do was fly his aircraft free and in silence to reach his destination safely took some effort. He should have made more effort with Jane. If only she hadn't asked about the medal. He heard the backdoor open and didn't move. She'd spot him then, brooding under her tree like a stalker.

"Merlin, are you still out here?"

Only his granny, his mom, and now Jane called him Merlin. Everyone else knew the name Blackie suited him better.

"Yeah," he confessed. "Just looking at the moon for a minute before I go."

"Are we still on for that dinner? I do owe you." Jane started down the steps.

"Better stay where you are. Snakes eat little bunnies like you."

"Where?" Her head swiveled from side to side trying to find the venomous reptile in her grass. If only she knew.

"It's gone for now. Tomorrow night. Dinner and dancing at Mulate's. Music starts at seven. I'll be over here early to plant those flowers. We'll have plenty of time to clean up before we go."

"That's a date then."

"Yeah, a date." Go figure, a real date with a good woman, something he never thought he'd have again.

Chapter Five

Merlin failed to ring the doorbell. Jane wouldn't have known he was out there on hands and knees by the newly revealed flowerbeds if she hadn't been wandering around her house with a bowl of breakfast granola in her hand wondering when he would show up. Much as she liked to sleep in on Saturdays, she'd gotten up early, put on khaki shorts, her pink T-shirt from the 10K run, and her sneakers, all to prove she wasn't such a slug when it came to yard work. She finished her cereal in a hurry and put the bowl in the sink. Grabbing the pot of coffee from the maker, she selected a sunny yellow mug and sauntered casually out the front door, across the porch and down to where Merlin worked.

Frilly, purple ornamental cabbages filled the center of each circular bed. Flats of plain yellow pansies and another variety, purple and white with markings like droll little faces sat beside where Merlin knelt. He picked up a six-pack of plants and gently squeezed one from the base of its plastic container. Tenderly, he placed it deep in a small hole and pressed the earth firmly around the stems. Why did that simple act make her mouth go dry?

"Coffee break," Jane said brightly.

"I barely got started here, but yeah, coffee would be good." He rocked back on his heels, folded his long legs Indian style, and accepted the mug without getting up. There he sat, his striking blue eyes catching the early morning light, his black beard another day thicker, right about the level of her crotch.

She poured. "I should have brought real sugar and milk for you."

"Black is fine. Your coffee is weaker than I'm used to."

Not sure if that statement was an insult, Jane nestled the coffeepot in a clump of grass and yanked a pansy from its holder. "Let me plant while you drink that."

"No! You'll tear the roots. Pinch it out from the bottom." He made a squeezing motion with his free hand a few inches from her breast.

Beneath her pink T-shirt, Jane's nipples puckered. Well, two could play this game. She wrapped her hand around the holder of one plant and squeezed. A spray of purple and white flowers squirted free. "Like this," she said, keeping her voice low and breathy while staring at the bulge in his jeans, a significant bulge, too.

"That's right, Green Eyes. Now put it the hole and tamp that soil tight around it." Merlin shifted, drawing his knees up in front of him.

She would so show him what she could do! Jane got on her knees and raised her rump in the air. She wiggled it in his face as she leaned over and pushed the pansy into the ground, firming it with pats of her hands. Only she'd forgotten about the newly installed traffic light requested by Councilman Freeman to make left turns into Cane View Estates easier for people who brought his townhouses.

This early on a Saturday, few cars passed, but those that did were stopped by the light and formed a short line in front of her house. A fisherman towing a bass boat with his SUV shouted, "Shake it, baby!" Two teenage boys in a pickup truck hooted and whistled. A white-haired lady returning from eight o'clock Mass at the Catholic church down the road took the time to roll down the automatic window of her bus of a Buick and comment, "Disgusting!"

Abruptly, Jane sat on her bottom, pulled up her knees, and buried her blazing face in her very dirty hands until the light changed and the traffic moved on. Merlin, however, fell back in the grass and laughed so hard he punctuated each guffaw with a fist pound to the earth. If she'd aroused him, it sure didn't show now.

"I guess I don't do provocative and sexy very well," she stated.

"You do it just fine, baby doll, even if you are dressed like a camp counselor. Jesus, Mary, and Joseph, I haven't laughed this hard in years. Feels good. Real good—like a lap dance."

How those blue eyes of his could sparkle when amused. "Well, macho man, I think you killed your chance of ever getting one of those from me. I'd hate to have you collapse onto my hardwood floors with a fit of the giggles. Coffee break is over. Get back to work." Jane seized the coffee pot and empty mug to take inside along with her humiliated self.

"Oh, honey, I never giggle. Come on, help me with the planting, but it might be best for you to keep your behind on the other side of the bed, the flowerbed, that is. I see Mass is letting out at Holy Mother, and we don't want to cause any elderly women to have heart attacks. This is the color scheme, purple in the front and back, yellow on the sides. Granny always did like to show her support for the LSU Tigers."

"Okay."

They worked in silence until all the flowers created a merry display of purple and gold. Merlin sprinkled some fertilizer, then attached a hose to the outdoor tap and gave the plants a good soaking. Jane could see the mischief in his eyes just before he turned the hose on her.

"Now for the wet T-shirt contest!"

Dodging did not help. The spray pursued her across the lawn and up the porch until she gained the safety of the front door. From a small crack she shouted, "I was going to invite you for lunch, but now you can just eat grass!"

Another spritz hit the door. "Can't anyhow. I want to go out to Harley's place and borrow his wood chipper. That's my step-dad, Harley David. Yeah, I know. He was born to be a biker and tries to live up to his name. We might as well make mulch out of the clippings. It should age a while before we put it on the plants though. The parish used to pick up yard waste the first of the month, so we need to get it done before then."

"Every six weeks now. The parish needed to save money, and this was one way of doing it," Jane corrected, opening the door wider. "We aren't supposed put our clippings on the curb until that week. I guess it will stay there until just before Christmas since we missed the last pickup."

"The chipper will take care of most of it. Say, you better get out of that wet T-shirt. I can tell you're cold. Don't want you to get sick before our big night out. Be ready at six-thirty."

Jane slammed the door on his wicked laughter.

By five p.m., Merlin had reduced a huge pile of branches to tiny chips and created an impressive mulch pile next to the garage. Jane admitted to herself she wouldn't have to pay for mulch for several years to come, not that she had a great deal of use for mulch. Still irked about the wet T-shirt, she stayed inside and used her laptop to work on the proposal.

Let him go for coffee at the hideous convenience store with the six gas pumps Bernard Freeman put up at the crossroads on the other side of the traffic light. Its glaring lights burned all night long blotting out the stars. The odor of fried chicken invaded her yard twice every day and the boxes often ended up in her ditch. No wonder the great horned owl that once called the pecan tree home had flown away. Even the name of the place offended—the Fast 'N Fun, as if it were some titty bar.

Merlin Tauzin was just a big, womanizing jerk. She'd thank him for his hard work by going dancing with him just this once, and she'd pay for both their dinners. Dancing, not her strong point, especially not Cajun dancing. Oh, she'd go out and gyrate around in a crowd, but at Mulate's serious dancers took the floor, each one outdoing the next with their footwork and twirls. The thought made her stomach nervous.

The annoying, distracting grind of the wood chipper ceased. She peeked through her kitchen curtain to watch Merlin put down a ramp and haul it into the electric blue truck possessing a color very close to that of his eyes. Those eyes turned her way. Caught!

"Six-thirty," he reminded her, got into the cab, and drove away.

Only an hour and a half to get ready! No, no,

plenty of time. No need to primp and impress this man. It wasn't as if he were some state senator with a vote that could give more money to improving the environment of Ste. Jeanne d'Arc Parish. But what to wear? Mulate's like most Louisiana dance halls called for casual. Jeans would be fine, but she found herself taking a dress from the closet.

The shimmering blue-green of the fabric ramped up the color of her eyes. It had a snug bodice but wasn't terribly low cut. The skirt, loose and flirty, would flare if she spun around. That called for wearing pantyhose. After her shower and blowing her hair dry, she put on a green lace bra and panties and struggled into the nylons. Bending before her mirror, Jane blended the lightest touch of bronze eye shadow on her lids and curled her lashes. Foundation, a few strokes of blush, a light slick of pale coral lipstick, and she declared herself ready to go once she curled the ends of her hair under and fastened the necklace made of chunks of recycled glass in the same shades as her gown.

Shoes, what to do about shoes? Flats would make her seem small next to Merlin. Her work pumps, too dowdy. Four-inch heels and she'd be a danger to herself and everyone on the dance floor. She settled on bronze-toned sandals with two-inch heels and stocked a small matching bag with a credit card, twenty dollars, her license, a lipstick, a pen, comb, tissues, and her ever handy pepper spray. You never knew when it came to men. A last quick spritz of hairspray, and done. She hadn't primped—much.

The doorbell rang. She'd half expected him to let himself in the backdoor, but he'd come around the front and filled that doorway as only a big man can. My God!

Merlin had shaved, showing off his impressive jaw. For a split second, he reminded her of someone she couldn't place, but oh hell, he looked toothsome. He wore a deep blue shirt that he didn't need to bring out the color those eyes and a loose black leather jacket over dark jeans. She expected to see his usual athletic shoes on his feet or maybe boots, but instead he wore black leather shoes, supple and shining, dancing shoes, the kind of shoes someone on *Dancing with the Stars* would wear.

"Ready to go?"

"As ready as I ever will be."

Jane turned to lock her door. I am in big trouble now—her last thought as Merlin took her elbow and guided her to his truck, but she said instead, "We could save gas if we took my car."

"No way, baby, no way. My legs would cramp up in a car like that."

Instead of letting her clamber into the high cab of his truck, Merlin placed his big hands around her waist, lifted her up, and snugged her into the pristine tan leather seat. "Buckle up now, bunny."

"I will, cowboy," she retorted, the thrill of being raised up so easily still making her toes curl, but she would never confess it to anyone.

He took the back road to Breaux Bridge, shooting past the half-harvested cane fields ten miles over the limit as if he knew every bend and straightaway. They passed Broussard's Barn where his mother and sister worked without a glance from Blackie. Its lot was beginning to fill. Generally, the place had good music, cheap drinks, decent bar food, and an atmosphere that still reeked of its early days as a speakeasy. People could and did get married there since the proprietor had his justice of the peace license. Being closer to Chapelle, Jane wondered why they didn't just go there, but he'd called the tune, the time and the place. Tonight, she would dance at Mulate's.

Chapter Six

With the place packed as usual on a Saturday night about the time the band began warming up, Merlin and Jane accepted a booth near the bar. Without asking Jane's opinion, he ordered an appetizer of boudin sausage balls, rye on the rocks for him and a red wine for her.

"How do you know if I eat pork products or want red wine?" she challenged.

He pondered for a moment. "Never seen you drink anything but red wine, and I figured if you eat duck and andouille gumbo you got nothing against sausage. If you don't like the appetizer, more for me."

"Are you going to order my dinner, too?"

"Nope, not now, but the Catfish Mulate's is great."

When the drinks and appetizer came, he ordered the specialty, fried catfish topped with etouffee, a stuffed potato, and coleslaw. Jane selected the same requesting that her catfish be grilled.

"You got it, honey. We girls have to watch our figures way, way more than a big, good looking guy like this," their middle-aged waitress said, giving Jane a wink. She plunked down a red plastic basket full of French bread and trotted back to the kitchen with their order.

Jane frowned. "Did she imply that I'm fat?"

"Nope. She was flirting with me."

"At her age!"

"I appeal to all ages, sweetheart."

"You know it infuriates me when you call me names like that, Merry. For my next drink I want a rum and Coke with a twist of lime. Make that Diet Coke."

"Now you just want to embarrass me by asking for that when I go up to the bar."

"Maybe, Lin."

Jane succumbed to two boudin balls. She'd dance them off. Merlin downed the other four before their dinner arrived. By the time they finished eating, twosomes crowded the small square of the dance floor, and a busload of tourists admired them from the sidelines. A couple of children who danced better than Jane ever would stole the show. Just the thought of going out there ruined her meal. She asked for a box to take half of it home. Merlin finished every scrap of his and mopped up the last drop of the pink sauce with a piece of crusty bread.

"Ready to go for a spin?"

"I'm not so sure…"

He pried her from the booth like a reluctant oyster from its shell, found an opening in the swirl of dancers, and moved them into place. Merlin held her close for the fast two-step. He led so masterfully she never made an error in footwork. She laughed as he spun her out and brought her back, looped his arms behind her and did a brief promenade before plastering her against his chest again. He let her have some space for a slow Cajun waltz with the triangle setting the beat, but gripped her tightly for the following country-western number. When the band called for a line dance to get the single women without partners out on the floor, he led her back to their booth.

"I could use that rum and Diet Coke now, and a trip to the ladies room," she said.

"Fine. I'll get that sissy drink for you. Don't take too long. The band will start another set soon. I kinda forgot how much I like to dance with a pretty lady in my arms."

"Thanks, I guess."

Jane wove through the tightly packed tables to the restroom while Merlin hunkered up to the very busy bar. Hunkered, hunky, hunk, she could not stop herself from thinking. There was a line. There always is outside a ladies room, but she finally got in and out after repairing her lipstick and combing her hair. Passing back through the packed dance hall, she heard a shout.

"Over here, Jane! Come sit a minute."

May Robin occupied a table with her sister-in-law, the one who made the cute lunch bags and bore the unfortunate name of Spring Robin. Even though the Cajuns pronounced her last name Ro-ban, they still teased her. Unlike red-haired May, Spring had "gone silver" with pride, actually more smoky blue, the color of her tightly-permed curls. With them sat Spring's son, the cold-handed Waldo. Even though Jane knew what was coming, she could hardly ignore them. She took the sole empty chair for a hopefully short visit.

"Miss May, Miss Spring, having a good time?"

"We only just got here. Jethro is getting our drinks," May answered, referring to her elderly brother. "The place is packed. I guess our waitress will get here eventually."

"Oh, I'm taking Mr. Jethro's seat! I should go back

to my own."

The band announced another song. Too late for her to flee.

"Why don't you and Waldo get out there and dance. He's light on his feet, believe you me," May touted for her nephew.

Those cold hands moved across the table and captured hers. Waldo had a long face that looked as if it never smiled. Handy for an undertaker, Jane supposed. He possessed wings of silver at the sides of his shoe polish black hair, and she wondered how he managed that unless he'd gone completely gray and dyed the rest, a good bet. Morose brown eyes rested on gray bags of flesh. Did she detect the faintest whiff of formaldehyde under the scent of his overwhelming cologne?

Waldo forced a thin-lipped smile more appropriate for the funeral parlor than a dance hall. "My aunt has told me so many good things about you, Jane. May I have the pleasure of this dance?"

"Um, thank you, Waldo, but I'm here with someone." Jane spied Merlin heading back to their booth with her sissy drink and a bottle of beer for himself. She waved frantically, and he nodded.

May Robin's mouth fell open revealing a little too much of her dentures. "You're here with Blackie Tauzin? Don't you know he's—"

"A war hero." Spring finished her sentence. "He can put his dancing shoes under my bed any day." Her light blue eyes twinkled behind a pair of wire-framed granny glasses. She ogled Merlin over the rims.

"Please, Mother, he's a psycho. All those veterans are. Before he went into the service, he was just another juvenile delinquent. Don't you recall he stole my hearse the day after I bought out Armand Duchamp when the old man wanted to retire?" For Jane's sake, he added, "I do own the business free and clear, but kept the Duchamp name. Somehow, Robin's funeral home sounded too cheery and lacking in dignity."

"Oh, Waldo. Blackie only went for a joy ride. No one takes a hearse to a chop shop." Spring fanned her hand in front of her face. "I always did like a man who rode a Harley. Maybe it's the black leather jackets, not like the one he has on tonight, but those tight-fitting ones."

Without releasing Jane's hands, Spring's son continued with his tale, "I wanted to press charges, but someone with pull got him off."

"He did no harm to that hearse and paid you back for the gas," his mother said.

"I believe he might have had sexual intercourse in the back. I found stains!"

"Could have been from leaky coffins," Spring suggested.

"My caskets do not leak! They are top quality."

Jane freed her hands after a brief struggle. "I should get back."

"You didn't tell me you and Blackie were a couple. There are things you should know," May said with a tad of hurt in her voice.

"Not a couple. So not a couple. Remember, I told you a friend helped clean my yard. He's the friend. I'm taking him to dinner as a thanks. That's all."

Jethro Robin made his way painfully back to the table with his long, bony fingers wrapped around four longnecks. Once as tall and thin as Waldo, he now bent over with a permanent crick in his back. A tiny pot belly rested just above his belt buckle. His hair had gone entirely white, but he still shared dark eyes, gray pouches, and a gloomy attitude with his son. Not much of Spring showed in Waldo. She was as plump and spritely as a, well—a spring robin.

"Thought they'd never serve me, making an old man with a bad back wait and wait." He slammed the bottles on the table so hard foam erupted from the tops and puddled down on the checkered oilcloth.

Ignoring her brother's ill humor, May cautioned, "That's very nice of him, Jane, but if you need any other help, ask me and I'll find someone."

"I considered asking him to haul my recyclables to the center in Lafayette, at least the aluminum cans since I can't seem to convince the council to move forward in restoring the program. He has a truck, and I don't think it will fit in my car."

"Don't do that. Waldo can put it all in his hearse," May suggested.

"Aunt May! I can't. What would people say if I place trash where their loved ones might someday rest? Think of the reputation of Duchamp's Funeral Home."

"If you can't see I'm trying to help you out..."

"Yes, of course. Jane, I would love to help you, but—"

"Oh, bring it all over to our place. We live in the city limits of Chapelle and still have our program. Just use our bin anytime," Spring offered.

"That would be wonderful! Thank you."

"All settled happily then. If you and Blackie aren't dating, then I can see no reason why we shouldn't dance together." Waldo took Jane in his icy clutches and led her to the dance floor.

He held her at arm's length doing a very proper waltz step, one, two, three, and one, two, three. Not quite able to follow his lead, she still stumbled along after two turns around the small space. On the third turn, Waldo stopped in his tracks as a big hand tapped him none too gently on the shoulder.

"You're dancing with my lady. You should have asked permission."

Waldo moved out of the stream of dancers but kept Jane's hand. Easily as tall as Merlin but much slimmer, Jane imagined her non-date could have picked Waldo up and spun him over his head like a majorette's baton.

"How very old-fashioned of you, Blackie. I am sure Jane can decide with whom she wants to dance," the funeral director sneered.

"Yes, I can," Jane asserted, wondering why she took Waldo's side when she wanted to be rid of him. Oh yes, because she was a modern professional woman, not a Victorian lady, that's why.

"Do you want to dance with this man, Jane?" Blackie said carefully, dangerously.

"Certainly she does. We were having a very pleasant time before you interrupted."

No, she wanted to escape Waldo's cold, cold grip, but on the other hand, she really did not want to encourage Merlin to think of her as his lady. That would be bad, very bad—maybe. "I, uh…"

Suddenly, Spring Robin popped up in their midst. "Why Blackie Tauzin, how is Olive doing in assisted living? I keep meaning to visit her."

"She likes it there, Miss Spring, and would love for you to visit her." Just like that, the threatening Merlin vanished and the one kind to old ladies appeared.

"I don't suppose a handsome young man like you would take an old lady for a spin around the dance floor? Jethro really can't manage too well anymore with his bad back. Oh, I do remember what a wonderful dancer your grandpa was. We stepped out a few times when we were young. I bet you have the same smooth moves."

"Mother, please!" Waldo begged.

"Yes, ma'am. I learned from him and my granny. Grandpa's dancing shoes used to be nailed to that very rafter before the last hurricane took the roof off this place. Granny donated them after he died. Don't know where they are now."

"What a sad loss, both your grandpa and his shoes. Well?" Spring Robin held up her plump, saggy arms.

Gallantly, Merlin swung the old woman into the dance. They glided by one turn before Waldo repossessed Jane and dragged her after the other couple. She noticed her just-a-friend held Mrs. Robin much more loosely, but they did make a cute couple with that curly, blue hair coming up only to the middle of his broad chest. Jane heard a few aaahs from the watchers. If Merlin wasn't careful, he'd have a queue of old women lining up to dance with him.

Waldo bent his stiff neck enough say over the music, "You should be careful, Jane. That man is a nut case."

"Maybe," a deep voice said. Moving faster than Waldo and Jane, Merlin and Spring came up beside them. "I just might shoot you dead for that remark. That's what us nut cases do. I want Jane back."

Stunned by Merlin's words, Waldo dropped his arms and, already a pale man due to his indoor trade, turned even whiter. A moment later, he found himself dancing with his own mother.

Back in Merlin's arms, Jane moved a hand under his black leather jacket, across the small of his back and over his hips. "You aren't packing."

"Nope. Since I got back from Afghanistan I can't hardly stand to hunt anymore, but if you keep that up, you'll have to ask me the Mae West question."

"What?"

"Is that a gun in your pocket, or are you just happy to see me?"

"Oh, that quote."

"I am happy to see you." He pressed her a little closer. Yes, obviously her nearness delighted him.

Changing the subject quickly as she could and pulling away a little, Jane asked, "Did you really steal Waldo's hearse?" She had no intention of asking him about the stains in the back of the vehicle.

"Yep. Just a joke. He was a prick then. He's still a prick. Wanted to have me put in juvie for a prank even after Granny went and pleaded with him not to press charges. I guess the judge had a sense of humor. He let me off with community service. I helped put in those flowerbeds around the church downtown. They still look pretty good. Anyhow, when Grandpa died, we took our business elsewhere."

"Good for you. Speaking of flowerbeds, would you like to bring your grandmother over to see ours, I mean mine, tomorrow? If you don't fill up at the retirement home brunch, we can have dessert together, the three of us."

"She'd like that. Thanks. I ordered us some bread pudding and coffee before I came over to rescue you from that shit, Waldo."

"I didn't need rescuing."

"Sure looked like you did, but even if you didn't, I got my jollies from seeing him almost shit himself when I threatened to kill him. Anyhow, dessert is waiting for us."

"Maybe I didn't want any dessert."

"That's okay. I can eat both servings." Merlin steered her back to their booth with a firm hand on the small of her back.

The warm bread pudding, hot coffee, a flat beer, and her greatly diluted rum and Coke adorned their table. Jane ate her portion. Why she continued to struggle with Merlin's high-handedness, she had no idea. He didn't appear to be the kind of man who could morph from Neanderthal to metrosexual very easily.

A fellow lingering at the bar came over with his date and asked if they'd like to exchange partners for a while. Jane knew where that idea came from. The other woman had scarlet lips, long blonde hair hanging halfway down her back, jeans so tight Jane could see her crack, and a tramp stamp on the small of her back revealed by her low riders that said, "Wanna See More?" Another tattoo riding across the top of her bulging breasts identified her as a "Honky-Tonk Woman". Unlike Jane, this gal apparently could dance in four-inch heels.

"Jane?" Merlin asked.

"Sure. I don't own you." There, she'd made her point.

"I'm Wanda, and that's good to know. Come on, tall, dark and handsome."

That left Jane with average-sized, red-haired, and

so-so looking Blaine who turned out to be a decent dancer because he didn't try any fancy moves beyond his level of skill. He seemed a nice enough guy, too. They talked a little. He worked fourteen days on, fourteen days off in the oil patch. When he got a paycheck, Wanda had no objections to going out with him. He knew enough to give his date some space.

"Yes," Jane said. "We all need space, but Wanda doesn't appear to be giving much of that to Merlin."

The honky-tonk woman had her arms locked around his shoulders and the rest of her body applied like wet paint to his body. As for Merlin, he rested his manly chin on the top of her head and just kept on dancing in his slick shoes. They stayed with their impromptu partners for the whole set.

When the band took a break, Wanda kept Merlin's hand. "Why don't we buy these nice folks a round of drinks, Blaine?"

"No, thanks," Jane said simultaneously with Merlin.

"I think we'd better be getting home. If you want to leave, Jane?"

"Yes, but great meeting you."

"You got a cell phone?" Wanda asked.

"Nope," Merlin replied. Jane knew he did, but he'd left it in the truck.

"A pen?" Wanda inquired, not giving up.

Jane opened her small purse. "I have one."

"Great!" Wanda used the borrowed pen to write her phone number on a paper napkin. "Maybe we can double date sometime. Personally, I think Blaine and Jane make the little ole cutest couple." She didn't elaborate on the kind of couple she and Merlin made, but Jane suspected "hot." Wanda shoved the napkin into his hip pocket.

Without comment, Merlin picked up the tab from the table and nodded good-bye. He preceded Jane to the cashier. She outdid herself dodging crowded tables to get there first and slap her credit card down on the counter. Merlin handed it back to her and replaced it with one of his own.

"But I owe you for the yard work!"

"Nope. What you owed me was the pleasure of your company for the evening. That's all I asked for, Jane."

The pleasure of her company—why did that thrill her down to the peep toes of her sandals? Oh-oh, maybe he'd expect more pleasure when they got back to her house. She had him figured out and her pepper spray ready all the way back to Chapelle. He didn't talk much, just turned on the radio, and kept his eyes on the road. She'd been watching his drinking in case she had to take his keys and drive the humongous truck, how she wasn't sure. However, Merlin confined himself to that one whiskey before dinner and half a beer after. Mostly, they'd stuffed themselves with good food and danced. Tired and full, sure Merlin had total mastery of the road, Jane dozed. The pepper spray fell from her grip and rolled under the front seat.

She woke when the big engine went silent. Groggy, she reached for the door handle, but Merlin stood there ready to help her down. He did that by putting his hands around her waist again and lifting. She should protest these peremptory moves, but somehow her will wasn't functioning at the moment. He walked her to the front door where a couple of moths made love to her glowing carriage lamp.

"I didn't say how pretty you look tonight." Drawing his fingers along her collarbone, he touched her necklace. "Great dress, but this I don't get—broken chunks of glass?"

His hand stayed right there. Her pulse picked up speed. "Recycled wine bottles."

"Oh. I know where you can find one made out of gum wrappers and pull tabs."

"Are you making fun of me, Merlin?"

"Nope." He lowered his head for the goodnight kiss, and he kissed the way he danced—with complete mastery. His hand slipped behind her head, holding her at just the right angle. He started out firm and commanding, then added a few fun flourishes of his tongue.

By the time he finished, Jane heard herself say, "Would you like to come in?" as if she'd pre-recorded the message.

"Not our third date yet. I don't want to rush you."

"Merlin, we haven't had any dates."

"We had dinner together the other night and again tonight."

"If you count those, you might as well say sitting on your stoop the first night we met was a date."

"I wouldn't go that far."

Pity. Shame on you, Jane. Get a grip. Mental chiding in full force, she answered, "Okay. Well, thanks for a nice evening. See you around."

"Tomorrow. I'm bringing Granny over to see the flowerbeds, remember?"

No, she didn't. That kiss had wiped out a memory circuit for sure. "Right. Tomorrow."

Chapter Seven

The growl of Merlin's truck announced Olive Tauzin's arrival. Jane recalled her from the closing on the house as a sweet old lady with fluffy white hair drawn into a tight little knob on the top of her head and round, dark eyes that filled with tears as they signed the papers selling the family home. Thinking the loss made Mrs. Tauzin distraught, Jane promised to take good care of the property.

"No, no, *cher*. You don't understand. I'm crying because you saved the place and won't tear it down like the other bidder."

Jane knew someone else had offered close to a hundred thousand for the corner property now near a stoplight. Her own bid of forty-five thousand seemed pitiful and unfair, but the house needed more than that amount in renovations according to a study she paid to have done before buying. She had to take out a second loan to get the job done. If the Tauzin home, built in 1875, had passed into those other hands, the convenience store and gas station would be sitting on this lot and not across the street on the other side of the light.

Regardless, Olive Tauzin seemed like the kind of old-timey woman who would make everything from scratch. Jane spent her Sunday morning baking a pecan pie using nuts gathered in the yard and stored in the freezer along with her mother's own recipe for an extra-flaky crust. She scalloped the edges with a spoon and in the end her masterpiece resembled a giant sunflower. Gathering lemons from the tree Merlin had observed had a real nice crop, she made fresh-squeezed lemonade with real sugar and put on a pot of coffee, dark roast, the way Cajuns liked it. She had no dining room, but the kitchen was spacious with plenty of room for a table and four chairs. A bowl of extra lemons held in a brown glazed bowl and accented with sprigs of the sweet olive now blooming wildly since being liberated from the vines sat in the center of that table. Glasses, mugs, plates, spoons, dessert forks and a pie server waited for the arrival of company.

Jane expected a knock any second at the kitchen door but instead, her front bell rang. She hurried through the house to find Olive Tauzin sitting on the porch swing and Merlin carrying a walker with yellow tennis balls on its feet up the steps.

"Oh, you should have come in the back way. It's shorter. So nice to see you again, Mrs. Tauzin."

"We're guests, not family. Call me Olive, or Miss Olive if you need to. I want to see the house. Merlin told me what a good job you did with it. How nice the floors turned out. Didn't know all that wood was under there. I made sure the tennis balls are on tight so I didn't ruin them."

Olive raised herself up on the walker her grandson placed carefully before her. A tiny woman, her black eyes as bright and curious as one of the squirrels in the pecan tree, she moved across the porch at a fairly good pace. Her lace-collared, flowered dress hiked up in the back as she bent over and showed a bit of her slip. She entered Jane's house, peeking into the small living room where Jane had laid down a tan and white cotton rug and furnished with two overstuffed chairs and a comfortably battered brown leather sofa. The television hid in an old cypress cabinet. Small local works of art enlivened the walls.

Olive thumped across the hall. "What do you call this room?"

A desk of dark cherry wood held her computer. A rug, faux oriental from Lowe's, covered the floor. Crowded bookcases covered the walls everywhere except the two window spaces and the small, corner fireplace.

"My library. I guess that's sort of pretentious."

"Nope, you got enough books for it. See, I told you she has class, Granny," Merlin said.

"Those fireplaces work now? We closed them up to keep out the draft," the old lady said. All four of the original rooms had them built into corners sharing the two brick chimneys on either side of the house.

"Yes, they do. Not that we need them very much in south Louisiana."

"Folks used to keep low fires burning to cut the humidity even in summer."

"Interesting, I did not know that. Sometimes on a rainy night I make a fire and run the air conditioner at the same time. I know I'm wasting energy, but…"

"Enjoy life while you can and don't worry so much," Olive advised. "Old age comes quick enough." She thumped off to the next room and, without a moment of hesitation, threw open the door to Jane's bedroom.

"A brass bed, I knew it," Merlin commented from

behind the two women.

Jane's eyes went immediately to her nightie and matching sea foam green robe hung over the footboard. Her silly, pink bunny slippers peeked out from under a bed skirt the color of spring foliage like shy, woodland creatures. In a hurry to start her preparations that morning, she hadn't pulled up the floral-sprigged comforter or fluffed her pillows. Her jewelry and makeup covered the top of a light oak dresser helter-skelter. Slung over a chair upholstered in fabric that matched the comforter her dress from dancing at Mulate's failed to cover the underwear on its seat.

"Green lace," Merlin said, his voice deepening with regret as if he'd thrown away a great opportunity.

"We don't mention a lady's unmentionables, even if she leaves them out where everyone can see, boy," Miss Olive corrected.

"Sorry, I had no time to clean this morning. I baked a pecan pie. Would you like some pie? Let's go to the kitchen." Jane shut her bedroom door the second Olive Tauzin's rear cleared the jamb.

"I want to see the other bedroom where Herve and me used to sleep."

For a cripple, the old lady could move. She flung open that door and registered her disappointment. "Not much in here."

Jane's dusty treadmill sat in the middle of the room facing a small, portable TV on a stand. "I haven't decorated in here yet, but when I can afford the furniture, I'll make a guest bedroom. The bath turned out nice. Would you like to see the bath?"

At least, she had taken the time to scrub that and put out fresh towels for her visitors in case either of them needed to use the facilities. Right next door, it had been added to the rear of the house just like the kitchen, hence her fear of streaking across the hall to her bedroom when Merlin lurked by her refrigerator the other night.

Not lemons but palm trees dominated the décor on the wallpaper and the appliqué on the guest towels. She'd retained the old claw-footed tub and pedestal sink, both refurbished, but added a showerhead and a curtain patterned in fronds that could be tucked in when she wanted to wash her hair. Otherwise, she liked to luxuriate in the deep, refinished bath, preferably with bubbles or scented bath salts in the water. The commode, however, was new. No way to get years of stains out of the old toilet. One of the workmen hauled that away to make a planter at his house.

"Nice," Merlin said, glancing from the oval framed mirror over the sink to the deep tub and back as if he fantasized about Jane covered in a froth of bubbles while he shaved his heavy, black beard.

Or maybe, she invented the fantasy. He'd be wearing only a towel, low slung on his hips. The mirror revealed his muscled chest covered in a mat of black hair, his swarthy face lathered in pure white shaving cream. He caught her watching and unleashed a lascivious smile that promised he'd soon be in that tub with her.

"Pie! Let's get out of here and have pie." With her heart beating way too fast, Jane led her guests to the kitchen.

Merlin got his grandmother settled while Jane poured the lemonade and cut thick slices of her pecan masterpiece. She awaited Olive's verdict. The old lady considered the dessert as if she were judging in a 4H contest. She stuck a fork in one petal of the crust and watched it flake off and drift to the plate.

Eyeing the filling, Olive said, "You used the Betty Crocker recipe with the three eggs and the light corn syrup, no?"

"Why, yes."

"I always used Steen's molasses. It makes a rich, dark pie, but your crust is good. You used pecans from my old tree. Most people won't bother to shell those little nuts, too small. They been spoiled by those huge, tasteless paper shell pecans. These are sweet, sweet." Finally, the judging done, Olive took a bite, nodded, and declared, "Tasty."

"Real sugar in the lemonade, too. I was afraid you'd use that artificial stuff." Merlin drained his glass and dug into his pie. Between large bites, he said, "Say, I'd like to go upstairs to my old bedroom in the attic and see what you did with it."

"The *garçonniere*," his grandmother corrected as she accepted a mug of coffee.

"You can slap a fancy French name on it, but us boys still slept in an attic with two mattresses on the floor and one rattling old air conditioner to make it bearable in summer."

Miss Olive sniffed. "In my day, no one had air conditioning, and we didn't complain. Go on if you want. You know I can't do those stairs no more." She accepted another tee-tiny piece of pie before they left the kitchen.

Jane and Merlin went out on the front porch and climbed the outside stairs to the traditional *garçonniere*. She explained as they went that some of the old boards had been replaced, but the contractor had carefully matched them with aged cypress to replicate the weathered gray color. As they entered the area, Merlin ducked his head to keep from bashing himself on the slanting roof beams. He glanced around with amazement.

"I've grown some since I last slept here. The trick is to remember to stay in the center of the room. If the place had looked like this in my time, Doyle and me would have thought we were staying at the Hilton. Gaw, you put in a bathroom."

"Just a small one with a shower, sink, and commode. I thought my brother might like to stay up here if he visits with my parents. What did you and Doyle do for—facilities?"

"Oh, Granny never locked the front door so we could go downstairs if we really needed to take a crap. She gave us one of those chamber pots to use, too, but mostly we just peed off the side of the stairs. Killed her hydrangeas. Nice bed."

Merlin sat on the single sleigh bed with a pull-out trundle in the bottom. He still had to lean forward a little to avoid the hand-hewn beams left showing between the slabs of the new insulated ceiling. As below, the floor had been redone and decorated in this case with oval rag rugs. A couple of cowhide chairs and a small flea market table sat near a tiny window. Two lanterns hung from the central beam, but came on with the snap of a switch rather than a strike of a match. On this fairly warm afternoon, the central air conditioning blew gently across the space big as the four original rooms below but narrowed by the slanting rafters.

Merlin lay down, put his feet up on the footboard

of the bed, and his hands behind his head. "I can see me here and Doyle on that trundle just listening to the summer rain beat on the tin roof. You ever been up here when it rains?"

"No, but I do hope you are comfortable there."

"Hey, my shoes are clean. The best, most soothing sound in the world. I used to dream about Louisiana rain when I was overseas." His eyes closed.

Jane ventured closer from the middle of the room where standing presented no problem. "Merlin, we shouldn't leave your granny alone downstairs."

"Sure, help me up."

She should have seen it coming but still offered her hand. He used his much superior strength to lever her on top of him.

"Did you wear those green panties for me last night?"

"Certainly not! They matched my dress, that's all." She braced her arms on his chest and pushed up slightly bumping her head on a beam.

"Sure, I know how important it is to match your dress and panties when no one is going to see it. Why hell, I pick my boxer briefs in the same color as my eyes." A grin pushed at the corner of his mouth trying to expand.

"It matters to women!" she protested, absolutely sure no fabric could ever duplicate that stunning shade of blue, but she wasn't going to ask him to show her.

He brought her face down to meet his. The kiss began with a flick of his tongue across her lips still a little sticky from the syrup in the pie. He coaxed his way inside her mouth, all the while raking her hair with his fingertips. She answered him stroke for stroke

A Trashy Affair

despite the rasp of his beard against her skin until they ran out of air. Surrendering, Jane collapsed against the hardness of his body.

"Tasty," he said, mimicking his grandmother. "You know why they put the Cajun boys in the attic? So they could go out, carouse, and sow their wild oats without disturbing the rest of the family."

"Out is the operative word. I doubt if those boys did any sowing right over their granny's head—which we are doing at the moment."

"No, we're not. Listen."

The unmistakable thump-step of the walker progressed across the boards of the porch right to the bottom of the steps. "What she got up there, Merlin, a bed?" Miss Olive shouted in her cracked old lady voice.

"Yep, a real fancy one, and a john, too. I'm going to use it, then be right down."

But Jane got to the bathroom first to finger comb her hair and make sure her lipstick wasn't all over her face. No lipstick problem. He'd licked it all off, damn him! But her lips glowed red from passionate contact and her chin bore a small pink patch from his stubble. She dabbed the beard burn with a cold, wet tissue. Not much help. Tucking the tails of her yellow silk shirt back into her black, tailored slacks and making sure all the buttons were closed, she turned the small space over to Merlin, ducking under his arms when he would have caged her inside with him. She rushed down the stairs to find Miss Olive rocking in the porch swing and took a seat beside her.

"Sorry we took so long. He was very interested in everything up there."

"I bet he was. Not to worry. My grandson ain't

taken much interest in women since he come back from the war this last time. That's not good for a young man. First time over there, he seemed okay, not now."

Merlin's heavy steps on the stairs alerted them. "Not talking about me, I hope."

"No, I was telling Jane how pretty the flowers are, purple and gold, my favorite colors." That pink, wrinkled face stayed perfectly innocent.

"Merlin, baby, go across to the Fast 'N Fun and get your granny some scratch-offs." Miss Olive fumbled with a net bag on her walker and took out a change purse. "Get me twenty of different kinds. You know, the casino bus comes twice a month to Magnolia Villa to take us Indian gambling, but I don't get out enough to get my scratch-offs," she informed Jane.

Her grandson waved the folded twenty away. "I got it, Granny." He loped off to do her bidding.

"He'll be gone a while. People certainly do like their fried chicken boxes and Sunday plate lunches. The line is out the door around this time. I just wish their trash didn't end up in my ditch. Oh well, can I get you more coffee, Miss Olive?" Jane asked.

"No, thank you, *cher.* I'm wearing my good drawers, not my diaper." She placed a wrinkled, veiny hand over Jane's lying on the swing. "I want to talk to you about Merlin. On the outside, he's this big, tough man, but inside he hurts. He won what they call the Distinguished Flying Cross in Afghanistan for saving six lives. He was coming back from an insertion of troops when he saw a squad pinned down with no way out. Why, he swooped right in and rescued six of those men, two of them riding on the struts of his helicopter. Got them to safety, called for help, but by the time another helicopter got there, the rest were killed. He can't get over not saving them all. I wouldn't know a word of this if the army hadn't sent the papers and the medal to us. Merlin won't talk about it, but his mama blabbed. Just made it worse that the town wanted to give him a parade, and he refused to attend."

"He should be proud of saving the six."

"That's what everyone thinks, but not him. He has lots of other hurts he holds inside from before he went into the army. You know about his mama?"

"That she's—simple-minded." Jane used Merlin's own term. Retarded sounded too harsh, special too precious.

"Yes, my Herve, being a small farmer, didn't have much insurance. I waited too long to go to the hospital trying to save on money. Foolish. Anyhow, nothing wrong with her body. She's *tres petite* like me, but pretty as a buttercup when she was young. I'll bet you a winning scratch-off Merlin didn't tell you my Jenny gave birth to him at just fourteen. A smart college guy, a young man who oughten to have known better, knocked her up. When Herve threatened to go to the police to report it, the boy's rich daddy comes running. Please don't ruin his son's life. Oh, he'll see Jenny and the child are supported until the kid reaches eighteen. A thousand dollars a month, he offered. Sounded good at the time. All our daughter had to do was say she didn't know who fathered the baby. They had a slick city lawyer draw up papers with one of those non-disclosure clauses. All three of us signed."

"No, he didn't tell me any of this. Merlin doesn't know who his real father is?"

"He certainly does. Smart boy, he figured it out by

himself, but I can't tell you. I doubt he will. We had to take Jenny out of school because she got a reputation for being loose after that, a girl who didn't know who fathered her baby. She would of earned only a certificate of completion, anyhow. We kept her close where we could watch over her and the baby until she turned eighteen. Then, Herve asked old man Broussard to give her a job at his dance hall. They were friends from childhood, so Broussard promised to watch out for Jenny. I guess he did his best, but she come up pregnant again. Harley David ain't much, can't keep a job, hardly raised a sweat on the farm, but he stepped up. Every night she works, he's at the bar watching out for her. All of them lived here, Jenny's second and third babies, then her baby girl's baby, too, before I had to sell the place."

"Merlin wanted the house. He said he was saving his flight and dangerous duty pay to buy it from you." Jane craned her neck to see if Miss Olive's grandson returned with the tickets. Not yet. She had a good view of the Fast 'N Fun now that the bushes were trimmed, more's the pity.

"Best he start over where there ain't so many sad memories: his grandpa wasting of cancer, his little sister catching a baby just like her mother before her, having to sell off the pasture and woodlot to a developer, then the cane fields to pay the doctor bills, Doyle going into the army. Not a damned thing Merlin could do about any of it, but he took each blow hard. He thinks he ruined his mother's life, should have stayed in college and made big money to pay our bills, and been here to prevent Brittney from going with that guy and Doyle from enlisting."

Jane watched Merlin emerge from the convenience store trailing several streamers of scratch-off tickets. "He's coming, Miss Olive."

"Only have one more thing to say. I like you, Jane, but don't you hurt my grandson. It's bad enough he bought a townhouse from that snake oil salesman, Bernard Freeman, and sits over there brooding day after day." Miss Olive pursed her lips as if she wanted to spit right on porch, but she held back. "My Merlin smiles when he talks about you. I haven't seen that smile in too, too long, so you be careful of him, you hear?"

"I'll try."

With that ground-eating stride and a fearless tendency to jaywalk in the Sunday traffic, Merlin joined them in no time at all. "I got twenty for Granny and ten each for me and you."

He broke blocks of tickets off the streamers, shuffled them like a blackjack dealer, and gave each a pile. Olive took three pennies from her change purse and handed them out. They scratched away in earnest until their knees and the porch floor glittered with silver flakes like an unexpected snow. One after another, Miss Olive threw the losing tickets to the ground until she finally came up with a two-dollar winner and then a ten. Merlin won nothing, but Jane revealed a doubler that earned her twenty. She handed her ticket to Olive Tauzin.

"Here, you bet I didn't know something, and you were right. I don't know nearly as much as I should."

"Yeah, you can be a showoff smarty pants sometimes," Merlin remarked, that grin straining to break out. "But you should never bet with Granny. She may seem delicate as a china teacup, but this woman is the steel spine of our family."

"I believe that. It's been interesting getting to know her."

"Everyone says so. She's surprising. You ready to go, Granny?"

"*Mais,* yeah, as soon as you drive me over to the store to collect my winnings. Thirty-two dollars. I think you bring the Tauzin family luck, Jane. But I need to be back at the Villa quick, quick for afternoon bingo. We'll talk again, *cher* heart."

With Jane moving ahead carrying the walker, Merlin transported his grandmother down the porch steps and set her between the handles. Olive batted him away when he tried to help her balance and offered to bring the truck onto the lawn to make it easier for her.

"Put ruts in this pretty yard? *Mais*, no. Go say goodbye to Jane and put some sugar in it. You got *merde* mouth since you come home from the army."

Unlike Merlin, Jane did not suppress her glee. "*Merde* mouth, quite the phrase. I love it!"

"Well, it's a shitty world most of the time. I work this week so I won't be around."

"On Thanksgiving Day, too?"

"Someone has to be on duty in case of emergencies. Lots of the guys have families. I don't. Mostly, we sit around the hangar, play cards, and eat pizza. Usually, the boss lets us off early as long as we wear our beepers."

"People eat pizza on Thanksgiving?"

"Only the lonely."

"Won't your mother be making a dinner for you?"

He shook his head. "She and Harley, Brittney and her little boy, Jayden, will eat with Granny at Magnolia

Villa. They put on a pretty nice spread from eleven to two, fancier than anything my mom can do, but it's over before I get back."

Why did this tug at her heart? The invitation came pouring out from the same source. "Look, I'll be alone, too. My parents moved back to Montana after they retired to take care of my grandmother who is just as feisty as yours, only she refuses to move out of her house. No assisted living for her. I don't have enough time off to fly up there. I plan to help serve the homeless at noon, but I ordered an all-natural, free-range turkey for myself, and I'll bake a pumpkin pie if you want to come over and eat with me in the evening."

"Will you have sweet potatoes covered in tiny marshmallows, green beans made with cream soup, and cranberry sauce from the can sliced along the ring marks?"

"No. Mine will be better for you."

"Okay. I'll take a chance. Here's my cell phone number in case you have a change of plans or get a better offer."

Merlin handed her a rather handsome business card proclaiming his position as a pilot for Rice Aviation Services, Inc. in sky blue letters on a glossy white background with a small, golden helicopter in the corner. He'd penned his personal number on the back. He seemed so prepared Jane wondered if he'd slipped one of these to Wanda, the honky-tonk woman. But, he didn't need to do that. He had Wanda's number on a napkin. What difference should that make to her?

"I won't change my mind. See you on Thursday evening around six."

"Yep."

Just yep. No thanks, no sounds great, just yep. What exactly was she to do with Merlin Tauzin? His granny called in her crackly voice, "Merlin, boost me up into this monster truck of yours."

"Coming."

And going out of Jane's life for most of the following week.

Chapter Eight

A week without Merlin Tauzin. Did that make her life better or worse? Hard to say and little time to think about it. After work on Monday, Jane stuffed her little hybrid with all the hoarded recyclables it could hold and drove into Chapelle to place the things in the Robin's bin. The city provided the Cadillac of recycling carts, high and sleek, black with the recycling symbol emblazoned in white on its sides and a hinged cover, nothing like the parish's orange boxes with the black lids that blew off in every storm. Jane argued that more people would recycle if the parish boxes had wheels and did not have to be lugged pressed against the stomach to the street or shoved along the ground. Folks out in the parish had long drives. Wheels would have made a difference certainly. As usual, the council ignored her suggestion. They already knew they weren't going to renew the recycling contract. Why bother to order better carts?

Jethro Robin hadn't yet rolled his cart to the curb on its sturdy, inset, smooth-rolling wheels. Tall, dark, and alluring, it sat in the carport beckoning to Jane. Since no one appeared to be home, she drove up beside the perfect container and began to unload. The very bottom of the Robin's bin held some aluminum cans and a few glass jars resting on a week's worth of the *Chapelle Clarion* newspaper. A few flattened cardboard boxes graced its sides.

Jane added several pounds of newspapers, a medley of jars, cans, and plastic containers, all topped with a gleaming mound of aluminum that included Merlin's crushed disks. She almost kept one for sentimental reasons, but believed there might be more in her future. The lid would not close. Using both her hands, she mashed the contents down as far as she could. Finally, the cover shut most of the way, leaving only a small slit showing a metallic grin like braces on a teenager. Totally satisfied, she returned home from her trashy rendezvous.

No lights shone in Merlin's townhouse, and he did not sit on his front stoop this evening. Jane found she missed him just a little. She erred by mentioning that he did not seem to be around when she ate lunch in the break room the following day with May and several of her other coworkers.

May immediately pounced. "I knew y'all were more than friends and neighbors."

"No, no. He is working this week. Only I expected him to be home in the evenings."

"Most likely he's staying out on the rigs and ferrying crews around," Angela Savoy said. Nineteen, nubile, and a newlywed, she had long, dark lashes to die for over amber eyes and a stream of deep brown hair flowing to the middle of her back. She took a diet milkshake from her calico lunch bag and shook it vigorously.

"I can drink it better when it's foamy and tastes more like a real shake. I lived on this before my wedding to be sure I could fit in my gown. Now I only drink it a few times a week. I can't let myself go now

I'm a married woman. May, this bag your sister-in-law made keeps it nice and cold. My Chad is offshore this week, too. He won't even be home for Thanksgiving. I guess I'll eat with my parents again."

"Merlin said he'd be in for the holiday." Quickly, Jane stuffed a corner of her tuna on whole wheat into her mouth before she revealed even more to the lunchroom gossips.

"My Chad says there are rigs he won't sleep on because the men are G-A-Y and get after you."

Jane doubted any man would try to creep into bed with Merlin or goose him in the shower. Remembering the threat made to Waldo Robin, she believed they would know enough to leave him alone.

Angela glanced over Jane's shoulder and lowered her voice. "Speaking of G-A-Y, here comes Nadia."

Not reacting to the entrance, Jane continued eating her half sandwich until Nadia's large hands dumped a floral centerpiece directly in front of her and smashed the rest of her lunch. A large white mum augmented to resemble a turkey with goggle eyes nested amid smaller yellow and bronze flowers and artificial autumn leaves. A plastic insert declared, "Happy Thanksgiving" in gold lettering. Another pick held a small, white envelope.

"These are for you, Marshall. I had to sign for them since May is in here. The reception desk should never go unattended," Nadia declared in gruff voice.

"I'm entitled to my lunch hour," May protested.

"Then get one of these women to watch the desk for you. Stagger your lunch hours for Christ's sake. If a citizen is showing their appreciation for parish services, the flowers must remain in the lounge for all to enjoy.

Got that, Marshall? No plants or bouquets on the desks. That is unprofessional."

"I believe these are personal flowers, Nadia, but I will leave them here until I go home."

"See that you do." With her stub of a blond ponytail bobbing aggressively, the president's assistant stomped out of the room.

Angela leaned close to the other two women. "I asked her once if she was a real blonde because I sort of like that shade she's got. I think Chad might go for me as a blonde, that's all I meant. You know what she said to me? Get down on your knees under my desk and I'll show you. I swear she did!"

Jane spoke up. "That's sexual harassment. You should report it to Human Resources."

"Sure, and get fired. The HR guy is just as afraid of Nadia as the rest of us."

"I'm not afraid of her."

"Then you are the only one."

"The card," May prompted. "Read the card."

Jane removed it from the holder and read the message to herself. "Looking forward to free-range turkey, whatever that is. Merlin." He made her smile in a way that caught May's eye.

"From your honey?" she asked.

"Just a friend." Jane removed the turkey centerpiece from her smashed lunch bag and stuck the card into its front pocket intended to hold change for a soft drink. Inside the sack, the other half of the smashed tuna sandwich oozed from its wrappings, but the organic baby carrots were still fine. She could use the tuna filling as a dip. Nadia would not spoil her moment.

"Sure, just a friend," May murmured. "Merlin

Tauzin didn't dance with you like a friend. He held you like this." May wrapped her thin, loose-skinned, age-spotted arms around her chest and massaged her back with her fingers. "That's not how he danced with Spring."

"No, but he held that tramp, Wanda, like this." Jane plastered her own hands tight to her breasts. She made her voice low and seductive. "Oh, Merlin, why don't you dry hump me right on this dance floor? Here's my phone number. Let me stuff it in your crotch."

The entire assemblage of women occupying the room burst into laughter and sure enough attracted Nadia back into their midst from wherever she lurked listening in the hall.

"Vulgarity is not permitted in the lounge," she decreed.

"No, we should keep it in our offices under our desks," Jane answered and watched her nemesis turn red in the face about the same shade as the felt wattles on the flower turkey.

"I'm writing you up for this."

"Sure, you do that, Nadia." Jane thought her file must be stuffed full by now, yet she'd never gotten a single written copy of any infraction to sign. Somehow, she looked forward to telling Merlin all about this and sussing out if he'd saved Wanda's phone number. She thought she could make him laugh again.

## Chapter Nine

At afternoon break on Wednesday, Nadia Nixon braced herself in the doorway of the staff lounge. Showing her large, square teeth, she smiled at the assemblage of coffee drinkers and snackers. Nadia's grin implied she would not mercifully rip out someone's throat with one quick bite but rather preferred to grind their bones bit by bit with her big molars. Usually, her smile appeared on Fridays at three-twenty, a time the staff had come to call "The Last Coffee Break," sort of like the Last Supper without the holy overtone. Someone had been betrayed to the woman and would get the axe. With the parish offices near to closing for the Thanksgiving holiday until Monday, the president's administrative officer moved the event forward accordingly.

The group fell silent. The decaf coffee carafe with its orange collar pinged against the mug held in Angela Savoy's shaking hand. One woman brushed the powdered sugar from a pack of tiny donuts off her purple blouse. Another picked at a rough cuticle until it bled as if making eye contact with Nadia would doom her like looking at the snake-headed Medusa. Only Jane met that glittering, heavy-lidded stare. For a tenth of a second, she thought Nadia had come for her, and she would not go with head hanging because she'd done nothing wrong.

"May Robin, may I see you in my office?"

A collective gasp escaped from the spectators. May, the oldest among them, the MawMaw who listened to their personal problems, the most pleasant and sympathetic of human beings, rose from her seat. Her usually spry tread faltered. She paled so greatly the splotches of rouge she wore on her cheeks stood out like twin red lights at a crossing. Nadia waved her to go ahead as if being supremely polite to the septuagenarian. As they cleared the doorway and began the walk to Nadia's office, one of office stoolies murmured *The Funeral March* and her closest crony pronounced, "Dead woman walking."

"Not funny, Tonette and Didi." Jane stood and confronted them.

"The old hag messed with Miss Nixon. At her age, May should know better. Besides, it's time she goes and someone else gets that plum job of receptionist," Tonnette, a squat brunette with a uni-brow, said. "All you have to do is sit on your behind and answer the phone, maybe give some directions. No big deal and much better pay."

"Not that the position will go to you, Toni." Didi, a very alluring, light-skinned African-American woman, tossed her red hair extensions as if she'd already gotten the job and had outgrown her association with Tonette. "The boss will want someone attractive up front."

She cracked her gum to make her point. That gum would have to be disposed of at break's end as Nadia did not approve, but then Didi, the mistress of one of the councilmen, frequently broke the rules without repercussions. Her lover made sure she got hired for an easy, low-level parish job and paid her rent on the side.

Didi finished her diet orange soda and threw the can into the wastebasket next to Jane. She stretched showing off a sleek yet busty figure encased in a leopard print jumpsuit, and with a jangle of her large hoop earrings, went back to doing whatever she did in the office besides servicing her district representative.

Jane fished the can from the trash. "This can be recycled, you know. It should go in here." She turned to put it in the plastic bin she'd placed in the break room, but the receptacle did not occupy its usual place.

"That's gone, too, just like May," Tonette told her with a thick-lipped smirk. "Nadia took it away when the old contract expired. Surprised you didn't notice."

"Then, I'll take it home. May's brother is letting me use his bin."

Jane crumpled the can with the bronze lipstick smeared on its top around the opening and followed Didi from the room. They went in opposite directions, however. She ghosted toward Nadia's large, corner office. Not long after the assistant's arrival, all the blinds had been removed from the glass-walled cubicles in order to facilitate a good work ethic, Nadia claimed. Now, no one could pick a booger or scratch a personal itch in private. Those with strong stomachs might witness a firing if they so wished. Miss Nixon hoped they would—to increase the fear factor, Jane surmised. Still, she stayed close to the wall at its bend where she would be the least conspicuous.

Inside the glass fishbowl, May's sagging face registered disbelief. Nadia handed her a message slip. She shook her head in vehement denial. Nadia expounded for a few minutes, then shoved a set of papers forward. It bristled with sticky notes where May should sign her name. May shook her head again, made the sign of the cross, and pleaded. A dumpy, bald old man Jane hadn't noticed from her angle, came from the far corner of the room and put his arm around May's shaking shoulders. Wofford "Woof" Langlois, himself, had come to witness the dismissal of a woman who had worked with him every single day of his extended time in office.

Nadia pulled a box of tissues from her drawer and plunked it down on the desk within easy reach. Woof offered one to May, who turned and cried on his white shirt instead. Nadia busied herself with the intercom. In a matter of seconds, two waiting security guards with the firm tread of storm troopers marched down the opposite hall and took up a place by the door. Woof gently turned May toward the desk again. With trembling hands, she signed the papers. Nadia handed her a cardboard box from a stack behind her desk. As May exited the office, the guards fell in by her side, each taking an elbow as they guided her back to the reception desk. They brushed by Jane, still clutching the orange drink can, without a glance, though May appealed to her with sodden eyes through running black makeup. Appearing a little teary-eyed himself, Woof scuttled back to his own corner office. Nadia hung in the doorway as if she wanted to do victory chin-ups.

"Enjoy the show, Marshall?"

"You cannot ever convince me May deserved to be fired."

"We put the old gray mare out to pasture, that's all. About time. She spent more time selling those lunch bags than doing any real work. You want to see what convinced her to take her retirement. Do step inside."

Nadia made a wide gesture of invitation.

Feeling like the proverbial fly, Jane stepped into her web. Nadia moved to her desk and handed over a message slip neatly typed. "Please call Miss Van Dyke regarding her bush immediately." A phone number followed.

"So? We get lots of garden club ladies upset when the parish road crews maul their plantings."

"The number is for that gay bar downtown. At best, May failed to screen my calls. At worst, she indulged in a tasteless, insulting joke."

Jane shook her head. "May doesn't type the messages. She writes them down. Granted, sometimes they are a little hard to read, but…"

"She types mine on that old IBM Selectric I requisitioned from storage since her computer skills are minimal. I told her I could no longer tolerate her shaky scrawl. Hey, she got a choice between a decent retirement or getting fired and made the wise decision. And that's not the best news." Nadia showed her big, square teeth again.

I'll grind your bones to make my bread, Jane thought, staring at her. She placed her hands on her hips and leaned across the broad desk. "Off she goes without so much as a word of thanks for her years of service or a farewell party?"

"Have one for her on your own time, Marshall. What, don't want to hear the good news?"

"I don't imagine it concerns me."

"But it does. Since the recycling program tanked, you have only half a job left."

"That's absurd. I'm working on a very important proposal that has to be finished by mid-December, and others will follow. I bring money to this parish for environmental projects."

"Yeah, yeah, and you can do that while manning the reception desk. Use the computer out there. God knows May hardly touched it. It's like brand new. Feel free to continue typing my messages on the Selectric, though." Her smile grew broader. Crunch, crunch.

"The phone rings constantly, and people come to the desk for directions. I can't work on a serious proposal with so many interruptions."

"Lately, most of the calls are about the garbage service your specs screwed up. You have to handle them anyhow. Or are you telling me you can't multitask? That handling a reception desk is beyond you? If so, hand in your resignation and save us all some grief."

Grief, hell. If she knew how to shake her booty, Nadia would be doing the happy dance right now to celebrate her triumph over Jane. House payment. Renovation loan. Car payment. Jane swallowed.

"Easy peasy. Of course, I can handle two jobs. When do I start?"

"Right now. The reception desk is unstaffed as we speak. So, chop, chop. Get out there. I'll be watching to see just how much money your proposals bring into this parish and if it even comes close to the salary we pay you." Nadia rubbed her big hands together as if she kneaded dough.

Jane wrinkled her nose. She could smell the bone bread baking already.

Chapter Ten

Could this day get any worse? Jane placed the silly turkey centerpiece on her kitchen table. It did make her smile a little. She poured her single evening glass of red wine and sipped at it while she put away her specially ordered free-range bird and the rest of the supplies picked up for Thanksgiving dinner on the way home. Clouds obscured the sunset, and she'd missed it anyhow while in line at the Winn-Dixie. Resisting the urge to polish off the bottle or call Merlin for a big, strong shoulder to cry on, she went for the soft bosom instead and dialed her mom.

"Hi, Mom. Happy Night Before Thanksgiving."

"Wish you could be here with us, honey. We're having the geese your dad and brother shot. How about you?"

"Free-range turkey, pumpkin pie."

"Sounds good. Are you having company?"

"Yes, just a neighbor coming over in the evening. I'll be serving dinner at the homeless shelter at noon."

"That's my girl, always concerned for others and the environment. I am so proud of you. Male or female?"

"What?"

"Your dinner guest. An elderly neighbor?"

"No, not Mr. Babin. He has lots of family. A guy from those new townhouses across the way."

How did her mother do it, sniff out the faintest hint of a man in her life from such a distance? Kathleen Marshall appeared soft and kind with her big, cushy breasts, warm smile, and lake green eyes. She still wore her hair long in a silver braid down her back, a remnant of her hippie days before she'd fallen for a young petroleum engineer prowling around the commune for a drilling sight. Oh, they'd done some drilling all right, Kathleen liked to say for shock value as they worked out compromises both could tolerate, wild goose for Thanksgiving being one of those. Geese were seriously overpopulating in some areas and throwing the environment out of balance.

"How did you meet this guy across the street?"

"I lectured him about throwing beer cans into my ditch."

"Good, good, whenever we can convert a man to our way of thinking, that's good. Who knows what comes next? Your father and I were oil and pure, fresh rainwater starting out, then…"

"Yes, I know. Merlin is just a new friend."

"Interesting name, Merlin. It means the falcon in Middle English."

Mom and her name lore, yet she couldn't come up with something better than Jane for her own daughter. "For *Jane Eyre*, my favorite novel," her mom said. "It's a great honor to be named for her." Sure, having Eyre for a middle name was great, too. People who hadn't read the book often assumed she'd been married and divorced at a young age.

"Well, Merlin is an interesting man, but not why I called."

"When will we get to meet him?"

"Possibly never. Mom, do you recall I've been telling you about Nadia Nixon, how she starts finding fault with an employee, dumps extra work on them so they can't finish their own, then fires them?"

"Yes." Her mother's voice went deadly serious with only that one word.

"I think I'm next on the chopping block. She's been picking at me lately and today, she fired May Robin and gave me receptionist duties instead of moving someone else into the position."

"You can't back down from bullies, Jane. Do your best and show her. If she fires you without cause, fight her."

Sometimes, Jane wished her mother hadn't been a protester in the Sixties. She only wanted to unburden herself, not develop a war against Nadia strategy, though that might not be a bad idea. Kathleen Marshall already thought ahead.

"If you lose your job, how long can you hold out financially?"

"Probably two months. I put so much into this house and still owe on my car. I never expected the recycling program to fail and the garbage contract to go so badly awry." Damn, her throat clogged and her eyes filled with tears. Mom had the protective instincts of an alpha female wolf and the senses to go with it.

"Don't cry, Jane. Fight! If worse comes to worse, you have a home here with us in Montana. I know you think of yourself as a Louisiana girl since you grew up there, but the world is a big place with lots of opportunities. You'll come stay with us and lick your wounds, then get right back out there saving the environment. I know you will. Louisiana doesn't deserve you."

"No, but Louisiana needs me. I appreciate your faith in me, Mom. I guess that's all I wanted to say. Have a good Thanksgiving."

"You, too, honey. Wish the same to Merlin from all of us."

"I will. Bye."

The instant the connection ended, Jane poured herself another glass of wine to clear her throat. One swallow into it and the phone rang. Probably her mother calling back with more thoughts on the subject of fighting Nadia. No. Jethro Robin's name came up on the caller ID.

"Hi, Mr. Jethro. Happy Thanksgiving! Thanks so much for letting me use your recycling bin. What can I do for you?" Jane strove to banish all distress from her voice and replace it with good cheer.

"Stop using my recycle bin. You took advantage of us. Why, I could hardly drag the danged thing to the curb."

"I'm so sorry." Never would she reveal the first load represented only a pittance of the stash of old newspapers, bottles, and cans waiting in plastic barrels in her garage. "Next time I'll wheel the cart to the curb. Would that be all right?"

"No, it would not. Besides misusing our bin, you betrayed my sister. Now she's out on her fanny at the parish council office, and you have her job. Word travels fast in a town like Chapelle."

"I don't want May's job. Nadia forced me into doing it. At least May has her full pension. If I get fired, I get nothing."

"Ask me if I care about you when my sister is

having a nervous breakdown. She's a childless old maid like you. That job was her world, so take your garbage somewhere else."

"It's not garbage. It's recyclable materials."

"You say!"

A scuffle ensued on the other end of the call. She should simply hang up and cut her loses. Spring probably wanted to get her licks in next.

"Give it up, old man! You hear me. Stop blaming Jane for what Miss Nixon did. Jane, you there?" Spring Robin's voice came over the phone.

"Yes. I'm sorry about overstuffing the bin. Honestly, I'd be glad to take it to the curb if Mr. Jethro would allow me to use it again. I want to have a retirement party for May at my house, too. How Nadia treated her was entirely unfair."

"Go in your den and watch the news, Jethro. Let us be. There, he's gone. It's Jethro's back. He carried the mail as a postal worker for years and injured it in the service of his country. Neither rain, nor snow, you know. He can't handle a heavy bin and won't admit it. Letting a little girl like you haul it to the street would injure his pride. Sorry, I guess you'll have to find another recycling buddy. I know how my husband is and shouldn't have offered in the first place."

"Sure, I'll try to find someone else and not overload the next time. Please believe me I had nothing to do with May losing her job."

"Sometimes I think Jethro's back isn't the only thing out of whack. What a crazy idea. No, *cher,* why would an educated woman like you with a special degree want to be a receptionist? I think May got things all turned around when you came to help her clean out her desk and then sat in her chair to take phone calls whether you wanted to or not. It is true working at the council office meant everything to my sister-in-law, but her brother doesn't know the half of it. One day, I'll tell you all about May Robin and her long-term affair with Woof Langlois."

"Huh?"

"Doesn't matter right now. You have a nice holiday, you hear, and if you see Merlin Tauzin give him peck on the cheek from me."

For several minutes, Jane stood in the middle of her kitchen with the disconnected phone in her hand. May with her garish red helmet hair, age spots, and warm heart had been the parish president's mistress, or maybe still was. No, Jane couldn't imagine that and did not want to, but her own mother kept assuring Jane that she and her dad maintained a vital sex life. Still, Mom had to be at least ten years younger than May. For a short time, the mystery took away the pain of losing the use of that sexy recycling bin and having to serve Nadia as a receptionist.

When her anguish returned, she thought of calling Merlin. His granny would know the full skinny on May and Woof, too. Jane checked the clock. She figured the Magnolia Villa residents probably dined about now. No, she could not, would not do either. She despised weak women who leaned on men for support, and gossip, even greatly warmed over, more than that. Simply having Merlin sitting in her kitchen tomorrow would be the world's greatest distraction from her woes. Tonight, she'd bake a pumpkin pie, maybe cook a few other dishes in advance, and polish off the rest of her wine.

## Chapter Eleven

Merlin Tauzin did fill a room just by stepping over the threshold. He must have walked over because Jane never heard him coming without that big-ass truck, whose roar could be distinguished a mile away. He knocked but walked right in afterward, perfectly at home, and held out a bottle of wine.

Without pleasantry or prelude, he said, "The man at the grocery store swore this would go with turkey, even the free-range kind."

Although Jane startled when he barged into the kitchen, she went back to making her radish rose garnishes at the sink, determined to be as casual as he was. "Good. Unscrew the top and pour some for both of us. Wineglasses are in the cupboard to your left."

"I need a corkscrew."

Did she detect a tad of insult in his deep voice? Jane took a closer look at the bottle, a nice California white zinfandel—with a cork. She removed her best corkscrew from her partitioned utility drawer and handed it to Merlin.

"See, you clamp it down on both sides, turn the screw, pull the levers up, and out comes the cork."

"I think I can handle this without all the instruction." He did, very deftly. Pouring two glasses, he asked, "You want ice in yours?"

"Ah, no."

She kept her eyes on the cutting board to hide her amusement. He came up behind her, very close, set the glass within her reach, then stayed there lounging against the counter and watching her work. His body heat alone would have distracted her, but he'd shaved before coming over and the spicy scent of his aftershave mingled so pleasantly with the aroma of roasting turkey that she inhaled deeply. Still wearing his R.A.S. uniform of pressed navy blue slacks, starched sky blue shirt with the golden company logo, and his name tag as if she might forget what to call him, Merlin looked as good as he smelled. What was it about a man in a uniform, marine, pilot, or UPS, that made him so damned attractive?

"Anything I can do for you?" he asked, leaning in.

"Sure, take these cans out to the garage. Put them in the orange barrel, please."

He scooped up the tins once holding pumpkin and condensed milk and loped off following her orders. Quickly back again, he returned to his position at the counter.

"You have lots of garbage out there. I need to get around to cleaning that garage."

"Recyclables. I'm storing them until we get a new contract for the parish."

"I thought you said Spring Robin would let you use her bin."

"Not anymore. Evidently, I abused my privilege by overstuffing her cart."

"Doesn't sound like Spring, more like that shit-ass, Jethro."

"*Merde* mouth, Merlin. You got that right, but they have only one bin between them. Why don't you sit down? The turkey won't be ready for another forty-five minutes. Here, have some crudités." Jane moved away from his body heat, took a pretty amber pressed glass plate from the refrigerator, and sat it on the pumpkin-colored tablecloth. The turkey centerpiece squatted merrily between two beeswax candles in wooden holders.

"Thank you for the flowers. They made me smile on an otherwise bad day."

"Glad you liked them. I thought they were a hoot, too. No boudin balls, huh?" he said as he took a seat. "Let's see here, raw broccoli and cauliflower, sweet pepper strips in three colors, celery, baby carrots, and cherry tomatoes. No chance this is ranch dressing in the center?"

"Lo-cal yogurt dip, but it tastes almost the same."

Merlin immersed a baby carrot in dip all the way to his fingertips and chewed it up. "Sure it does."

The trouble with the man was she could never tell if he joked or not, he suppressed his smile so well. She rushed to assure him that he wouldn't starve at her table carefully set with the silver she'd inherited from her paternal grandmother, her pottery dinnerware with the lemon pattern, and amber-colored goblets that matched the relish tray picked up cheaply at the K-Mart. You worked with what you had and could afford in her book.

"Don't worry, you won't go hungry. We have pear, pecan and blue cheese salad, fresh green beans sautéed with caramelized onions, cranberry-orange relish, some of those great whole wheat rolls from Pommier's bakery, pumpkin pie, oh, and rice dressing made from a recipe May Robin gave me. You'll like that, I think, even though I substituted brown rice."

She couldn't help it. The mention of May choked her up. Jane turned rapidly back to the cutting board where she sliced the last radish and dumped it into a bowl of cold water with the others. She gripped the side of the sink and tried so very hard to keep her shoulders from shaking. Merlin's big hands came to rest on either side of her neck. Maybe if he really was crazy, he'd snap her spine and put her out of her misery, a mercy killing.

"Did I upset you by being sarcastic about the—crudités?"

"No, no. Nadia Nixon fired May yesterday over some prank I am sure she had nothing to do with. At least, she let May take her retirement. I'm going to have a retirement party for May here as soon as I can since we can't do one at work now."

"Nice of you." His large thumbs began a gentle massage of her tense shoulder muscles.

"But now, I have to staff the reception desk. I don't know how I'll do that and still be able to write my grants or get the recycling program going again if I can't leave the building to muster group support. I mean, every time the matter is discussed at a council meeting, all the mention it gets in the newspaper is a couple of sentences in the last paragraph no one reads at the end of the article. I have to do something to rally the public, so I wrote a letter to the *Clarion*, but they haven't published it yet."

"They won't print it. Bernard Freeman takes out a full-page ad every Sunday to advertise his realty business. That's a big deal to a little rag like the *Clarion*. Freeman is against the recycling program, considers it a waste of money. The paper can't afford to offend him. Besides, he builds a bunch of his developments on old landfills. I'll bet he already has a deal with Burl Oubre to take over the dump when it closes sometime in the future. Granny said that was good cane land Burl inherited, but he was too lazy to farm it and turned it into a trash heap."

"You know a lot about local politics."

"My family has lived here over two hundred years. I think we've figured out how this parish works, but you, baby, are a newcomer. You don't stand a chance."

"I have to keep fighting. I hate that Bernard Freeman represents my district!"

"Me, too. Don't you love the way he gets a Cajun accent during election years when everybody in Chapelle knows his folks came from Texas in the Fifties to work in the oil fields?"

"May Robin told me Bernie wormed his way onto the council by marrying old Leroy Mouton's daughter. Leroy 'Lambo' Mouton must have been the town's most beloved politician."

"He was a good guy, but I can't say the same for the son-in-law who took his place."

"Yet, you bought a townhouse from Freeman."

"Only way I could keep a piece of Tauzin land."

"Sorry I bought this house out from under you."

"Don't be. I would have lived in it as is. You did better by the house. Look, I can tell this stuff means a lot to you. You are so tense. Your back is all knotted up." His long thumbs worked on her stiff neck. "Come on, sit down in the living room for a while, and let me give you a massage until that turkey is done."

"Okay." Jane caved far too easily in her own

opinion. How weak could she be? Merlin steered her toward the comfortable, scarred leather sofa without ever removing his hands and pressed her to sit on the worn cushions. Oh, ecstasy as he worked those thumbs across her back. She needed another diversion right now before she became putty in his hands. Her hand groped for the TV remote.

"I know. We can watch the rerun of the Thanksgiving Day Parade with the big balloons. That will cheer me up."

"Sure, if it helps you relax, babe."

She found the channel. Gigantic cartoon characters and their tiny human handlers filled the screen. "Oh, look, my favorite dog balloon. Oooh, you're very good at this, Merlin." His fingers ran along her ribs, almost tickling but not quite.

"My mom taught me. She wanted to get a masseuse license but couldn't pass the written test. The names of all those muscles confused her. Too bad because she would have been good, and it would have gotten her out of Broussard's Barn. Lie down flat, and I'll do your legs."

Not a good idea, but she complied anyway. Sometimes, a girl just needed a good—massage. He used the sides of his hands to chop up and down her calf muscles, slid her dress up to her behind and worked on her thighs. Had she chosen her clothes knowing this might happen, no hose, her green lace panties, slides that simply dropped off her feet as he rubbed her arches?

Earlier when she considered wearing the jeans and shirt she'd had under her apron when serving the poor their dinner, she thought the holiday occasion and maybe Merlin deserved better. Out came the plum-colored knit dress with the cowl neck and long sleeves. Simple and appropriate for the chilly, gray day, the knit did mold nicely to her breasts and bottom, but not in a sexy way certainly. She'd added earrings shaped and colored like autumn leaves and a matching pin locally crafted to the ensemble. Merlin hadn't told her she looked nice, not that it mattered. What did matter? His magic fingers found all the right spots one after another.

He slid his hands under the knit of her dress and drew her panties down over her buttocks. Her bra clasp opened and fell to the side.

"You'll enjoy it more this way. Usually, a person would only have a towel on at this point unless you're getting a massage at the airport."

"We're not at the airport."

"Nope. You'd be naked beneath that towel and my hands would be under it."

He removed her panties, spread her thighs, and moved one of his legs between them. The other stayed on the floor as he smoothed her hind cheeks over and over. His hands moved upward taking her dress with it to the sides of her breasts, then over her head and onto the floor. Jane shivered.

"Cold?"

"Not at all. Merlin, are you enjoying this, too?

He pressed his erection against her buttocks.

"I'll take that as a yes. Would you turn off the TV? I can't do this in front of the entire Beaver Springs High School marching band."

"You have the remote."

"So I do." Jane unclenched her fingers from the instrument, stopped the parade, and tossed it aside.

Suddenly, she felt one of Merlin's long fingers in an unexpected place and tensed around it.

"Just seeing if you are ready."

"Right now I'm juicier than that turkey in the oven. It's been a while for me." Heck, she'd almost come around that single finger.

"Me, too." He didn't pause to suggest they remove to the bedroom or roll onto the rug. One hand got his belt buckle open and his zipper down while the other continued to stroke the side of a breast. He shoved his uniform pants and underwear down to his knees and mounted her from behind. His shaft slid easily into her wetness longer, harder, deeper than any finger could. Odd position, but curiously arousing—as if she needed to be more stimulated. Neither of them took very long. Her orgasm arrived with explosive fireworks more appropriate for the Fourth of July than Thanksgiving, but she was giving thanks for this, absolutely.

Merlin followed with an aaah of great relief. He collapsed over Jane but kept his arms braced to keep from crushing her into the cushions. After a couple of minutes, he set his clothes right and turned her naked body over to hold against his chest. Inhaling the clean scent of his starched shirt and natural male musk, a great combo for a new masculine cologne, Jane burrowed against him hiding half her body against his side. One breast refused to tuck in. He fondled it.

"You have great breasts. Sorry I didn't get to see more of them this time."

"I come from a long line of big-busted women. I have to watch my weight to keep them a normal size. Eat a little too much and it goes right to the boobs."

"And that is a problem? Um, speaking of problems,

I didn't use a condom. Should have, didn't. Got carried away. But I'm clean. I had a full physical before I got my discharge from the army, and, well, I haven't felt much like doing this since I got back from Afghanistan. There hasn't been anyone else."

"Not even Wanda?"

"Who?"

"The hootchie mama at Mulates. You didn't call her and set up a date?"

"Nope. I forgot about that napkin and washed it with my jeans. It shredded all over my laundry."

"What a pity."

"I don't think so. Jane, I was careless. How about you?"

"No worries. I'm on the pill and haven't been with anyone in a couple of years, since college to be honest."

"But you are still prepared like a good boy scout."

"More like an eternal optimist. You never know when something good will come along to enjoy. Boy scouts prepare for disasters. Were you ever a boy scout?"

"Hell, no. I guess I just proved that." Merlin hung his head a little.

Ping. Ping. Ping.

"The turkey is ready, but I'm not so sure I can get up."

"I'll get it. I'm dressed. Take your time and don't feel you need to put your underwear back on for me." Merlin eased her off his chest and onto the sofa cushion.

Jane watched him go tucking in the tails of his sky blue shirt as he went. She took a minute, stretched, finally found her feet and stood to gather her clothes.

Tempting as it might be, at least for Merlin, she intended to wear a bra and panties to dinner. She straggled into the bathroom, washed the important place, and dressed again. Fortunately, knits didn't wrinkle. Her makeup remained unmarred. They hadn't even kissed and yet every inch of her felt satisfied. But now, the aftermath. Could she face him across the silly turkey centerpiece? Only one way to find out.

Jane entered the kitchen. Merlin had his back to her as he worked a carving knife on the turkey. He'd lit the candles, poured water and wine, and centered the pear salads on both plates. The microwave dinged, and he set down his carving tools to remove the casserole dish holding the green beans and onions. The cranberry-orange relish sat ruby red and ready to eat on the table. He looked her way, green beans in hand, and saw her staring.

"What? I washed my hands first."

"Somehow, I expected to find you seated with knife and fork in hand waiting to be served. I never would have guessed you'd be so handy in a kitchen."

Now, he grinned. "Granny," a one word explanation. "She would wait on the men hand and foot if they spent all day in the fields, but if a guy was just lying around the house, he'd better know how to set a table and carry a dish from the stove. The rice dressing is still in the oven, and I put the rolls in to warm."

"Do you cook, too?"

"Some. Not lately. I'm hell on dirty dishes though. This bird should be ready to eat in a minute." He laid a severed leg to one side and began carving slices off the breast.

"Oh, I was going to put it on a platter with pretty

garnishes."

"I ate two of the radishes already because I'm starving. Get the platter."

Jane took down the old Spode plate with a big brown turkey at its center, a treasure from the Episcopal Church garage sale. Merlin turned the uncarved half of the turkey sideways, tucked a radish rose under its wing, another under its butt, and the last where its head should have been. He placed the platter on the table.

"There you go. If someone walks in right now, they could take a picture of the perfect Thanksgiving."

Jane took a couple of bunches of parsley from the fridge and stuffed them under the beautifully browned carcass, then turned off most of the kitchen lights to allow them to enjoy the candles. "Now they could. We are ready to eat. But first we should say what we're thankful for."

His face troubled in the candlelight, Merlin held her chair, then went to his own. Jane began the ritual.

"I am thankful for this beautiful land that deserves to be preserved for future generations and for the company I have with me this evening."

"Amen," said Merlin, crossing himself. "Let's eat."

"It isn't a prayer. Your turn."

"I'm thankful for what I shouldn't mention at this table even though it looks like I won't get dessert."

"Of course, you will. I made a pumpkin pie."

"Not that kind of dessert. You put your underwear back on."

Jane waited a beat, and here came his smile, rolling out slowly at first then expanding. She got up, went to the oven, took out the tray of rolls, and lobbed one at him. Merlin caught it mid-air and placed it primly on the little dish intended for that purpose.

"Turkey?" he asked.

"White meat for me."

Putting the pear salad to one side, he placed several slices on her plate and added a mix of light and dark meat to his own. She brought the basket of rolls to the table and the dish of rice dressing, passing it to him. Merlin took a hearty amount. He tried the bird.

"So this is what natural, free-range turkey tastes like. Almost as good as my mother's Butterball."

Jane waited for a teasing smile, but it did not arrive. She frowned. "You know those turkeys aren't natural. Their breasts are so big if they fall in a water trough, they drown."

"I did notice this one is a little skimpy in the chest, unlike you."

"It isn't skimpy. It's natural. This bird ate wild grains and roamed free."

"And still ended up on our dinner table. I don't see the difference."

"It died happy, okay?"

"If you say so—though it is hard to tell if a turkey is happy."

Jane glanced up from a bite of pear salad, and there gleamed the delayed grin across the table. "Turkey truce?"

"Sure. Jane, this is the best Thanksgiving I ever had."

"Yes, the holidays don't usually come with sofa sex."

"Granny would say that is not proper table talk, but yeah. More than that."

"Thought your mom was a good cook."

"She is, but big, fancy meals fluster her. Harley drinks a few too many. She burns or breaks something. He gets on her about it. Granny weighs in on Mom's side. Brittney tries to sneak out to meet one of her skuzzy boyfriends, gets grounded. Grandpa is in the bedroom dying slowly and quietly. Doyle just keeps his head down. I hope he's doing that in the war zone tonight and eating a real dinner in the mess hall, not sucking down a turkey and gravy MRE in the middle of nowhere like I did my first year over there. "

"I'm sure he is. Where would you be in all that family turmoil?"

"Out on the porch swing waiting for it to blow over. Like Merlin the Magician, I vanish. You. What does your family do for Thanksgiving?"

Jane broke open a roll and watched the steam rise like it held a vision of Thanksgivings past. "Not bad, but maybe kind of quirky. We always have wild game, geese, maybe turkey or ducks. Mom can tolerate hunting if all the meat goes to feed someone. No trophies at our house."

"Same with everything Grandpa and me ever brought down or caught. The rice dressing is good even if it is brown." He showed his appreciation by taking a second helping.

"Thanks. You know, I went to a Christmas party Bernard Freeman held for the parish employees last year. He has an entire wing of his house dedicated to his hunting trophies from all over the world. The ones he hunted on exotic game ranches didn't bother me too much, but that polar bear mounted standing up—as if those poor creatures didn't have enough trouble with global warming."

"Sounds like Bernard. Getting a license to kill one costs a bunch. That way he can show off his wealth and his hunting skills at the same time. I doubt the bear stood up and attacked him."

"Me, too. My dad will get a black bear license now and then, but he'd never kill any dwindling species—or my mom would kill and stuff *him*. Try your salad." She nudged the greens toward him.

"Good, fancy, the beans, too, and the cranberry stuff."

"Anyhow, my brother, Heath, would be sitting across the table deviling me about something like not eating the Rocky Mountain oysters if we were up at Grandma's in Montana. He's six years older and always acted like he owned me, but he's gotten better since we've grown up. I always wanted a baby sister."

"Be glad you never got one."

"That bad?"

"Yep. When she sent me off to the store for scratch-offs, I'm betting Granny told you all about the deal they cut with my father to get me some child support."

Jane hoped the dim lighting hid her blush. "She did mention it." And won *her* bet.

"Brittney is as lazy as they come, always doing just enough to get by in school and in life. When she got into her teens she took note of that thousand-dollar check coming from the lawyer each month. She knew to ask my mom for things she wanted about that time, but Granny said the cash was to go to my food and clothing and other needs. Guess it sounded like a good deal to Brittney. She found an older guy to sucker and knock her up when she turned sixteen, then cut the same deal for Jayden, her boy, only none of the extra goes into a college fund for the kid like it should. She buys herself clothes and jewelry. Granny made my sister finish high school or she would have quit. Brittney is *canaille*, you know, tricky. Pretty like my mom if you can tell under all that makeup. I doubt she'd work at all if Harley didn't force her to get a job."

"Sad. You have no idea who Jayden's father is?"

"I was in flight training when all this happened. They won't tell me. I guess they figure I'll go berserk and kill the man. I only hope it isn't the same guy who got to Mom, and Jayden isn't my half-brother."

"Do you think that is a real possibility?"

"Could be. That scuzz-bucket's morals haven't improved over the years. My nephew is tall for his age and long in the face like me." Merlin pushed away from the table and took his half-filled plate to the sink. "Great food."

Nothing could make her ask his father's name. "I'm sorry I killed your appetite with all my questions."

"I was on seconds, so no problem."

Jane, still on firsts, got up, too. Desperately, she wanted to restore the ease between them. "I'm going to make coffee and cut the pie. Would you go into the living room and start a fire? I'll bring dessert in there."

With a tiny quirk at the side of his lips, he said, "I thought we did that earlier."

Good, the Merlin she was coming to know and love—make that becoming acquainted with—had returned to her kitchen. He began clearing the table, rinsing dishes in the sink.

"I can wash them if you want."

"Just put everything in the dishwasher except the

108

silver."

"We didn't have one of those. I like this kitchen a lot better than Granny's and the woman in it, too."

He kissed the back of her neck as she carried the leftover cranberry-orange relish to the refrigerator, and the pressed glass dish nearly fell to the floor. His hands came around to cover her breasts as he nuzzled her neck. Here, on the kitchen floor, the two of them wallowing in cranberry sauce—a scene much too vivid entered her mind.

"Ahem, you were going into the living room to start a fire."

"Trying."

Considering that her hands held a breakable object with a great deal of splatter potential, she gave him a little bump with her hips. "Go."

"That seems more like encouragement to stay right where I am."

Jane stretched to put her burden on the counter. He tugged her backside tighter against his crotch with his hands still hot and hard across her chest and rested that big chin of his right on top of her head.

"I warn you I am entirely capable of lobbing this dish of sauce over my head and right into your face if you don't let me go, Merlin. Then, I assure you we will have no dessert of any kind, just a cleanup on aisle one." Thank God, the man could not read her previous thoughts.

Not releasing her, he seemed to consider for a moment before dropping his hands. "Yeah, I think you would do it."

"Damn straight! Now light that fire or go home."

His hands fell away from her bosom and left her

feeling chilly and alone. She didn't turn until his heavy footsteps retreated to the living room, a battle won—or maybe lost. Jane finished wrapping and storing the leftovers while the coffee perked. She cut the pie and arranged the plates on a tray with the coffee cups, skimmed milk, and real sugar for him. As soon as the coffee finished dripping, she poured the cups, and taking a deep breath, headed for the living room.

A small, pleasant fire burned in the hearth. Merlin sat on the leather sofa with the remote in his hand flipping through channels. Was she a tinge disappointed that he hadn't stripped and spread his long body out on the tan and white striped cotton rug in front of the fireplace simply to surprise her?

"Nice job on the fire."

"Not a boy scout, but Grandpa and me did camp out when we went hunting and fishing. Now do I get dessert?"

Were his blue eyes twinkling, or did they simply reflect the flames in the fire? Maybe she had been too harsh telling him to go home when that was the last thing she wanted him to do. Jane handed him the slice of pie without comment. He ate every last crumb before fixing his coffee with sugar and lightening it with milk since she'd made it strong to suit him. Jane did the same, skipping the sugar. Conversation appeared to have died the same death as the free-range turkey. On the television, the roar of the crowd cheering for a football team neither of them cared about filled the void. Merlin finished the coffee, placed the cup on the tray, and stood. Jane jumped up, putting her cup aside to remove all barriers between them.

"Would you like to stay the night?" There, she'd

said it, simply blurted out the ultimate invitation. Did she see a moment of panic flash across that seriously manly face?

"Uh, no. I mean I have to get up before dawn because I'm flying offshore tomorrow, and I put in a long day before I got here. Tired. Lots of tryptophan in that free-range turkey. I doubt if I'd be able to do much good for either of us. Wouldn't want to wake you early in the a.m. Great meal, honeybunch. Thanks for inviting me."

Merlin went to the front door and worked the lock to make his escape. Jane followed, staying him with a hand on his forearm, wondering if she felt a slight tremor there.

"Would you like to take some leftovers? Come to the kitchen and let me fix some for you." And rewind time to a half hour ago when his hands covered her breasts, and she felt his desire hard against her backside.

"I won't be home until late Sunday night, and the stuff might go bad by then. Feed the homeless or something. See you around, Jane."

Outside, a thick autumn fog lay across the land like a smoke screen. He stepped onto the porch, took the steps in two big strides, and disappeared into its cover, Merlin the Magician, poof, vanished in the mist.

Chapter Twelve

Jane swore she recognized the heavy breathing of Merlin's big-ass truck as it idled at the traffic light in the wee hours of the morning. Bad to know what a man's truck sounded like so you could pick it out like your baby crying in the nursery. Not that the noise awakened her. Despite a heavy turkey dinner, relaxing massage, and some great recreational sex, because that's all it was, she hadn't slept well.

Around three a.m., she got up and made a list of people to invite to May's impromptu retirement party on Sunday afternoon and supplies she would have to purchase for the fete if she could pull it off by then. She loved lists, making them, ticking off each item completed. They made her feel well-organized, in control, moving steadily forward toward a goal. After that, back to bed to toss and turn some more.

Why bother trying to sleep? She didn't have to go into work today, could take a nap in the afternoon if she wanted. Jane left her covers and went into the kitchen. The coffee she'd made for Merlin still sat warm in the carafe because she'd forgotten to unplug the machine. She poured a cup, tasted its bitterness, and added milk and two packets of sweetener. Gazing into its murky depths, she berated herself for being too assertive in pushing Merlin away and then being foolish enough to ask him to stay overnight. No wonder he'd spooked.

She knew what "See you around" meant. He'd probably spent his night trying to piece together Good Time Wanda's shredded phone number.

Moving on as one must, Jane ate a large piece of pumpkin pie for breakfast, justifying it as a nice balance of fruit and carbs. After that, she removed the turkey from the fridge and tore the meat off the bones, chopped it fine, bagged it to make turkey salad sandwiches for the party, and stored the carcass for soup later in the day. Contemplating the cranberry-orange relish, which made her think of Merlin, she considered tossing it into the garbage disposal, but that would be wasteful and the Marshalls did not waste. She found a recipe for cranberry-orange quick bread in one of her cookbooks, made double the batter, and folded in the relish along with some pecans from her tree. If it turned out, she could serve that on Sunday, too. Still in her robe and slippers, Jane went out into the mist being thinned at last by the sun and harvested lemons, lots of lemons. She squeezed out all their juice and stored it to make fresh lemonade.

Once the kitchen clock showed a decent hour for calling, she started on her list of guests for the party. Obviously, some had gone out of town for the holiday, but most of the women she reached indicated their readiness for some relief from cooking and football games. Spring Robin asked if she could bring her daughter, Wendy, and her three grandchildren. Sure, why not? May doted on them. Spring also wanted to supply a cake with an appropriate message. Fine with Jane. She suggested the guests purchase a retirement card and put gift cards inside of them since time grew short for shopping, though they could do something else if they wanted. Several promised to bring food, even better.

She diced the celery and carrots from the relish tray, added chopped onions and the minced parsley garnish to start the stock with the carcass for her mother's turkey-corn-noodle soup. Throwing in frozen corn, noodles, and some of the meat, she had soup ready for dinner along with the leftover whole wheat rolls. After keeping him out of her mind all day, the buns reminded her of Merlin catching one in the air with his large hands, his large hands on her breasts, his large…" Backsliding again after so much progress made.

By seven p.m., Jane crawled back into bed never having gotten out of her robe all day, then forced herself out again. Her trash in its big, green container needed to be on the curb tomorrow. She collected two bags of garbage, and glad of the early dark, went outside to place them in the container and haul her heavy can from the edge of the garage, through the resistant gravel of her drive to the roadside. She dusted her hands upon completing the task. There, she didn't need no stinkin' man who smelled of masculine musk and starched shirts to help her. Her eyes moved in the direction of Merlin's townhouse. No lights burned in the windows. At least, he hadn't lied about being gone. Shit! Now, she would spend another night remembering how his blue eyes glittered in the firelight, how his hands clasped her breasts, how the length of him felt inside of her. Oh, take two aspirins and go to bed, Jane Marshall!

\*\*\*\*

Though tormented by erotic dreams, Jane did sleep,

only to wake hot and bothered. She took a warm shower, washed her hair, and declined to shave her legs today, maybe never again for any man, but only for herself since the idea of hairy legs on a woman disgusted her despite her mother's teachings. She dressed in jeans and a plain blue T-shirt, no logo of any kind, and began to blow dry her hair. Clang, clank, chug. She heard those sweet sounds over the noise of her hairdryer, turned it off, and bolted outside to witness her first trash pickup in ages. The B. O. truck passed right on by to pause at the stop sign.

"Wait! Wait! You forgot my trash. See, it's in a green can exactly like you wanted." Jane ran after the truck and latched herself on to one of the handholds for the garbageman as if she could tow the vehicle back to her driveway.

"Ma'am, you gotta get off. It ain't safe."

"Not until you take my garbage." She wished she had a chain and padlock to bind herself to the vehicle as her mother once did to a bulldozer being used to take down old growth forest.

"You done gots the wrong can. I told you a black one. See here, it has to have a hook bar to fit on the lift. These things is heavy. I can't be putting my back out to heave yo' can. Mr. Burl, he says he ain't payin' no workmen's comp claims."

"But you said to get a green can. I have a witness."

The garbageman's eyes rolled, showing their whites, as he stared at the neatly pruned bushes in case Merlin should appear any second now. Jane wished he would. She glanced hopefully across the street. No dice. Ridiculous, she could handle this matter easily.

"I had a witness. You misled me on purpose."

The B.O. employee gave her a big-shouldered shrug that pulled his large belly above the safety belt he wore. He readjusted the harness. "Can't use that green one. I'm telling you nice as I can," he told her in case Merlin should overhear, Jane was certain.

"Wait. I'll put my trash in a lighter can even I can lift. Would that do? Just give me a few minutes."

Another shrug and he leaned against the truck, took out a half-smoked cigar from his pocket, and lit it. "Go on and get it."

Jane dashed to her kitchen and seized the tall waste can under her sink. She carried it to her garbage receptacle and went in armpit deep to retrieve the two trash bags inside. The first she smashed down into the waste can as far as it would go, then balanced the other on it like a giant muffin top. With the second bag tucked under her chin, she carried her load to the idling garbage truck and thrust it at the driver.

"See, if a small woman like me can handle this, I am sure a great, big man like you will be able to dump it in the truck.

"Okay." He took a moment to toss the butt of his cigar and grind it out with the toe of his work boot, took her kitchen waste can and threw it, contents and all, into the back of the truck. He pulled the lever to rotate the waste.

"No! I need my can back."

"Well, it's gone fo' sure now, little lady."

Tears of frustration gathered in her eyes. Bad enough when Merlin called her little lady, let alone this guy. Her entire body trembled with rage. She'd like to pummel this man, tip him into the maw of the garbage truck, and hit the switch.

The garbageman interpreted her watering eyes and tremor in another way entirely and took pity. "Now don't you cry, ma'am. I'm gonna tell you a little secret. You don't gots to go out to the barn for a black can. New ones done come in finally. You gets one on Monday."

Jane eyed him suspiciously. "That's what Ethel tells me every time I call B.O. to complain."

"I ain't Ethel. I'm in the know. Dry yo' eyes, little lady. Weep no more."

"Thank you for the information." Jane squinted at the name embroidered on his dark blue uniform shirt in orange thread half-obscured by smut. "Lemonjello? Is that right?"

"Yeah, my mama musta been smoking something when she named me. Most folks call me Mellow for short. See, this is the best job I could get after the sheriff let me out of the pokey. I gots to do what Mr. Burl says. You understand."

"I do. My name is Jane Marshall, not little lady."

The driver stuck his head out of the cab window. "You done flappin' yo' gums, Mellow?"

"Miss Jane, that's my brother, Oranjello, O.J. for short. Yeah, coming. Drive on."

Jane returned to her house and added "kitchen waste can" to her list of party needs from the Wal-Mart out on the highway. She appreciated that K-Mart stayed in its spot on the edge of town and usually tried shopping there first, but she had to admit Wally World offered a better selection for festive occasions, much cheaper than the Hallmark store on Main Street. Since she planned to get May a hundred-dollar gift card, she must pinch her pennies somewhere.

A thought occurred as she finished applying makeup for her foray out to the shopping center by the interstate. Miss Olive might enjoy getting out of assisted living for an afternoon to join the party. Not that Jane would do it simply to please Merlin and gain his attention. She genuinely liked his grandmother, surprising in so many ways. Olive Tauzin probably knew May. They were of an age. She made the call.

"*Mais,* yeah, I want to come. I know May Robin from way back though I have a couple years on her. We went to the same high school. I do love a good party. Will you have music? I can't dance no more, but I sure do love to listen and tap my feet."

"Sorry, no music. Not in the budget. The party starts at two. It's a surprise, so don't tell. Should I pick you up around one?"

"No need. The Villa's van will bring me, like having a chauffeur to do for me. Lots to like about this place."

"Attitude is everything."

"*C'est vrai.* Thanks for inviting me, baby. We have birthday parties for the geezers here all the time, but it is nice to get out."

"Glad to have you. Off to get the decorations," Jane said when she sensed Olive would keep her on the phone chatting about life at Magnolia Villa.

"Bye-bye, *cher.*"

\*\*\*\*

Jane waited tensely. The guests filled her living room and kitchen, overflowed into her library. Now if only Spring had been able to convince May to come for a conciliatory visit. The sight of the older woman's betrayed eyes lingered in her memory as they'd cleaned out her desk, and Jane settled into the receptionist's chair used so long by its former occupant that it molded to her skinny behind and so felt lumpy and uncomfortable to a younger, more rounded derriere.

The women of the council office went all out for May's party, short notice or not. A rice cooker and crock pots holding meatballs and mini-cabbage rolls sat plugged into the outlets on the kitchen counter. Jane put an extra leaf into her table to hold all the sandwiches, her turkey salad, ham, and tangy pimento cheese, and a huge assortment of sweets, the cranberry bread, chocolate chip cookies, pastel mints, pralines, and tiny pecan pie tarts. Even Tonette brought some pretty decent homemade peanut butter fudge. Didi, who did not cook, stopped on the way to pick up boudin sausage and sliced it into rings on the cutting board. Jane considered leaving the snitches off the guest list along with Nadia, but figured she had nothing to hide. Didn't Miss Nixon tell her to have the party on her own time?

Jane saved a place for the cake Spring intended to smuggle to the event in the trunk of her car by filling it with the turkey centerpiece, now disassembled and revamped without its goggle eyes, red felt wattles, and yellow beak. With any wilted flowers discarded and the rest placed in a pretty green recycled glass vase, it thriftily served the purpose. Pitchers of lemonade on the table, soft drinks in a cooler, coffee ready in a borrowed Party Perk, check! Black plates, cups, and napkins bedecked with a colorful confetti and streamer design and the words "Happy Retirement" in yellow placed on the table along with forks and spoons, check! A large basket brimming with cards containing gift certificates placed next to the guest-of-honor chair, check! Now, they only lacked that honoree.

"Here they come," Angela Savoy announced from her spy place by the front window. The crowd went silent as the car turned into the side road and moved up the gravel drive. The passengers didn't come to the back door like old friends but walked around to the front and rang the bell. Jane opened the door and embraced the wide-eyed May who immediately noticed the "Happy Retirement" sign hung across the hallway. All the ladies jumped out of their hiding places and shouted, "Surprise."

She managed to whisper, "May, I don't want your job. Not with all the tales you've told about the crazies and the threats received over the years. How did you ever do it?"

"It's a special talent, being able to handle people," May replied. "One that I cultivated over the years. Everybody assumes being a receptionist is easy."

"I know it's not."

May's niece, Wendy, and her children surged forward and escorted the woman of the hour to her designated chair. Spring brought in the cake and displaced the turkey flowers. Jane provided the honoree with her drink of choice, and the opening of the cards began. Some were funny, the majority sentimental, bringing tears to May's eyes. Most favored Wal-Mart for a gift, but May received a nice selection of restaurant meal tickets, all with notes inviting her for a lunch or dinner, and a few gas cards, too. Didi gave her a gift certificate to the local naughty nightie store, adding more red to May's already rouged cheeks and great guffaws of laughter from the women.

"How do you know? This might be the first one I

use," May quipped, bringing on additional chuckles.

"For true," Merlin's granny said from her perch on the other comfortable chair. "You got no idea what hanky-panky goes on at Magnolia Villa now that the old men got those little blue pills—only they don't remember you in the morning." Chortles erupted all around.

May's oldest grandniece, a beautiful blue-eyed girl out of high school a year or two, carefully paired the greeting and gift cards together, saving all the envelopes to make the task of thank-you notes easier. Finally finished with the abundance of good wishes, the ladies dug into the food, none of them holding back on seconds or mentioning a diet, except Didi who had to keep herself svelte for the councilman and Angela who seemed to be lacking in appetite.

One by one, the guests departed, most of them leaving their food contributions behind for Jane and May to split. Spring, her daughter, and three granddaughters began ferrying containers, the gifts, and remaining cake to the car, leaving the kitchen a quiet and private place for the first time in hours.

May squeezed Jane against her bony frame. "Thank you for doing this for me, honey. I know none of my trouble was your fault, but a person looks for someone to blame at first. I should have retired years ago before this happened."

"Nonsense. You did a great job, how great a job I am finding out. What will you do now?"

"No idea. Buy a travel wardrobe with my Wal-Mart gift cards and hit the road, maybe. I won't even have to pay for gas or food on the way."

"Sounds like a good plan to me."

"Jane, could I ask a very special favor?"

"Anything." As soon as the word escaped her lips, Jane knew she should have held it captive.

"Would you go out with Waldo just once and give him a chance? Like me, he's had no luck in love. He didn't marry until he turned thirty-five, about the same age I messed up my life. His first marriage lasted ten years before she ran off with a casket salesman. Married again when he was forty-nine, but that babe only wanted his money. Undertaking is a very lucrative business, you know."

"So I've heard." Jane's brain churned desperately trying to produce an excuse not to grant May her wish. She wanted to say that she and Merlin were a couple, hardly the case since the Thanksgiving debacle. No, couldn't use that reason.

"He wouldn't build her a house away from the funeral home and made her sign a prenup. That floozy only gave him a few of years of her life. Neither one of his wives had any interest in having children. Waldo is all alone, like me."

"Neither of you are alone. You both have Jethro and Spring, Wendy and her three daughters. I can tell the girls love you." How they felt about their uncle was another matter entirely. Jane overheard one of them call him "Creepy Uncle Waldo" just this afternoon.

"Wendy, sweet as she is, is part of the problem. When that baby girl came along ten years after Waldo, Spring simply stopped paying much attention to her son."

"Spring and Wendy do have a lot in common, I could tell. They both have those light blue eyes and sunny natures, always smiling and joking, at least here at the party. Waldo is more like his father. Maybe that's why."

"Yes, Waldo is Jethro's son all right. That's why he needs someone like you who is cheerful and positive to bring out the best in him. Please, Jane. May I tell my nephew you'd like him to call for a date?"

"Like might be implying too much. Just say I'll go out with him if he wants."

"Thank you, dear." May gave Jane a peck on the cheek and left a small smear of coral lipstick behind.

The youngest grandniece poked her curly head into the kitchen. "Come on, Auntie May. Grandma says the car is all packed. We're waiting."

This time, May used the backdoor. With dread of the call from Waldo occupying her mind, Jane wandered toward the living room intending to pick up any party trash left behind. Before she arrived, Angela Savoy stepped out of her library.

"Oh, Angie, I thought you'd left with the others. Come back to the kitchen and take some of these leftovers home to Chad."

"I have to talk to you. I guess being Catholic, I need to confess."

Jane drew back. "Not to me! Tell a priest."

"I have, but I can't make things right again. Oh, Jane, I'm the one who left that ugly note on Nadia's desk and got May fired. I didn't mean to. I only wanted to get back at the Nixster for what she said to me. Now, I've messed up your career, too. You can't do both jobs. Everyone knows Nadia is gunning for you next. Look, anytime you need to work on a project, I'll fill in at the reception desk if I possibly can." Angela wrung her hands in front of her belly, a little pudgy despite her dieting.

"From what you say, Chad makes good money and can support you. Why not go in, tell Nadia, and get it off your chest? Yes, she will fire you on the spot, but maybe May and I can get back to our old jobs. I am sure the retirement paperwork hasn't gone through yet. Besides, you do have some business school training. If you want to work again, I'll give you a reference."

"I can't get fired, Jane. I'm pregnant. They won't let me get on Chad's insurance for six months until pre-existing conditions are ruled out." Angela patted that poochy belly tenderly. "The baby pre-existed the wedding, too. I mean, we were getting married anyhow, so I thought, why not? That's what we should name the kid, Whynot Savoy."

"Oh, don't stick a child with a name like that! It might turn out like Waldo Robin. Weird names, not good." Jane simply couldn't shake the idea of the upcoming date with the undertaker, even with this startling confession to provide a distraction.

"Creepy, isn't he? May kept trying to fix me up with him before I got engaged to Chad. She said Waldo was his grandfather's name and her brother, Jethro, insisted on using it. I heard her talking you into a date with him. Loud as she is, maybe her hearing is going. *Pauvre bête* as my mawmaw would say."

After this expression of sympathy, Angela raced along nearly breathless in her haste to convince Jane not to turn her in to the CAO. "Anyhow, I've been trying to keep my weight down so no one will know for a while. Even with my husband's good salary, having a baby without insurance will put us in the hole so I have to use my parish health insurance. Please, please understand why I can't tell Nadia now. After the baby comes, I plan to quit anyhow. I'll make things right then. I promise."

"Too late for May by then, though maybe she should get free of the council office, but I guess I can hold out against Nadia for a few more months if you help me at the desk." For the second time today, Jane knew she shouldn't promise a friend anything. "How far along are you?" she belatedly asked.

"At the end of my fourth month. Only five more to go. I might have to name the baby after you if it's a girl."

"Oh, don't do that. Just have a fine, healthy baby— and stop dieting."

"Great, I've been starving for the last month. Thank you, Jane." Angela added a dab of sparkling pink lipstick to Jane's cheek before dashing to the car in case her friend might change her mind and call Nadia if she didn't hurry and escape.

A crackly voice hailed Jane from the depths of the overstuffed chair in the living room. "I'm still here. My ride ain't shown yet. Couldn't help but eavesdrop since I can't get up without some help."

Olive Tauzin, she'd forgotten all about her. During the party the women took turns sitting by the elderly woman's side to talk. Wendy's girls ferried food and drink to Miss Olive so the old lady didn't have to get up. Unabashed, Olive informed everyone in the group that she had her Depends on and could have as much coffee as she wanted. Jane had greeted her upon arrival and got Olive settled before her hostess duties kicked in, but whenever she looked over at that white head, the woman appeared to be having a fine time.

"You know, *cher* heart, you too nice to people. Both that Angie and May just played you good."

"Oh, I don't think so. Angela is genuinely afraid, and medical costs are nothing to overlook, especially when a couple is only starting out."

"Then, she should of thought first before she played that joke. Now, you and May are paying the price. Not to mention May Robin used your guilt to get Waldo a date. She always had a loud voice, and the years haven't made it any softer. Unlike me, maybe her hearing is going. I can still listen to a cockroach scuttle across a tile floor and nail it with my slipper from bed."

"They have cockroaches at Magnolia Villa?" The thought appalled Jane who wondered if she should speak to the management at the place.

"Not so many. Those big ones get in during summertime no matter what anyone does. They don't like the heat no more than the rest of us. The Villa sprays, but I consider a quick death by shoe or slipper better for all concerned. I have days I wish *le Bon Dieu* would stomp on me and get it over with. You got any more coffee?"

"I'll get you a cup. And Miss Olive, I think you still have plenty of life left in you."

Olive Tauzin shot out her little bird claw of a hand and kept Jane from leaving on her caffeine run. "I thought you and my Merlin had something going on, you know. Now you gonna dump him for Cold Hands Waldo?"

"Lord, no! Since I promised May, I'll have to go out with him once and once only, I swear. May cares a lot about her nephew and is trying to help him meet someone."

126

"Ha! That's her own guilt working on her. Wendy is adopted, and May helped her sister-in-law get a girl child. That pretty baby put Waldo in the shade, not that he wasn't lurking there already even at ten. Funny you going on and on about how much Wendy looks and acts like Spring Robin. I swear half the people in this parish don't know who their daddy is and a few don't know their mamas, neither. I do, but I'm not saying. Now about you and my grandson…"

"As for me and Merlin, I think your grandson took what he wanted and left."

"Got in your panties, huh? Well, I take that as a good sign for both of you. He ain't shown much interest in women since he mustered out of the army. Before he enlisted he liked the ladies fine and often. The military made him grow up some, but this keeping to himself ain't like him, no."

"Really glad I could help him with that problem," Jane said with a little taste of sarcasm tainting her statement. Miss Olive didn't appear to notice.

"And you, Jane, nice, pretty girl drying on the vine. By your age, the only unmarried men left in Chapelle to date are divorced or perverts. That Waldo, a man who can't hold on to a wife: who knows what he does with those corpses? I told Merlin, you don't take me to his funeral home when I die. Get me cremated and scatter me in the bayou right behind this house. That's where I belong. Pope don't like it, too bad. I figure *le Bon Dieu* be able to find me no matter where I'm resting."

Jane shook her head. "I'm only twenty-four, Miss Olive, not forty. I still have lots of time to find a man if I want to marry. Let me get you that coffee? How do you take it?"

"Black as the Devil's soul and sweet enough to save him. Real sugar, none of that fake stuff that's putting the cane farmers out of business."

Jane tried to move away, but Olive held on to her arm with surprising strength. "Don't give up on Merlin. I'm asking you, Jane. He needs you way more than Waldo Robin and can make you a happy life together once he gets over the war."

At last, she released Jane, but a van pulled into the drive and tooted its horn before the coffee delivery. A moment later, one of the aides from Magnolia Villa pounded on the front door. A burly, black woman, she carried a folding wheelchair.

"Miss Olive, I'm gonna put you in this to hurry things up a little bit since I got two more to pick up after. Ma'am, could you bring the walker?"

"Shit, back to decaf," Olive mumbled. "Sorry, for the *merde* mouth, Jane." As the aide lifted her frail body and strapped her into the chair, she said in parting, "You give Merlin another chance, you hear?"

This time, Jane made no promises. Hadn't Merlin's granny said she'd been suckered twice already today? She followed Olive to the van and handed the walker to the aide to stow. Miss Olive couldn't get a hold on her belted into her seat as she was, but she still leaned forward and said, "Swear you will, Jane," almost desperately.

Jane sighed. What did one more promise matter? She would keep Angela's secret, go out once with Waldo no matter how much he repelled her, and make one more attempt to show her interest in Merlin Tauzin. "I will."

Olive leaned back in her seat like a sleepy child

suddenly out of energy. "Now I can die happy. Take me back to the Villa, Melba."

"You ain't dying, Miss Olive. You just got the osteoporosis and too much sugar and caffeine in yo' system. Now, you behave for me." The driver got behind the wheel and took her charge away.

Jane returned to her kitchen to continue the cleanup. Really, her guests hadn't left much for her to do. They'd taken their dishes with them and filled her storage containers with an excess of food, now stacked in her refrigerator. She put plastic wrap over the generous chunk of cake Spring left on the table. Her portion read, "Happy." "Retirement" had gone home with May. Happy, that remained to be seen. She sure wasn't thrilled about going out with Waldo or throwing herself at Merlin again or being a receptionist/environmental project manager.

By the time she'd policed the house and found all the stray paper cups and crumpled napkins, emptied her regular waste cans full of party plates gooey with frosting, darkness prevailed outside her door. Leery of snakes, she hauled the bulging bags of trash to the rejected green receptacle. At least, she could use it for storage until the new can arrived.

Before she could stop herself, she stepped out of the shadow of the old pecan tree and looked across the way to Merlin's townhouse. A lamp burned in his presumed bedroom window. So, he'd finished his shift and come home. No flowers sent to her after Thanksgiving. No phone call to see how she did or if the party went well even though the hour wasn't that late. Sure, Merlin Tauzin could make her happy in at least one way, but great sex one time did not a relationship make. Okay, tomorrow after work, she would take him a plate of party leftovers, fulfill her vow to Miss Olive to make an effort, and consider that promise complete. She walked back with hands fisted at her waist simply daring any lowdown snake to get in her way and slammed the kitchen door.

****

Merlin saw Jane appear briefly by the side of the house as he sat in his dark living room with the TV for company and a second beer in his hand. By the light of her driveway lantern, he watched her stare in his direction, then put her hands on her hips and stamp back to her door. He could tell she was pissed, probably at him for leaving the way he did. He had no words to explain that didn't seem cowardly, so no sense in calling her.

Doubting that flowers would smooth over his actions either, he finished his drink and went to get another using the illumination seeping from his open bedroom door upstairs to find his way. He half hoped Jane would encounter some nasty wildlife on her way to the kitchen and she'd call for help, but that shotgun slam of the door probably scared off any critter within a mile. Just went to show he wasn't the man he used to be, or he'd go right over there and say, "Baby, I'm back," watch her get mad for calling her "baby" and his casual attitude. Then, he'd kiss that angry snarl right off her face and take her to bed. But, not tonight, maybe never.

Chapter Thirteen

Monday, and Nadia Nixon waiting by the time clock. What a great way to start a work week. Jane pasted a pleasant smile on her face and handed the CAO a paper plate bearing a large chunk of retirement cake before she reached for her time card.

"What's this?" By Nadia's grim expression, Jane surmised people rarely brought her treats unless they made her a special Ex-lax brownie which the woman both needed and deserved.

"A piece of May's retirement cake. Since I knew you were running a marathon this weekend from the staff newsletter, I didn't bother to invite you, but a good time was had by all."

"It says 'Happy' on it. What's that supposed to mean?"

"That someone else took home the 'Retirement' part. Enjoy!"

Happy that you got rid of an old woman who loved her job, happy that the proposal to clean up the oil well site would probably be sent in late and thus earn a rejection, happy that you can screw up people's lives at will. Thinking all of the above, Jane moved past the woman who looked like she'd been built of bricks to go to her office.

"Wrong turn, Marshall. You need to be out here to take calls and greet the public, remember?"

"Just going to put away my purse and lunch bag and transfer some files over to this computer first."

"It's seven-thirty. We're open, and the phone is ringing. Assume your position."

Jane wanted to retort, "On my knees and under your desk?" but she buried the urge beneath her triple mantra of mortgage payment, car loan, renovation costs, and took her seat in May's ancient chair. The first calls she fielded, easy enough transfers to various staff members. Most of the desk action consisted of buzzing employees in and out of the inner offices. Unable to get at her files, she had plenty of time to muse that if a psychotic gunman broke into the courthouse and tried to slay Nadia, Woof, or an ex-wife, she'd be the first one to die when the rampage began. How did May endure this? Maybe she had less imagination to run rampant.

Evidently, the riled and the crazy got up a little later in the day. A commuter on his way to Lafayette nearly hit a cow in the road. "Living or dead," Jane asked logically.

"What difference does that make? Stupid beast very nearly got me killed."

"Well, I either call animal control to wrangle it or public works to clean up the mess."

"It stood in the center of the Old Chapelle Road and threatened my vehicle near the abandoned Cajun racetrack. How about I go back and shoot it? That should solve your dilemma."

Monday and lack of coffee made some people testy. She headed down that path herself. "Alive, then. I will take care of it. Thank you for calling the Ste. Jeanne d'Arc parish council office." She passed the information on to Animal Control.

The next, a woman's thin, hysterical voice whispering into the phone, "The aliens who can see through my walls are going to bomb the library. You must stop them."

Jane got her address and debated whether to call the cops or the EMT's. Someone forgot to take their meds this morning. She settled on the police in case the bomb might have a real basis. They were not happy about the alert.

"That's old Rachael. She calls with these loony tips twice a week. May never bothered us with them."

Still, the woman needed help. Jane asked for an ambulance to be sent to that address. And so it went all morning. Angela spelled her at ten-thirty, allowing Jane to fill her coffee mug and transfer her files onto a flash drive she could use on May's computer or at home. Clearly, she'd have to do the Super Fund proposal on her own time if this were a typical day. Pictures needed to be taken of the site, but how to get out from behind the reception desk? She guessed she could do the photos on Saturday. Taking a second cup of coffee with her, she assumed her position again.

Nadia checked on her briefly under the guise of using the public restroom across from the desk. Jane had her proposal up on the computer and worked away diligently, refusing to glance up. On her way back into the maze of offices, the CAO leaned over the reception desk to stare at the screen and spied the coffee mug.

"Unprofessional, drinking coffee where the public can see you, and if you swill free coffee all day, you'll have to pee and leave your desk."

"Like you just did? Don't you have a restroom near

your office? Wouldn't it be more efficient if you used that one?"

"Where I choose to void is not your business. In the future, confine yourself to one cup of coffee on each break and use those breaks and your lunch hour for your bathroom visits."

Nadia's breath puffing in Jane's face reeked of the special blend she brewed in her own office and sipped all day long. Jane picked up her mug. The impulse surged to toss the remnants into the CAO's face. She summoned her indebtedness mantra, calmed, poured the dregs into a waste can, and hid the mug in a drawer.

"I'm writing you up for this and your insubordinate attitude."

Jane held her tongue and returned to her proposal writing. Going red in the face, Nadia stood there waiting.

"You have to buzz me in, Marshall."

"Yet another reason why you should use the interior restroom, Nadia." Jane hit the buzzer and sent her on her way. Hmmm, this position did come with some power after all.

Angela relieved her for lunch at one. Jane spent the time eating alone in the break room. She used the employee bathroom near Nadia's office and fell to the temptation to poke her head through the CAO's half-open doorway and report, "I did my lunchtime void as you suggested, Chief."

"I do not require a report on your bodily functions." Nadia stood, turned, and poured coffee from her private stock into a stainless steel travel mug. The block of cake with most of the icing licked off sat on the corner of her desk. Suitably, only the letters PP remained. She resumed her seat and swiped up the remaining frosting on a thick finger. Without taking her steely gaze from Jane's face, she sucked the finger clean. "Either come in and shut the door, or get back to work."

With a thought in her mind about cobras hypnotizing their prey, Jane bolted back to the reception desk where Angela greeted her with, "Thank God you're back. I so gotta pee. Because of the B-A-B-Y," as if no one in the office could spell. The pregnant woman dashed into the public restroom before returning to her job.

The first joy of the afternoon—a call from Waldo Robin.

"Jane Marshall's office, please."

"This is Jane."

"Oh, good! I got your message from Aunt May that you wanted me to get in touch about getting together. No need to be shy. You could have called me the way modern women do when they want a man, I mean, a date."

"I can't take personal calls at work. Catch me at home." Only postponing the inevitable, Jane disconnected.

The next time she answered a call, an irate voice shouted into her ear, "What for you took my crazy Tante Rachael to da psych ward? Everybody know she nuts but harmless. Who is gonna pay for dat ambulance? Better be the parish, you hear you me?"

Feigning ignorance, Jane took his name and number, said the parish president would get back to him, and prayed for the day to end. Eventually, it did.

\*\*\*\*

Her new trash receptacle waited at the end of the driveway when Jane arrived home. Full of rapture, she left her car right there and went to hug the can's solid, square sides. She inhaled its new plastic smell. Opening its kind of flimsy lid, she admired the pristine interior soon to be filled to the brim with her very own garbage. Now to see how this baby handled. Jane swung it around and began to push it toward the garage. The cheap wheels caught in the gravel. She applied more force and got the can rolling again. A few feet later, another jam occurred, this one more stubborn. She put her back into it and gave a mighty shove. One of the wheels popped off and rolled free onto her lawn.

"No! No!" Jane gathered the stray wheel and tried to stick it back on the axle, but the plastic hub had split. It held for a few inches, then went rogue again. Finally, she placed the wheel atop the can, turned the receptacle to drag position, and drew it backwards to the garage. The slim metal axle dug a line into the driveway as she went. Parking it next to the sturdier green can the Senegal trash collectors had used, Jane transferred the party trash bags to the new one. She'd figure out how to get it to the curb on Thursday.

Entering the house, she rushed to catch a ringing phone before giving it any thought. The measured, lugubrious voice of Waldo Robin said, "Hello there, Jane. Can we talk now?"

"I just walked in the door from work, and…"

"I only want to confirm our plans for a date. Friday night, dinner and dancing at Broussard's Barn. I find the place more authentic than Mulates. Too many tourists go there these days, but Broussard's is still an undiscovered treasure. Pick you up at six-thirty unless I get a call to retrieve a body. Will that work for you?"

She wanted to say, "Tell it to the Tourist Commission," but kept her word to May. "That would be fine. See you, then." She disconnected. Nothing in her promise said she must stay on the phone making chitchat and gushing over the details of their evening together.

Making a salad and boiling some noodles, Jane fixed a meal featuring leftover cocktail meatballs over pasta. She sort of regretted using the last of the cake to take a poke at Nadia, but plenty of other goodies beckoned. Reminding herself that she'd end up a size 42DD cup if she indulged in too many sweets, she confined dessert to a pecan tartlet and a single chocolate chip cookie accompanied by two cups of coffee. Ah, the caffeine rush she'd been missing all day.

Okay, she'd kept Angela's pregnancy a secret. The girl would surely spill that any day and get one burden out of the way. The origin of the off-color note must remain buried for now, but she did hope Angela would fess up when she quit to become a stay-at-home mom. She'd set the date with Waldo for better or worse. Now to get up her courage and approach Merlin's door for the giving of the second chance requested by Miss Olive.

Jane took down two of her signature lemon-decorated pottery plates and arranged one with an attractive display of sweets. The other she piled high with turkey sandwiches, little cabbage rolls, meatballs, and cold boudin sausage. Stretching plastic wrap over both, she backed out her kitchen door and moved across the lawn to deliver her load to Merlin. He did not sit in his accustomed place on the stoop. The sun had sunk below the horizon without much fanfare this evening. No need to watch it, she supposed.

She used Cane View's glaring parking lot lights, the ones that blotted out the stars, to make her way across the street. The second she set foot inside the gates, Merlin's outside lamp flicked on and his door opened as if he'd seen her coming and wanted to invite her inside his place. Jane felt gratified for a few seconds as she crossed the lot until a small woman stepped out. The petite lady turned to face Merlin who stood in the entrance.

Whoever she was had dark brown hair liberally streaked with blonde hanging halfway down her back in long, loose waves, very striking against a tight, stretchy black top that emphasized her delicate bones. A short, black skirt with a slit up the back clung to her shapely rump. The other woman wore dark hosiery with seams running up the back, the kind you'd hold up with a sexy garter belt, and high heels, also black, that did not nearly elevate her to Merlin's height. She ran a dainty, almost child-like, hand over his big, stubbly chin and said something in a low, scratchy-soft voice. He put his hands on her tiny shoulders and lowered his head. She placed a kiss on his cheek.

Plates in hand and no place to hide, Jane froze in mid-parking lot. Then, Merlin spotted her of course. His hands remained on the woman's shoulders, but he called out, "Jane, come on over here," as if she had some other destination and wandered around parking lots with food in her hands every night—to feed stray cats, perhaps. That's how she'd probably end up if she stayed in Chapelle, a pathetic cat lady, if she didn't want to live over the mortuary with Waldo.

So now what? Come and meet the woman he'd spent the day with, probably in bed, not on the sofa, the lover his granny had no notion of as she tried to match Merlin and Jane? She would deliver the food, go home, and consider that promise null and void.

Stepping forward and managing a big smile, Jane held out the plates. "Leftovers from the party on Sunday. Since you will be home all week, they shouldn't go bad. Too much for me to eat. Here you go. Just leave the plates on the porch when you're finished."

Why, oh why, had she used real plates instead of paper? Had she harbored some kind of subconscious wish he'd come to her kitchen door to return them and stay? Nothing for it now but to hand him her nice pottery dishes and make her escape.

Merlin turned the woman around to face Jane. Her aging face crinkled into a happy smile that deepened the lines beside her nose and emphasized the crow's feet at the corners of a pair of rather lovely, but vacant brown eyes very heavily made up. From the bottom step of the townhouse, Jane caught a whiff of the menthol cigarette smoke that permeated her clothes and her gorgeous hair. My God, she had to be at least forty. Didn't women that old know not to wear red lipstick, some of which marked Merlin's cheek? He'd spent the day with this cougar, but didn't want to stay the night with her?

Before he could open his mouth, the woman began to gush, "Is this your sweetie, Merry? Are you Jane? Mama said Merry had a sweetie."

Jane looked over the woman's head and said, "I thought you hated being called Merry."

"No, he doesn't. I called him Merry from the day he was born, my cute little Merry bug."

The dense black of his stubble could not hide the red creeping up his neck to his cheeks. "Jane, this is my mother, Jenny David."

"Oh! Nice to meet you, Mrs. David."

"Jenny, everyone just calls me Jenny. See." She pointed to a nametag pinned to the scooped-neck, stretchy black top. A pushup bra squeezed her small breasts into two arcs popping above its neckline. Anything else she said got lost in the roar of a motorcycle rounding the corner at the stoplight.

"Sorry, I can't hear you, Jenny. I don't know why they can't put mufflers on those things."

"Because that would ruin the fun," Merlin shouted over the racket as the big hog turned in at the gates of Cane View.

"That's Harley, my husband, come to take me to work. Over here, honey!" Jenny David waved frantically as if the rider might not see her. No chance of that.

He pulled up right in front and got off his bike. Loosening a leather jacket stowed on the back of the motorcycle and similar to the one he wore hanging open he held the garment for his wife. "Come on, Jen. We're running late, and it's getting chilly."

A good ten years older than Jenny, Jane judged, the man with the wind-reddened face nesting between long, untrimmed sideburns that merged with a chest-covering gray beard got his passenger settled before saying, "I guess you're Jane."

"My stepfather, Harley David." Merlin came down the stairs and took a helmet off the rear if the bike.

Tenderly, he fastened the strap under his mother's chin. "You promised to wear it."

"Harley doesn't." She pouted like a first-grader.

"Well, baby, I got a very hard head." Harley reset the flat, leather cap a la Marlon Brando he wore instead. He leaned toward Jane, or rather the plates she held. "I got me the munchies, you mind?"

Digging his fingers under the plastic wrap, Harley helped himself to some boudin. Jane recognized the sweet scent of pot clinging to the facial hair and the Grateful Dead T-shirt that spanned across his vast belly.

"Be my guest. I brought this for Merlin."

Harley wagged a piece of sausage at his stepson. "If she can cook, she's a keeper. Sorry, we got to run." He shoved the remainder of the boudin into his mouth, remounted his bike, and took off with his silver ponytail flailing in the wind and his wife clinging to his back.

"Part of my family," Merlin said flatly.

"Interesting."

"You could say that ten times over. Looks good." He nodded at the plates.

"Here you go, then." She finally handed over the dishes. "You're letting bugs in." Jane pointed to his open door.

"Yeah, right."

He gave the plates back to her and went to click the door shut. Obviously no invitation to come inside would be forthcoming. Merlin reclaimed the food.

"My mission is complete then. I vowed to foist leftovers upon you, and I have. Time for me to go." Had all their ease and banter dissolved like the fog on Thanksgiving Eve?

His big jaw struggled to find a tidbit of

conversation. "Um, I saw you got your new trash can finally."

"Yes, it's a piece of crap. One of the wheels already fell off."

"I could come over and fix that for you."

"I'll manage. Maybe Super Glue will take care of it."

"That won't work. I don't mind doing it."

"No, you've done enough. I mean in cleaning my yard, mulching, planting. I still feel I owe you."

"Nope, we're square." Finally, he managed to acknowledge the alligator in the bayou, metaphorically speaking. "Ah, Jane, about the other night. I did want to stay, but I don't sleep very well. I toss a lot and get up in the night. I'm not a good bed partner." To say the least.

"Sure, no problem." She half turned to go.

He stopped her once more by saying, "I'd like to take you out again, maybe to a movie in Lafayette on Friday night."

"Sorry, I have a date to go dancing at Broussard's Barn that evening."

His stubbled jaw dropped, and she enjoyed the sight. Waldo was good for something after all.

"I thought you weren't going with anybody."

"What can I say? Suddenly, I'm popular. See you around, Merlin." She hastened away before he could ask the name of her escort and left him standing with two of her good plates in hand. If he truly wanted to see her again, he'd return them washed and in person. She'd given him a second chance along with the leftovers, but she did not have to make it easy for him.

Chapter Fourteen

Merlin Tauzin took a long time to eat those leftovers. Jane caught no sight of him the rest of the week. The weather turned gray and nasty with a chilly drizzle that refused to turn into a real rain. Neither of them spent any time watching the sun set. Jane heard his truck come and go, watched his lights turn on and go out, but the man himself might as well have been invisible.

She came home on Thursday to find her trash can not only fixed, but sporting a whole new set of wheels, chrome-spoked and rubber-rimmed, that slewed glittering through her gravel to the curb like a Coast Guard cutter pursuing drug runners. Her nice dishes, washed, sat on the kitchen steps. Coward—but he had left a note wedged between them.

"Thanks for feeding me. I fixed your trashcan. We are still even. Merlin."

His writing, like his hands on her back, stood out strong and bold in black ink on a piece of paper torn from a notebook. She started to toss it, but ended up shoving the folded, single sheet into her desk drawer, keeping a final memento from Merlin the Magician. The message light blinking on her extension phone caught her eye. Maybe, he'd called, too, to see if she'd gotten home, found the plates and the repair.

No such luck. The recorded voice of Waldo Robin

reminded her of their date on Friday and the pickup time, then launched into a recitation of his schedule. "I have a wake tonight and a rosary at eight a.m. before we take the deceased to the church at ten. Burial at noon. I should be free and clear by two, excluding any emergencies. I am so looking forward to having you in my arms again—on the dance floor of course." He ended with a forced chuckle.

Jane pushed the delete button. That message she had no desire to keep.

****

Friday came whether she wanted it to or not. After another tedious day of answering phones and trying to do her real job in snatches, Jane truly did not feel like tripping the light fantastic with May's nephew. She considered canceling and rescheduling, but that would only postpone the agony for another week. Her glass of red wine helped numb her nerves for the ordeal. She shrugged out of her work clothes, bushed her teeth, and considered what to wear to Broussard's Barn, best described as a venerable local dive of a dance hall. Jeans, the boots she'd bought in Montana, and a blue-checked cotton shirt, tucked in, belted, and buttoned up to her chin seemed about right. For whimsy, she added non-matching silver earrings, one a small accordion, the other a *frottoir*, a rub-board, both essential to the kind of music the Barn offered.

She supposed an undertaker would be punctual, though the dead were in no hurry, and Waldo was, right on the dot of six-thirty. With relief, Jane noted he did not drive the hearse, but instead a deluxe edition Cadillac. Somehow, that seemed even more wasteful than Merlin's big-ass truck, which could at least haul stuff like giant trashcans and probably pull tractors out of the mud, too. Still, when Waldo helped her into its fine white leather interior, she appreciated not having his cold hand on her elbow for more than a few seconds. Merlin wrapped his big, warm mitts around her waist and lifted her in and out of his rig despite her protests that she could very well enter and exit on her own—though it would have been a rugged and revealing climb in a short dress.

Unfair to compare the two men since Waldo had a quarter century on Merlin in age. To give the funeral director credit, he maintained a slim body though Jane suspected he inherited that from his mail-toting father. He wore khakis paired with a pale blue dress shirt open enough at the throat to show the very top of a pristine, white undershirt. His long sleeves ended with French cuffs held together with what Jane at first glance took for gold nugget links, but on closer inspection turned out to be miniature skulls, very overdressed for an evening at Broussard's Barn.

"Interesting cufflinks," she said as Waldo got behind the wheel.

"A little undertaker humor. I find it is better to put the fact of my trade right out there rather than hide it."

Jane nodded. She wished his black hair with the silver wings and slight widow's peak did not remind her so very much of Grandpa in the vintage *Munster's* television series. At least, he combed it straight back and did not part it in the middle in old-timey vampire style. Grandpa, no, he wasn't that old, but he could have fathered her at a not very young age. Why May thought they'd make such a great couple eluded Jane.

Easy listening music surrounded her in sound as

soon as the engine turned over with the strong purr of a sleeping lion, not a roar like Merlin's truck. She hummed along to avoid making conversation. The sequence of tunes sounded familiar and very uplifting.

"Do you like the mix?" Waldo asked. "Put it together myself to play at the mortuary and made a copy for the Caddy."

Oh right, the songs played in the background at the last viewing she'd attended for old Leroy "Lambo" Mouton's funeral. Jane stopped humming. Somehow, singing along seemed disrespectful. "Very nice," she mumbled.

They cruised through the town of Chapelle with perfect enough timing to miss every one of the five traffic lights: entering town to slow folks down, two on either side of the green where the Church of Ste. Jeanne d'Arc sat, one at the school, and the last upon leaving town in a vain a attempt to make people stay a while. Outside the city limits, they did have to stop at the light slung across the road at the huge Hartz Technology campus. It sort of balanced the new signal by Jane's house, though Hartz needed it to allow its many employees to come and go while the Cane View light served more as a convenience for its residents and a way to remind passersby they could stop right there at the Fast 'N Fun for fried chicken and gas.

Waldo used the delay at the light to move one long, thin arm from the wheel and lay it across the seat where Jane sat a little hunched forward, eager to get to the Barn, escape the Caddy and mood music for mortuaries. She believed the last time a guy tried that move on her she'd been in high school. The cold hand inched toward her shoulder. The light changed. They moved out with

Waldo's hand dangling still closer.

"Watch out for that dog!" Jane screamed. The hand snapped back to the wheel, the Caddy swerving a little in the process.

"Where?"

"Oh, it ran into the cane field across the road."

She supposed she might have gotten them both killed, all in an attempt to get Waldo's hand back where it belonged, but since they had just pulled out, she doubted it. Her date made the turn onto the secondary road that would take them to Broussard's Barn with his hands stuck tight to the wheel and his teeth gritted in his long, pale jaw.

They arrived without mishap and parked in the far corner of the large oyster shell lot because Waldo did not want his car scratched or dinged by the trucks, large and small, SUV's, and rusty beaters parked closer to the building. Strings of clear bulbs illuminated the space and left the rear of the place in near darkness except for the lamps burning dimly in front of the doors of an old motel to the back where rooms rented by the hour. Fallow cane fields closed in on either side of the property and beyond them the venerable Broussard homestead still stood despite its hundred years and more.

They entered according to custom through the nineteenth century general store where canned peaches older than its current proprietor still held shelf space. The goods that really moved, snuff, cigarettes, and condoms, sat behind the cash register protected by Old Broussard and various weapons known to be kept under the counter but rarely seen. The arsenal supposedly consisted of a Louisville Slugger, a shotgun, and a pearl-handled revolver.

Old Broussard was an institution himself and nearly as large as a real one. His hind cheeks overflowed the cane seat of a bentwood chair. His vast stomach filled out bib overalls with a bulk like a laughing Buddha and strained a soiled white T-shirt beneath it. A standing joke said an Old Broussard died of a heart attack when his heir reached the required weight to replace him. Nevertheless, the family provided the current mayor of Chapelle and many others powerful in ways no one wanted to ridicule. Old Broussard, certified as a justice of the peace, performed marriages in the store. Oddly, many locals chose to tie the knot there, then step through the connecting corridor to the dance hall and celebrate their union. Quite the scandal when the local librarian eloped to the place with Bob LeBlanc one boozy Mardi Gras Eve. No chance Jane would ever wed here.

From blubbery lips sunk into several chins, Old Broussard greeted their arrival with a *"Bienvenue a Broussard's"* and held out a sausage-fingered hand for the five dollar each cover charge, a relatively new fee. "Now you get one free drink wit' dat. Y'all pass a good time," he added as he handed Waldo a ten in change and two tickets for the drinks. The couple descended into the frenzy of the dance hall.

At this early hour, customers already filled the tables nearest the large dance floor. Some patrons had taken the four-tops and shoved them together to accommodate all of their friends. A group of wiry black men calling themselves The Salty Beans warmed up on the spacious bandstand that once hosted jazz bands out of New Orleans during Prohibition. While there was only one way into Broussard's Barn, it possessed many ways out, great for accommodating the fire laws, but having their origins in its speakeasy days.

Finding a space near a side door, Jane and Waldo sat and considered their options for dinner. Judging by the offerings on the two-sided laminated menu, the music drew the crowds, not the food. Choice of fried catfish, shrimp, crawfish, or oysters served in a basket with fries and a cup of coleslaw or ensconced in a loaf of French bread po-boy style, same sides. Boiled crawfish available in season with corn and red potatoes. This wasn't the season for mudbugs. A long list of half-pound burgers with various toppings filled the second column and the back merely listed all the beer and booze available from Broussard's bar.

Okay, the giant ball of cholesterol or fried seafood, Jane considered. Most Cajun places did fried really, really well. She settled on the shrimp basket. Waldo dithered about the wine list consisting of a choice of house red or white, but he wanted a Broussard Burger, the Barn's specialty. Jane's selection called for white while his would go better with red.

"Order a glass of each for our free drinks. You really don't want to see the bottle," Jane advised.

"Oh, you've been here before, a nice young woman like yourself—alone?" His tone implied perhaps she was not as nice as his aunt claimed.

"No, I came with a bunch of women from the office for the music as you said."

"Ah, I see." Waldo held up his arm and began snapping his fingers. Jane half-expected frost to fly from the tips. "Waitress, where is our waitress?"

She came up behind the undertaker. "Yeah, wadda

you want to drink?'"

Jane did the double-take. She knew Merlin's mom worked here, but somehow didn't expect to run into her. But, the voice wasn't right, this one tough, not childish. She took a closer look as the waitress stepped around Waldo. Not Jenny David, but her younger clone with an identical hair style and blonde streaking, dressed in the same Broussard's Barn serving attire but exposing the tops of bigger, plumper, younger breasts. The overdone makeup matched, but instead of coming across like a girl trying out her mother's red lipstick and mascara, this babe looked hard despite the lack of Jenny's facial lines. Her nametag read "Brittney," the sister Merlin wished he never had.

Suddenly less imperious when confronted by their surly server, Waldo ordered the two glasses of wine and went ahead with their orders as if dearly wanting to minimize contact with the waitress. That seemed fine with her. "Gotcha," she said before moving off toward the bar and kitchen.

"Allow me to apologize for the terrible service here, but Chapelle has so little to offer in the way of fine eateries. The next time we should go into Lafayette."

"Hmmm," Jane responded. No more promises to May, no next times, she swore to herself.

The music cranked up with the accordion and fiddles taking the lead and the rub-boards coming in behind, one played with the spoons and the other with inch long picks like stainless steel fingernails for a different sound. A fast-paced zydeco two-step, some people danced as couples and others appeared to simply jerk their bodies around to the rhythm.

"Shall we dance?"

"Ah, no. Let's wait until after we eat, okay?" The longer she could draw out the meal, the less time spent in Waldo's frigid grasp.

Their waitress plunked down the wineglasses and left without saying a word. Jane sipped her drink, a white jug wine with a sour edge. Gauging by Waldo's expression, his beverage did not taste any better. Still he did the whole sniff and swill in the mouth routine so thoroughly to impress her, Jane had to hold in a laugh. As if Brittney would take it back for a better vintage.

"As I said, the music is the thing here." Waldo clinked his glass against hers. "Here's to a pleasant evening in good company."

"Hmmm," Jane said again with a slight acknowledging smile.

The food came quickly in green plastic baskets served with the same crude panache. Plonk! "Enjoy" and their waitress retreated. Jane imagined the grill and the deep fat fryers never stopped churning out big, greasy burgers, golden fries, and lightly battered seafood from the time the music started until the Barn shut down at two a.m. She gave the kitchen credit for using huge, fresh shrimp and a superb, flaky coating as well as fresh cut potatoes for the steaming fries. The coleslaw, very peppery, was not to her taste, but then, no one came here to eat vegetables.

Waldo divided his immense burger in half like a prissy spinster wearing white gloves and bit into it. A glob of grease and mayo looking very much like a bird dropping splurted onto his pale blue dress shirt. Only making the spot larger, he tried to wipe it away with a paper napkin.

"Embarrassing."

"Don't worry about it on my account. Maybe we should leave so you can go home and soak your shirt in cold water."

"Oh, no! I've had worse things splattered on me," he countered.

Jane did not want to think about what. She reconsidered dipping her fries into ketchup. No, fine just as they are. She ate slowly, holding each shrimp between her fingers and nibbling down to the tailfins as she watched the musicians put on a gyrating show. One glance at Waldo told her she should have cut the shrimp into pieces and eaten them with a fork. Not repelled at all, he watched her lips as they progressed along the length of the large crustacean. Dang, finger food turned him on! How could she turn him off again? She bathed the fries in ketchup until they appeared to swim in blood, let some of the sauce drip on her checked shirt, and hoped she wouldn't have trouble getting out the stain.

Blotting her chest, she said, "I can be a very messy eater."

His dark eyes sunk deep in his skull watched her hand dabbing at one breast as if she masturbated just for him. She tossed the napkin aside in a hurry. "Let's dance!"

"I thought you wanted to finish eating first."

"The food will keep. I want to move." Yes, far from Waldo.

Without his mother and aunt watching, he cast away decorum and clutched her close to his bony chest as soon as they reached the edge of the dance floor. Jane pushed away.

"It's a fast one. We should be dancing like this." She spun off by herself about three feet away and began swaying her hips and snapping her fingers, tossed in a few twirls and sidesteps as Waldo observed standing almost still amid the dancers. He headed forward, his arms outstretched.

"No, I am sure the music calls for closely held partners."

"Not!" she said and backed into the guy behind her.

"Hey, watch it, babe," the guy objected as she kicked his ankle with her boot heel. "Oh, hi, Jane."

"Blaine, so good to see you again. You with Wanda? I'd like her to meet my date, Waldo Robin. Maybe we could switch partners again like we did at Mulates."

"She's around somewhere. We already hooked up with Dylan and Linzey here." Shouting above the music, he nodded at his current partner who held her arms up high and shimmied down low. Her straw cowgirl hat sat on top of a brunette extravaganza of big hair. Amazing how she could get that close to the floor in jeans so tight and still rise again without landing on her ass.

"Hey, Linzey, we're switching partners, okay?" Jane slithered between the dancing couple and tugged Blaine to one side leaving the brunette facing Waldo with his arms still extended. "Waldo, I want to dance with my old buddy, Blaine, for a while. You take Linzey for a spin."

"But I came to dance with you."

"The night is still young. Off you go."

Determined not to give in on the style of dance,

Waldo drew Linzey into his grasp and began a fast foxtrot around the floor. He held his new partner tight enough to get a feel of her enhanced breasts against his chest and knock her hat to the back of her head. Linzey, possibly stoned and in her own little world, went along with it.

"So where's Merlin tonight?" Blaine asked.

"Waldo asked first, unfortunately."

"Sorry to say he looks like a real stiff. Old and smells kinda funny, too."

Jane watched Waldo with his upper torso held rigid, but his feet moving fast like a Celtic dancer. "Eau de Mortuary," she answered.

Blaine laughed, thinking she jested. "Well, Wanda will be disappointed. She's still a little ticked Merlin didn't call her."

"He's been offshore and washed her number with his jeans."

"I done that a few times. Always wanted to kick myself afterwards. I never did get yours." Jane didn't offer it now either.

The set ended and the leader stepped to the microphone. "Next one is a line dance for the ladies. Gentlemen take a seat and watch them show their stuff. Girls, I don't want to see a single one of you sitting at a table. And here we go, one, two, three."

Waldo took his seat and started in on his burger again, careful to enrobe its oozing bottom with a napkin first. Jane stayed on the dance floor even though she didn't know the steps and made her turns and directional changes a half beat behind the others. When the music stopped, she drifted slowly back to their table. The fries had gone soggy in their puddle of catsup.

"I could certainly use something to drink."

Waldo held up a hand and snapped his fingers. Brittney passed nearby with a tray full of draft beers and ignored him. "This will be easier if I simply go to the bar. Another white wine?"

"No, a rum and Diet Coke."

He nodded somberly and weaved through the crush to the bar. Jane realized she missed Merlin teasing her about her choice of beverages. Well, she'd turned him down for another date, and he considered them even. Shortly, he'd be offshore again. Bye-bye, Merlin, no second chances for either of them.

Waldo returned with her drink and a beer for him. Jane drank it quickly and asked for another to make dancing the next set with her date more bearable as Dylan and Linzey, Blaine and Wanda kept their distance. Evidently, Waldo did not appeal to the honky-tonk gal the way Merlin had. She downed a third before they ventured out on the dance floor again. One thing you could say about the mixed drinks at Broussard's Barn, their bartender did not skimp on the alcohol, and it helped. Lit up and numbed from the inside out, Waldo's hands did not feel as cold to Jane, nor his rib cage as skeletal. Still, she wanted out of his arms.

They danced near an exit with a restroom sign and an arrow pointing outside. No lie, she needed the facilities and a break from being crushed to Waldo's chest. Pushing away from her partner's grip, she said, "Moment. Gotta pee." She could tell by his down-turned mouth that he did not approve of the way she expressed herself and would have preferred her to say, "Excuse me, please. I need to use the Little Girl's

Room" with a simper.

Well, screw Waldo. No, don't screw Waldo ever. Jane made for the door held open for her by one of the many burly Broussard boys who worked the place as bouncers. "Knock when you need back in," he said, combing a greasy ducktail that went out when Elvis died.

She found herself in the parking lot by a small, cement block building, plain and primitive as a john found in the wilderness areas of national parks. Better than the wooden outhouses of yore, she figured, knowing that Broussard's Barn once had separate sets for whites and the black performers and kitchen workers. The women's side wasn't totally filthy yet, just short on toilet paper and previously occupied by people who forgot to flush. Jane made sure she had plenty of paper going in, enough to coat the seat and wipe, too.

She sat there for some time enjoying her freedom from Waldo and the cool, stiff breeze coming in under the tin roof long after she concluded her business. The wooden stall had lots of interesting reading material: insults, comments, and phone numbers scratched into its thick, gray paint. "For a good time call..." "Dottie sucks Dick." "Elvis lives in Erath." A truck engine snarled as it passed the building, making its doors shake. She swore she recognized Merlin's big-ass Ford, but put that down to wishful thinking.

A couple of girls way drunker than her staggered in and pounded on her door. "Get out, we both gotta puke." She got out fast, washed her hands to the tune of dual barfing, and went outside still reluctant to knock for re-entry to the dance hall. Waldo stood a short distance away in a shadowed area with his back toward her away from the light over the restroom door. Shit, he'd followed her and waited to pounce again—but no. His chilly hands rested on the shoulders of their waitress who turned away from him and enjoyed a smoke break. The wind carried his words and the whiff of menthol cigarettes back to Jane.

"My date is as cold as a redfish on ice, baby. I think she might be of the same persuasion as Nadia Nixon since she certainly doesn't like the feel of a man's body against hers. After I take Jane home, I could come back at closing and get a room. It's not like you haven't done it before. I'm a generous man as you know, but I like to get my money's worth."

Before Jane could step forward and say their evening together had ended, she felt the body heat behind her and saw the long shadow cast by its owner, Merlin Tauzin in person and truly pissed. He moved right by her without a word and knocked those hands from his sister's shoulders. Only the woman wasn't Brittney.

Jenny Tauzin turned and spoke up in her soft, smoke-scratchy voice. "I'd like to help you, but I can't no matter how good it feels. I'm a married woman and once you marry, you can't go with other men, my mama says. Baby boy, you come to pick me up tonight? Where's Harley?"

"Feeling under the weather, Mom. He called and asked me to come."

Jenny gazed up at her son with a sweet smile. "I don't get off until midnight. Is that okay?"

"Sure, Mom. I'll sit in the bar area like Harley does and watch out for you. The crowd can get rough here on weekends."

"That's nice. See you inside." Jenny stubbed out her cigarette. "Back to work."

Jenny made her way to the restroom exit, knocked, and stepped back into the writhing turmoil of the Barn. Meanwhile, Waldo worked his way slowly backwards as if he intended to hide behind Jane while Merlin talked to his mother. He did not move quick enough. Merlin turned, took a few long strides forward, and jerked him closer by the collar of his dress shirt. Of similar height but greatly outmuscled, Waldo shrank down a few inches to avoid meeting the man's blazing blue eyes.

"Never touch or talk to my mother again. You understand?"

"I thought she was Britt...no, one of Broussard's working girls."

"Yeah, like every man in the parish doesn't know his girls hang by the bar and don't wear waitress outfits. This is for my mom." Merlin cocked a fist.

"Don't hit me!" Waldo covered his long face as best he could with his hands, so Merlin drove his fist into the flat but flabby stomach of the undertaker. The hands flew to the side opening up room for an uppercut to the jaw. "And for my sister."

Jane knew she should intervene as a civilized bystander, a Good Samaritan, but her delighted brain kept repeating, "Date with Waldo over. Check." Must be the alcohol.

Waldo's head snapped back and rebounded in time to meet a blow to the nose. "And for what you said about Jane."

"Assault, assault," Waldo managed to scream

before his knees hit the oyster shells and his beer and burger dinner made its way from gut to ground.

The side door banged open, and the Broussard bouncer charged out wielding a baseball bat. "What's going on here! Blackie Tauzin, that you?"

"Yeah, Slick. This jerk-wad hit on my mother, insulted my sister and Jane over there."

"Police, you need to call the police. I want to press charges," Waldo wailed, still kneeling over his self-made puddle.

"Now, Mr. Robin, you a regular here and know the cops don't get ever get called to Broussard's Barn. We handle shit in our own way. Don't you be telling me neither, you don't know the wait staff is off-limits. You pay for your pleasure here, yeah. Tell you what, let me help you up. We go over to the bar, get an ice pack for that nose, give you a whiskey for the pain on the house. Who knows, maybe one of our ladies will feel sorry enough for you to give a freebie if you still got the urge. What say?"

"I want to press charges." Waldo's words came out muffled by his rapidly swelling nose.

"You want to find yourself floating in a ditch tomorrow morning? That what you said?" Slick thumped his bat against a calloused hand for emphasis.

"No. I'll take that ice and whiskey."

"Good decision." The bouncer extended the bat to help Waldo up rather than offer his thick, hairy arm.

"Come along, Jane," her date ordered.

"I don't think so, Waldo. I'll call a cab. Don't ask me out again. And I'm not a lesbian."

"Frigid, then."

"Not half as much as you."

The door into the barn opened. Zydeco music and the shuffling sound of boots on the dance floor poured out along with a few gasps as Waldo entered followed by Slick.

"Nothing to see here, folks. The man fell down in the parking lot. Shit happens." The bouncer stopped in the doorway and offered Merlin a bit of advice, too.

"Better come back at midnight. I'll watch out for your mother, Blackie."

"Thanks, Slick."

That left Jane alone with Merlin on the dark side of the parking lot.

"Since I'm leaving, I could give you a lift. If you want to stay even with me, you can give me a ten for gas. I'm parked right behind the restrooms."

Despite the near darkness, she could sense a grin tugged at the corners of his lips. "You know, a ten would fill half my car's tank."

"That so?"

"Yes, but I would like a ride, thank you."

She followed him around the back of the cinderblock building and admitted to feeling that thrill when he lifted her into his truck. They rolled out of the lot and rode in silence until they reached the outskirts of Chapelle and got caught by every light. By the church, she noticed his hand with the knuckles turning purple resting easy and commanding on the wheel. Impulsively, she took it and laid a healing kiss on the bruises.

"Merlin, you should learn to use your words, not your fists."

"I'm not so good with words."

"A lucky thing tonight you knew the bouncer, or

you'd be in jail right now for assaulting Waldo, upstanding local businessman that he is."

Merlin snorted. "Yeah, right. Great guy, Waldo. I ran with Slick in high school, but even so, the result would have been the same. Broussard's Barn is our own local Vegas. What happens there stays there."

Merlin moved the truck through the black district of Chapelle, quiet by day but throbbing with life on a Friday night when the hole-in-the-wall clubs lit their neon beer signs and knots of folks moved along the sidewalk from one bar to another. No one bothered them, not even when they had to idle at the long light on the other end of town by the run-down strip mall. She felt safe with Merlin in a way hard to rationalize with her very women's libby upbringing.

"Yeah, Slick and me on our bikes, no one messed with us," he volunteered.

For a moment, Jane envisioned two adolescent boys, one lanky, one chunky, pedaling their bicycles along the country roads abloom with yellowtop and pussytoes until Merlin said, "He helped me steal the hearse."

"And the stains in the rear?"

"Some of his grandfather's girls volunteered to show us the ropes."

"So not riding bicycles or deflowering virgins, then."

"Motorcycles, muffin. The virgins came later. What, no rebuttal on the muffin?"

"Nope." Because she felt like a muffin right now, warm and soft with a sweet, jelly filling.

"My granny was so eager to get me away from bad company she found the means to send me to college. I had good grades, but enough detention to keep me off the honor roll and out of the Beta Club. I do regret I got bored with higher education and didn't finish. But no, I wanted action. Got more than I bargained for."

They arrived at her house. Merlin pulled around to the back under the deep shadow of the pecan tree. Out of the shelter of the cab, the wind howled and whipped Jane's hair into her face as he lifted her down.

"Change in the weather coming," he said.

"Want to come in for a while?"

"Not tonight. I have to go back to the Barn for Mom and Brittney. Tomorrow, maybe."

Jane lowered his face down to hers and gave him a kiss, deep and hard, enjoying the brush of his stubble and his hands going around her back drawing her in tight against him.

"Waldo doesn't know what he's talking about when it comes to you."

"I'm glad you realize that. Tomorrow for sure?"

"Yep."

Second chance offered and accepted. Check.

## Chapter Fifteen

Clad in last night's clothes and high rubber boots, Jane went out early to photograph the site of the leaking waste pit reported months ago by a squirrel hunter heading for a copse of water oaks. She hiked in to spare her car on the crude access road. With the dike around its edges broken in several places, dark puddles dotted the landscape. The wind, pushing a cold front into place, riffled the surface of the oily, black substance the pit still contained. Beyond the tree line half a mile away ran the bayou teeming with fish, turtles, and waterfowl. This place needed to be cleaned up, and soon. She'd collected soil and water samples earlier when she could still leave the office and had the results ready to plug into her report. Now, she recorded pictorial evidence for her document and headed home before the rain hit.

Having no intention of dragging pollutants into her house, she shucked off the boots at the front of the garage and made her way across a scattering of small pecans more painful to tread upon than pebbles. "Ouch, ouch—ouch, ouch," she muttered with each step.

Strong arms gathered her up from behind. If she didn't know his very scent by now, she would have screamed. "Merlin, you can put me down."

"Sure, I love hearing you make that little ouch, ouch noise, cuddles." But he did not release her until they reached the kitchen steps where he set her down gently at the top.

"I didn't expect you so soon. I went out to take pictures of the waste pit we need to get cleaned up." She took her little digital camera from her shirt pocket and suddenly recalled the ketchup stains down her front. "I'm not injured."

"No, I recognize ketchup when I see it. Blood has a coppery smell and dries black. Still, you shouldn't go places like that alone. They find bodies in those pits all the time."

"None out there today, not even a snapping turtle to worry about. Wildlife deserted the area some time ago, but thanks for your concern." On eye level with him, she could not resist rasping her thumb along his unshaven jaw. He caught it in his teeth and shook her digit like an overgrown puppy for a second before letting go.

"Ready to play, are we?" Jane asked.

"After lunch. Holy Mom is holding a hot link po-boy sale today for a benefit. Granny asked me to get her some, so I bought enough for us, too."

He held up two white paper bags clutched in one fist. If she hadn't been so busy sniffing his neck and taking in the aroma that should be labeled "manly" when he carried her, she would have caught the smell of barbecued sausage exuding from the sacks. She already knew the contents: a hot link sausage poking out the ends of a short bun, a bag of chips, an off-brand can of cola, and a peppermint candy to sweeten the breath after eating, the ingredients that raised funds for many good causes in the area. Sad to say, her stomach rumbled as it never did for salad.

"Now I owe you for gas and lunch."

"Don't worry about it. Like Waldo, I think I'll get my money's worth."

Jane opened the door before they ended up rolling on the lawn among the fallen pecans. Merlin made himself at home popping the tops of the soft drinks and laying out the spread while Jane got glasses and ice. A little orange grease leaked from the end of the sausage when she took a bite and landed on her chest. She didn't bother wiping it away this time.

"This shirt needed to go in the wash anyhow. No sense wearing clean clothes to visit a cesspit."

"You can take it off anytime. All right by me." His smile tugged at his lips. His blue eyes glittered in kitchen light she'd turned on as the sky outside darkened. Tempted, she was very tempted to do exactly that, but held him off with, "Right, you'd love that."

"I would, especially if you have on that green lace bra."

"Sure, I wear my best undies to tramp around polluted sites."

The first pattering of drops began to fall covering the noise of crunching potato chips. Neither one of them forgot to use the mint at the end of the meal. A long, low roll of thunder stretched out like a sexual groan followed by an orgasmic flash of lightning.

"You ever been upstairs when rain is hitting that metal roof?"

"No, it's more of a guestroom. I don't really use the space except for that and storage."

"I do recall you had a bed up there. Come on."

Merlin led her through the house, out the front door, and up the precarious wooden stairs to the old *garçonniere*.

165

"Loud," she said as the rain beat down harder, maybe mixed with a little hail.

"Soothing when it lets up a little, great for napping." He eyed the sleigh bed. "Not made for two."

"No, it's a guestroom, not a bachelor pad."

"Not a problem." He stooped to draw out the trundle bed and tumble her onto its fresh sheets. "You fit just fine."

"So where do you plan to nap?"

"I don't plan to nap at all. Let me help you out of that awful stained shirt." Straddling her, he started on the buttons and got down to the bra in a hurry.

"Plain white cotton. You disappointed?"

"Nope. Because it will be out of my way in a second. There. Nice, very nice, 36C."

"How did you know that?"

"Read the label, sugar baby. I didn't really get to see them last time."

"All I got to see was the leather of my couch. Then, you left."

"I had my reasons. You want me to go?"

Like the storm outside, they'd been building toward this since last night. No way would she let him walk now. Jane sat up letting him get a good look before she stretched the dark T-shirt over his head and used her hand to smooth down that black hair from his head all the way down his chest to his belt buckle. She grappled with its oversized buckle embossed with a motorcycle. He released it and himself with one tug and a quick unzip. No briefs. He searched his hip pocket for a condom before kicking off his jeans and taking his athletic shoes with them. No socks either. The man came ready for action.

"Unless you've been with Wanda, you don't really need to use that."

"Wanda who? Jane, I want you to feel safe with me so I'll use it."

"Then, allow me."

She took the packet he'd torn open and smoothed it down the length of his hardened shaft all the way to the root, a treat for both of them evidently because he nearly upended her stripping off her jeans and socks. Her panties were pink cotton, but bikini cut. Like the bra, they didn't stay on long enough to matter. Then, he began to work her with those long fingers inside and out while he pressed her back and seized a nipple in his mouth. Jane nibbled along his neck and shoulder as he bowed over her, but like the rain that started gently and turned into a storm her bites grew stronger as her urge increased.

She raked her nails down his back and cupped his buttocks, trying to force him to enter her now, now, now! Stubborn as he could be in all ways, he kept that thumb in motion on her pulsing clit, his fingers filling the space inside, merely turning his head to take the other breast for a suckle. Jane beat on his back with both fists. "In, in, damn you!"

He raised his head long enough to say, "Ladies first." Lightning struck nearby adding to the charge in the air. Unable to hold back any longer, she came with an electric surge that arched her back.

"That's my little darlin'," he said.

"Oh, you—you…" Words failed her because now he sank deep into her moist warmth and began building on what he'd wrought. He took his time and when she bucked again, picked up the pace for the final thrusts before shuddering down into her arms. She stroked his back in apology for her scratches and laid gentle kisses along his prickly cheek. He mumbled something into her shoulder.

"What did you say?"

"You for sure ain't frigid."

If he admitted anything else he wasn't going to own up to it. Merlin rolled off on her far side, and Jane, feeling chilled by his loss, spooned around his body warmth. She tugged the quilt from the top of the bed over both of them though his long legs hung out over the edge of the trundle. The rain gentled, only a light pattering against the metal roof now. Soothing, yes, it was. She put an arm over him and could tell by the regular rise and fall of his chest he'd gone to sleep. Instead of feeling insulted, she put her worries aside, burrowed her face against his nape and relaxed into a long overdue nap.

Chapter Sixteen

A strong arm smashed Jane against the side of the sleigh bed. Merlin thrashed entangled in the sheets and quilt. A strong shaft of sunlight from the small attic window illuminated the side of his desperate, black-bearded face.

"We're going down! Do you read me? Six aboard, my gunner wounded. Do you read me?" He spewed out coordinates and the ID of his chopper, repeated the call for help again and again. Sweat ran down his back. Tremors shook his body.

Jane wrapped her arms around his quaking torso from the rear. Locking her hands over his pounding heart, she whispered in his ear. "You aren't over there anymore, Merlin. Come back now. Come back to Louisiana, to your old room in your granny's house where you are safe. You had a bad dream. Wake up."

He calmed. The tension went out of his body, and he sank back onto the small mattress as Jane released him. She stroked his lank, dark hair back from his forehead. His eyes opened, so bright a blue in the patch of sunlight.

"Did I hurt you?"

"Only a small bump, nothing much."

"Were you scared of me?"

"No, only scared for you."

He lowered the lids of his eyes like a child unable

to face his mother after doing wrong. "This is why I can't stay the night, Jane. I do things in my sleep. The dream comes, and I rip down my drapes or break a lamp and only find out when I wake up."

He shivered as the sweat on his body dried. Jane straightened the quilt and drew it over him. She stroked his hair again. "Does this happen when you are offshore? Isn't that dangerous?"

"Usually I stay in the trailers at Intracoastal City, but plenty of guys out on the rigs have been to Iraq and Afghanistan. Hell, the man who owns the company where I work flew helicopters in Nam. They get it. And I'm not likely to put a dent in any of them. They can take it, but you—any woman, I could hurt."

Jane shook her head. "I don't think so. From what I've seen you are a protector, always trying to save someone else and getting pissed when you can't. Would it help if you told me about what happened over there?"

"You can't understand."

"No, I don't imagine I can, but sometimes it helps just to tell someone what's bothering you."

"That's what my shrink says. You want me to go now that you know I really am crazy?"

"No, I think it's great that you are getting help."

"I'm working on the self-medicating, the beer I mean. I've gotten a lot better since—recently."

"Get dressed, come downstairs, and talk to me over coffee."

She got up and gathered the scattered clothing, found her socks and panties still stuffed in her jeans, but her shirt and bra halfway across the room. She caught him looking as she bent over to cover herself. The glint of interest, the slight smile on his face gave her hope.

"How about when I finish, I sit on the bed and watch you dress, huh?"

"Fine by me, but if you pay too much attention you will end up naked again."

Jane found one of his oversized shoes and lobbed it at him, like he cared.

"You know, you're still half-naked and your boobs jiggle when you do that, hot stuff. Go on and throw the other one."

"Don't tempt me to whap you over the head with it." She walked over to where her shirt and bra lay crumpled on the floor and intentionally turned her back on him to put them on.

"Party pooper."

"Coffee in the kitchen, five minutes." Despite the sternness of her voice, she went down the stairs smiling.

Merlin joined her before the pot stopped perking. She put out the real sugar for him and the skimmed milk. He fixed his mug after she poured and kept his eyes on the white milk swirling into the blackness of the brew.

"Do you really want to know?" The way he said the words implied, "Must I?"

"Yes. Begin at the beginning." She doctored her own coffee with a little sweetener.

"Okay, so I quit college, join the army, go into helicopter training for a year, and find I have a talent for it. I could set a squad down anywhere on a dime and get them out again with change to spare. With a name like Merlin, they started calling me the Magician. Troops wanted to ride with me. First hitch overseas, I never took a hit to my aircraft, brought all my guys back safe. A year stateside, then back to Afghanistan again, only this time with my great record, I get assigned to the toughest region, the worst terrain. It's harder now getting the men in and out in one piece. Some are wounded. Some don't make it all the way back."

"Not your fault, Merlin. You did your best." By the bleak demeanor of his face, Jane figured offering a hug right now would hardly make a difference in his outlook. What happened to him was too big for a warm squeeze of the shoulders. For now, she stayed put and used her coffee to keep her suddenly cold hands warm.

"Rocket propelled grenades everywhere, have to be dodged, and that's more luck than skill. Anyhow, I do a troop insertion, take off for another load, but on my way back I see another squad down there really getting pummeled. I take it on myself to go into a hover and wave them aboard. Only got room for six and if they all climb in we won't get off the ground. Their sergeant calls out some names. The chosen men scatter for my copter while the rest lay down covering fire. I pull out with two of them still on my struts. We take some hits to the aircraft, but I get the hell out of there. Almost get back to safety when my ship goes down. I go into autorotation, land as best I can, and look over to see my gunner bleeding bad. He dies because I had to be a big hero. Left a pregnant wife."

"You saved six," she said softly.

"You think I did? Really? The rest of that squad got cut up bad. The rag heads decapitated the sergeant, mutilated the rest of the men I left behind. About the time my commander is pinning the Distinguished

Flying Cross on my chest, all six of the men I brought back die in another aircraft hit by a missile. Jane, all I did was get my gunner, my good friend, a husband, a father by now, killed. And they wanted to give me a parade for that when I got home."

Merlin sunk his head into his hands. His big shoulders heaved as if he carried a boulder between his blades crushing his back toward the ground. Tears leaked out between his fingers and left darkened spots on Jane's cheerful yellow tablecloth.

That hug she'd subdued earlier, such a small thing, so powerless in the face of his grief, she offered now, going behind him, offering the press of her warmth against his shaking back.

"You can't know the extra days those men lived had no meaning. They might have talked to a loved one for the last time, conceived a child, saved someone else's life in whatever time they had. My mother believes we are all connected in a grand cosmic scheme that we cannot comprehend. From her point of view, nothing is ever a waste. I think she might be right."

"Wish I could believe that. Gotta go, Jane. I need to get my act together. I'll call."

He stood without facing her, simply let her arms slide down his back releasing him, and walked out her kitchen door. Embarrassed by his tears, she guessed, but she would gladly have wiped them away, taken him into her bedroom, and held him tight.

Chapter Seventeen

Of course big, bad Blackie Tauzin did not call. He'd shown her his weakness, his shame. Well, he could run but he couldn't hide, not when he lived right across the street and his truck made enough noise wake any dead ancestors who might be buried on Jane's property. Jane sighted the rear end of his big-ass truck as it left the Cane View lot and disappeared down the road when she went out to get her Sunday *Clarion*.

After a leisurely breakfast spent browsing the newspaper and still no sign of her letter about restoring the recycling program, she put on some clothes and set to work on her proposal. Appending the pictures, she filled in the rest of the documentation and put it on her flash drive to take to work on Monday. If she could find the time to proof and fine tune the entire form amid answering calls, directing people, and buzzing the staff in and out of the offices, she'd print the required multiple copies and mail it by Friday well ahead of the deadline. Take that, Nadia Nixon! Jane swore the woman doubled her out-of-office business simply to force her reluctant receptionist to stop work and hit that damn buzzer—as if terrorists or anyone else planned to storm the parish council offices.

Dinnertime came and darkness, still no sign of Merlin, no roar of his truck, no phone call. At ten p.m. as she considered giving up and getting into bed—

alone—his unmistakable Ford returned home. After waiting a half hour to give him a chance to call, she ran a brush through her hair and put on a little lipstick, but she refused to primp for Merlin Tauzin. He'd have to take her in her day-off duds if he wanted her. As Waldo implied, a modern woman could make the first move, and that she would do. She crossed the street since it seemed Merlin wasn't planning to, skirted his truck parked aslant in the white lines of his space, and rang the bell. To her surprise, he came to the door rather than trying to hide out and filled that space in the frame as only he could. One of his hands clutched a tall aluminum beer can.

"Hey, Jane. Kinda late, huh?" He swayed and braced himself by putting the other hand on the doorknob.

"You were going to call me."

"Didn't say when. Did I?"

"Anytime today would have been fine. May I come in?"

"Ah, sure." He stepped aside and followed her into his small living room. A large, black leather recliner sat in front of a flat-screen TV almost as big-ass as his truck. Merlin dropped into his seat and gestured Jane toward a card table with two folding chairs that sat in the dining area beneath a Cane View-supplied lighting fixture having four frosted glass globes decorated with pink rosebuds.

Jane sat, crossed her legs, and tried to keep one foot from shaking with impatience. "Did you have a nice Sunday?"

"Less see. Oh, yeah. I took Granny to Mass at Holy Mom's, had dinner with her at Magnolia Villa, went over to my mother's place and watched football with Harley, had a few beers. Thass about it. You?"

"I finished my Super Fund proposal, did some laundry, and waited for you to call."

"Thass good. I got to leave early tomorrow for Intracoastal. Figured I'd call when I got back, see." He tired to suppress a burp, but it got by him. "Excuse me."

"Didn't you tell me there is some rule about twelve hours between bottle and throttle?"

"Only beer. Be fine by the time I get to work." Merlin craned his head back and finished the last drops in the can. He crushed the aluminum in his fist. "Las' one. Here, to put in your recycle barrel." He offered it to her on his open palm like a fine, glittering jewel for her delectation.

Jane rose and took his offering. She stroked his long jaw, stubbly even after a Sunday morning shave. "I worry about you, Merlin. I truly do. Drive safe."

"I'll call. When I get back."

"Sure. Don't get up. I know the way out."

She kissed his cheek and left before she cried. All the way across the parking lot, the road, her yard, she kept thinking, "Second chance gone." Didn't appear he wanted one after all.

\*\*\*\*

Merlin Tauzin doubled over in his recliner. He wanted to vomit and probably should to get the alcohol out of his system before morning. The trouble with being Catholic was the family and the Church would be really upset if he killed himself. Liquor took longer than a gunshot to the head or stretching on a piece of rope, but it got you buried in holy ground with everyone standing around saying, "What a shame." Hey, an insight about his drinking. He should write that down to tell his shrink.

Jane left in such a hurry she failed to close his front door. He watched her progress back to the old homestead. See Jane run. Run, Jane, run. Be safe, Jane. Safe from me.

\*\*\*\*

Before dawn, Jane heard Merlin's truck take to the road. She prayed to God and her mother's cosmic powers that he had sobered up and would arrive safely at Intracoastal City. Maybe that was all she could do for him now or in the future. She strove to put Merlin out of her mind, but when she pushed her trashcan with its fancy wheels to the curb on Thursday night, he might as well have been standing by her side offering her another smashed beer can for recycling. He invaded her dreams and crushed her hopes for both of them.

Rising early from a restless night, she planned to get to work before seven-thirty and run copies of the proposal prior to punching in and well before Nadia took up her post by the time clock. CLANG, CLANK, CHUG. The garbage truck blocked her drive as Mellow crossed the street and wheeled her neighbor's container to the lift. Jane waited patiently behind the wheel of her little hybrid. She gave the garbage men a friendly finger wave. They glanced away and pulled the truck up to the stop sign without taking her trash. Throwing her transmission into park, she got out and cried to them, "You forgot to take my garbage!"

Mellow let go of his handhold on the back of the truck and trudged toward her. "Can't, Miss Jane. Mr. Burl says you done modified yo' can so we can't take it no more."

"I don't understand."

Mellow studied the steel toes of his work boots. "I was telling the other collectors how nice your container rolled and how I wished all our cans had wheels like that, and Mr. Burl, he overheard. Said was I putting down the quality of his receptacles. I sez, 'No sir, just saying.' And he sez, 'If you know what's good for you, tell that woman she can't mess with my cans without I cut off service.' I didn't mean to cause you no trouble."

"That's okay. I'll ask Mr. Babin if I can use his can again. Just don't let that slip to Burl Oubre. There's probably an ordinance against it."

"I won't. This mouth is shut." Mellow pinched his big lips together, went back to the truck, and motioned to his brother to move on.

Another setback in the garbage wars, but she would not let that ruin her day. She had her proposal polished shinier than an oil slick and would get it in the mail today to redeem a small part of Ste. Jeanne d'Arc Parish, which was her job, not answering telephones. Jane glanced at her watch. Oh hell, thanks to her talk with Mellow, she'd get to work on time, but not early. There went her lunch hour, the only time she could get away from the reception desk to run the required copies of her forms.

\*\*\*\*

Jane almost welcomed Nadia's nit-picking and frequent trips to the bathroom in the waiting area. The harassment kept her mind off of Merlin, his pain, his problems. At one p.m., she asked Angela Savoy to mind the desk in order to allow her to use the big office copier to spew out six collated copies of the original document. She'd still have plenty of time to shove them into a large, brown envelope and get them in the mail. Angela, having given up dieting for the sake of the baby, now showed her pregnancy but made no announcement to her fellow employees or confession to Nadia Nixon. Jane supposed she never would. One day Angie would "get sick" at work, take the day off, pop that baby out, and quit as soon as her parish insurance paid the delivery bills at the rate this was going.

In the small copier room, Jane sat on top of several stacked boxes of paper and waited for the last page to print. Very careful not to spill or leave any crumbs, she drank coffee and ate an energy bar. Setting her scanty lunch aside when the copier finished, she checked each document to make sure no pages were missing or misprinted, then clipped each one together and shoved them into the pre-addressed envelope. She tossed the wrapper from her lunch into the wastebasket full of old toner cartridges that should be recycled, tucked the forms under her arm, and headed, coffee mug in hand, to the door only to run headlong into Nadia Nixon.

"Angela told me you were in here working on your lunch hour."

"Just some printing I needed to get done and of course, I couldn't desert my post at the front desk to do it."

Nadia's grim lips twisted as if she suppressed a smirk. "Are you trying to bring the labor people down on us? Next thing you'll say is we denied you your lunchtime. Thirty minutes is mandated by law, and we generously allow an hour. I see your scheme. In a day or two, I get served for making you work without a break. Won't happen on my watch. Marshall, you are fired."

Nadia plucked an empty paper carton from a corner and chest-passed it to Jane. "Clean out your desk. I'll have your pink slip ready in a jiffy. Don't bother trying to claim unemployment either with the file I've kept on your transgressions."

Jane knew she'd been set up for this moment, yet like a pickup truck stuck on a railroad track, she couldn't get out of the way of the locomotive. "You're firing me for working?"

"For not taking your mandatory lunch break."

Jane nodded toward the wastebasket. "I had lunch, coffee and an energy bar. The wrapper is in there and my mug still has coffee in the bottom."

"You cannot eat and work at the same time. Get it? I never thought you were dense before today, Marshall. Go to your desk and pack. The guards will be along to escort you from the building." Now, Nadia allowed the full extent of her victory to show on her face with the baring of her large, square teeth in a huge grin. Executing a tight, military turn in the small space, she left to fill out the paperwork. Another Friday, another victim flattened beneath her heels.

As the shock passed, Jane realized Nadia had made one mistake. In her haste to announce the firing, she'd failed to tear the grant forms out of Jane's hands. Most certainly, all her work would have been put through a shredder in order to concoct further evidence that the environmental project manager neglected her duties and had not completed and submitted the documents. Jane placed the brown envelope, address downside, into the bottom of her box and holding both it and her head high she marched to her former office and emptied the personal contents on top of it.

Her next stop, the reception desk, required her to pass the cubicles of the lower-ranked employees. No one spoke to her, but she heard the whispers, "Nadia fired Jane," fearful and implying "Who's next?" Didi said gleefully to Tonette, "That means the receptionist job is open again."

At least her circumstances made someone happy. The guards waited for her. Really, she had nothing more to do than take her purse and empty lunch sack out of a drawer and place them in the box. Nadia allowed no plants, personal pictures or mementos, and Jane had what mattered most in the bottom of the box under her files of complimentary letters, references, and news clippings about her various projects.

"I'm so sorry, Jane. I should have said you went out for lunch. I didn't know you could get fired for working." Angela dabbed at her eyes with a tissue.

"This would have happened sooner or later. Have a healthy baby, then get the hell out of this place," Jane advised.

Nadia paraded through the door and waved a sheaf of papers in Jane's face like an ugly cheerleader taunting an opponent with a pair of pompoms. "Sit, Marshall. Sign here and here. This packet explains your COBRA rights. Read it and sign."

Before putting her name to anything, Jane read the top form, "Dismissed for refusing to take a lunch break as mandated by law." She took a pen from the desk and wrote in the space below the accusation, "Because of being assigned extra duties outside my job description, I was unable to complete my regular work during normal working hours. Jane E. Marshall."

Nadia's infuriated face reddened at the rebuttal.

She ripped off the pink copy of the form and threw it on top of the belongings in the box. Her square-fingered hands rooted beneath it weeding out the articles on Jane's achievements. She flipped open a folder, read a letter of praise, and snorted. "Jane Marshall is thoroughly devoted to making this world a better place," she read in a pinched and mocking voice before letting the folder fall closed.

"Those are my personal files if you don't mind," Jane said before the woman could delve any farther.

"I don't mind. You'll need all this claptrap to get another job. Just don't put *me* down as a reference because I'll let them know the kind of person you really are."

Jane stood, clocked out at two-fifteen, and allowed the guards to escort her onto the elevator. "Sorry, Miss Jane," one said sheepishly when they arrived in the lobby. The other held the heavy courthouse door open for her and her box. She made her way alone to her car.

Driving directly to the post office, she paid for the mailing of the grant forms out of her own soon to be empty pocket. From there, she headed straight for the unemployment office to file a claim because no matter what Nadia said, she could collect if she fought hard enough—and she would.

Chapter Eighteen

Jane reached home before she let herself cry. Once she got all the water out of her system, she made a pot of the herbal tea her mother claimed calmed the nerves and started crunching numbers. Car and mortgage payments paid for the month. Check. Enough in her account to cover the renovation loan, utilities and the other two items until the end of January. Check. After that, finances got dicey.

If she got on the ball and did her taxes early, her return might cover another month. The sympathetic woman at the unemployment office had given her an estimate of what she might be able to collect but warned, "The parish fights all claims, so be prepared to hold out on your own for a while." If she received an unemployment check by February, her house note and utilities would be covered, possibly the car loan, too, but not the renovation payment. Since she'd used her house as collateral for the renovation money, chances were the bank would end up owning it.

Jane plugged in all the numbers, squeezed her eyes tight when they blurred, opened them and faced the facts. If she didn't want to lose her house to the bank, she needed to get it on the market priced to sell immediately. Good possibility if she found a job in the next two months, she'd have to relocate anyhow.

Digging in the desk drawer, she located the

Realtor's card. The varnish hadn't dried on her floors before Daisy Derouen, Chapelle's most aggressive seller of houses, drove carefully up the gravel driveway to avoid dinging the black Jaguar bought with the commission from selling billionaire Jonathan Hartz his huge estate. Daisy offered to help her flip the newly renovated home for a large profit and already had a potential client in mind. Considering what Merlin said, that client must have been Bernard Freeman. Not even tempted because she wanted a home, not money, Jane accepted the business card pressed into her palm by the manicured hand with nails polished bright red to match the Realtor's professional blazer.

"Call me if you change your mind, honey." With a quick check of the silk scarf that held her lacquered blonde hair in place and a jingle of the gold charm bracelet hung with tiny houses and one small palace to mark the Hartz sale, Daisy prowled off down the road in her expensive ride. Periodically, the Realtor called to see if Jane remained happy in her new home or needed quick cash. Daisy was about to have her day. Jane punched the number into her phone.

"Daisy Derouen, Realtor, how may I serve you?"

Jane explained her plight: lost job, need for a quick sale, possible relocation.

"So many people losing their homes right now. Sad. You did right to call me, honey, before the bank puts you out. Why, that client I suggested before might still be interested. He wants the property more than the house, but with all the work you've put into the old place, I am sure he'd move the house to another location. I have a showing out your way tomorrow morning, and I'll be by with my signs and a contract. If

I can get in touch with the buyer, who knows? I might have an offer for you that will cover your investment and make some money for the both of us right away. See you bright and early!"

Jane imagined the Realtor licking her red lips with her pink tongue as soon as they disconnected. Feeling miserable, she put the tea aside, poured a large glass of red wine, and went outside to watch the sun set. No telling how many more she'd see from her own front porch. The spectacle wasn't the same in Montana with its high mountains and brief twilights, no prolonged blaze firing the clouds a potter's orange, painting them pink and edging them in gold. Her thoughts and her vision strayed to the Cane View townhouses. Tonight, Merlin missed a good one.

****

Merlin Tauzin got in late Sunday and went to bed dead tired, not drunk. Not that he hadn't been tempted to get off the road and have a few when the traffic backed up for miles because a truck hauling cane to a mill got its wheels stuck in the soft shoulder and overturned blocking all lanes. Instead, he opted to stop and play a little video poker to keep his hands and mind busy until the highway opened. A week of flying always cleared his head, and he thought Jane might give him another chance if he said the exact right words.

On the long drive, he worked out what he would say to Jane if the big war hero he was supposed to be could get up the courage to cross the street and apologize for his inebriation the last time they'd spoken. Well, she'd spoken. Mostly, he'd slurred his words and burped. After he told her about how he'd gotten his buddy killed trying to pull off another Merlin the Magician feat of flying magic and then cried like a pitiful child who'd lost his mommy, he figured he wouldn't see her anymore. Who needed a man that disgusting, that weak? So why not get buzzed with Harley? Bad move. He should have known someone like Jane who saw beauty in broken chunks of glass and saved every aluminum can would think he could be salvaged.

Since she came marching into his life to chew him out about littering, he'd felt better, more sure he could overcome his dark moods, control his drinking. She made him smile, even laugh a little, made him want to go dancing again and enjoy a nice meal in her company. Of course, he played up the macho man image just to tease her. Tomorrow, he would tell her all that when she came home from work and sat outside to watch the sunset. He went so far as to check the Weather Channel to make sure the sky would be clear and the night fine for sitting in the swing on the front porch of the house he'd once called home. She'd made the place so cozy he could see himself living happy there again. And if Jane wanted to talk after he'd said all these things, they would talk some more—about their future together.

In the morning, he experienced an absurd urge to sing in the shower, not a good idea with his voice, and shaved as close as he possibly could. He wanted to call his shrink and tell the dude he'd had a breakthrough. He did want to live after all. Checking his watch, he thought better of it. Men with fancy degrees didn't get up this early to go to work, but Jane did. If he watched from his upstairs window, he'd see her leave in the tiny, energy-efficient car that would give him leg cramps to drive.

After, he'd go downtown and get her some flowers at Beau's Blooms even though the two gay guys who ran the place gave him the willies. Beau Regard always told him he had beautiful eyes when he went in there. That was enough to make him buy supermarket bouquets for his mom and granny, but he'd overcome his discomfort for Jane. Since the turkey centerpiece made her smile, maybe sunflowers would be right for sunset watching? He'd make himself ask Beau for suggestions because gay men, being closer to their female side, knew about such things.

Seven-fifteen. Jane should be leaving for work about now. He went to the window simply to watch her pass. What the fuck! A Daisy Derouen Realty sign with its perky red flower logo squatted in the middle of the flowerbed he'd made for Jane. Another faced the side street. He *had* scared, disgusted, and disappointed her. Now she wanted to move, to get away from him and his darkness and his cowardly tears.

Merlin threw on a pair of jeans, a fairly clean T-shirt, his running shoes, and raced to intercept her before she left the house. If Jane wanted to talk, if she needed words, she would get a bushel of them right now special delivery. The hell if their confrontation made her late at the office. He jaywalked through the line of work traffic backed up at the red light, jumped her ditch, and headed straight for the flowerbed where he uprooted the Daisy Derouen sign. He sidetracked to rip the second sign from the lawn and moved around the back of the house. Jane's little hybrid car sat parked by the ramshackle garage. Good, he hadn't missed her.

He tried the kitchen door, still locked, and pounded

on it hard enough to make the little panes set in the panel rattle rather than go into the garage for the key. She came to the door dressed in the pink sweat suit and the bunny slippers that made her look so cuddly. Her eyes appeared puffy, her hair disheveled, and maybe he'd gotten her out of bed, but that did not prevent him from throwing the signs at her feet and saying, "What the fuck, Jane! What the fuck!"

"*Merde* mouth, Merlin. You want coffee? I'm going to make some." She shuffled away, not a scared little rabbit at all, and began filling the pot with water.

A thought occurred to him. "You sick? I guess we could talk later, but we have to talk about this."

"No, now is good. I have no choice really. Sit down. Don't trip over those signs with your big feet." She measured the coffee, set the pot to brew, and brought two of her yellow mugs and the real sugar to the table.

Not frightened, not angry, not disgusted at him when she should be, what the hell was going on? He propped the realty signs in a corner and took a seat. He'd come to apologize and he would, the sooner the better.

"Look, Jane, I know I terrified you when we were up in the attic. You probably still have a bruise. What I told you, how I acted, must make you think less of me. Then, I don't call and I get drunk. I understand your disgust, but you don't have to move. Say the word, I'll stay on my side of the street. If you want, I'll pay to have new locks put on your doors so you know I can't get inside to bother you. Just don't go away from me. I mean because of me."

Jane looked him in the eye. He glanced aside. She

reached over and turned his face toward hers and did not let go.

"Merlin Tauzin, do you realize how many times you said I and me in that outburst of words? Other people have problems, too, Merry Man. Yours are not the center of the universe. Nadia Nixon fired me on Friday for working on that proposal during my lunch hour. But I got it in the mail despite her. At best I can hold out here for two months without losing the house. Needless to say, Chapelle, Louisiana, is not crawling with jobs for environmental project managers. My only chance is to relocate and find another job before I go under and the bank takes this place."

The same way he intuitively knew how to get out of hot situations in Afghanistan, he realized the solution. "I'll buy the house. Name your price. You can stay here as long as you want."

"Don't you have a brand new mortgage on your townhouse?" She dropped her hand from his face, and he was kind of sorry she'd let go because her thumb had been caressing his newly shaven jaw whether she was aware of it or not.

"Yep. How much did the parish pay you, Jane?"

"I made forty-five thousand a year."

"Not bad."

"Did you imply 'for a woman'?"

"Nope, not unless you can read minds. I make a shitload more than you. The oil industry pays just fine. I can afford two mortgages. Deal?"

Jane turned away, busied herself with pouring coffee and setting out milk. She rummaged in the refrigerator, opened a cabinet, and held up a loaf of raisin bread and a jar of peanut butter. "Breakfast? I'm out of eggs and thought I should start economizing right away."

"I'm not picky. I eat most anything. Now answer me. Do we have a deal for the house?"

"I wasn't brought up to be a kept woman. If I found out you went deep into debt because of me, I'd never forgive myself."

"I want to keep you here, yeah. I can sell my townhouse easy if me having two mortgages bothers you. Then, I could move upstairs. You saw what I got in the way of furniture, but I'd need my king-sized bed if I can figure out how to get it up those narrow steps. My offer stands to change the locks downstairs if you are afraid to have me so close."

Jane slammed the peanut butter jar onto the table. "I'm saying it one more time. I am not afraid *of* you! I am afraid *for* you. I worry you'll drink too much and die driving that big-ass truck. I'm scared you'll pick a fight with someone tougher than Waldo Robin and get yourself shot or stabbed. I fear you don't take care of yourself or eat right. That's what scares me."

"If I lived above you, you could keep an eye on me and make sure I don't do any of those things." A smile tugged at his lips. He did not think she would take it well, but the damned thing escaped anyhow, so he just kept talking.

"You could cook nourishing meals for me and pay whatever you can in rent if you don't want to be kept. Hell, you could become an ecological consultant and use that little library you have for your office. I'm gone half the year anyhow. I don't need much room. This could work."

Jane bowed her head, defeated by his cogent

arguments he hoped. She put two slices of raisin bread in the toaster and lowered them into the heated coils. Then, she came up fighting.

"Half those townhouses are still empty and brand new. You won't get a good price for a used one. As for me cooking for you, I think you'd get tired of healthy eating, and it smacks of traditional housewifery. Wipe that grin off your face."

"Housewifery, huh? Nothing wrong with that, honey pot. My granny was a housewife all her life. I bring home the bacon. You fry it up in a pan and make me feel like a man. Is that how the song goes?"

"No, no, it is not." The toast popped along with Jane's temper. She threw two slices onto a plate and shoved it in front of him. "Eat."

"Aren't you going to spread the peanut butter for me? Isn't that what good housewives do?"

Jane grabbed a butter knife from a drawer and slathered a slice with peanut butter. She held it up in her palm and aimed right for his face. Merlin caught her wrist. "If you do that, honeybunch, I'll expect you to lick it off my lips."

She let the piece of raisin toast drop back on the plate and sank into a chair. "Sorry. I'm super-sensitive right now. I hate feeling helpless and at the mercy of people like Nadia."

"And men like me. Personally, I think you should have gone for it. I would love peanut butter anywhere you care to put it." He took a big bite of his breakfast.

"Cut it out. I know you say things like that just to get a rise out of me."

"Glad you can tell when I'm kidding."

"Not always. I don't know what to do or what to

say anymore."

"Tell me what you want. I'll see you get it."

"I want my job. I want my house and a recycling program for the parish, but all those things are gone."

Merlin finished his piece of toast and spread peanut butter on the second slice. "I already told you how you can keep your house. Call Daisy Derouen and set up the sale. As soon as it goes through, I'll see about those other two wants. I might throw myself into the deal as *lagniappe*, that little something extra."

"Your townhouse…"

"I guarantee I can get out of my mortgage."

Jane took a deep gulp of black coffee as if fortifying herself. "Merlin, I don't want you to threaten or hit anyone. Bernard Freeman will send you to jail even if Waldo didn't. You can't assault a councilman and get away with it."

"Not a drop of blood will be shed, his or mine. I can be very persuasive." He got up and put more raisin bread in the toaster. "See, I'm making breakfast for you. I can be housebroken, too."

"I believe the persuasive part. Okay, deal on the house. I have to sell it anyhow and know you wanted it badly. You'll take good care of it. Thanks in advance for letting me live here until I find work."

"Believe you me the council will beg you to come back to your old job." The toast popped. Merlin plated it and added the peanut butter. He set the slices in front of Jane. "*Et voila!* My first astounding feat—preparing breakfast for a woman."

He made Jane smile. Good enough for now. Too bad one of her wants had not been Merlin Tauzin. That would have been so easy to supply.

Chapter Nineteen

Daisy Derouen never let time lag between an offer and a sale. On Friday, she met Merlin and Jane beneath the antique clock outside the First National Bank of Chapelle and escorted them into the boardroom where the lawyer waited to do the closing. Before letting Jane take her seat, the Realtor drew her aside.

"Honey, I am sure I can get you a better deal if you'll wait a week. The other buyer is in Africa hunting lions right now and is a tad hard to get on the phone. I know he'd double this offer he wants that land so bad."

"Mr. Tauzin is paying me enough to cover my mortgage, the renovation costs, closing fees and your commission, plus letting me stay in the house until I get another job. There is no better deal than that."

The little houses on Daisy's charm bracelet jingled like gold coins chinking into a sack. "But there could be if you want to put this off a week or so."

"No, I'm ready now. I want Merlin to have the house."

"The customer is always right. Here we go then."

The humorless lawyer recommended by Daisy from the firm of Lasky, Jefferson, and Babcock ran through the details of the sale and transferred all of Jane's debt onto Merlin's big shoulders with dispatch. She remembered feeling queasy when she sealed the deal on her first mortgage and the huge renovation loan thinking she'd signed her life away. Close to true now that she'd lost her job. Merlin, however, didn't break a sweat. His blue eyes possessed a clear, cold quality unmarred by alcohol consumption. Though he'd come to watch the sunset with her every evening in the past week, he left his beer at home, turned down her offer of wine, and returned to his place not long after total darkness fell. Taking in every word of the transaction, he nodded at the right places and put his name on the papers, here, here, and here.

"Mr. Tauzin, you do understand that until the sale of your townhouse, the bank will hold the papers on your Ford as collateral for the pending twenty-thousand dollar down payment?" said Mr. Jefferson.

"Sure, no problem." He handed over the title to the big-ass truck.

Jane's hand flashed out and tugged the title from the lawyer's hand much to the attorney's annoyance. "Merlin, your truck! You can't do this."

His grin appeared like the first star of evening in the night sky. Daisy Derouen sucked in her breath either because she feared the sale would fall through or she was simply stunned by Merlin's transformation from dark and surly to handsome and sexy. Jane had no idea which. She'd gotten so used to both sides of the man the lightning changes no longer caught her off guard.

"No worries, sweetness. We'll have this all cleared up by the New Year."

"But your truck *is* you, what you'd be if you were a truck, I mean. Big, rugged, electric blue, ready for anything, and a little overbearing. How will you get to work if you lose it?"

"I know you wanted to say 'a lot overbearing', so thanks for that, but it's only a vehicle, babe. You'd loan me your car if I needed it, right?"

"Right, though I can hardly imagine you behind the wheel of my hybrid."

"Ahem," the lawyer said. "I do have another closing in an hour. If we could proceed."

Merlin removed the papers from her grip and signed his truck over to the bank for the time being. He took the new mortgage, rolled it in his fist, and tapped the wad of papers against the flawless, polished surface of the boardroom table. "That's that."

Rising, Merlin shook the lawyer's hand and gave Daisy a peck on the cheek that left her so flustered her charm bracelet tinkled. "Want to go to lunch and celebrate, Jane? How about the Golden Dragon Chinese Buffet since you think I need more vegetables in my life."

"Okay, if you promise not to eat only the brown side of the buffet."

"The brown side?"

"Yes, fried egg rolls, fried fish, popcorn shrimp, breaded sweet and sour pork, sesame chicken, etc."

"I think they have boiled shrimp and crabs on Fridays. I'll bring the truck around." Happy as a Cajun could be on his way to a seafood buffet, Merlin strode out the door deeply in debt and not a bit concerned about it.

The lawyer packed his papers and briskly left the room. Daisy put an arm around Jane's shoulders and gave her a hug. "My, my, my, maybe you did make the better deal if you're going to be living with him. I'd heard Merlin Tauzin burned out in the war, but I'd say he has risen from the ashes."

"No, he will be upstairs. I will be downstairs. We are not living together."

"Whatever you say, Jane, but I sure wouldn't miss out on that opportunity. Good luck with your future, honey."

**\*\*\*\***

Like Daisy, Merlin lost no time sealing his deal. Louisiana provided great weather for moving on Saturday, one of those freakishly hot December days without a cloud in the sky. Harley came over bright and early to help disassemble the king-sized bed and lug the recliner and big-ass TV into the rear of the truck. They filled in the gaps with boxes of odds and ends and a filthy duffel bag containing most of his non-work clothes. His uniforms, a suit, and a few dress shirts made the trip bagged in plastic on the dry cleaner's hangers and slung over his leather chair. Merlin backed the entire load across the front lawn as close to the outside stairs as he could. The two men got the oversized chair into the *garçonniere* and the television before Harley remembered he had to be somewhere.

"Probably somewhere with less work to be done," Merlin remarked to Jane who hauled the boxes and the duffel bag upstairs. "I can get the bed frame parts and the two box springs up there, no trouble, but you'll have help with the mattress."

He took the lead up the narrow stairs with Jane pushing the unwieldy burden one step at a time from behind. At the small doorway, Merlin fought the springs to fold the mattress over and both of them shoved it inch by inch through the opening. Once on the other side, it snapped open and fell flat with a thud.

Merlin wiped the sweat on his forehead with the back of his hand. "I think I like it there just fine." Taking Jane with him, he fell back on the mattress and shut the attic door with one swift kick.

"Fair warning, I'm taking off my shirt." He did exactly that, peeling the sweat-soaked garment off his chest and over his head. It landed in a ball in the general vicinity of the shower. Merlin tucked his hands behind his head and showed off a smoothly muscled chest on a body a little too thin for his size. A mat of black hair plastered down over his pecs. "Look all you want since I got a good gander at yours last time."

Jane, who had been staring up at the rafters after her exertions, rolled onto her side. "You really expect me to be so inflamed with passion by the sight of a hairy chest that I'd jump you?"

"Nope, but a guy can hope."

"The only way that would happen is if you took off your pants, too."

Off came his jeans, his athletic shoes going with them, and no briefs to bother about at all. "See, I'm already inflamed by that suggestion."

"Impressive," she admitted, drawing a fingernail lightly down the length of his erection and making it jump like a bass to bait. She cradled his balls and massaged them with her thumb.

"Condom in the rear pocket of my jeans. You'd better suit me up and get mounted because if you keep doing that I will not last."

Jane found the sheath and smoothed it down his length. He shivered. "Cold?"

"Nope, just get into position quick, and take your top and bra off first. I want to watch your girls jiggle.

Oh, just so you know, this has nothing to do with your rent. It is part of the *lagniappe* I mentioned."

"Something extra for you or for me?" Perversely, Jane stripped off her jeans, panties, and shoes, but remained in a buttoned-down pale blue shirt with long tails and her bra. She straddled him and began moving over him very slowly.

"For both of us." His hands cupped her hind cheeks, helping her along, up and down, for a few strokes before they wandered up under the shirttails to her bra hooks. He opened them with a fairly nimble move, pushed the bra away, and moved to the front to tease her nipples and stroke her breasts. His eyes closed.

"What, is unbuttoning the shirt too much work?"

"I have a good imagination. Just keep doing what you're doing, sugar tits, maybe pick up the pace."

Jane tweaked his brown nipple in its nest of dark hair.

"Baby, if you think that turned me off, you are so wrong."

He bucked up against her and pumped his hips relentlessly letting her know that now no longer in control, she only went along for the ride. She was losing it, losing it very rapidly. He pulled her upright by the back of her open collar and rubbed her clit as he pounded into her. She came with a long, drawn out moan as extended as her orgasm. Only two thrusts behind, Merlin released with a final hard thrust and a great gasp. He hooked his fingers in her shirt collar and drew her down to rest on his heaving chest.

"Leaving the shirt on worked out really great for me. You?"

"Oh, yes," Jane answered, still panting.

"I always knew when to seize an opportunity. You know what I could use now—lunch."

Jane raised her head. "You expect me to get dressed and trot downstairs to make sandwiches right this minute? Really?"

"Nope, I'll spring for pizza. Order two large with everything and extra cheese. Forgot my manners. Get one with whatever you want. We can have them for both lunch and dinner unless you want to get chicken from the Fast 'N Fun."

"Unlike fried chicken, pizza has some redeeming qualities paired with a salad and some fruit. Let's stick to that. Say, did you remember to empty your refrigerator at the townhouse? Men always forget that little detail. You won't get a sale if the entire place stinks of rotten food."

"Nothing in it but beer, and I gave that to Harley for helping. He promised to save the cans."

Jane found her jeans and panties and climbed into them. When she couldn't refasten her bra without taking off her shirt, Merlin helped her out. Placing a kiss on the back of her neck, he said, "I'm going to take a shower. Don't forget to phone for the pizza, extra cheese."

She heaved her sneaker at him just as he shut the door to the tiny bathroom. He laughed out loud, a good sound, music to her ears actually.

Jane went downstairs to do some washing of her own before placing the order, setting the table, and pouring tall glasses of lemonade made from her bumper crop of lemons. She assembled the rest of the meal and waited.

Fresh, clean-shaven, and smelling great, Merlin arrived in the kitchen about the same time as the pies. He eyed the salad and apple wedges before opening the top box, then the second one. "You forgot the extra cheese."

"No, I did not. The last thing you need is extra cheese, but both have everything on them, only mine has no jalapenos. Fair enough?"

"Yep." He loaded three slices on his plate. "Looks like extra veggies on this."

"Yep." Jane took two pieces, her limit for a lunch.

"I think I might need to get one of those little refrigerators for upstairs."

"You can use mine, yours, ours. Whatever."

"I want you to keep your doors locked at night and take that key out of the garage. I stay up all hours and lately, I got my appetite back again. I can keep some snacks and cold drinks upstairs if I get my own fridge."

Jane watched him over the lip of her lemonade glass. "Still don't trust yourself?"

"Right."

\*\*\*\*

Regardless of what Merlin thought, Jane noted he slept soundlessly above her that night. He showered in the morning, went to church with his granny, had Sunday dinner at Magnolia Villa, but did not go to his mom's trailer to watch football with Harley. Instead, he invited Jane upstairs to watch Louisiana's team on his TV because "that one you have downstairs hidden in the cabinet is simply pitiful."

Jane curled in his recliner while he disassembled the trundle bed under the rafters only bumping his head twice and holding in the curse words. Football players jumped out at her in high-definition.

"I'll move this to your junk room, the table and chairs, too. I think I need a computer table under that window."

"I don't have a junk room!" she protested. "That's my exercise space."

"Yeah, I saw the dust on the treadmill."

"So I go to the Pink Power Palace, the ladies gym in the strip mall. I like to socialize while I exercise."

"If you can talk, that isn't exercise."

"You sound like Nadia," she pouted.

"Maybe, but I'm better looking. I'd like to use the treadmill before its gears rust. I'm supposed to work out to kill the blues."

"By all means, do." Jane bunched her legs and put her arms around them in the big chair. Merlin merely picked up the neat bundle she made and sat her in his lap.

"Don't be mad now. Come on, uncurl. Let me make you feel better."

The two-minute warning sounded for the first half. He used that time for foreplay, longer because of all the penalties and time outs, and concluded with an amazing twenty minute halftime performance without ever leaving the recliner.

Still, Merlin would not let Jane stay the night. He did not disturb her rest until he turned on the shower before dawn and clomped down the stairs to leave for work Monday morning. His truck roared off on its way to Intracoastal City, and Jane snuggled into her covers happy he left sober and well rested.

Chapter Twenty

The denial of her unemployment claim came on Monday. Knowing weeks would pass before she got a hearing, Jane filed her appeal immediately. If nothing else, the bad news threw her into a frenzy of list making. Search for jobs on the internet, check. Update resume, check. Call people to ask them for a good reference, check, check, check. Exercise, check. Removing the dust, she used that treadmill to stave off any hint of depression. When her gym membership ended on the thirty-first, she did not plan to renew. Every penny counted now.

She could not, absolutely could not, stay here living off Merlin and retain any pride at all. In return for his kindness, she used some of her excess energy to fix up his *garçonniere* just a bit to make it more Merlin. Since inactivity drove her crazy, she channeled that positively to make his space more of a home.

Because she'd already paid for the plane ticket long before Thanksgiving, she planned to go to Montana for Christmas. Her parents knew she'd been fired, and the pressure would be on to have her move in with them and look for work in the northwest. She should kiss Louisiana goodbye after the way she'd been treated, but her heart was here, and that heart inexplicably beat hard for Merlin Tauzin.

When Merlin returned on Sunday after dark, she

expected him to go immediately upstairs and lock himself in for the night. After he'd seen what she did to his manly territory, he might reconsider, charge down those stairs and give her another "What the fuck!" verbally only. Why should she dress up for a dressing down? Jane took a bath and got comfortable in her pale green robe, nightie, and her pink bunny slippers. She jumped when he knocked on her front door upon arrival instead of going to his room.

"Just wanted you to know I'm back in case you heard noises upstairs."

He did look toothsome with his black stubble and his slightly wrinkled flight uniform, the sky blue shirt ramping up those blue eyes even more. Totally aware she did not look her best, she went for it anyhow. "Want to come in for a while? Did you have dinner?"

"I ate before I headed home, but sure, I can visit."

Not the answer she anticipated. He took a seat on her scarred leather sofa and squinted at the show on the television. "What's playing?"

Jane sat next to him and picked up her cup of herbal tea, her evening drink of choice lately. "PBS, *Masterpiece Theatre.*"

"You do know the Sinners are playing a night game right now?"

"Didn't think of it, but feel free to turn the channel. Are you sure you wouldn't like a snack?"

With the remote in hand, Merlin flicked through the channels until he found the game. "Ahead by seven. Good. What kind of snacks do you have?"

"I have some of the pizza from last weekend that I haven't picked the jalapenos off yet."

"That's still here? Sounds great. I used to live on

those all week, then go out for Chinese every Friday, fried chicken Saturday, and dinner at the Villa on Sunday. Heat it up for me, honey bunny. No, no, go for the field goal!"

"Nice to have you back, Merlin."

"Right." His eyes stayed on the game.

She heated the pizza and added lots of red pepper flakes to get his attention. Upon delivery, he did take notice. "Ai-yi-yi, that's got some kick." He gave her a sly glance away from the television. "I like it when you take it up a notch, pumpkin."

Alarmed, she said, "Pumpkin? Am I putting on weight from lying around the house? I've been using the treadmill to stay in shape."

"From here your shape looks good to me, Jane, but if you want to be sure, you can open that robe and let me form a more personal opinion."

"Oh, eat your pizza."

He did, but warned, "Halftime coming up, and you know what I can accomplish in a halftime. Damn! I knew they wouldn't make that two-point conversion. But still, ahead at the half. Let's go."

"Where?"

"Up to my place and the king-sized bed."

"It's late. I'm not dressed!"

"Like that matters."

Merlin threw her over a shoulder and started for the outside stairs. Jane put up a token protest by beating on his back with her fists and kicking her heels. But really, wasn't seduction better than falling to their death from that staircase? He opened his door and stopped dead. She slid down the front of his chest.

"What's this?"

"I'm not used to being idle. Those rag rugs didn't go with your recliner. I bought the new ones on sale. Found a great deal on the black lacquer computer desk on Craig's List. The wife said it showed dust too much and the husband delivered it. They threw in the desk chair, too. The electrician traded out the lights for me and gave me a good deal on the replacements. You needed something more contemporary than the lanterns. I installed the stainless steel bars between the beams for you to hang up your clothes and the red storage boxes are only from Wal-Mart, but you can use them for your underwear and T-shirts. They fit really neatly under the slanted roof and make a good use of space. Oh, and I got the little refrigerator and microwave cheap from a college student who graduated this month. I put up some shelves for canned goods and snacks, too. No charge for my work, but you might count it toward my rent. All the bills are on the desk. I know you are good for the expenses."

"Yeah, I forgot for a while that I am good for some things."

Merlin walked around and took in the changes to his space: the modern, geometric-patterned rugs in black, red, and gray, the sleek, stainless steel lighting fixtures that resembled inverted pie plates, the glossy desk, the red storage units. He took a closer look at the last, bending low to avoid a bump to the head and opened a drawer. His extra underwear lay neatly folded alongside some brand new boxer briefs deep blue in color.

Still standing by the door in case he made a move to boot her down the stairs, Jane continued to babble, defending and explaining all her choices. "I used the size off your old ones which are in such poor condition no wonder you rarely wear any. The blue doesn't nearly match your eyes though. You needed new athletic socks, too. Well, you left all your clothes smashed together in that grungy duffel bag so I put them away. I washed the bag, and you can use it to haul your dirty laundry downstairs to my washer and dryer. I mean your washer and dryer."

She paused long enough for him to get a few words out. "Our washer and dryer. Tell me I don't have red and black matching towels."

"The ones you had in that box were practically rags, and no, a nice shade of gray and very fluffy. I put the beige ones from here in my bathroom where they blend."

"Red pillows and a shiny black spread on my bed?"

"You had no bedspread at all. Old army blankets do not count. The pillows are accent pieces. The new sheets are pale gray." She stopped talking and tried to read his expression. Bemused? The word did not really fit Merlin Tauzin. "You don't like it?"

"Actually, I've never had a place this nice and don't know what to say. I think it will grow on me. Thanks, Jane." He seemed to struggle with the simple words, swallowing, and dropping his glance to stare at the new rug underfoot.

"Maybe I shouldn't have done this, but I was going stir crazy, and I wanted you to have a special space. After I leave, you'll move downstairs, but you could keep the attic as your man cave." Man cave, now that phrase fit Merlin perfectly.

His head came up again as he mouthed a strong denial. "Yeah, but you aren't leaving—unless you really want to go. I cannot save the whole world." He said those words as if repeating by rote something his shrink told him. "But, I can save you and this little piece of earth you stand on, Jane. Then, you can get on with saving the universe in your own way. Believe me. Believe in me."

She moved from the doorway to where he stood by the huge bed. Jane cupped his face and ran her thumbs across the stubble on his jaw, a gesture becoming all too familiar to her.

"I've lost faith in myself, not you. Lately, I've bungled everything, the garbage contract, the recycling program, my job. But, I do believe in Merlin Tauzin. Let me stay up here with you."

He did not give her a direct answer. His kiss stung from the hot peppers on the pizza. The heat coursed through her body all the way to her toes, making a significant stop to set a fire between her legs. Parting her robe, he made short work getting rid of her thin nightie and paring her down to nothing but the bunny slippers. He weighed her breasts in his hands.

"Yep, I think you are putting on weight. They seem a little bigger than the last time I had the pleasure."

As always, he used a sexist remark to hide his feelings, but Jane did have that much figured out about Merlin Tauzin. "Are not! You'd better go downstairs and lock up because I plan to be here all night long."

He did not make her leave.

Chapter Twenty-One

Merlin watched Jane make his breakfast. The sight gave him nearly as much pleasure as a full night's sleep, not counting the hard-on at three a.m., and Jane lying right beside him. He made it quick and enjoyable for her, too, he believed. Being Jane and having to assert herself, she declined to cook him three fried eggs over easy, bacon, and biscuits even though he indicated the kind from the can were okay when he left an envelope full of grocery money and a list of foods he liked before leaving last week. Instead, they would share an omelet chock full of fresh vegetables he helped chop: green pepper, onions, mushrooms, some sautéed spinach, and little bits of broccoli. He told her to keep that last item on her side of the pan. At least, she bought eggs and not some substitute.

He knew the toast would be brown bread and the milk skimmed, but she had purchased some dark roast coffee and orange juice. She would hear no complaints from him. Anything Jane prepared beat cold pizza or leftover oriental noodles, his usual fare. He could gorge on bacon offshore if he wanted. She'd greased the pan with a tad of butter. So what if the stuff in the little container on the table held some kind of heart healthy spread? He hadn't felt this good in well over a year.

"Get that toast and put in some more bread, would you?" Jane asked him as she sprinkled some shredded two-percent cheese on the omelet and carefully folded it over in the pan. Vegetables tumbled out of its fat center.

He did her bidding. "See, I can be trained."

"Now, if we can break you of three a.m. booty calls." She cut the omelet with her spatula and slid three-quarters of it onto a plate for him. "*Bon appetit.*"

"You didn't seem angry at the time." Merlin winkled out a piece of stray broccoli from the eggs and put it on her plate.

"I wasn't. You do know how to get to the point, or points, pretty quickly, I'll give you that. And you could learn to like broccoli."

"Nope." He dug into the rest of the omelet.

"Any plans for the day?"

She left herself wide open for innuendo, but he passed on that. He had other things to handle besides Jane, even if she did look as delicious as his breakfast in her sunny yellow top, same color as the tablecloth. The two would blend if he took her on the tabletop, but he needed to put that thought aside. Merlin paged through the Sunday paper still on the table from yesterday.

"I have people to see. The *Clarion* never printed your letter about recycling, did they? I might stop by their office on my way to the dry cleaners."

Her eyes, green as troubled waters, searched his. "Please don't make a scene or hit anyone. The letter doesn't matter anymore. I'm canceling my subscription at the end of the month."

"Great sex and a good breakfast make me mellow. I probably won't kill anyone before noon."

She did not take his comment lightly. "I know, but be careful of what you say and do."

"No need to worry. Today, I plan to do a little magic. That's all."

\*\*\*\*

After breakfast, Merlin drove straight to the real estate office of Bernard Freeman. Considerably more plush than Daisy Derouen's one-room establishment always cluttered with pictures of houses for sale and homes sold, Freeman's space resembled an attorney's office with brochures advertising Cane View fanned on a mahogany coffee table beside a leather binder showcasing other properties he represented. Merlin sank into a comfortable chair in the waiting area.

Bernie's receptionist/secretary, a shapely, blue-eyed young woman probably right out of community college and eager to use her newly minted schooling, made a show of asking his name and purpose before checking to see if her boss was in and available to Mr. Merlin Tauzin. She nodded several times as she took her orders over a fancy headset. The inner sanctum where the councilman resided had large glass windows with vertical blinds on the outside behind the young woman. They were tightly closed as if part of her duties included keeping them that way at all costs. The secretary offered coffee or water.

"No, thanks." He and Bernie played the making-the-other-guy-twiddle-their-thumbs game for a while longer. The receptionist fiddled with a stack of papers, dropped them on the floor. When he moved to help her gather them, she said, "Stay where you are! I mean, don't bother getting up." He guessed his presence or his reputation made her nervous.

Finally, the Realtor and politician opened his door and welcomed his guest with an outstretched hand and a jovial smile. The two men were of the same height and build with Bernie gone a trifle soft in the middle. Neither attempted to out macho the other on the handshake. In fact, they disconnected after a brief touch. Entering the office, Freeman immediately put the desk fit for a Middle Eastern dictator between himself and Merlin and played with the buttons on his phone in a slightly nervous manner.

"Sit down and tell me how much you are enjoying that new townhouse. You have a friend or relative looking to buy at Cane View?"

"Nope. I need to sell my place back to you, preferably this week before I go offshore again." Merlin remained standing.

The cordiality vanished. "I gave you a special price on that place, anything for one of our brave war veterans. Now you want me to buy it back. I'd say you are on your own if you can't pay your mortgage."

"My mortgage is not the problem. I found a house I like better. The townhouse is like brand new, and I'm already moved out. I can't see what the trouble might be in your taking it back."

Freeman expelled an exasperated breath. Merlin thought he detected the taint of bourbon in the air. Had the Realtor taken a nerve-steadying shot of liquor before seeing him? Great, the jitters would work in his favor.

"That's not how the real estate business works, young man," Bernie said as if talking to a simpleton.

"You built the places, and you sell them. You did give me a great deal, so now you can buy it back, sell it for the full price and make a bigger profit."

"What if I am not interested in doing that?"

Merlin beckoned to the Realtor. "Come out from behind that big-ass desk for a minute."

Freeman glanced over his shoulder at a rear exit door as if gauging an escape.

Merlin reassured him. "I won't touch you, I swear. Stand right here next to me at the window."

Freeman edged around the desk. Merlin, back turned, faced the glass with his arms relaxed at his side. The Realtor clenched his fists as he took a place next to him.

"Tell me what you see."

"Two grown men standing together staring at a piece of glass like idiots."

Merlin, looking straight ahead, smiled in a way neither warm nor friendly. "I see two bastards who look remarkably alike. Note the blue eyes, an unusually bright shade, heavy beard, the exact same height and build. You've gone gray in the past few years, but I remember when I was in high school your hair was black, black, black. Like mine."

The councilman refused to see any resemblance. "I'm not a bastard. I know who my daddy is, and he married my mother."

"I also know who my daddy is. I recall the day I figured it out. You worked one of the fairs passing out Vote for Leroy 'Lambo' Mouton cards and shaking hands. My grandfather accepted a card, but declined a handshake. He took me to the festival and let me go on some of the adult rides because I'd gotten so tall. Doyle and Brittney doing the ones for little kids stayed with Granny and Mom. Only still in grade school at the time, but I pointed out I had the same color eyes as that man, and we looked kind of alike. Could you be my daddy? I was always on the lookout for that man. Grandpa turned away and said I shouldn't want to be related to that snake in the grass, a *personne traitre.*"

"I am sorry your grandfather had a poor opinion of me, but your childish observations mean nothing." Still, Bernard Freeman kept staring at the glass as if mesmerized.

"When I got a little older, around twelve, I found the papers agreeing never to divulge my father's name in exchange for child support. The lawyer was discreet. You are not named in the document, but your own father had to sign it. My mom used to go on and on about how handsome my daddy was, just like me, but I must never, never, ever know his name. For her sake I pretended to be in the dark, but Granny could tell I'd figured it out."

Bernie broke eye contact and returned to the safety of his desk. "Harley David is your daddy. He raised you."

Merlin followed him and this time took the previously offered chair, sliding back into it and stretching out his legs completely at ease. "Nope. Harley treated me decently but did not adopt me. Granny wouldn't allow it. She had no sons and wanted the Tauzin name to go on, especially after Grandpa died. You know, not being born at the time, I did not sign that agreement."

"Divulge anything, and I will see your family is ruined."

"Grandpa is dead. Granny lives in Magnolia Villa. You already took their land. Will you go after my mom's double-wide and Harley's motorcycle next, maybe my nephew's tricycle?"

Freeman took a bottle out of his desk drawer and sat a shot glass with the logo of a big game hunting organization on it beside the deluxe bourbon. He kept the drawer open. Merlin thought the man might have a weapon concealed there. It wouldn't be needed, only Bernie did not know that.

"Your family would make pathetic trophies, like shooting coots in a pond. You give out my name and I will sue for every penny we gave your family to keep quiet. That would come to $216,000, plus the delivery fee since they wouldn't go for the abortion, two years of wasted college, and bailing your sorry ass out of jail when you were seventeen," the councilman sneered.

"Yeah, I see you are familiar with the deal. My shrink says I acted out to get your attention. Bet it looked good to the public when you helped out a poor boy in trouble, didn't it?"

"Then, your granny comes crawling to me to send you up the road to the university and swearing she won't ever ask for anything else. She might as well have chucked that money in the bayou and thrown you in after it for all the good giving you a chance at a college education did."

"I agree with you there. See we can agree. With an election year coming up, I just want to offer you another chance to do something right for the parish. Drop your objections to the recycling program, support it wholeheartedly, and reinstate Jane Marshall as Environmental Project Manager for the good of the parish."

"Hmmm, Ms. Nixon told me Jane Marshall lost her job for failing to complete an important project that would have brought the parish a large amount of grant funds. I cannot support incompetence in government."

"As it turns out, Jane was fired for working on that proposal during her lunch hour. She put it in the mail well ahead of schedule. I think the parish will find itself with money it has no idea how to handle without Jane after the first of the year."

"Jane, is it?" The councilman leveled a finger at Merlin. "You're the one who bought her house out from under me while I was in Africa. Now you want me to bail you out of a double mortgage. I get it."

"And I get that you are isolating old Woof Langlois, taking away all his supporters at the council office, making him look bad with things like the poor trash service so you can run against him next fall. But, you don't have to worry that I'll tell anyone who bred me on a fourteen-year-old girl. I would never break my grandpa's word."

Merlin picked up a picture in a silver frame from a corner of the desk. Two tall, black-haired sons stood beside their father with their hands clasped on the back of an antique settee. Two lovely daughters sat next to their mother in the front of the men. He studied the photo for a moment, then turned it toward Bernie and held it up under his long jaw, another trait he'd inherited from Freeman. He tapped the glass protecting the group portrait.

"Nice family. I would fit in perfectly right beside you, but that would throw the balance off, I'd say. No, sir. I plan to support your candidacy by going to every rally, standing up tall to ask you questions, standing beside you to have my picture taken. Why I might even run that photo of you and me as a paid ad in the newspaper saying I will vote for you. Big war hero supports Bernard Freeman. You like to play the Cajun angle, but you believe we're all stupid and naïve. I think people will figure out who my daddy is without my saying a word."

Watching Merlin with cold, blue eyes, Freeman poured the bourbon and took a sip. "I understand you have a drinking problem."

"Not anymore."

The politician removed another glass from the drawer and filled it. "I find a little lubricant makes the gears run smoother. Have a drink. It's probably better than anything you've ever tasted." He slid the drink in Merlin's direction, close enough for the scent of premium alcohol to tickle his nostrils.

"No, thanks. I had my last beer a week ago."

"That long? You think can stay sober until the election comes around?"

"That's not your concern."

Merlin held up a large hand that would have matched Bernard Freeman's right down to the scattering of black hair on the knuckles and the shape of the thumb if the other man had held his up for comparison. He ticked off his demands by folding down three fingers one at a time. "You buy my townhouse. You re-hire Jane. You support recycling. All easy for a rich, influential guy like you. If you could see your way clear to getting Nadia Nixon fired that would be good, too." He folded down a fourth finger. Now, his hand made a fist.

"We need her to clean house after the mess Woof made at the courthouse. I mean the public has paid the salary of his mistress for forty years. Do you condone that?"

"Old news about Woof and May Robin. I understand she did her job well. Besides, I think everyone in the parish already knows Wendy Robin Plaisance is their daughter, but they like Woof and May too much to hold it against them."

Freeman's blue eyes brightened with speculation. "I did not know that."

"I forgot you're an outsider from Texas. Considering the dirt in your own past, I wouldn't be using that against him in the election. You think about telling Nadia her cleaning services are no longer needed, no?"

The politician shook his head with something like regret. "You realize, Tauzin, you could have parlayed that victory parade the city offered you into a political career. I'll take back the townhouse. As you said, I can make a greater profit on it when I'm not catering to a war hero for a little feel-good publicity. Okay on the recycling program. Reconsidering my position on that, finding the money to make the parish a cleaner place, will go down well come election time. I'll see what I can do about Jane and Nadia, but I'm not the only one who gets to vote on that. Let's drink to our agreement." Again, he inched the glass closer to Merlin.

"My grandpa wouldn't shake your hand, and I won't drink with you either. Let me know when we're ready to sign on the townhouse. You pay the closing costs."

Merlin walked out much happier than alcohol could have made him. The young secretary had lost all her formality, and in fact appeared to be ill judging by her shaking hands and a face gone pale. He asked with a glance at her nameplate, "Can I get you some of that water, Courtney? No need to be scared of me."

"It's not you." Her youthful voice quavered. She disconnected her headset and placed it on the desk. "He told me to leave the line open in case you attacked him. I was to call the police. I think he forgot all about me listening. Is my mother really Great-Aunt May's child?"

"If your mom is Wendy Robin, yes. Sorry you had to learn that from overhearing. My granny told me in high school. I guess she wanted me to know other folks had secrets in their families to make me feel better about myself. It didn't work. Look, ask your Granny Spring about this before you mention it to anyone else, okay? I said everyone knew already to protect Woof and May, but I'm not sure. Why don't you tell the great and mighty Freeman you don't feel well and go home? Oh, and if I were you, I'd be looking for another job. You don't want to work for this snake."

She nodded. "Thanks for the advice, Mr. Tauzin. I'd vote for you if you ran for office. You were really strong in there."

"I appreciate your thinking so. Quit today."

Now to take on the managing editor of the *Chapelle Clarion*. After Bernard Freeman, a piece of chocolate cake with whipped cream frosting on top.

\*\*\*\*

Merlin firmly shook the hand of Wallace Burch, managing editor of the *Clarion,* followed him into his office, and immediately took the offered seat but rejected the coffee. Wally Burch with his rotund belly, gray walrus mustache, and round glasses resembled an out of shape Teddy Roosevelt. He cultivated the old time image by wearing a dark vest over his white shirt with the chain of a gold pocket watch stretched across his paunch

"I hope you are here to reconsider that victory parade. Your grandfather, a good man, would be so proud if he still walked among us. More and more of the boys are coming home now. We thought we might include them all, but you would still ride right up front behind the Ste. Jeanne d'Arc Flames Marching Band. The Ford dealer is willing to lend us a Mustang convertible for your ride." He paused a moment to really assess the man sitting across from him. "You look better than the last time I met with you, Blackie."

Merlin nodded. He recalled when Burch came to the door of the townhouse to lay out the plans for the grand "welcome home to our hero" procession: two high school bands, the convertible, a troop of Boy Scouts carrying American flags, a flatbed Mardi Gras float transporting area beauty queens dressed in red, white, and blue who would toss mini-flags and beads in the same colors to the crowd.

He answered his doorbell in the clothes he'd slept in the night before with his breakfast beer and cold pizza in hand. Unshaven and rude, he'd made Burch, the committee chairman for the parade, stand on the steps to say his piece, then said, "Not interested," and slammed the door in the man's past presidential face.

"I feel better, but I still don't want a parade. Thanks for the offer. The other guys might be interested so your plans would not be wasted. No, I came here out of concern for the recycling program."

Wally's bushy brows raised. "How so?"

"I believe Jane Marshall sent a lengthy letter to the editor explaining the issue and trying to rouse some support since she felt the newspaper had not covered the situation adequately."

The editor immediately went on the defensive. "We have limited space and must pick and choose what to run. With the advertising revenue and even our stories lost to the internet, our paper is smaller than it once was."

"But you do believe recycling is a worthy cause—because I understand your valued customer, Bernard Freeman, is about to change his mind and bring the issue to the council again. I spoke to him just this morning. Printing Jane's letter would be a nice start for his campaign to save the program. Why, I'd like to take out an ad the same day it appears, say this coming Sunday, to run right under the letter. Maybe a full-color swamp scene with egrets, alligators, and such, along with the caption 'Keep Ste. Jeanne Parish beautiful. Support Recycling.' Half page, and I'd like the proof by Thursday."

Wally Burch held up his hands. "Wait a second. Let me see if we ever got this letter you mentioned." He buzzed a lesser editor. "Stan, did we get a letter from Jane Marshall about recycling?"

Stan's voice came across loud and clear. "Sure. Very well-written. You told me to put it in the circular file."

Wally glanced at Merlin to see if he knew circular file meant the same thing as trashcan. He did, but kept his face stoic. Jane might have to rewrite that letter, but it *would* be printed.

"Actually, the letter came in as an e-mail, so I dumped it in the virtual trash. It's probably still there. You can't get rid of anything on a computer."

"Get it out of the circular file or wherever and run it on Sunday."

"You got it, boss."

"Sorry about the misunderstanding. Stan and his computers. He's always losing documents and having to find them again. Stop by the advertising department and discuss the layout you want with them. You'll have to put a name on it, this being a political issue."

"Not my name, say Falcon Enterprises."

"Good enough. Tell them I said to have the proof ready *before* Thursday."

The editor stood to get Merlin moving out of his office. In a few minutes, he'd be on the phone confirming the flip-flop on the recycling issue with Bernie. They shook hands again.

"Thanks, I know my fa—my grandpa would approve. He loved the land."

Jesus, he'd almost said "father" with Freeman on his mind. As Jane liked to say, "Recycling program saved, check. Letter to paper, check." But, he still had to drop off his dry cleaning and keep an afternoon appointment with his headshrinker way up in Alexandria at the VA hospital, a two-hour drive both ways. He imagined his PTSD specialist doing handsprings of joy over his progress.

Chapter Twenty-Two

"Where were you? You never came home for lunch. I worried about you! There's a sandwich in the refrigerator if you're hungry."

The little chicken hawk attacked the big, white rooster again, this time in their own kitchen. Merlin needed to remember his name meant falcon. He started to tell Jane she wasn't his mom, the way a surly teenager might reply, and stopped himself. She worried about him. He formed a softer reply.

"I had a lot of stuff to do."

"And you couldn't call?"

"Well, there's that law about not using cell phones while driving, and I couldn't have it turned on at the hospital."

"Hospital? Were you ill, visiting a friend, or what?"

He'd let slip about seeing a psychiatrist before, why couldn't he just say the words? "I—um—had to drive to Alex to see my shrink at the VA hospital. I go once a week when I'm not offshore. He says I'm doing good."

"Oh, Merlin."

That earned him an undeserved hug for keeping a regular appointment. What would happen when he told her the real news? Something better than a hug?

"Put some coffee on—please. I have lots of things

to tell you."

He got the real sugar out for himself and the fake stuff for her, took the milk carton from the refrigerator and put it on the table before he indulged in the simple pleasure of watching Jane prepare coffee. The slightly burnt aroma of dark roast filled the kitchen. He settled into a chair and beckoned Jane to the other seat with a crook of his little finger.

"That gesture could be considered sexist, Merlin." But, she sat anyhow. He sort of wished he'd pulled her onto his lap.

"I know, sugar lips. Bernard Freeman is buying back my townhouse and agreed to support the recycling program. Your letter will run on Sunday above a pretty ad asking people to save the environment. Best of all, you have a good chance of getting your job back, and maybe Nadia will be fired. I can't guarantee those last two, but don't let your parents convince you to stay in Montana past Christmas. You have a life waiting for you right here. So, check, check, check, check."

"Incredible! But why all those checks at the end?" Jane poured the coffee and took her seat again.

"You do that all the time, even when you don't say the word aloud. You make coffee and your lips move: water, check; spoons, check; mugs, check. My shrink would say you want to impose order on a chaotic world, but I think it's cute. I often wonder if you do that when we're in bed together. Foreplay, check; orgasm, check; cuddle time, check." He rested his big chin in his hands and grinned at her.

"I do not! You make me so crazy in bed I can't think straight." Jane searched the table for something not too breakable, messy, or lethal to throw. She settled on a spoon and flung it at him. Merlin batted it aside.

"Hey, regaining my sense of humor is a sign of recovery. Don't knock it. Making you crazy in bed is good, right?"

"You know it is. Tell me how you accomplished all this?"

Merlin sat up straight and waved his hands in a mystical gesture. "No bloodshed, few harsh words uttered, only my special brand of magic—and a magician can never reveal his secrets."

****

Of course, Jane did not accept his answer. He didn't break after that especially long and satisfying bout of sex following his revelations. She continued to wheedle, cajole, and plead all week. No, he told Freeman he would honor his grandparents' promise, and he meant to, but he did enjoy Jane's means of persuasion.

Thursday night, they sat down to a New England boiled dinner made with a picnic ham, cabbage, carrots, potatoes, turnips, and onions. Not bad, but needed seasoning. He shook some Tony's Cajun spices over his portion. Frozen yogurt topped with fresh strawberries for dessert, good, too.

With all that hulling, vegetable scraping, and paring the garbage strainer in the sink overflowed with the papery skins of the onions, the core of the cabbage, the peels of the potatoes and turnips

As Jane dealt with the dirty dishes, he tried to show his housebroken ways by emptying the garbage into the kitchen trashcan and taking the bag out to the receptacle by the garage.

"You got anything else needs to go to the curb," he

asked. "It's garbage night."

"Let me empty the wastebaskets in the bathrooms and my office, then take the stuff next door to Mr. Babin's trashcan." Jane rinsed a dish and put it in the washer.

"Why? Did the wheels on your bin break again? I can fix it."

"No, Burl Oubre is making up new rules to hassle me since I spoke against giving him the garbage contract. He says if my cart has been altered, his men can't pick it up. Ridiculous, I know, but I simply do not care anymore. I mean how much longer will I be here?"

"As long as you want, a lifetime maybe."

She cocked her head at him, but he could not go any farther than that right now. He wasn't completely well, had not fulfilled all his promises to her yet. "I'm taking the bin to the curb, and they *will* pick up our trash."

"Don't be rough on Mellow and O.J. They have to do what Oubre tells them. Mellow has a record and can't get any other kind of job."

"Mellow and O.J.? You made friends with these guys?"

"Better than making enemies. I tried with Nadia, too, but she befriends no one."

"I'm taking the trash to the curb. Hurry up and get the rest. Looks like rain again tonight."

Jane unhappily complied. When Merlin returned from the garbage run, she had the phone in hand. "It's your granny. She wants us to come have lunch with her at the Villa tomorrow. I'm supposed to wear red, and she wants you in a suit."

Merlin took the phone. "What the heck, Granny? Is

it dress up day at the home? A surprise. I do not like surprises, you know that. But, I'll love this one. Right. Tell, or we won't be there. Okay, okay, fine. Eleven before the frozen yogurt machine runs low."

He set the phone back in its cradle and smacked his forehead trying to bring life back into perspective. "She won a family portrait gift certificate from Stella Musemeche playing *bourree*. Stella should know Granny is a killer at card games, but evidently her mind is slipping. Great, we get to have lunch with my family. The red dress is so all of the women blend for the photo, men in dark suits. Do you have a red dress, or do we need to go shopping, too?"

His pained tone made Jane laugh out loud. "You are spared a shopping trip. I do have a red dress, though it is a dark red. That okay?"

"Makes no never mind to me, babe."

A gentle rain tapped on the windowpanes like the fingers of small children. "You want to go upstairs and listen to the rain?" she asked, soothing him.

"Hell, I want to do more than that, lady in red."

She offered her hand, and he took it. They actually did listen to the rainfall on the metal roof for a while before getting naked and going at it. He'd been sleeping so well in Jane's company, he dozed off without concern after they finished.

But, Mother Nature can be a real bitch. The storm intensified and threw down hail hitting that roof with a sound like machinegun fire. His gunner was hit, dying. He had to get him to safety. He called in his coordinates, cried for help.

Then, Jane talked him down to a soft, safe landing in her arms. She had twice his courage, staying through

226

all that. Would she remain permanently with a nut case like him if he asked?

How could he risk losing what they had now by popping that question?

Chapter Twenty-Three

CLANG, CLANK, CHUG. Merlin jumped off the treadmill, letting it run, and bolted for the street. Sure enough, the garbage truck ignored their receptacle and rolled up to the stop sign to make its turn.

"Hey, you sonsabitches, you didn't take my trash!"

"Sorry, sorry," Mellow said, his big belly shaking like his namesake Jell-O at Merlin's rage. "That receptacle done been altered. We can't take Miss Jane's can no more."

"This is no longer Miss Jane's can. It's mine, crazy Merlin Tauzin's garbage can. Take it before I shove it up your ass."

Jane shuffled up behind him in her robe and the bunny slippers, which had slowed her down. "You aren't crazy, and this is not Mellow's fault. Let them go. I give up."

She clung to Merlin's arm. When he shook her off and headed for the garbage truck, pushing the cart before him at ramming speed, Mellow's eyes popped wide.

"What you say, O.J.? If this Mr. Tauzin's receptacle, can we take it?" he called over the rumble of the truck engine. O.J., not leaving the safety of the cab for nothing, stuck an arm out the window and gave a thumbs up.

"See, we takin' your can. We takin' it right now.

Let me get it up on the lift. There it go, all that nasty garbage into the truck. You have a good day now, Mr. Tauzin." Mellow climbed onto the back of the truck, and they got the hell out the crazy white man's way.

"Merlin Tauzin, you listen to me." Jane grasped his jaw to make her point. "I never want you to call yourself crazy again. If you keep saying that, using that, people will believe it. You are not insane."

"I was again last night." There, he stated it simply, the reason why he could not ask her to commit herself to him permanently.

Jane smoothed his deep frown lines with her fingertips. "No, you had a bad episode and we dealt with it. Merlin, I could never love a crazy man."

"Yeah, that's what I think, too." He reversed the garbage can, sent it spinning toward the driveway, and followed after it at a trot, running away.

Jane placed her hands on her hips. Cars passed on the street. She didn't give a damn if all of Ste. Jeanne Parish saw her standing there, unemployed, in her bunny slippers. She had just told Merlin Tauzin she loved him. He'd taken her words and twisted them to fit his own warped image of himself. Well, if he thought he could get away with that… She went after him.

Damn him! As she came around the back of the house impeded by her footwear, he scooted out the front door and went upstairs. Jane kicked off her slippers and ran after him barefoot. His sweats sans any underwear lay in a heap by the bathroom door. The water already beat against the sides of the small shower, but the door remained unlocked—negligence or an invitation? She shed her robe and nightie intending to find out. He'd already soaped his long body and had his head stuck under water, an ostrich hiding in the sand but with his black plumage still very noticeable. Under her care, he'd lost some of his gauntness. That pleased her immensely, but did not let him off the hook.

Beating on the glass enclosure, Jane shouted, "Did you play the crazy card with Bernard Freeman and over at the newspaper? Did you?"

"Can't hear you." He had his eyes shut tight as he lathered his hair.

Jane opened the enclosure and stepped inside. Cupping her hands around her mouth she repeated, "Did you play the crazy card with Bernard Freeman?"

He turned and flicked his hair, shampoo, and water out of his face. "Well, hello there."

"Do not get distracted simply because I am here naked. Did you play the crazy card with Freeman to get your way?"

"Nope. He might have thought that in the beginning of our discussion, but not by the end. Okay?"

"How about at the newspaper? Did you threaten Wally Burch?"

"Not there, either. I told him Freeman would back recycling, and I bought an ad. That's all."

"Truly?"

Merlin made the sign of the cross, carving it out of lather still on his chest. "Cross my heart and hope to die."

"Stop that! I don't want you dead for any reason."

"Good, because I'm feeling very alive right his minute." He nudged her belly with his erection. "Kind of tight in here, but we have this handy little ledge."

He swept the plastic bottles of shampoo and body wash off the shelf and replaced them with Jane.

Spreading her legs wide, he scraped some of the soap from his body and worked it into her cleft, circling the hot button of her clit over and over. She rested her hands on his broad shoulders, partly for support, and partly to dig her nails into his flesh as her arousal grew. He put his wet lips on hers, worked his tongue into her mouth and his penis into her honey hole, flicked both of them in and out, in and out. Jane moved to grasp his hips and urge him on. They both came before the hot water ran out.

She rested her head on his chest. "A crazy man could not make love like that."

"How many crazy men have you been with, Jane?"

"Oh, get out and let me wash my hair. We have to get ready for our photo shoot."

By the time she finished her shower Merlin had scraped away his dark beard and put on the blue boxer briefs she'd bought for him. "I guess I should wear a T-shirt under my dress shirt, huh?"

Wrapped in a towel, she went to him and played with the dark hair on his chest. "You don't have to for me." She sniffed, taking in his brisk, manly scent. "I like the way you smell, too."

Suddenly, she pulled away. "Oh, my God, I used your shampoo and body wash. Now I smell like a man."

Merlin drew her close. He nuzzled her neck. "No, you still smell like Jane to me. It's my aftershave you're enjoying."

"No, I think I'd be very attractive to Nadia right now. I have to go downstairs and rinse off again."

"Do what you must, but don't be too long. We have to pick up my entire family and cart them to Magnolia Villa before the frozen yogurt runs out, remember?"

"Right. I'm on it." She headed toward the door.

"Jane, you better put on your robe. I heard a tugboat whistle while you were in the shower. My guess is the bridge is open for a barge, and traffic is backed up at the light. No sense in giving a show unless you charge admission."

"See, I'm the crazy one, made crazy by you." She dropped the towel and bundled up in her nightie and robe before taking the stairs as fast as she could and disappearing into the house.

****

"Will this do?" Jane twirled around in her deep red dress, showing off for Merlin. A draped bodice crisscrossed her chest, flattering her breasts but not exposing them. She filled the neckline with an enameled necklace of green holly leaves and red berries purchased from a museum catalog back in the days when she had the money to do that. Never a big fan of ass-hugging dresses, Jane's skirt flared just above the knees. She'd taken the time to make sure all the ends of her bob turned under and carefully matched her lipstick to her dress color. No red shoes though, her black work pumps would have to do.

"You make me want to stay home and peel you out of that getup, holly berry."

"And you clean up very nicely yourself."

He did. The dark suit only made his eyes seem bluer. Wearing the classic white shirt-red power tie combo, he could use the photo to run for public office tomorrow.

"I've been told that before, but we don't have time to fool around right now. Let me give you a boost into the truck. You'll have to ride in the backseat once we pick up Mom and Harley, Brittney and Jayden. Harley won't fit back there." He held the kitchen door open for her and pointed the way.

"I shouldn't be going along anyhow. Maybe I should just…"

"Get in the truck."

He helped her in the usual way by swinging her upward, but paused in mid-arc to steal a kiss. Jane believed she might never want to come down, but at last broke it off and used her finger to remove the red lipstick from his smile. He put her down, strapped her in, and climbed into the driver's seat.

"Brace yourself for the full-court press of my family."

They drove to a trailer park so well-established large oak trees separated the single and doublewides. Harley's motorcycle sat parked in front of a fairly new double at the very end of a row. Merlin's stepfather had already blown up the inflatable snowman and Santa Claus, pegged them down on the small patch of brown lawn, and hung blue Christmas lights along the eaves of the trailer. A wreath of plastic holly decorated the door. Merlin barely stopped when a small boy in a red sweater and a cute matching bowtie clipped to the collar of his shirt bolted from the tiny porch and raced to the cab door.

"Nonc Merry! You come to play with me?"

Merlin got down and helicoptered the kid above his head. "That's Nonc Merlin or Nonc Blackie to you, Blue Jay." The child around four years of age laughed and flapped his arms like a bird.

"Put him down, Merlin. He'll pee his pants, and

then I'll have to get him cleaned up again. You have no idea how hard it is to take care of a kid."

Brittney David made her way carefully down the trailer's three front steps. A bright red dress wrapped tight as a bandage around her body and matching red satin four-inch heels made the short trip precarious. A web of lined stretch lace across the bodice kept the outfit within a half-inch on the modest side by confining her breasts. Jane had not seen Brittney in anything but her waitress uniform, but somehow the choice of clothes did not surprise her. Evidently, heavy eye makeup was not a Broussard's Barn job requirement, only something the young woman enjoyed wearing along with siren red lipstick and several cheap gold chains. She flipped her long dark hair with its blonde streaks over her shoulders.

"Give me a boost up, bro," she said to Merlin.

"If you tell J.J. not to call me Merry."

"For crying out loud, the family always called you Merry until you started that broody crap in middle school and said to you wanted to go by Blackie—like a horse or a dog."

"Tell him or split that dress trying to get up there."

"Okay, okay. J.J., sweetie, you call this mean man Nonc Blackie from now on."

"Nonc isn't mean. He's fun." Back on his feet, the boy looked up at Merlin with adoration in his Cajun dark puppy eyes and a happy smile on his long, narrow face. His mother had brushed his short black hair into a peak running along the center of his head and gelled it into place in the latest male hairstyle fad.

"I sure am. A million laughs." With that comment, he cupped his hands around his half-sister's butt and heaved her into the backseat of the truck. She squealed until she landed.

"Buckle the boy in first. We don't have enough seat belts back there for all of you. Where's Mom?"

"Late as usual. I did her makeup, her hair, and laid out her clothes and everything, but still late."

Jane made her own way into the backseat before Merlin could lay hands on her. She watched horrified when his mother appeared in the same dress, shoes, and makeup as Brittney wore. The only difference in appearance was her heavily sprayed upsweep of hair. At least, Jenny possessed the thinness to wear the gown, but it didn't flatter her older face. Harley came to her elbow before she tried to totter down the steps. Gallantly, he carried her to the truck, set her inside like precious cargo, and fastened her seatbelt. That left Jane unbuckled since Brittney had seized hers and snapped it shut.

Huffing a little from his exertion, Harley took the shotgun seat next to Merlin. He'd combed his side whiskers and beard to a fine fluff, slicked back the hair on top of his head and tucked his ponytail into the back of his black suit coat. If he also wore a red tie, the beard obscured it. Half turning in his seat, he said, "Nice to see you again, Jane. You meet the rest of my family."

"Sort of."

"Yeah, I waited on her and Waldo Robin out at the Barn. I guess he's looking for his third wife. You must like them long and lean, Jane, but believe me, you are not his type. You don't look like you could show a man a good time."

"I wouldn't say that," Merlin answered, making Jane wish she sat close enough to punch him. "Let's get this done," he said in a voice that might have been calling for the start a military mission. He turned over the engine and let it roar them out of the trailer park.

Before they reached the highway taking them to Magnolia Villa, Brittney shook out a cigarette from a pack concealed in the tiny handbag that dangled from her wrist on a thin chain.

"You want one, Mom?"

Jenny nodded and reached out a hand, but Merlin interrupted. "No one smokes in my truck. I don't want the stink to get in the upholstery. I swear if you light up, Brittney, I'll leave you by the side of the road."

In a snit, she crammed the pack back into its cramped space. "I guess that means you don't smoke, Jane."

"No, never." She wished she could move over but her hip welded to Brittney's in the crowded backseat.

"Didn't think so. All I ever hear from Granny anymore is how classy Jane is. Jane speaks so nice. Jane dresses like a lady. You should be more like Jane."

"You should," Merlin muttered.

"Children," Harley said with a chuckle. "Now grandchildren are a better deal. Right, J.J.? That stands for Jayden Justin for Justin Bieber, that boy singer."

"I like the Bieb," Jenny piped up in her childish voice. "I have a new red dress, Jane, a mother-daughter dress. Brittney picked it out. I like red."

With a little lump in her throat, Jane answered, "It's lovely."

"I told you so," Brittney shot back at her brother.

He declined to speak again until they arrived at Magnolia Villa nestled among big beds of multicolored pansies and entwined by pleasant walkways paved for wheelchairs. Merlin handed each of the women down, only lifting his nephew who took off like a bottle rocket for the main lobby. Jayden backpedaled halfway there.

"They got yogurt here!" he crowed before charging the doors which he could not open until an adult came along, but not for lack of trying.

Olive Tauzin, her walker to one side, sat positioned on a paisley-patterned sofa flanked with potted palms in clear view of the doorway. She wore a red velour pantsuit embroidered with a cheerful montage of cardinals and holly across her fallen chest, her hair in its usual cottony white topknot but trimmed with a crimson ribbon around its base. A young man wearing a dress military uniform held her big-veined hand. The sight of the stranger stopped J.J. in his tracks so suddenly both Jenny and Merlin nearly knocked him down.

"Doyle!" they shouted simultaneously. Merlin let his mother do the hugging and squeezing first as she repeated, "My baby, my baby" over and over, but Jane could tell he itched to embrace his half-brother. Once Jenny let loose, he gave a quick, manly kind of hug and followed it with a solid handshake.

"Get you, kid brother, all slimmed down and grown to be a man. Who let you out of Afghanistan?" Merlin's blue eyes had a glitter to them close to tears.

Jane surmised Doyle had been a chubby child and most likely resembled the round-faced Harley without all the facial hair. He surely did not bear any likeness to Merlin who towered over the stubby young man. Both had blue eyes but Doyle's were round, a strangely innocent baby blue like the ones on the biker, but not a hint of danger in them. His lips, full and small, mimicked the ones hidden in Harley's beard. Jane would have called him baby-faced, but the army had honed Doyle down and brought out his cheek bones. The soldier had medium brown hair shaved down nearly to the scalp, not the very dark brown of the Tauzins, and no sign of a heavy beard. When Doyle smiled, his face lit like a child's at Christmas, and Jane saw a hint of Jenny in him.

"Aw, Granny wrote my commanding officer and claimed she was dying and need to see her grandson for Christmas one last time. I expected her to be lying in a hospital bed when I got here. She said to come straight to the Villa and not to call anyone when I got in. A person driving this way gave me a ride from the airport."

Very pleased with herself, Olive Tauzin chirped, "I thought you didn't like surprises, Merlin. Guess you do now."

"Yeah, this is great, but are you really sick?"

Olive threw up her withered hands. "At my age, I could go any time, don't you know?"

Harley worked his way in to give his son a few backslaps and declare how good he looked in his uniform. J.J. still held back until Doyle knelt and said, "Maybe you don't remember me. You were a tee-tiny baby when I left for training camp. I'm your Uncle Doyle."

He reached out a hand to ruffle the boy's hair, but Brittney slapped it away. "Don't you mess up his do before the picture." She made amends, kissing her brother's cheek and leaving a large red splotch behind.

"Should I call him Uncle Doyle?" J.J. asked cautiously of his mother.

"Sure, Doyle is just Doyle. He's not always changing his name and his mood."

"They got yogurt here," the boy confided to his uncle.

"Can't wait to have some and my mother's cooking. The army doesn't feed us like she does."

"Then, you young people run ahead and get a big table before those bridge club bitches take the last one. They think they're too good to play *bouree*. Food is great here, Doyle, and I don't have to cook or clean up. So glad to have you home for a while. Go on, I'll get there eventually." Olive waggled her walker into place and hiked herself into position.

They took over a table for eight and got J.J. a booster seat. Small salads already sat at each place along with a glass of water and a second ready for iced tea from a pitcher sweating on the table linen. A large black woman came to take their orders.

"Hi, Melba. Nice to see you again," Jane said.

"You, too, ma'am. Miss Olive been talking about this get-together all week. Now after y'all eat, we got Milly Olinde set up in the library to take your pictures. The gift certificates were bingo prizes, but Miss Olive done snookered Stella Musemeche out of hers."

"If Stella wanted it so bad, she shouldn't have put it on the table. Besides, it's only good for one eight-by-ten family photo. You know Milly will take a dozen different poses and try to sell you more. What's for lunch?" Olive asked.

"Being this is Friday, the stuffed tilapia is a good bet. We have the loaded potatoes, a big one as the main dish or a little one on the side. Also got baked chicken legs with a mac and cheese side and a Salisbury steak come with whipped potatoes. The vegetable is green beans. For dessert you got your choice of a sugar-free brownie, apple pie, or the yogurt. Anybody want a cup of seafood gumbo for a starter?"

"I'd like a vat of seafood gumbo," Doyle replied.

"I'm bringing you a great, big bowl, soldier boy."

Everyone but Harley and J.J. decided on the tilapia. Harley went with the giant stuffed potato, and Brittney ordered the chicken with mac and cheese for her son who wanted yogurt but had to clean his plate first. She decked the boy out with a large linen napkin tied around his neck. The rest were trusted not to spill. They finally got to dessert after many interruptions by aged veterans who wanted to shake Doyle's hand and slap Merlin on the back. Old ladies smooched them on the cheeks and left behind their lipstick to the point that the men's napkins looked blood-stained from wiping it off. Melba served J.J. his yogurt and the guys their apple pie with a topping of the same. All the women went for the sugar-free brownies.

At the end of the meal, Brittney stood and ran a hand down the front of her dress. "Oh, no! My belly is pooching out. We should have gotten the pictures taken first. Mom, is your belly pooching out?"

Jenny regarded her stomach very seriously. "I don't think so. It only stuck out when I had babies in there."

Harley put his arms around both women. "Come on, you both look beautiful. Let's get this picture taken."

He guided them to the Villa's tiny library, its shelves filled with old Reader's Digest condensed books and dog-eared, donated novels. Relieved that

Brittney hadn't upset the plan for the day by refusing to pose with a poochy belly, Jane followed behind appreciating Harley's value to the family for the first time. He may not have been a hard worker, but he had a soothing, silver tongue amid that bush of beard.

Milly Olinde had her lights set up around a settee in the same muted paisley pattern as the rest of the Villa's furnishings. Small, quick, and slim in her skinny slacks, Milly dressed all in black from the flats on her feet to her long-sleeved, turtleneck top. Radiating a brilliant professional smile and greeting them like old friends, as they might well be in a town as small as Chapelle, Milly positioned Olive in the center of the settee. She placed the daughter and granddaughter on either side with Jayden sitting cross-legged at their feet. Arranging the men behind them, she made Merlin the center of a pyramid with stocky Doyle and Harley on either side. Jane hung back behind the photographer.

"Don't forget, Jane," Olive prompted.

"She's not family," Brittney objected.

"I want Jane in my picture. It's my gift certificate."

"Look, Brittney is right. I don't belong in this picture. Why don't you take it as is?" Jane stepped deeper into the shadows cast by the bright lighting.

Milly raked her fingers through her already spiky blonde hair. "You would throw the balance off. Let me get this shot and think about it." She pronounced the usual "Say cheese!" and took three quick snaps.

"Okay, I got it. You two ladies—I do swear you look like twins, not mother and daughter—stand on either side of the settee. You, Jane, sit with Miss Olive and sort of center yourselves on the couch. Guys stay where you are."

She went behind her camera again. Merlin's hand slipped onto Jane's shoulder and stayed there as Milly blinded them with the flash again and again. "Nice," the photographer proclaimed. "I got some great shots. Now, how about a few extra poses? Maybe the four generations, granny, mother, daughter, grandson? Or couples. When was the last time you had a picture taken together? How about all these handsome men together?"

"Yes, the four generations. Get up, Jane." Brittney took her place as Merlin's hand fell away from her shoulder leaving a warm spot behind.

"I gotta pee." Jayden wiggled his behind on the floor.

His mother reached down and plunked him on the settee. "Hold it in a few more minutes."

"I want more yogurt."

"Hold it, and you'll have some."

He did long enough for Milly to get her pictures, but immediately wet his pants as soon as he stood.

"No yogurt for you! You made a spot on Granny's carpet. Now I must clean you up."

J.J. sobbed from both humiliation and lack of yogurt as his mother yanked him from the room.

Olive Tauzin leaned forward and shouted after them, "I don't give a damn. Not my carpet. Let the boy have his yogurt. It's not like nobody ever wet themselves in this place. Doyle, fetch J.J. some yogurt for when he comes out the bathroom. Have some more yourself."

Like a man accustomed to taking orders, Doyle left for the yogurt machine.

Unperturbed, Milly said, "Happens all the time

when you photograph kids. No big deal. So how about a couples picture? I brought some scenic drops along in case you're tired of the library setting: sunset, azaleas in bloom, apple blossom time, waterfall, beach." Milly dragged the frame supporting the drops into place and checked the lighting.

"Sunset, Jane and me and the sunset," Merlin replied, catching Jane off guard.

"I believe she meant Harley and your mom."

"Apple blossoms," Olive said almost dreamily. "If they want one with a sunset, fine, but I think Merlin and Jane should be among the apple blossoms. Then, Harley and Jenny and the azaleas in bloom. Humor me, y'all."

Milly positioned Jane and Merlin sideways with the blazing sunset behind them and his arms folded around Jane's waist. "Do I know a couple when I see one? Yes! Now, Jane put your hands over his. Don't let them dangle at your side. That's it. Let's do this one serious. No smiles. Great. Click, click, click, and on to the apple blossoms. Face each other. His hands on your waist. Your hands on his shoulders. Look into each other's eyes. Good. You two are very photogenic. You'll want multiple copies of these. Next couple."

"Mama, can I have a beach, too? Harley takes me to Destin sometimes," Jenny pleaded.

"Sure, baby." Olive patted the settee and asked Jane and Merlin to sit beside her. "Now watch that wet spot on the carpet. No need to get pee stink on your shoes. Thanks for making an old lady happy today."

"Glad to do it, Granny."

Merlin pecked her wrinkled cheek. Jane murmured the same sentiment. About the time Milly finished with Harley and Jenny, the others returned, Jayden in his damp little boy pants but licking frozen yogurt in a cone and Doyle doing the same.

Brittney, maybe concerned about her poochy belly, carried nothing but a sour expression and some water stains down the front of her red dress. "We got to go. I didn't bring extra clothes for the kid. That Melba person gave me a towel to put down on your precious car seat, Merlin. I tell you these stains had better come out."

"Go on, then. I'm worn out from being a glamour puss." Miss Olive mounted her walker again.

Getting ready for the next group waiting in the hall, Milly said, "Now, I'll be sending you the proofs by e-mail. Who has e-mail?"

Merlin raised his hand. "Got a laptop."

"Great, then you can show the others. Write your address on this form. I know you are going to love these. I tell you with all these digital cameras around, a girl has to hustle to make a living. Remember, my photos will not fade away to nothing over the years. They are heirloom quality. Wait until you see my selection of frames."

"That's all good, but don't you forget to credit my gift certificate," Olive reminded the photographer as she moved her walker forward.

They parted from Olive at the double door entry of the Villa and got everyone into the truck again with Jayden positioned carefully on his towel and belted in, a tall for his age little boy already outgrowing car seats. He fell asleep on the way back. With his duffel bag stowed in the truck bed along with Harley who wanted him to have the front seat, Doyle chatted with Merlin, not about war but of old times growing up on the farm.

Including Jane, the soldier told her, "Kids bullied me in grade school. You know, the pudgy kid with the squatty body. I tried to laugh them off, but one day the bully king decided to wipe that smile off my face and knocked out one of my baby teeth. Merlin, he says to me, you tell those brats you're Blackie Tauzin's brother. They don't want to know what Blackie will do to them if they bother you again. With Merlin being so many years older and up in middle school that worked really great."

"What did you do to them, Merlin?" Jane asked as if he might confirm a history of violence.

"Nothing, because they didn't want to know what Blackie would do. By the time I got to be thirteen I already had a tough attitude and a beard coming in, pretty scary to third-graders. I knocked out a few baby teeth myself in grade school when I got teased about not knowing my real daddy. After that, I just lived on my reputation. Once I got the motorcycle and started hanging out with Slick Broussard, everyone left me alone."

"Except the girls," Doyle snickered.

Jenny said softly, "My poor little boy came home crying from school, wanting to know who his daddy was, but I couldn't tell. No, I couldn't tell. He got into fights. My poor boy."

Merlin pushed the truck up another ten miles an hour. Harley lay down in the truck bed in case the cops came after them. No sense attracting even more attention than being ten miles over the limit would do. They got back to the trailer park in record time and unloaded. Merlin did not get down. He let Doyle and Harley do the lifting. With a wave out his window, he sped home with Jane still in the backseat amid her choice of belts to buckle. She leaned as far forward as the seatbelt would let her.

"That was awkward."

"Yeah, I hate when my mom gets upset about my grade school years. So what? I had to get tough fast. That's what Harley taught us, but it didn't come to Doyle naturally like it did to me."

"I meant the picture taking session. I did not belong there. Brittney was right."

"My sister is a bitch. Granny wanted you there, and I want—what Granny wants." He kept his eyes on the road. She should have been grateful for that.

"Those couple pictures must have made you uncomfortable."

"Nope. We watch the sunset together. I wanted a picture of that in case you go. The other was for Granny."

"Go where? Not one reply to any of my job inquiries yet." Jane flopped back against the seat.

"No rush. The Council won't do much business right before Christmas. In January, they will see the error of their ways and want you back to run the new recycling program and administer that grant I know you'll get."

"You have more faith in me than I do."

"Yeah, I'm beginning to think that's the way this works."

"What works?"

"Nothing. Look, I'm going to drop you off, change my clothes and pack, then go back to Mom's to spend the weekend with Doyle before I have to go offshore. I'd invite you, but we'll only be sitting around eating

Mom's cooking and telling stories on each other. I'll leave from there on Monday morning, okay?"

"That's what you should do, spend time with your brother, only don't drink—" Jane stopped herself. She wasn't Merlin's mother, wife, or fiancée—only his too easy lay, and had no more right to tell him how to behave than honky-tonk Wanda. "Never mind."

"I won't drink at all. God's oath," he responded as if he really needed her to know that.

"Good. We might not see each other when you get back. I'll be flying out at six a.m. that Monday for Christmas in Montana. I don't want to wake you early after you get in late Sunday."

"I don't mind getting up to take you to the airport."

"No, you'll be offshore again when I get back. I'd better leave my car in long-term parking."

"If that's how you want it."

No, that's not how she wanted it. She'd rather have him drive her to the airport, kiss her goodbye long enough to embarrass the other passengers, say he loved her and would miss her, and be there waiting when she got back. Wasn't going to happen with Merlin. She should make it easier on both of them by creeping away quietly and driving herself home after the trip.

He turned his truck into the gravel driveway. Helping her down, he held her briefly against his chest before turning her lose to go into the kitchen while he walked around front to his loft leaving her again.

Chapter Twenty-Four

Nine days without Merlin seemed like a month when Jane had nothing to do with her time except check her e-mail hoping for a reply to her job inquiries. Sunday morning, she ate a light breakfast of coffee, orange juice, whole wheat toast, and strawberry jam and scanned the newspaper Christmas ads for an inexpensive gift that might appeal to Merlin. If worst came to worst, she could always buy him a gift card for gas, though she couldn't afford enough to entirely fill the tank of his big-ass truck.

And there it was—her long letter pleading the benefits of restoring the recycling program in Ste. Jeanne d'Arc Parish and asking for public support. Right below it taking up precious editorial space ran a full-color ad of a gorgeous swamp scene she recognized as the work of a talented local photographer. It promoted the same message and purported to be paid for by Falcon Enterprises. An ad like that cost plenty. Merlin was not cheap, nor did he lie. He'd closed on the sale of his townhouse the previous Thursday and gotten back the title of his big-ass truck the same day. While the ad dazzled her, the townhouse transaction relieved Jane of the worry that her problems would result in his financial ruin.

She tore out the page to save, noticing as she flipped it over that the backside had a picture of

Bernard Freeman and his perfect family wishing his constituents a Merry Christmas and a Blessed New Year. Much as she wanted to use that portion to start her fireplace, the reverse side meant more. In fact, she would get dressed and walk over to the Fast 'N Fun for another copy of the Sunday paper to get a tear sheet for framing. Christmas gift problem solved.

\*\*\*\*

Monday morning, Jane parked on the lot of the church of Ste. Jeanne d'Arc as everyone did who wanted avoid the new parking meters on the street and still shop in the two-block row of downtown, locally-owned businesses. She cut across the church green, its ancient live oaks currently bedecked with a frenzy of flying angel figures that lit up brilliantly at night to celebrate the holiday season.

Strolling along Main Street on a brisk morning that complemented the carols and pop holiday songs emanating from some of the small shops, Jane paused to peer into the two barred windows of LeClerc's Jewelry and Watch Repair. Mr. LeClerc seldom placed any jewelry of great value right up front, but he did sometimes feature locally handcrafted merchandise placed with him on consignment. She could still window-shop if nothing else. One window displayed a Christmas special on diamond earrings, some so tiny one had to squint to see them in the setting. In the other, a pyramid of glass cubes caught her eye. Each one held a small animal figurine within its clear walls. On the very top, a silver falcon swooped suspended within its confines. Merlin.

But, first things first. Without entering the jewelry shop, she went next door to Sweat's Gallery and Frame

Shop, a relatively new business proving Chapelle held some fine but previously unacknowledged artists in its midst. Zola Sweat, who claimed her last name was pronounced Sweet, bedecked her walls with local art: swamp scenes, Louisiana celebrities, sketches of Cajuns past and present, and views of the church across the street in various mediums. While she occasionally collected a thirty percent commission on a piece of art, her real income came from framing LSU and Sinners football memorabilia and anything else people wanted preserved under glass like Jane's news clipping. Zola lived above the store and came clomping down the staircase in her clogs when the bell over the door rang.

A big-boned woman with her black hair parted in the middle and hanging to the center of her back in a coarse, curly tail, Zola claimed the clogs helped her bad back. Today, she wore a hand-woven caftan, multi-hued, from some small African nation. Tomorrow, she might favor an orange retro polyester pantsuit. No one knew what to expect from Zola since she'd blown into town from New Orleans where she'd earned a living as a quick portrait artist on Jackson Square before Hurricane Katrina. Trapped in the horror of the Super Dome refuge, she told any and all she "ain't a-gonna go back there." Her race mixed, her opinions outspoken, Zola added lots of color to Main Street.

"Hey, Jane. How ya doing?"

"Not so great. Unemployed and Christmas coming on. I'd like to have this framed, but nothing too expensive." Jane laid out the newspaper clipping carefully handled to prevent any creasing.

"Aluminum frame, plain back mat, and non-glare glass be okay? I'll give you a twenty percent regular customer discount. Sorry about your job. That's government for you. If someone does good work, they are the first to go. If they louse it up, they get a pat on the back. 'Brownie, you're doing a heck of a job,' my big, fat ass. I'll never forget that one after Katrina."

"Me neither. Thanks for the deal. Can I have it by Saturday? I'll be going out of town for Christmas and need to get it wrapped for someone."

"Sure, all the autographed posters of Joe Dean Billodeaux can wait. Would this someone be Blackie Tauzin?" Zola raised her thin-plucked, dramatic eyebrows and pursed the thick lips set in her tawny face. The little polymer parrots mounted on her hoop earrings swung back and forth inquisitively.

"Maybe."

"No need to be coy with me, but you should be more careful now that you live by a stoplight. Miss Lolly says she saw Blackie carrying you up that outside staircase on her way home from perpetual prayer. Sinning going on according to her, but what do old maids know?"

"We were just fooling around."

"I'll say! I envy you. I doubt there's a man in the world big enough to carry me up the stairs—except maybe Rev Bullock, but being a minister and all, that ain't his kind of thing. The newspaper called here to get Roger Darby's phone number to see if they could use this picture in Blackie's ad. The ladies over there spilled about this Falcon Enterprises business. So are you and Blackie cohabitating?"

"He brought my house and lives upstairs for the time being. I couldn't keep up the payments. He's letting me stay there until I find a job. Then, I'll be moving on."

"Not what I heard, honey, but the grapevine don't always bear ripe fruit. Jane, this parish needs people like you—and me—to shake things up a little bit. Don't pack your bags too soon, okay?"

"I'll do my best. See you Saturday."

Jane went out the gallery door and into the jewelry store. Like most of the old brick buildings along Main Street this one was long and narrow running back half a block. An alley with parking areas separated it from the businesses the next street over. With a jeweler's loupe attached to his spectacles, bald-headed Mr. LeClerc sat in his office far to the rear. Customers ran a gauntlet of tempting display cases, ropes of pearls in this one, colored gems in the next, diamonds farther on, to get to him. Few people came in for watch repairs anymore, but he would replace a battery in a cheap, disposal watch for seven dollars. Having tried to do this herself only to find the hands of her Timex on the floor, Jane came here most often for that particular service.

He betook himself to the counter for her benefit. "Here comes the lucky lady,"

"Hardly. I am currently unemployed. How much for these cubes with the animals in them?"

"Very reasonably priced at twenty dollars and right up your alley. The figurines are recycled cast aluminum. For each one sold, a dollar goes to wildlife preservation. I favor the sea turtles myself. I've sold a lot of those. Great stocking stuffers."

"No, I want the falcon."

"Bring it here. Free gift wrap."

Jane brought the cube to the back of the store and sat down in the area reserved for the selection of class rings. The seat, an old-fashioned fainting couch, contributed to the standard joke that parents went weak after hearing the prices. The phone rang and another customer arrived to pick up a repaired necklace, all contributing to a delay in the wrapping.

Jane got up and wandered over to the antique hutch that housed the bridal selections of fine china, crystal and silver, each one labeled with the name of the bride and groom. Her eyes skimmed over the cut-glass vases and sterling serving pieces suggested for wedding gifts. She lingered by the showcase of engagement rings, but nothing special attracted her. Still by the time Mr. LeClerc handed her the little white box with its topping of curly red ribbon and his gold business sticker, she began feeling mildly depressed.

Not that she wanted fancy china or a crystal vase or a large engagement ring, all unnecessary for a happy life her mother would say. If Merlin did not return her love, she could not force him. He had been good to her, and she hoped her small gifts would brighten his rather stark life. Not a single photo, framed picture, or small piece of art moved with him from the townhouse to her, no, his new house. Her living room walls hung with wonderful items purchased from Zola's gallery, all done by rising young artists who might someday be famous. Over her brass bedstead she had fine art prints of Van Gogh's irises and Monet's water lilies. How did he live without art and beauty in his life? They were simply too different, too far apart ever to meet in the middle.

"Merry Christmas, Jane. I know the New Year will be better for you." Mr. LeClerc beamed at her like a character in the last scene of *It's a Wonderful Life* when the whole town comes together to save George Bailey's bank.

"Thank you, but I won't count on it."

At home, two vital pieces of mail waited in the box—a letter fixing her unemployment hearing for January seventh and an invitation to interview with an environmental company in Billings, Montana, during the week between Christmas and the New Year. If they offered her a job, she could hardly afford to turn it down on the chance she would get six months worth of unemployment support. Even if she won her challenge against Nadia and the parish, having work trumped living off the dole any day of the week. She needed to get on that treadmill and run off her new low before she went on a crying jag again.

Chapter Twenty-Five

Dammit! Jane made a clean getaway. Merlin thought sure he'd hear her get up and shower at four a.m. in plenty of time to go downstairs and give her the sendoff she deserved, maybe a hot breakfast made while she got ready to leave, definitely a kiss sizzling enough for her to remember while she was gone. But, she'd skipped the shower and left in her rinky-dink car that turned over with a faint buzz like a bumblebee.

Between foul weather, stopping for dinner, and another wreck on the highway, he got in around ten last night. Her lights were out downstairs, and with a long day of travel ahead of her, he'd tried to be a considerate lover and let her rest, only to have her sneak away in the dark. What if someone offered her a job in Montana or her brother introduced her to some of his friends, and she returned to Chapelle only to pack her belongings and leave permanently before he found the right time and the right words?

When he got downstairs only a little artificial Christmas tree centered on a red tablecloth occupied the kitchen table, not Jane, her yellow mug, or her breakfast dishes. Tiny wooden ornaments decorated its branches and a petite manger scene sat beneath its lowest branches. Two gifts, both for him, lay nearby. She'd wrapped the long, thin one in the Sunday Comics and made a bow out of twine. The other, a box from

LeClerc's, resembled the one he had for her. He ripped them open, saving the twine and the bow from the jewelry store because Jane certainly would. Smiling, he held the cube with the falcon in flight in his palm. She did know the meaning of his name, then, understood him better than he'd thought. As for the framed ad and letter, he wasn't much for art but this had real meaning. It said he'd kept his promise and supported her one hundred percent.

The Fast 'N Fun opened at six a.m. He jogged across the street to grab a couple of hot sausage kolaches and a jumbo coffee. Hearing Jane in the back of his mind say, "Have some fruit with that," he picked up a bottle of orange juice, too. While waiting in line, a cardboard display of Christmas wrapping paper, stick-on bows, and tape caught his eye. He let two truckers move ahead and went back to select a pack of cheerful holly wrap like the necklace Jane wore for the picture session, a red bow, and tape in case he couldn't find any around the house. Milly Olinde promised to deliver his picture order around ten, and he wanted his gifts for Jane to be ready, wrapped, and sitting under that little tree when she returned even if he wouldn't be there to see her open them.

Milly made her delivery right on time, and for what he paid her, she should have included the gift wrap, but he hadn't thought to ask. Viewing the selection of photos on his laptop down at Intracoastal City, he quickly figured out she made a bundle on frames, but hell, he wasn't going to shop for them. He selected plain black for the family shot, wood rubbed with gold leaf for the sunset pose, and silver like the one in Bernard Freeman's office for the apple blossoms. The last was a little too sweet for his taste, but women liked that sort of thing. Jane sure looked pretty in her red dress against that fluffy white background and the way she looked up at him, he could stare at that all day.

He made a pile of the framed photos and managed to wrap the holly paper around them without too much trouble, but the damned bow wouldn't stick. He sat in his room looping tape around his middle finger to put on the back of the ribbon when he heard a car door slam. Could be a neighbor or even across the street. He applied the tape loop and mashed the bow onto the top of the irregularly-shaped package. Done! Below him, the kitchen door opened and closed. Someone moved around the house. Cautiously and as quietly as he could, Merlin made his way down the stairs and let himself in the front door. He smelled coffee brewing, followed his nose, but should have used his eyes. Tripping over a suitcase left in the dim hallway, he crashed into a very solid wall.

Jane appeared with a meat fork held defensively before her. She dropped it immediately and ran to his side or rather his place on the floor. "I'm sorry. The house was so quiet I thought you might still be asleep. I should have put that in the bedroom. Are you okay?"

"Yep." He shook his head, got up, and flexed all the joints in his body. "Nothing broken. How come you're here? You should be in Dallas by now."

"My flight was cancelled. Dallas is backed up because of a blizzard in the west, and my next stop is Denver where the airport is completely closed. I'm told I won't get home for Christmas. Come into the light and let me look at that bump on your head."

"Aw, you know I'm hard-headed, sweetheart. Let it

go."

"Kitchen. Now."

"Yes, ma'am. Coffee would be good. It's a cold, gray day out there."

Washing the small wound on his forehead and dabbing antibiotic cream on it, she fussed over him, and he liked it. She brought him coffee with real sugar and didn't tell him to get his own milk. Better yet, he had Jane all to himself for Christmas. Then, he took note of the red on the tip of her nose and the puffiness of her eyes, and the way her subtle eyeliner had been wiped away.

"Jane, you been crying?"

"A little. All I wanted for Christmas was to be with my family. It seems this year, I won't get anything I truly desire."

"I know a man with a big-ass truck who can get you to Montana."

"No, Merlin! That trip would take three days at best, and you'd miss Christmas with Doyle. We could get caught in a storm and not get there at all. What would be the point of that?'

"Are you done naysaying? I need to pack so we can get started. I can have you in Dallas late afternoon. We check with the airport. If you can get into Denver, I'll put you on the plane. If not, we drive there next. If that airport is still closed, we go straight on to Bozeman. It's a good plan. Consider it part of my Christmas gift to you. I have another one upstairs. Oh, and thanks for mine." Merlin stood, ready to head out.

"You opened your presents before Christmas?" Jane said as if he'd committed sacrilege.

"Wasn't any note telling me not, no. The clipping

is great if I can figure out how to hang it on those slanted beams, maybe on a wire run in between them. The falcon, I really like the falcon. It's up on my desk right now."

"Glad they made you happy, but—"

"No buts. Give me a few minutes, and we're on our way."

"If I'd known this would happen, I'd have given you a gas card," Jane mumbled.

"I wouldn't have enjoyed that half as much. Hurry up, daisy! Get ready to leave again. You got about fifteen minutes to use the bathroom and repair your makeup."

He left before she could come up with more objections. He'd get her there safe and sound, he would. Dumping his dirty laundry on the floor of his room, he freed up the duffel bag and stuffed it with handfuls of underwear, a couple of pairs of jeans, T-shirts, heavy socks, and every really warm item he owned: a navy peacoat, a couple of flannel shirts, gloves, a knit cap, a sweater made by his granny and never worn. Add his shaving kit, an extra pair of shoes and some work boots. Shove Jane's Christmas presents in there along with two other small boxes and good to go.

Still looking doubtful, Jane stood in the kitchen with her rolling suitcase and a heavy red wool coat slung over her arm. "Are you sure?"

"I'm feeling pretty positive lately. Let's go."

Chapter Twenty-Six

Despite a chill breeze and threatening skies, they cleared Dallas by early evening, leaving behind a still clogged airport. Merlin pushed on with Jane asleep on his shoulder far into the night, finally stopping for rest in Norman, Oklahoma. In the morning, they stoked up on the free breakfast offered by the hotel and headed into a wind strong enough to tangle with a big-ass truck and try to push it off the road. They made Denver by early evening, stopping there because Merlin said he had something he wanted to do in the area. Though he would never admit it, Jane suspected his arms ached from holding the truck on the road.

Denver, a city that knew how to deal with snow, had its main roads plowed, but the airport remained closed. She swore Merlin seemed pleased about that. He made a phone call, asking the person on the other end if he'd arrived too late for a visit, hung up, and told her he had to go out. Seeing his face go bleak, Jane put a hand on his arm.

"Where?"

"I'm going to see my gunner's widow. I should have done it when I got home, but didn't have the guts to face her."

"Would you like me to come with you?"

"Yes."

That one word answer told Jane enough. She got in

the truck and helped him follow the directions to a street still two feet deep in snow and lined with small homes. Merlin's big tires crunched through this insignificant barrier and carried them up a driveway beside a house with a large blue spruce in the yard and a small pine tree, the size a single woman could manage, sitting in the picture window, its Christmas lights glowing in the night. Margo Bailey opened the door immediately because who could miss the sound of Merlin's truck bearing down on them? She held a toddler, newly bathed with his red hair slicked back and clothed in footie pajamas patterned with little airplanes. They waded toward her across an unshoveled walk.

"Sorry about that. My father keeps saying he'll cover over and dig me out, but he hasn't made it yet. Come in out of the cold. So nice to meet you, Merlin Tauzin, after all my husband said about you. Can I offer you some coffee, hot chocolate?"

"No, thank you, we can't stay. This is Jane Marshall, my uh…"

"Friend and tenant," Jane said. "Merlin insisted on driving me to Bozeman to be with my parents for the holidays when the airports closed."

"Yes, I thought he'd be that kind of guy, always there for a person in a crisis." Curvaceous with dark hair framing her pretty face, Margo Bailey had wide blue eyes that held less happiness and more wisdom than she should have possessed at her young age. She led the way to the room with the Christmas tree and a single stocking hanging on the fireplace.

"I can't put gifts out yet, not until Santa comes tomorrow night, or he'll get into them." She hugged her son affectionately. "Say hi to Mr. Tauzin, Scotty." The child hid his round blue eyes in his mother's red sweater.

"I guess I'm pretty scary. I haven't shaved in two days. He looks like his daddy and has the same name."

"He's at a shy age right now. Yes, we had another name picked out but after...anyhow, I decided to name him Scott Jordan Bailey, Jr. for his father. My husband said if we had a girl we should name her Merry after you."

"Now that would be terrible to do to a little girl. Good thing the baby turned out to be a boy." Merlin kept his eyes on the child, unable to look directly at the widow, glanced at Jane, and came back to the boy.

"I want to thank you for keeping his father alive long enough to come home on leave and give me this baby."

Jane would have described the expression on Merlin's face as agony when he looked at her before blurting out, "No, don't say that! I got him killed trying to save those other men, and they were shot down later, all of them dead. Scotty died for nothing."

Frantically, Merlin dug in the pocket of his navy jacket, unbuttoned but not taken off because he wanted to flee back outside into the freezing night as quickly as possible. "I want little Scotty to have this. It won't replace his father, but..." He offered an open box holding a medal, a propeller on a starburst hanging from a red, white and blue ribbon, the Distinguished Flying Cross.

Margo folded his hand over the box. "No, you keep that for your own son someday." She gazed sideways at Jane when she said those words. "I have the Purple Heart and the Bronze Star for Scotty. We both know my husband could have died over there any day of the week by being in the wrong place at the wrong time. You tried to save some lives. He would have said 'Go for it, Magician'."

Merlin's head came up. "He did, those very words just before...but it doesn't change that he died, and I didn't. They try to shoot the pilot and got him instead because I swung my chopper around at just that moment to pick up those other guys."

"Listen to me, Merlin Tauzin. I want only two things from you. Stop blaming yourself and stay in touch. I'd like Scotty to know a man who flew with his father." With her blue eyes tear-filled, Margo wiped her face on the back of her little boy's pajamas, the ones with the airplanes on them.

"I can do that, stay in touch. I swear." He met those brave, blue eyes for the very first time.

"No need to swear. I believe you. Now, coffee, cookies?"

"No, we need to go. Maybe on my way back, I'll stop by again and take the two of you to dinner."

"If you do, I'll cook. Scotty is a bad little boy in a restaurant right now, always wanting to get down and throwing his food on the floor."

"Kids his age are like that. I have a nephew a little older. Okay, Jane, long drive ahead tomorrow. Let's get some rest."

Margo Bailey, still holding Scotty, saw them to the door. She coaxed a bye-bye wave from the boy which brought a smile to Merlin's weary face. He trudged into the snow, breaking a better path for Jane, opened the door to the truck, went around and started the engine to warm the cab. Jane hung back a minute.

"Thanks for telling him that. Maybe he'll be able to sleep at night now."

"I'm glad I could help. You are more to him than he can say, you know. He must have looked at you half a dozen times as if you were holding his lifeline."

Jane shook her head. "But he won't say."

"He got these words out, and that must have been hard. Don't give up on him, Jane."

"People keep telling me that. I'll try a little longer."

"Come on, woman! We're wasting precious fossil fuel here," Merlin called.

Somehow, those words made her feel better, too.

\*\*\*\*

Jane braced herself for the nightmare, stayed awake anticipating Merlin's thrashing and frantic calls for backup because the visit with Margo Bailey must have brought every excruciating minute of his ordeal to the forefront of his mind. She waited to talk him down, then put her arms around him and hold him for the rest of the evening. She could afford the loss of rest because no way would he allow her to drive Big Blue through the snow, and she could sleep while he steered.

Merlin slept deeply, barely moving by her side, allowing her too much time in the darkest hours of the night to think of their relationship if he ever admitted they had one. He'd certainly been unable to define it for Margo, the understanding widow of his best friend, mother of a sweet, fatherless boy, but that pretty-faced woman pegged Merlin perfectly. Always there for a person in a crisis. That said it all. Would he now feel an obligation to care for Margo and Scotty, enter their lives and stay there permanently, maybe offering marriage out of guilt or a growing affection after several months of contact?

"How jealous and petty can you be, Jane?" she muttered in the dark. If Merlin could leave her that easily, he did not love her in the first place. She waited, not realizing she'd finally fallen asleep until the sound of Merlin in the shower made her open her gritty eyes.

They got another early start following the trail of freight-hauling big rigs that heated the paving of the road and cleared the interstate. Out of Colorado and into Wyoming, they moved steadily north through steep, rolling hills where snow fences held back the drifts from the traffic below. The sky stayed a frigid pale blue until Merlin's truck crossed into Montana. Wooly, gray clouds rolled in, and the flakes began to fall hard enough to warrant using the windshield wipers. At a pit stop for gas, bathrooms, and hot coffee in Billings, the convenience store owner, a Sikh with a beard and turban, warned them the road ahead would be closed by the blizzard before they reached Bozeman. He might have been an all-seeing, all-knowing swami because his prediction became true right outside of Livingston where the big-ass truck got shunted onto a side road by a line of orange traffic cones and closed gates across the interstate.

Merlin held their vehicle slow and steady on the loop of back roads they traversed. He made his way down the middle of the road certain he'd see the headlights of any oncoming cars through the heavy sheet of snow, and they would notice the sharp, blue-white glow of his LEDs in plenty of time to pull aside. Jane, not so certain, dug her nails into the leather seat cushion and held her breath on every turn. When the inevitable happened and another insane driver trundling along through the heavy weather in a big SUV approached, Merlin began his gradual journey toward the side of his lane. As the SUV pushed past, the big tires of the truck hit ice and went into a slow fishtail toward a huge snow bank. The truck's rear end thumped against something hard and straightened out again in Merlin's skilled hands. Still, he stopped, backed up slowly, and turned on the spotlights across the top of the cab.

"This is really no time to check for dents," Jane chided.

"It's not dents that worry me. We hit something way sturdier than a pile of snow."

He drew on the black knit cap that made him look like a thug or a longshoreman and his gloves, buttoned up the navy peacoat, and got out to do an inspection. Jane watched as he probed the snow bank. An icy crust fell away from a white fender where the truck hit. Beneath that, two black tires canted into the air as Merlin gradually exposed the rear of an old van nose down in a shallow ditch. He swept off a softer covering and revealed a large rear window. The spotlights penetrated the interior. Without hesitation, Merlin climbed into the rear of his truck, cleared the snow off of his toolbox, and took out a hammer. Shielding his eyes, he smashed the van's window and cleared the jagged edges of glass with his coat sleeve.

Jane opened her door. "What on earth are you doing? That's vandalism!"

He reached inside the stranded van and lifted out one small body, then another, two rosy cheeked, well-bundled unconscious children. He laid them in Jane's arms.

"Try to wake them. Keep them in the fresh air."

He returned to the van and snaked himself inside, returning with a groggy woman and dragging her through the opening. Lightly slapping her flushed cheeks, Merlin urged her to breathe deep.

"Where's my husband, my kids?"

"Your children are over there with Jane. I don't see any man around."

"He went…he went for help after we slid off the road. I kept the motor running for heat. Got so sleepy, the children all quiet in the back."

Jane jostled the larger boy, the smaller girl with her knees. "Wake up, wake up, wake up, please, wake up." For your mother, for Merlin, for me.

Shoving his duffel aside, Merlin helped the woman into the truck. He rummaged under a seat and brought out a thin square of silver cloth, flipped it open. "An emergency blanket, warmer than it looks. We need to keep the windows down for a while. We'll look for your husband along the way. Jane, how are the kids?"

She started to say unresponsive when the boy opened a pair of large gray eyes so beautifully fringed with long, dark lashes they should have belonged to his sister. "Mom?" he said.

"Right here, baby. Come under this cover with me."

Merlin made the transfer from Jane's lap. "Don't let him go to sleep again, okay? Jane, keep the daughter up front and work on her. We'll search for the dad as we go."

With everyone stowed, he killed the spotlights that made a blinding white wall of the falling snow and eased the truck forward. Slowly, it crunched along, one mile, two. They approached a short bridge over a small river.

"There," he said, stopping the truck by a break in a drift going down to the water. A flicker of light went on and off like the tail of a firefly. Once more, he turned on the spotlight but saw nothing. Getting out, he moved carefully to the brink of the hole. The light flickered again.

"Help me!"

"We'll get you out." Into the bed of the truck again, he found a length of yellow nylon rope and tied it to the silver knob of his trailer hitch. "I'm throwing down a rope. Can you pull yourself up?"

"Don't think so. My arm is broken."

"Can you tie it around yourself or just hang on?"

"Yes, I'll try."

Merlin gave the unseen man a few moments before starting the truck again. He angled its body across the road until he could go no farther. Leaving the cab, he pulled the rope up the remainder of the way until a hunter's cap appeared on the verge, then the head and torso of a man clinging on for dear life with the rope doubled wrapped around a gloved hand. Merlin offered a strong shoulder for support and helped the fellow to the truck. He got his burden into the backseat and placed the husband under the blanket with his family.

All the while, Jane continued to pat the little girl with the rosy cheeks of a baby doll and a fringe of blonde curls peeking out beneath her pompom cap as if she were burping a baby. "Breathe deep, breathe deep, breathe deep." The child gasped and vomited on her shoulder and the back of the leather seat. "Oh, I'm so sorry, Merlin. I did not see that coming."

"Makes no never-mind at all. Be back in a minute."

He retrieved his rope and coiled it into the toolbox, took out some rags, and handed them to Jane. "Please tell me there is a hospital in frickin' Bozeman because I'm driving a fuckin' ambulance right now, not a truck."

"Said a bad word," the little girl murmured.

Merlin laughed. "I do think she'll live."

"Mommy, want Mommy." She held out her hands toward the backseat. Jane hoisted her over to join her family.

"There is a hospital not too far off the main road."

"Thank the Lord God and Baby Jesus for that. Everyone ready? We got thirty more miles to go in this crap. Another reason you should stay in Louisiana, Jane. No snow!"

"And the others would be…" she thought but did not say.

Chapter Twenty-Seven

Rescuing and dropping the entire McAllistair family off at the hospital to be treated for carbon monoxide poisoning, hypothermia, and the single broken arm set their arrival time back two hours. On Jane's directions, Merlin turned into an old neighborhood that had hit rock bottom judging by the huge, rundown houses turned into apartments momentarily made lovely by the coating of snow. They stopped on a street in the process of clawing its way up again with a row of beautiful restorations. Midnight approached by the time they parked in front of a three-story Victorian home with fish scale shingles ornamenting its gables and dainty spindles enclosing a generous porch. Considering the many lights in the windows, Jane's family, all of them, waited up.

Someone had cleared the walkway to the front door earlier in the day, but six inches of new snow now filled the gap. Merlin lifted Jane down and sent her ahead while he retrieved his duffel and her suitcase, hefting the first over his shoulder and carrying the luggage without the assistance of the sissy wheels. The tall door decorated with a sizeable holly, fir, and pinecone wreath opened. A sparkling chandelier hanging from an ornate ceiling medallion illuminated the family standing in the hall. Not humble Cajun cottage people and definitely not trailer trash, they pressed forward to embrace Jane. Merlin stayed on the other side of the threshold like a vampire who needed an invitation to enter.

"We thought you were dead in a ditch!" exclaimed an elderly lady, who most likely had been Jane's size once but had been boiled down to tiny by age. She wore a soft powder blue quilted robe with matching slippers and gazed at Merlin with Jane's green eyes set in a soft lacework of wrinkles. Her straight white hair, beautifully cut and styled, gleamed under the light from the fixture. "Come in, come in, you'll catch your death of cold, not to mention upping the size of our heating bill."

A second set of green eyes belonged to an earth mother of a woman with large, soft breasts swaying beneath her red flannel nightgown covered over with a plaid wool shawl, and fluffy gray socks on her feet. A braided rope of silver hair lay over her shoulder. She stepped close as Merlin entered.

"You must be Merlin, the falcon. Yes, I can see the spirits of the air in those eyes. I'm Kathleen Marshall, Jane's mother."

Not knowing what else to say, he responded with, "Nice to meet you, ma'am."

The grandmother snorted, but ordered a shaggy dark-haired young man approaching thirty forward to help with the bags. A close-cropped beard framed his face. He stood with his graybeard father, both tall and amber of eye, sharing a strong family resemblance and waiting for the women to stop hugging and gabbing so they could get a word in edgewise. Obviously, both had stayed dressed in heavy jeans, boots, and flannel shirts in case they had to mount a rescue mission in the middle of the night. The Marshall males sized up Merlin like wolves considering whether to admit a new member to the pack. He stared right back at them, not about to cower or show his soft underbelly even if the grandeur of the house unnerved him.

"Heath, the luggage," the grandmother repeated again. "You know where Jane's room is. The one at the end of the upstairs hall is for our guest."

Jane's brother came forward and participated in a minor tug of war over the suitcase. Merlin let him win, but he hung onto his duffel. "I'll carry it up. I should get some sleep before I turn around and head back to Louisiana tomorrow."

"Absolutely not! You are not going to spend Christmas Day on the road. Take off your coats and come into the front parlor instead of standing in this drafty hallway. Visit with us a while, then you can sleep in as long as you like tomorrow. That's the one advantage of not having any grandchildren yet. No need to get up early to open the gifts. Now, why so late?" Kathleen Marshall helped Jane out of her heavy red coat and sniffed at the collar. "Did you have to stop because you were carsick? When we got your call from Billings, I said you should have stayed the night there with the weather getting worse."

"No, Mom, a little girl barfed on me after we rescued her family, or rather Merlin did. That's why we're so late," Jane explained.

She began to unbutton Merlin's jacket since he hadn't made a move to take it off. Tugging on a sleeve, she forced him to put down the duffel and relinquish the peacoat. She hung it on the brass hook of an impressive coat rack complete with a mirror, a seat for removing boots and topped with a rack of huge elk antlers providing extra space for an array of knitted scarves and mittens. He removed his black watch cap, placed it on one of the prongs, and smoothed his ruffled hair with one large hand.

Jane steered him into a high-ceiling room with a ten foot Christmas tree and a fire burning bright in the hearth. He expected mahogany antiques but found comfortable easy chairs with hassocks and a long, deep coffee-colored sofa where he took the offered seat. His booted feet touched the edge of a black bearskin rug beneath the coffee table, actually a flat-topped chest so worn with use its painted pattern was difficult to discern. Before claiming one of the armchairs, her father offered Merlin his hand for a firm shake.

"Roy Marshall. You already met my wife, Kathleen, and my mother-in-law, Ellen Draper. Heath will be back in a minute. That sounds like quite a story you have to tell."

Merlin nodded and said not a word. When Heath returned and threw himself into the other armchair, the women lined up on the sofa like tiny birds perched on a wide branch with Jane next to Merlin. She did the squawking.

"We had to leave the highway in Livingston and came across an old van covered with snow in a ditch. Merlin broke the back window and carried two children and a woman out. They had carbon monoxide poisoning, but we got there in time. Then, we found the husband where he'd fallen into a ravine when he went too close to the soft edge of the road in the snow. His arm was broken."

Heath, legs up on an ottoman and hands behind his

head, said kind of snarky, "I suppose you went down there and carried him up on your mighty back."

"Nope. Because that would be dumb, leaving the women and children alone and maybe getting trapped down there with him. He was conscious. I threw him a rope and towed him out with my truck as far as I could, then pulled him the rest of the way. If he hadn't been signaling with a flashlight, I suspect we might have driven right on by, and no one would have found him before a thaw."

"Merlin saved four lives tonight. The doctor said so at the hospital," Jane answered, flashing a glare at her brother.

"Four rescued. Three more and I'll be even."

Looking into Merlin's eyes, Jane caged his long, bristled jaw in her hands and shook his head side to side. "No, you do not get to keep score. Only God is allowed to do that, and I am fairly sure He is pleased with you."

Kathleen Marshall peered around her daughter. "Do you see, Roy, they have a cosmic connection. I knew it. And exactly how do you know that God isn't a Goddess, Jane?"

Her brother laughed. "Yeah, Jane, what do you know? Mom, I think they call those vibes sexual attraction these days."

"Sometimes I hate you, Heath Cliff Marshall!" Jane shot back.

"Heathcliff—like one those seagulls on the old Red Skelton show? My granny loved to watch the reruns." Merlin actually smiled, imagining Jane's hostile brother with his arms tucked in his pits like a bird.

"Oh, my yes! Mr. Skelton could be so funny

without being dirty like the comedians today. The other bird was Gertrude. We could have named Jane that," her grandmother twittered.

"No, Mother. Heathcliff as in *Wuthering Heights*. You know that. Have you read it, Merlin?" Kathleen waited for his answer.

"Nope. We had a list we could choose from in school. I did *Red Badge of Courage* instead."

"Did you like it?"

"Not much. The kid ran away and let his fellow soldiers down."

"It is an anti-war novel, you must understand. Now, *Jane Eyre* is my favorite book, which is how Jane got her name. Have you read that?"

Merlin settled for shaking his head and suppressing his grin. "So, Jane Eyre Marshall. What else don't I know about you?"

"She's afraid of spiders and snakes," her brother offered.

"That I already figured out, thanks."

"Quiet, Heath. Honestly, you sound like a six-year-old. She wouldn't fear them if you hadn't put them in her bed and her shoes all the time. They are simply creatures of the earth we all share. Well, feel free to borrow my copy of *Jane Eyre* while you are here, Merlin. You have much in common with Mr. Rochester."

"Mom was an English lit major and taught at the high school level once she went back to college and got her ed credits," Jane explained. "Could we leave the literary discussions for tomorrow? Merlin is tired. I am exhausted. See you in the morning."

Jane rose and took his hand almost protectively.

"Let me show you the way."

"Separate bedrooms under my roof," her grandmother called after them.

Cheeks burning, Jane got them out of the parlor. Merlin grabbed his duffel in the hall, and they started up the staircase with its banister garlanded in evergreens and red bows. She stopped outside his bedroom door. "See, I told you my family wasn't perfect. Overbearing brother, nutty mother, very opinionated grandmother, and a quiet, stay out of it kind of dad. Oh, you scored big with Gran knowing about Red Skelton."

"Yeah, they love me at Magnolia Villa. Still, your family is a lot better than mine. This house—"

"Is all Grandma has left. The Drapers lost their fortune in the great stock market crash of '29, the year she came into the world. The place was falling down around her after my grandfather died and before my parents moved back here and made repairs. It's a grand money pit. Give me a minute to get in my flannel nightie, and I'll join you. Not very sexy, but this place is so damned drafty."

"No, we should honor your grandmother's rules."

"What the…"

He stopped her with his kiss. Touching, feeling, lip-locked, they lingered in the hall until Heath caught them in the act and said, "Get a room. No, don't! Get to your rooms, your separate rooms. Mom and Dad will be up here in a minute."

"*Parting is such sweet sorrow*. Shakespeare," Merlin said.

"*Get thee to a nunnery*. Hamlet," her brother replied, and they parted.

\*\*\*\*

The wind howled around the house like wolves closing in on prey and shoved paws of frigid air under the aged window frames. Tired as he was from fighting ice and snow, Merlin could not rest. Strange how quickly he'd become accustomed to having Jane pressed against him at night whether they had sex or not. The down comforter on the four-poster bed settled snugly around his body keeping him plenty warm, so that wasn't the problem.

Not thinking to buy pajamas somewhere along the way, he kept his briefs and a T-shirt on in case he had what Jane called his "episodes," putting a nice name to it. If he started to rave and run into the hall, her family would know him for a nut case, but at least he wouldn't be a naked nut case. Much as he respected the aged for their wisdom and endurance despite life's tragedies, he wanted the comfort of Jane.

Rolling out from under the feather blanket, he put his bare feet on the cold floorboards and with goose bumps rising on his flesh made his way to the door. Cracking it open, he surveyed the hall illuminated along its length by a couple of nightlights. He'd watched Jane go into her room strategically placed between her parents and her brother almost like the way the old Cajuns guarded their daughters from men like him. No sound out there, not even a mouse. He cracked a grin at that Christmas Eve chestnut. Carefully moving to her door, he tried the knob—unlocked as if she anticipated he might join her. Entering and closing it softly, he let his eyes adjust to dimness, no tripping over suitcases this time. Beyond the lace curtains, the snow had stopped, and though the wind still whipped the treetops, a cold moon shed some light on the rumpled covers of the bed.

No Jane. He went back to the door, opened it a crack and listened. Below, the ping of a microwave sounded. Having trouble resting herself, she'd gone to make some chamomile tea he was sure. He didn't flatter himself that she missed him too much to sleep. Shutting the door again, he got into her bed and fit himself into the warm spot she'd left behind. He put his arms around her pillow and wrapped in her light, fresh scent, he slept.

Chapter Twenty-Eight

Jane left the kitchen with herbal tea in hand and started the return to her room when her grandmother called out from the rear parlor where she slept now that the stairs had become too much for her. "Jane, it that you?"

"Yes, Gran. Just making some tea. You want some?" She peeked inside the room to find her grandmother sitting up in bed, light on, a book opened on her covers.

"I would. My arthritis isn't letting me sleep, and those pills upset my stomach."

"Take mine. I'll make another."

By the time she returned with a second cup, her mother sat by the bedside in a little needlepoint chair helping Ellen remove the gloves she wore to soothe her knotted hands. Her grandmother wrapped her fingers around the warmth of the cup and took a sip. "Good, thank you, Jane."

"You want some, too, Mom?"

"No. I heard people talking and came down to see if I was needed. Mother's ears, you never lose them after you have kids. You couldn't sleep?"

"You know how it goes, exhausted but can't rest after all the stuff going on." Jane set her tea on the nightstand and brought a matching chair to place beside her mother. The fact that her grandmother had once

279

sewn well enough to make the floral seat covers wrung her heart. Arthritis took that skill from Ellen and left her unoccupied and peevish.

"You miss Merlin in your bed. It is perfectly fine with me if you want to sleep with him." Her mother patted Jane's hand in understanding.

"Kathleen, do not encourage her! This Merlin, well, he seems rather unrefined for a college educated young woman."

"Opposites attract, Mother. Remember the petroleum engineer and the hippie who wanted to save the earth?"

"Only too well. I could never divine what a normal man like Roy saw in you unless it was all the free love you were spreading around in the Sixties."

"Joining the commune was not about free love! We wanted pure air, food, and water."

"And drugs."

"We did not pollute our bodies with drugs. Well, maybe a little pot, and there was that one LSD trip, but nothing on a regular basis. Oh, Jane, the last owner sold the commune land for condo building a few months ago. Soon the apple orchard where your father and I were married will be bulldozed, gone forever. Remember, we used to take you and Heath for picnics there whenever we visited from Louisiana." Her mother took a tissue from the sleeve of her nightgown and dabbed her eyes.

Jane nodded. "The hillside with all the gnarled old trees is a beautiful place."

"If you had married in a church like regular people instead of barefoot in an orchard this would not be a problem. The place would still be standing," her grandmother snapped. "Now you've distracted me. I meant to talk to Jane about this Merlin fellow. He is rather a great big brute, isn't he?"

"He's a hunk, in my opinion," Kathleen said.

"Yes, crude and hunky on the outside, but inside he cares deeply for his family and the land. He torments himself about things he cannot fix or change. Merlin is trying to get my old job back and restore recycling in the parish. He bought my house to help me. I mean there is much more to him than his looks and his big-ass truck," Jane tried to explain.

"Such raw language, Jane. Well, I'll give him credit for helping you and for loving his grandmother and Red Skelton, but otherwise…" her grandmother started in again.

"The man is a freakin' war hero, Mother. The Distinguished Flying Cross, flies helicopters for a living, two years of college, no real criminal record, only a small brush with the law in high school and a sentence of community service. Jane is twenty-four, and the man pool is drying up, especially in a small town like Chapelle. Don't you want to see your great-grandchildren?"

"Of course I do, but this man—"

Jane held up a hand. "Wait, wait! How do you know so much about Merlin?"

"Google, a great big article in the hometown newspaper about him when he came home from the war all decorated with a DFC medal and the silver star, too. A contact of your father's at the police department checked on him for us. Well, you wouldn't tell me anything about him. I got curious."

"Because I wanted to avoid having everyone judge

him before you met him. You might as well know he suffers from PTSD, has terrible nightmares and some depression all because he served his country. He is gradually getting better."

"Yes, war destroys more than countries. You know how I feel about war, but when I looked into his very striking blue eyes, I saw a man who had always been a fighter of one kind or another. Mother, you can't deny his bravery."

Her grandmother sniffed, but not as she had earlier in the evening. "I thought you saw the spirits of the air in his eyes, Kathleen. A tissue please," she said, but the elderly woman's voice wobbled.

Jane handed Ellen a tissue from a porcelain caddy on the nightstand. She took a deep breath and a sip of her rapidly cooling tea. Fat chance she'd get any sleep after this discussion.

"I wrote to your grandfather all during World War II. We were high school sweethearts before he got drafted. I married him the minute he returned from the war—nothing fancy but in a church, not an apple orchard." Ellen's eyes blurred with nostalgia.

"I was eighteen and wore a gray suit with a white orchid on the collar. He was twenty-one, so handsome in his uniform. But he fought at Normandy and had nightmares about that for the rest of his life, though they faded with time. Do you remember, Kathleen? He'd get to feeling low in early June and shut himself up in our library for a day or two and drink. I'd hide the guns."

Kathleen nodded. "Another reason I'm anti-war."

"Your father worked so hard rebuilding the family business. Having a purpose helped, he said. Of course, we couldn't sell supplies to miners anymore. That market was long gone. He branched out at the store. Do you recall our lovely gift department? I used to select the items. Then late in his life along comes these big box stores and poof! No more business. You'd think there would be some customer loyalty to a store that gave free gift wrap and delivery, but no. I'm not sure which killed him, losing the store or the trip we made to the World War II monument that made him cry."

"I think flying helps Merlin to cope, Gran. He's given up drinking."

"Of course his hawk spirit would be soothed by open skies," Kathleen remarked.

"Nonsense. It's Jane who made a difference in his life. Even I can see that."

Glad the little snit with her mother had dried Gran's tears, Jane stood. "I should try to sleep."

"Go to Merlin. Love is all that matters. I could see how he feels about you in his beautiful eyes," her mother said, placing gentle fingers over Ellen's lips to hold the protest back.

The dappled, arthritic hand pushed the fingers away. "Those eyes of his are getting awfully crowded with all the things you've seen in them, Kathleen. The point is do you love him, Jane?"

"Yes, though how I fell for a man with a big-ass truck I will never know."

"Then go with my blessing, too."

"Thanks, both of you."

She went upstairs and headed directly for the last room at the end of the hall. He'd left the door unlocked. She smiled tenderly and entered. Missing. For a moment she thought he'd gotten in his truck and fled her family, but no, she would have heard the roar of his huge Ford engine in her deepest sleep. His duffel still sat half collapsed on the freezing floor, the clothes he'd worn earlier heaped beside it. Maybe he'd put on something warmer and gone for a walk. Snow would be a novelty to him even though he'd been cursing it for hours. Or maybe just a trip to the bathroom in the middle of the hall. She checked that out. Not there. Might as well go back to her own bed.

She found Merlin, a very rugged version of Prince Charming, clutching one pillow to his chest and hogging the other, sound asleep. Jane slipped in beside him very tempted to put her icy feet on his backside. He slept so deeply and needed the rest so badly she refrained and settled for reclaiming half a pillow and placing her arm over his side.

"Jane," he murmured and tucked the arm under his without completely waking.

Now that she had what she desired, sleep came quick and heavy, but when she woke far too late in the morning, Merlin the Magician had vanished again.

## Chapter Twenty-Nine

He left her bed as soon as he woke and placing a kiss on Jane's cheek, went to the bathroom to clean up, but didn't shower for fear of waking her and everyone else in the house. With four days growth of beard, he fit right in with the men of the house in looks if nothing else. They knew he wasn't good enough for their family, especially for Jane. He realized that himself when he entered their house and saw how they lived. Hell, if they got to know him any better, the whole bunch of them would convince her not to return to Louisiana at all. He should let her go, stop trying to get her to stay in Chapelle until he got his act together.

In his isolated bedroom, he put on his heaviest jeans, thick socks and boots, a dark blue T-shirt, and topped it with green, blue and white flannel. Rummaging in the duffel, he found the Christmas gift and laid it aside on the bed while he shoved his dirty clothes on top and cinched it shut. An early morning Santa with a black beard, he threw the sack over his shoulder and took it and the present downstairs. Setting the duffel in a corner by the front door, he went into the parlor.

The tiny LED lights on the tall, fresh tree glowed amid the branches. Had the Marshalls left them on all night? He placed the gift for Jane far under its bows and noticed on the way up that all the decorations were homemade or handmade: glittering curlicues cut from aluminum pie tins, reindeer made from clothes pins, beaded candy canes, needlepoint angels, and a little picture frame created from puzzle pieces containing a snapshot of Jane in first or second grade with almost the same haircut she wore now.

He held it up for a closer look and nearly tipped the tree over when a hearty voice behind him said, "Up early? Great. I'm making waffles for the ladies who are all still in bed. I heard them down here having a hen party around two a.m. How are you with a skillet? I need a man on the bacon. This way to the kitchen," Mr. Marshall beckoned.

Merlin steadied the wobbling fir tree. "I can manage a frying pan."

He followed the leader down the hall past a closed door. Roy Marshall put a finger to his lips rimmed by that short, gray professorial beard and mouthed, "Mother-in-law." They entered a large airy kitchen, and Roy quietly closed the door behind them.

"Your skillet, sir." He presented Merlin with a heavy piece of cast iron.

"My granny had one just like this. My mother owns it now. Where's the bacon?"

Roy pointed to a slab on the cutting board. "Slice it thick and fry it greasy since I'm cooking today. When you're done, pour the fat into that orange juice can. Kathy puts it outside to harden, then rolls it in seeds for the birds."

Merlin turned up the gas under the skillet giving it time to heat while he cut the bacon to order. The view from the window over the sink showed a large backyard full of mature, leafless trees coated with an icing of snow and a backdrop of dark firs similarly capped. Bird feeders, wind chimes, and shining glass baubles hung from all the low branches. He suspected the drifts hid other yard art probably made from scraps. A pair of nuthatches crept up a bare trunk toward a wire basket filled with suet, and chickadees flitted with other small birds, dashing to and from the feeders and back into the bushes again.

"A wonder the birds aren't chased off by the decorations and all that tinging," he remarked.

"They get used to the noise exactly like us. Food trumps fear in the dead of winter."

Merlin laid the bacon on the well-seasoned cast iron. In moments, the fat began to spit and sizzle. He turned the first batch over with a long fork Roy put in his hand. A second door on the far end of the kitchen opened, and Heath entered yawning from the hallway that skirted the other side of the staircase.

"I smelled bacon. When's breakfast?"

"After you squeeze the orange juice and make the coffee, son. We're treating the ladies today." Roy retrieved a bottle of maple syrup from a shelf and poured it into a saucepan. "Hot syrup is the way to their hearts." He put it over a low flame. "That and fresh orange juice, so get squeezing."

Reluctantly, Heath took a bag of oranges from the fridge, began cutting them in half and reaming out the juice. He took a half-hearted break from that to set up a fancy coffeemaker with enough buttons on it to please a barista. Roy whisked his from-scratch waffle batter in a huge yellow bowl and tested a griddle ready to produce four deep Belgians at a time. Merlin drained the bacon on paper towels and started another batch.

He thought people like this would eat in a fancy dining room, but a large butcher block table surrounded by six ladder back chairs filled much of the space. Placemats made from woven reeds and a large wooden bowl filled with fresh fruit showed the family ate here often. He could see where Jane got her nice ways. The light, color, and warmth were the same in her small kitchen.

"Not much of a talker, are you, Merlin?" Roy said as he poured the batter.

"Nope. Jane said the same about you—that you were quiet."

But not today. Jane's father chatted away nonstop.

"I live with three women who never stop talking. They only think I'm quiet. Once Heath moved out, no way I could compete. I have to get my talking out when I teach my geology classes." Roy rummaged in a drawer and took out flatware and white huck cloth napkins with a lacy blue pattern woven in and out around the edges. He set the table, went back to check his waffles, and figured he had enough time to light a candle in a small warmer and set a little white pitcher of hot maple syrup on it.

"Yeah, Jane always wants me to use my words." Merlin finished frying the bacon, poured the grease into the juice can, and turned down the flame. He set the skillet aside to cool.

"Which brings me to what words you might want to say to my daughter. What are your intentions toward Jane, young man?"

"Yeah, what are they? I heard a lot of creeping around last night," Heath chimed in belligerently.

Jane's brother severed another orange with a very

sharp knife taken from a block full of them. The amber eyes of father and son bored into Merlin's heart. He was not prey. He did not run—except from Jane when his feelings got too strong to handle.

"If I was good enough, I'd ask her to marry me. She deserves better."

"Damn straight," Heath agreed.

Roy Marshall sampled the batch of bacon. He chewed thoughtfully. "Good job. Not burnt, meaty, rich. Despite this house, we aren't wealthy, just comfortable. We don't think we're better than other folks. Now, I got the impression last night you despise cowards, but isn't this a form of cowardice? Not asking so Jane has no chance to turn you down—or accept."

"Right! Man up or get out." Heath pressed a button on the coffeemaker and filled a metal pot with steamed milk. Artfully, he made himself a latte letting the steam rise in Merlin's face.

Eye to eye, Merlin said to Jane's brother, "Unless you have proposed to a woman or dodged an RPG, do not tell me to man up." Heath leaned back a little but refused to budge.

They might as well have been exchanging growls when the far kitchen door opened and Jane entered wearing bunny slippers and a fluffy pink chenille robe far heavier than she wore in Louisiana. Though she hadn't dressed, Merlin noticed she'd put on makeup and fixed her hair.

"*Bon jour*, bun…Jane," he said casually, relaxing his stance and stepping away from her brother. He almost slipped there and said something sexist.

"Merlin, are you intimidating my brother with your crazy act?"

"Maybe."

"Good, he deserves to be taken down a notch. Waffles! Dad, you are so great."

"With hot maple syrup and some very good bacon fried up by our guest."

Roy rated a big hug. Evidently, bacon got you nothing. Or maybe Jane didn't want to hug him in front of her family. He had no time to consider which because the other door opened to let in a slowly progressing Ellen using a three-pronged cane. Kathleen walked behind her. Both women were attired exactly the same as last evening.

Merlin pulled out a chair for Jane's grandmother who responded with, "How nice of you. I will limber up later in the day. I always wake with stiff joints."

"He does nice things like that all the time," Jane hurried to say.

Not to be outdone, Roy provided the same service for his wife, but Heath let his sister seat herself. Roy opened the waffle maker.

"Four perfect waffles. One for each of our ladies and the last for our guest. Sit down, Merlin. Be at ease. Heath, get the butter while I start another batch. Place your orders for coffee and fresh-squeezed orange juice. After breakfast, pictures and presents!" Roy rubbed his hands together with pretend avarice. "Wait until you see what I got for you, my goddess." He kissed the top of Kathleen's silver head.

My goddess, good. Bunnikins, most likely bad. And no escape from learning how classy people celebrated Christmas. Merlin guessed it wasn't with twelve packs of Bud topped with a red ribbon like the ones he'd left for Harley and Doyle.

Chapter Thirty

After a breakfast that turned into brunch, the ladies scrambled to get dressed before Roy started snapping pictures. Jane reappeared in a soft, clingy forest green cashmere sweater over brown wool slacks, short black boots on her feet and her holly necklace around her throat. Kathleen helped her mother into a ruby velvet pantsuit with a froth of lace at the neck and placed little red gems in her earlobes for the special occasion. Once Ellen had settled on the couch, she went off to don a voluminous caftan of red and gold brocade and wrap her braid into a crown atop her head. She tucked sprigs of real holly snipped from the Christmas decorations into her hair and returned to the parlor looking like the spirit of Christmas Past in all her splendor. As she sat next to her mother, the toes of her flat gold slippers peeked out from under her ensemble. While the gifts were still wrapped Roy, the family shutterbug, snapped a picture of his ladies and one of the Christmas tree.

"Stockings first!" Kathleen announced gleefully.

Merlin, taking a seat next to Jane again, found a long, lumpy hand-knitted red sock fringed with gold balls around the top resting in his lap. The others merrily dumped out small packages from theirs and laid into them. Favorite candies, scented soaps, paperback books, small bottles of perfume and cologne, sacks of premium nuts and exotic teas emerged.

Heath, already unwrapping and indulging in a piece of a chocolate orange, glanced over at the stocking still lying across Merlin's knees. "Something wrong with yours?" he asked.

"Ah, nope. I didn't expect anything is all."

"It's not much. We didn't know you were coming until yesterday and with the weather so bad, we had to make do with things around the house," Kathleen apologized. "Please," she gestured for him to dump his stocking.

All eyes on him now, he began opening the small gifts: a package of buffalo jerky, some elk sausage sticks, a little box of chocolates, a jar of huckleberry jelly, an obviously used paperback copy of *Jane Eyre,* and, filling most of the heel and toe, a knitted red and white striped wool scarf of some length unfurling endlessly like a magician's trick.

"This is great, all great. Thank you."

"I added the *Jane Eyre* last night after I heard you hadn't read it. I get used copies at the library book sale to give to people and always have a good supply. The jam is mine. I gather my own organic huckleberries. My mother made the scarf. She can't do fine needlework anymore, but she knits hats and scarves for the homeless."

Knowing how ridiculous he would look, Merlin wrapped the long, candy-cane striped scarf around his neck. "Love it, ma'am."

Ellen beamed at him. "Wait until you see what's under the tree for you."

He waited with dread while the family exchanged bigger gifts, though they tended toward lovely editions of classic books, DVD sets ordered from Public

Broadcasting, and gift cards for museum shops for the women with hunting-fishing sort of stuff for the men like antique lures and certificates for outdoors stores. A bulky package delivered to Merlin revealed a hat and mittens to match his scarf. The cap had a large red pompom on top.

He nodded at Ellen. "Now I'm ready for a Montana winter." Thank God he would never need to wear the striped ensemble in Louisiana where people knew him as Blackie.

Heath tossed him a box. "From me and Dad. We make and collect them."

Merlin opened his package to reveal a horn-handled hunting knife with a pretty nice heft and balance. He tossed it from hand to hand. "Sweet," he said.

"One of our best," Roy assured him. "You seemed like a man who could appreciate a fine knife. Take good care of it now."

"I swear I will."

"Here." Jane took two packages from under the tree and handed them to the men in her family. "For your collections."

They unwrapped two small knives with large alligator teeth for handles that obviously pleased them. Jane's family certainly had more going for it than intellect. Her presents for her mother and granny turned out to be necklaces formed of handcrafted silver gingko leaves.

"Jane, you are unemployed! I do love it, but you shouldn't have spent the money," her mother scolded.

"I bought them before my job imploded. Enjoy."

"One more way back here," Heath said. "No name

on it."

"For Jane from me." Merlin winced a little when he confessed that. He'd planned to be miles away by now, safe from any repercussions in his big-ass truck.

Jane smiled at him as if the clumsy wrapping and the stick-on bow outshone every other gift she'd received. Then, she stripped off the paper and stared at the photographs, the one of her and Merlin staring into the fake sunset on top, then the apple blossom extravaganza, and the family grouping.

He felt the need to explain. "Jane and me, we watch the sunset together most nights when it isn't cloudy. My granny wanted her in the family picture and really liked those apple blossoms for some reason. I mean, I got different photos as gifts for the whole family like one of my mom and stepdad on a beach." Brittney would be happy with her family picture that excluded Jane, he knew.

"Well, pass them around, Jane," her mother prompted. "Oh, my," she said as the frames made their way from her hands to Ellen's gnarled fingers.

Merlin studied his boot toes. He knew what the Marshalls would see: his mother and sister in their cheap, inappropriate dresses, Harley with all his facial hair still looking like a biker even when he wore a suit, himself pawing their daughter with his big hands around her waist.

Ellen studied one of the photos. "Heath, go into the library and put on my Andrews Sisters' album. I want *Apple Blossom Time*." As her grandson left the parlor, she confided. "He installed the sound system all by himself. We can get music in any room, even the bathroom, but Heath is the only one who can operate it."

Of course, the Marshalls had a library, probably crammed floor to ceiling with books, and a damned good sound system, too. The old sentimental song from the World War II era filled the air. "*I'll be with you in Apple Blossom Time. I'll be with you to change your name to mine.*" Ellen's green eyes grew watery.

"Clayton and I married during apple blossom time, the first one after he came home from the war. They played this at our reception."

Jane's eyes misted over, too, but Kathleen let her tears flow and splash on her caftan turning the red brocade dark. "Our apple orchard where Roy and I married will soon be gone, uprooted for condos."

Helpless before so many emotional women, Merlin said, "I'm-uh…sorry?" not sure if he meant to sympathize with Jane's mother or apologize for the damn picture that set them all off.

Roy Marshall raised his wife and took her into his arms. "Don't cry, my lovely. You have one more gift to open." He took a flat packet from inside his flannel shirt.

Kathleen dried her eyes against his shoulder. "What's this?"

"Open it and see."

"A deed?"

"To our orchard. I convinced the owner to parcel out that piece of land for me. It's too hilly for easy building. The trees are old but still produce. I thought we might open a cidery, plant some new trees, grow a small business as a hobby. The condo developer said he planned to call the street into the place Apple Blossom Lane and needed some real ones to back up the name."

"Roy Marshall, you are going to get some tonight!" Kathleen embraced her husband and placed a big kiss on his lips.

Heath cringed, but Jane turned toward Merlin with her misty lake green eyes. "Isn't this perfect?"

"We should drive there after dinner and show the place to Merlin!" Jane's mother exclaimed.

"You know my hybrid won't make it up that hill in this weather," Roy said, shaking his head. "We'd have to dig Heath's truck out."

Merlin, uncertain what he'd put in motion, parted the ecru lace curtain over the tall parlor window and checked the depth of the snow where his truck sat. Heath's vehicle, a modest red single cab, some foreign brand, sat in the driveway up to its axles and capped with a foot of the white stuff, but he and Jane had arrived later in his jacked-up rig.

"You want to go, I've got a truck can get you there, ma'am."

\*\*\*\*

The women got busy in the kitchen and produced a full turkey dinner by 2:00 p.m. Naturally, the Marshalls did have a fancy dining room right next to that library. The huge mahogany table with twelve matching chairs and a massive sideboard wouldn't fit in any normal-sized house. While a centerpiece of all natural greens, berries, and pinecones graced its center, the beeswax candles glowed in many branched silver candelabrums. At least the menu was familiar to Merlin, being nearly a duplicate of the one Jane prepared for him on Thanksgiving right down to the cranberry relish. No foie gras or snails in garlic butter like the rich might eat. He'd tried both once and didn't much care for either.

"Are you enjoying the turkey, Merlin? It's wild game. We hung and marinated it in advance," Kathleen said.

"I know it died happy, ma'am," he answered. All but a grinning Jane seated next to her grandmother across the table stared at his remark. "I mean being in the great outdoors and free until its last days."

"When I blew its head off," Heath added. "No birdshot in this baby. Right, Dad?"

"Yes, we both took the limit. Got a freezer full of them."

"They're coming back in Louisiana, mostly in the north part of the state. I'd like another one of those tasty rolls. I'll bet you made them yourself, Miss Kathleen." Laying on the butter never hurt according to Jane.

"Oh, you southern boys with your Ma'ams and Misses. Just call me Kathleen. I did make them from scratch and froze them for the occasion. We don't like to be in the kitchen all day on Christmas. Your choice of fresh apple pie or real pumpkin from our own garden for dessert. Made them yesterday."

"I must have some of both."

"I do wish you could stay longer," Jane's grandmother said. "With the roads the way they are, you could drive Jane to her job interview in Billings. I'm so hopeful that she will soon live closer to us, and we'll see her more often."

"What job interview? I thought we agreed you'd wait and see if the parish would rehire you come the New Year when the recycling program starts up again." Merlin watched the guilt rise in the form of a blush on Jane's face from directly across the table.

Next to him, Heath bumped his elbow. "I talked to

some people I knew in Billings to get her the interview. Pays more than any parish job. I'm fairly sure my sister will be moving to Montana shortly unless she gets a better offer."

Merlin took a moment to control his temper. When he spoke, he addressed Jane's grandmother. "I'm sorry I won't be here to do that favor for you, Miss Ellen. I have a three-day drive ahead of me, and I'm on duty flying as soon as I get back. She'll have to call and let me know how that interview goes, yeah." He shot one of his black glares at Jane, however.

"Time for pie and coffee," Kathleen said brightly. "Place your orders now. Merlin, I know what you want. How about the rest of you?"

Everyone decided on small pieces of both. Jane and her mother carried in the plates holding the slices garnished with real whipped cream and a dash of cinnamon. Ellen poured coffee from a tall porcelain pot that matched the platinum-rimmed dinnerware and prepared each cup from the cream and sugar set.

"My wedding china," she told Merlin with a fond smile. "I'm going to leave it to Jane because she will never get any of her own."

"Because it's conspicuous consumption, not because she won't marry," Kathleen hastened to add. "I certainly never had any."

After that exchange, the conversation died off. The men cleared the table with Merlin joining right in, but he spoke not a word. Afraid he would break or scratch something, he declined to help with the hand washing and drying of the fine china and silver, but offered to scrub the pots and pans and let the rest of the family digest their meal in the parlor.

Jane stayed in the kitchen with him drying each one as he finished. "What's wrong, Merlin? You haven't used even one sexist endearment all day."

That forced a small smile from him. "So you miss it, sweet thang—or should I say 'my goddess.'"

"That's Mom and Dad's endearment, not ours."

"Oh, so we exchange endearments, but don't mention major life changes like moving to Montana, huh?"

"I knew you'd be upset and had no reason to tell you unless they offered me the job. I can't keep living off you like some Fifties housewife because that is not who I am."

"Sure you can. You could cook and clean and have my babies and stay home."

Jane brandished a newly cleaned saucepan at his head. "Say that once more, Merlin Tauzin, and I'll let you have it."

Obviously, she missed the joke. He twisted the pot from her hand and set it aside. "If we didn't have a parlor full of people, I'd carry you upstairs and show you…" How much I love you, but he never got that part out before she verbally attacked.

"Neanderthal!"

Kathleen poked her head in the doorway. "Nearly ready to go to Apple Blossom Hill? Wait until you see how beautiful it is there, Merlin." She'd changed into tan wool slacks, snow boots, and a long, brown knit tunic with gold embroidery around the neckline and hem, but obviously still rebelled against wearing a bra.

"I'm ready *tout de suite.* Let me get my coat and keys."

"French, I love that!" Kathleen said as she led them

from the kitchen.

Merlin stalked to the ornate coat rack and shrugged into his peacoat. He checked the pockets for the keys and the small box, both still there. While reaching to retrieve his black watch cap, Ellen summoned him to the parlor. He tucked his hat in a pocket and went to see what she wanted.

"Come here, dear boy. I'm not going along because I do fear falling, but you must learn to dress for the cold. Bend down." When he complied, she wrapped the striped scarf around his neck several times and pulled the hat with the pompom down over his ears. "And don't forget your mittens."

"No, ma'am." He shoved them deep into the opposite pocket of his jacket figuring he could switch them out with his driving gloves in the truck.

Wearing her long, red coat, fuzzy white mittens and a cap made of the same furry yarn with pompoms on the strings that tied beneath her chin, Jane appeared in the archway of the parlor. On her, the outfit looked cute, but she smirked a little at his appearance.

"Heath shoveled a path to the truck. We should get going. It gets dark early here."

He didn't want to look at himself in the mirror of the coat rack when he passed, so he kept his eyes on Jane. He knew the exact moment when she noticed his duffel by the door. She spun and faced him.

"You were going to run out on me this morning! I can't trust you to stay, and you have the gall to get that beak of a nose out of joint because I didn't tell you about the job interview." Jane stamped outside, slamming the door in his face so hard that when he opened it again, the large Christmas wreath lay on the porch.

Merlin replaced the wreath on its hook and held the door for Kathleen and Roy to pass. The couple exchanged glances the way the long married often did—as if they could read each other's minds. His grandparents used to do that kind of thing. Probably, he would never get to that point with Jane where they understood each other so well words weren't needed. She should know why the job interview and her lack of faith in him mattered more than his going home early for her own good so as not to embarrass her in front of her family. He'd blown it with her again.

As Merlin walked down the narrow path scooped in the snow to his truck, Heath mocked, "Looks like we've found Waldo," referring to the picture book character given to wearing red and white stripes and a pompom cap.

Merlin got right in his face. "I know a man named Waldo I truly despise. Never call me that again, you hear? It's Merlin or Blackie and nothing else. Now get in the truck, Heathcliff." He opened the doors.

"Touchy," Heath said.

"You leave my brother alone." Jane pointedly climbed into the backseat without assistance.

Looking rather pleased, Heath joined her there. Roy lifted his short, round goddess inside and took the shotgun seat. He gave the directions going south out of town to an area where the earth lay disturbed under shallow drifts between stakes in the ground marking out the plats of the new condos. A steep hill without a road rose directly behind the graded area. The twisted black trunks of old apple trees spread out in even rows, their branches so coated with snow they might have been in bloom.

"Want me to take you to the top, because I could do that," Merlin offered.

"No. We should get out and walk to spare the roots of the trees. Jane knows where we're going," Kathleen told him.

As soon as he unlocked the doors, Jane and Heath got down and raced off nimble as arctic hares. Their warm breath sent white plumes into the air as they ran. Merlin started after them, but Kathleen held him back.

"I'm going to need some help getting up there. It's icy, and I don't want to break a hip anymore than my mother does. Gentlemen." She hooked one arm around her husband's elbow and snagged Merlin with the other. They set off at a sedate pace.

"Talk to him, Roy."

"Son, we know you're brave. You proved that by serving your country. But, there is also emotional courage. Sometimes, you just have to put yourself out there and say what's on your mind."

"Even when a woman just told you off?"

"Oh hell, yes. How do you think I got Kathy to marry me? She was screaming at me about raping the earth with my oil wells, and I got on my knees and said we might have different opinions on that issue, but I knew we loved each other and could make it work."

"And we have," Kathleen added.

"I have to say marrying a very opinionated woman will change you," Roy continued.

"For the better," his wife said.

"You don't have to tell me that. I already noticed. Are you saying I have your blessing?"

"We're saying go for it. Go, go, go." Kathleen

dropped Merlin's arm and gave him a little shove forward toward the spot where Jane and her brother waited by the biggest tree with a long, low spread of branches in the center of the frozen orchard. "That's where we were married. I can't think of a better place."

Merlin strode forward. He shed the absurd hat, stuffed it in his pocket with the mittens, and replaced it with his black watch cap. Unwinding the scarf, he shoved that inside his coat. When he took his chance, he did not intend to look like Waldo, any Waldo. Reaching Jane, he dropped to his knees as suddenly as a hawk stooping from the sky above and grasped her hand in its fuzzy, white mitten.

"Jane Marshall, will you marry me? I love you and never want to be without you for the rest of my life. I know I'm not good enough, but have mercy." He took the deep blue velvet box from his pocket, flicked it open, and offered her the ring he'd carried for two weeks, unable to find the right time or the right words to present it. He believed the first part of the proposal went well, but wasn't sure about the rest. Too bad because that was how he felt—unworthy and at her mercy.

Jane's other hand flew to her mouth, then fluttered in the air. "Oh, get up, get up. It must be ten degrees out here. You'll freeze to the ground, and your jeans aren't lined. I'm wearing mittens. How can I be wearing a pair of Gran's mittens at a time like this? I didn't expect a proposal, not now, not at all!"

Still clutching her hand and completely perplexed, Merlin rose slowly. "Is that a no or a yes? Should I put this away?" He offered her the ring again.

Jane pulled off a mitten with her teeth and held out

her ring finger. Her dad got a picture on his digital camera just before she remembered to spit out the mitten and say, "Yes, oh yes!"

That one would make the family album whether she liked it or not. The most embarrassing photos always did, but Roy took another of Merlin placing the ring on Jane's finger and kissing her before the backdrop of real apple trees lacy with snow. He made them pose again in the same stance as the fake apple blossom picture and then another gazing outward down the valley with Merlin's arm around Jane's shoulder.

There might have been more poses, but Heath began to complain, "Dad, it is cold as a witch's tit out here. Can we go now?"

"For shame, Heath Cliff Marshall. Some of my best friends are witches, very nice ones, though I don't go in for that sort of thing myself," Kathleen reprimanded him.

"Sorry, Mom. Still freezing. The sun is getting low."

Reluctantly, Jane covered her hands with her mittens. Merlin fished out the scarf, wrapped it around his neck and the lower half of his face, grateful for its warmth if not for its style. Kathleen claimed both her husband and Merlin to assist her again as the way had grown icier and more tricky going down. Heath and Jane went ahead. Over his wife's head, Roy whispered to his son-in-law to be, "If Jane takes after her mother you will never be disappointed in bed."

"I heard that. My silver wolf is absolutely right," Kathleen agreed. Merlin nodded and did not let on what he already knew.

Back at the house, Jane immediately ran to show

her grandmother the ring. "Most unusual," Ellen said as if she might have preferred something more traditional.

Merlin took Jane's hand and displayed the ring. "Mr. LeClerc designed it for me. The center diamond isn't very big, but it is perfect and old, so the cut has more sparkle than most today, the jeweler told me. It belonged to my Granny. She gave it to me after she met Jane and claimed she couldn't get the ring over her knuckle anymore. I should give it to my bride someday."

"I do understand that." Ellen gazed down on the swollen joints of her own ringless hands. "I'll save mine for Heath."

"Shouldn't she have passed it along to your mother or Brittney?" Jane said with just a twinge of guilt.

"No. My mother could lose it, and Brittney would sell it. Granny knows that. I had it reset. These little yellow stones in the half circle around the diamond are topazes. They represent the rays of the setting sun. The emerald slivers running along band, that's supposed to be sugarcane." Seized with a moment of doubt, Merlin asked, "Do you think it's too gaudy? Mr. LeClerc said he'd take it back if you didn't like it, but he seemed fairly sure you would."

"I love it right down to its recycled center stone. It's unique, like you." Jane grasped his bearded chin to lower his head for a kiss.

"Manly yet sensitive like your father," Kathleen sighed. "Where is my own dear man?"

"In the kitchen setting out the leftovers for dinner," Heath answered. "I think we should eat before it gets anymore sickly sweet in here."

"Your day will come, Heathcliff. I guarantee you

me," Merlin said.

They ate. They listened to the Mormon Tabernacle Choir on PBS and watched *It's a Wonderful Life* playing endlessly on another channel. When Jane and Merlin decided to go up to bed at exactly the same time, no one commented. They chose to spend the night in Merlin's designated room at the far end of the hall away from parents and brother and kept the lovemaking quiet. In the morning, he told Jane to stay in bed and tucked the feather comforter tight around her. He wanted to make an early start without waking anyone. She listened to his big-ass truck roar toward the sunrise until she could hear it no more before going back to sleep.

Merlin Tauzin went back to Louisiana sure of one thing. Jane would be coming home to him.

Chapter Thirty-One

Merlin waited for her at the airport gate. Jane saw him standing at the foot of the escalator as she left the security area. He looked up, clean-shaven, fresh haircut, and wearing a blue dress shirt open at the collar with new khakis possessing a razor-sharp crease. The middle-aged woman with whom she'd shared the cramped seats on the small jet from Dallas said, "Wish he was waiting for me."

"I'm afraid he's all mine."

Impatient with the queue forming at the escalator, she took the stairs straight into his arms. After a gratifying kiss long enough to draw embarrassed stares from other passengers, they walked hand in hand to the baggage carousel to wait for the beep and roll of the luggage. Jane studied his long face. The electric blue eyes held something she'd never seen there before—happiness backed up with an instant broad smile that said the same.

"You look wonderful, Merlin."

"You, too."

He lied. She had poorly concealed circles under her eyes, chapped lips slathered with gloss, and a pale face amped up with a little blusher. No matter how hard she tried, her curling iron failed to turn all the ends of her straight hair under in a becoming way. She wore a touch of gold jewelry donated by her grandmother, her engagement ring, and a slinky black travel knit ensemble guaranteed not to wrinkle. Unfortunately, the coffee she'd spilled with her nervous hands on the plane left stains on the apple green turtleneck shell she wore under it. With the jacket worn buttoned, only she would know the difference, but still.

Having spent the night in Dallas in order to arrive early enough for the unemployment hearing today, she'd let her nerves keep her up going over and over what she would say. Her mother rehearsed her for days as if preparing her for a Supreme Court testimony, always emphasizing that her daughter needed to do this for her fellow employees. Kathleen had some experience with the process having once been fired for her unorthodox views, but she'd proved beyond a doubt that her personal beliefs did not intrude into her classroom. Not only had she won against the school board, she'd collected compensation and a settlement as well. A less rigid community college soon gave her a contract. Jane prayed, not for her sake so much as for Merlin's, that her outcome would be as successful. What if recycling was not restored? What if the parish did not rehire her? She refused to be a drain on his resources.

They drove back to Chapelle in the big-ass truck, though he could have used her hybrid. She declined to mention that. Other things mattered more.

"Thanks for taking today off to meet me. Did you get to see Doyle again before he left?"

"Yep. I feel good about his chances of coming home now. While we were on our way to Montana, he met up with a girl who'd been writing to him, one of these deals to support our troops they set up at Holy

Mom's. They went to high school together, and I think he had a little crush on her, but being a fat kid with mostly just nice going for him, he didn't stand a chance. Now, he's a trim man in a uniform who wants to start his own trucking business once he gets out of the service. She has secretarial training and could run an office. Courtney Plaisance, you know her?"

"Yes, a very nice young woman, pretty, too. She's May Robin's grandniece. She came to the retirement party."

Merlin answered, "Right," as if he held something back, but he continued. "She was working for Bernard Freeman when I went to visit with him, but I set her straight on what kind of snake he is. She quit. Looks like she might be part of our family in the future. Having someone to come home to makes a man overseas a lot more cautious and a lot less stupid. I doubt if they would have called me The Magician for my exploits if you'd been waiting for me."

"Then, we probably would not have met at all since you would have been a different man. I love you as you are." She did mean that, but knew her answer came out distracted by the looming hearing.

"Your dad said you'd change me for the better."

"No, you will change yourself. You already have."

"Thanks for canceling that job interview."

"Heath was pissed, but my mom said I had to follow my heart."

"I like your mom. Heath, well, he wants to look out for you like I should have for Brittney. I understand that. Don't slug me now, but you need not go through with this hearing. Like I said before if your old job doesn't come back, start your own consulting service

309

out of your home office. I'm putting the house in both our names."

"Merlin, you are still keeping me. I need to do this."

Getting to know her better, he did not argue the point. "You want to stop for something to eat or go straight home?"

"Let's pick up May and see if she'd like to go to lunch. The least we can do is feed my only witness. The others were too afraid to testify on my behalf. Retirement does have its privileges."

May received them with every curl of her red hair in place, her cheeks rouged, and her scrawny body draped in what seemed to be a lifetime's accumulation of good jewelry, from her small diamond hoop earrings to her numerous gold bangles and necklaces to a large gemstone brooch pinned to the jacket of her dark green suit. They went to eat at a sandwich shop near the unemployment office, which had a fancier name, the Office of Workforce Development. No one called it that. A person went there when out of a job to file for a check, but rarely to find new work.

Jane picked at a salad with a dozen medium-sized shrimp in it. Merlin had a steak and cheese. May delicately ate the four triangles of a club sandwich and told them what she intended to say. Jane nodded and thanked her. Stomach clenching, she walked with them to the hearing. Merlin waited outside the glass-walled room. Nadia Nixon already sat inside, grim in her prison warden gray, and escorted by Didi LaRoche, who resembled a newly arrested prostitute in her tight, low-cut attire. He watched Jane and May take places on the opposite side of the table and gave them a thumbs up that drew a shaky smile from his fiancée. An officious, gray-haired woman, thin as a sword, entered with a file and a clipboard and claimed the head of the table. A second HR employee followed her into the room, but sat discreetly on a chair in the corner—a witness, person to call for help if things got out of hand, perhaps. The hearing began.

"I am Sharon Leger. I will be your mediator today. The proceedings will be recorded for accuracy." Ms. Leger noted the date, time, and those in attendance. "You may speak first Ms. Nixon. Ms. Marshall, please do not interrupt."

"Jane Marshall was a problem employee, insubordinate, late for work, unable to complete a crucial proposal in a timely manner. And she ordered shoes online during working hours."

Jane gasped and started to refute, but Ms. Leger held up a hand. "You will have your turn. Were these infractions documented? Was the employee given time to correct her behavior?"

"Mostly, she was insubordinate to me. The other employees liked her, and our parish president showed a fondness for Jane. He did not allow me to write her up, but I brought Miss LaRoche as a witness to those behaviors."

"Oh, yeah. I saw her ordering things online all the time. Jane was real snotty to Miss Nixon and came in late lots of times." Didi dug in her little gold bag for a pack of gum and shoved a stick into her mouth. "Sorry, my mouth is dry."

"Is that all you have to say, Miss LaRoche?"

"Ah, no. She was a lousy receptionist. Jane only wanted to work on her fancy grants, not deal with people and phone calls at the front desk, which is an important job, too." Didi puffed out her chest. Jane swore the woman had gone up a bra size since she'd been gone. Her breasts nearly spilled out of a red surplice-wrapped dress that tied beneath them with a gold cord. "I'm the receptionist now. I know how the work should be done, and Jane didn't do it right."

May hissed through her shining white dentures. "As if trash like you could ever properly represent the parish."

"Silence! My file shows that Ms. Marshall held the position of parish environmental project manager. Why did she staff the front desk?"

Nadia jumped in, perhaps regretting she'd brought a witness. "We are shorthanded due to staff cutbacks. Everyone is expected to help where needed. Since the recycling contract was not renewed, Jane had less to do than anyone, but she did not accept her new duties gracefully."

"What about time cards showing her tardiness? Do you have those?"

"No, but the main issue here is her using her lunch hour to complete a proposal because she neared a crucial deadline and hadn't done all the work. Employees are required to take a lunch break for their health and wellbeing. It is against the law to do otherwise, but I caught her running copies. I fired her immediately for this infraction. As far as I know, she neglected to finish a proposal that would have gained funds to clean up a polluted site in the parish. Jane Marshall was a bad employee. I'm done." Nadia planted her large fists on the table with a hard rap.

Ms. Leger nodded to Jane. "Your turn."

"I'd like to let May Robin speak first. She served as receptionist at the council offices before I was forced into her role."

May eagerly spoke up. "I served at the front desk for forty years before Miss Nixon accused me of perpetrating a crude joke on her and ordered me to take my retirement or be fired. Always a lady, I would never have done such a thing. I carried myself with utmost propriety and dressed in a seemly manner."

May rolled her light eyes at Didi. "I believe I was set up to be discharged either because of my age or because Miss Nixon really wanted to be rid of Jane and conspired against her."

"No conspiracy theories, please. Have you anything relevant to Miss Marshall's case to reveal."

May adjusted her jacket and sat up very straight in complete contrast to Didi whose long, crossed leg and slim, arched foot dangled a four-inch stiletto heel with a gold rose above the open toe of her shoe. "I accepted my retirement since I didn't want to make trouble for Woof, I mean President Langlois. Jane was immediately pressed into my position. At first, I thought she wanted the job, but it pays less than hers, so I changed my mind about that. The desk is very busy and would not allow anyone to work on a serious project while staffing it. Miss Nixon knew that. I think she was out to get Jane because everyone liked her and hated Nadia."

"Speculation. Anything else?"

"I only want to say that Jane Marshall worked hard and was rarely tardy. If she came in late, she stayed late. She took work home to complete without being compensated for that time because there were not enough hours in the day for all she had to do—and that was before Miss Nixon put her on the desk. That's all."

Ms. Leger jotted a few notes and looked at Jane above her half-framed glasses. "Thank for your testimony. Ms. Marshall, let's hear from you."

"Yes, thanks, May." Jane took a deep breath and tried to remember her rehearsed speech, but the accusation about the shoes, unexpected and untrue, rankled in her mind. "First of all, I own fewer than a dozen pairs of shoes, and I do not order them online—though I have seen others in the office do this." She stared at Didi's outlandish heels available nowhere in Ste. Jeanne d'Arc Parish.

"Give me their names, and I'll see they are fired," Nadia growled.

"As if I would ever do that under these circumstances!"

Ms. Leger stifled a faint smile. "Let us put the shoe issue aside as Ms. Nixon has no concrete proof of that allegation. Go on."

"As May said, I always made up my time if I arrived late and frequently took projects home to complete without charging the parish for those hours. Once I was commanded to take over the front desk duties, I continued to work even more at home and did finish and mail the project in question. While government slows to a crawl over Christmas, we should be hearing from the EPA soon, successfully, I hope."

Jane took a deep breath before continuing. "It is true I was working on my lunch hour to complete the project. By being assigned another full-time job as well as my own, I saw no other way to get it done. I think in the private sector, this would have been seen as admirable, but I was fired within minutes of Miss Nixon finding me in the copy center and marched from the building. I didn't attempt to injure the parish in any way or claim extra compensation for my additional work. That is all I have to say."

Jane had forgotten parts of her speech. Too late now. Ms. Leger turned off the recorder, finished her notes, and stood, dismissing them all.

"You will get written confirmation of the outcome. If a decision is made in Ms. Marshall's favor, she will receive all of her compensation to date and be eligible for six more months at which time it may be renewed if she cannot find a comparable job." The woman and her shadow companion left the four adversaries alone.

Didi unwound from her chair slowly, taking a minute to get her balance on her high heels. She placed a hand on a small baby bump now clearly visible beneath her red dress. "I guess I need to give up nice shoes soon. Don't want to fall and injure my precious bundle."

Sashaying out the door and giving Merlin a lingering look, Didi added a little extra bounce in her booty simply because an attractive man sat there to admire it. Nadia blocked Jane's way with her square, unattractive body.

"I don't see why this matters to you, Marshall. Look at you with your gold jewelry and that fancy ring on your finger. Seems like you, May, and Didi are all somebody's mistress and don't need to work for a living like me."

"This is my engagement ring, Nadia, and I know you wish me well." Jane quirked her lips at her long time nemesis. "But, I would have fought you regardless for—truth, justice, and the American way." Not what she wanted to say, it came out sounding ridiculous.

Nadia wagged her stubby, blonde ponytail back and forth. "As if those things ever existed, except in the minds of puny idealists like you. Save the earth, my ass. Around here it's drill, baby, drill."

"Excuse me, but you are in my fiancée's way." Merlin rose behind Nadia like a dark thunderhead about to loose a bolt of lightning into a stagnant, gray pond.

She got out of Jane's road but fired off a final shot. "Yeah, I heard you were running with crazy Merlin Tauzin. Good luck with that."

Jane answered, "You know what, Nadia? I wish you love, any kind you prefer."

Red in the face and unable to find a retort, the parish chief administrative officer followed her pregnant snitch from the building. May tapped her spindly fingers together in silent applause.

"I think you won, *cher* heart. I'm going to tell you two a secret no one else knows. Woof isn't running for office again. His wife has Alzheimer's and doesn't so much as remember his name. We're going off together once he finishes this term. Elvira, a hard woman, never would give him a divorce. She said she'd ruin him politically and get him excommunicated from the church. Divorce, not such a big deal now, but way back then, yes. Our love can't hurt her now. Their children will take care of her, and when Elvira passes maybe I'll finally get a wedding band instead of lots of good jewelry to keep me happy."

"You and Woof, I still can't believe it," Jane said, gossip confirmed by the person involved.

May smiled at Merlin. "Your granny knew

everything all along and probably most of the parish except for newcomers like Jane. You are a good man for keeping a secret, Blackie, a good man all around. Bernie had his snake eyes on Courtney and was already starting to make moves on her. She came and talked to me for a long time. I told her she should go for the man with the big heart, not a huge, swinging dick—unless the guy has both."

May cackled and elbowed Merlin in the side. "I think our families will soon be joined, and I could not be happier. Bernard Freeman will run for Woof's office now, but I don't expect him to win, especially if word gets around about his pregnant mistress—and I think it might. Receptionists see and know a lot."

"Didi? I knew she owed her job to one of the councilmen, but Bernie Freeman with his perfect wife and kids? She seems too tacky for him."

May patted Jane's cheek with her age-spotted hand. "You are so sweet, always thinking the best of everyone and everything. Sometimes that pays off." She pinched Merlin's big chin. "Mostly it doesn't. Bernie started fooling around on his wife as soon as the flowers withered on old Leroy Mouton's grave. I suspect he took his pleasures out of town up until then. Woof and I used to run into him at some of our hideaways. But, when a man breaks loose after years of being on a leash, sometimes he goes right to the first shiny thing he sees and puts his mark on it. That Didi, she has no class. Come on. It's after three, I'm buying the drinks."

May wanted to treat them to strawberry daiquiris at a drive-thru bar on the way to her house. Merlin refused on the basis of being the driver, but Jane, nerves shot, accepted. After they dropped off May, she leaned against Merlin's comforting shoulder and sucked the alcoholic red slush in her go-cup with a straw.

"I'm not so sure we won. After all, I did work on my lunch hour. And that stuff about Woof and May, Didi and Bernard. I can't take it all in."

"Forget about it. What you need to do is get naked and spend the rest of the day in bed with me, kitten."

Ah, Merlin, cheering her up with a sexist remark. She responded in kind. "Sounds like a perfect idea to me, my great big Cajun stud. Can you drive this big-ass truck any faster?"

Chapter Thirty-Two

Jane positioned her framed photographs on her home office desk. No more Nadia to tell her how unprofessional that was. Sunset to the right, apple blossoms to the left, and the family portrait in the middle. She smoothed out her copy of the newspaper clipping with the letter about recycling and Merlin's ad of support, then folded it neatly in half to place in a file folder. Bernard Freeman's perfect, smiling family gazed out at her. What a sham!

She contrasted it with the picture of Merlin's mildly dysfunctional family and found she preferred them, quirks and all. At least they were genuine, their faults up front. Something about the two pictures nagged at her, maybe the same pose with the men behind and the women on the couch. No, Milly's pose was typical of most groupings. Then, she saw it, how Merlin would fit neatly into the Freeman family as the oldest son standing right next to his father—Bernard Freeman—same height, same eyes, same big blue-black jaw. How could she have missed it? Among the Tauzins, Merlin stood out like a hawk raised by two little hens and a very feathery rooster.

The phone rang. Merlin, making them tomato soup and toasted cheese sandwiches in the kitchen, picked it up. Not merely a junk call, someone engaged him in conversation, probably his granny or mother. Good. She needed a minute to accept her discovery. In fact, she needed some air. She went quietly out the front door and inhaled the cold dampness of January. The purple and gold pansies in their bed flourished despite the weather. Walking to her mailbox, she picked up its contents and took the *Chapelle Clarion* from its slot. She ran her eyes down the headlines on the way back. *Recycling to be restored.* Jane dashed to share the news with Merlin.

She found him in her office staring at the evidence of his birth, the folded piece of newspaper directly under his family's photograph. His face appeared pale beneath his stubble, and his eyes bleak as a winter's day.

"You know," he said.

Jane nodded. "I figured it out by the resemblance just as you must have. I should have seen it sooner."

"My family made sure we weren't seen together. I went to public school, his sons to private. I get a chance at the local college. His boys attend Tulane. Best of all I go off to war where I have a good chance of getting killed and ending the problem of my existence altogether. You want to give that ring back now that you know I'm the son of a man we both despise?"

"Never crossed my mind. You are more Tauzin than you ever will be Freeman."

"Before you decide, you might want to hear the rest. My grandparents were the salt of the earth. Mom can't help how she is, and even Harley has his better points. Doyle is a good guy, but Brittney is out of control. That was her on the phone. She's pregnant again. This time she wants me to confront the father and get her a better deal. She figures he'll be afraid of me."

"The same man? Please, not Bernie." Jane put a hand on his arm, steadying them both.

"Nope, thank God for small favors. She says she probably caught that night we were at Broussard's Barn by giving Waldo Robin a pity fuck after I beat him up. See, he wasn't after my mother at all. He thought she was Brittney."

"Is he Jayden's father, too?"

"Yep, so she tells me now. What a sucker. Even at sixteen Brittney knew how to manipulate men. Waldo was still married to his second wife who was looking for a way out of that prenup that would take him for a bundle. My sister, a high school girl and pregnant, could have given her all the ammunition she needed. He paid up to keep Brittney quiet. She claims he let her alone until I punched him out, so it's my fault he took comfort in her arms again. Yeah, right. He just wanted to screw my little sister for some revenge."

"You don't know that. Even Waldo has feelings, deeply buried, but still there."

"Sure you still want to be part of my family? Can your kin endure a scandal?"

"It's not up to them, but I did tell them about your origins as far as I knew at the time. My mother thinks you should bring the man to justice who took advantage of your mother. My dad says the fellow should be roped, tied, bobbed, and branded for what he did to Jenny."

Merlin nodded, and Jane thought she noticed a smile trying to get out on the edge of lips. "I like that last idea and appreciate your mother's viewpoint. Neither will happen at this late date. I think your mom in a mellower moment might say to let karma take care of Bernie. So, you're still willing to marry me?"

Jane cupped his long jaw in her hands and stroked with her thumbs. His eyes closed like those of a contented tom cat. She put her lips on his and when she finished the kiss, said, "I will. Now, how is that lunch coming, my gourmet chef?"

"The sandwiches are slightly burnt on one side, little chickadee. I forgot to turn them when Brittney called. After we eat, I'm going to see Waldo and let him know money won't buy him out this time. Not what Brittney wants from me, but I really don't give a damn."

"I'll go with you."

"No need."

"Just in case you forget to use your words, Merlin."

He shrugged. "I have my temper under control—pretty much, but your presence would be appreciated. Welcome to the Tauzin family."

"Oh, I nearly forgot. At last night's council meeting, Bernard Freeman moved in favor of restoring recycling and got the rest to agree. They are putting the bids out now. He claims my letter convinced him to change his mind, but I am beginning to see how you might have worked your magic."

Merlin grinned in a rather predatory way. "I may have more of Bernie in me than I'd like. Keep the secret quiet. Exposure is a terrible thing for magicians and politicians both."

****

Directly after dining on tomato soup and slightly burnt cheese sandwiches, they drove to Duchamp's Funeral Home, Waldo Robin, Director. Fortunately, the undertaker was unoccupied with either embalming or conducting a funeral. Exuding a sympathetic air, he showed them into his office where the wall shelves displayed the best in crematory urns. A large bouquet of white lilies in a remarkably similar vase graced his impressive black desk. In the background, Waldo's mix of inspirational music played softly recalling to Jane's mind their single disastrous date. The bruises from his brawl with Merlin had healed, though Waldo's long nose possessed a new bump. Jane thought it gave a little interest to his gloomy face.

The undertaker beckoned them to comfortable chairs, folded his cold hands together, and said, "First, let me congratulate the two of you on your engagement. I read the notice in the Sunday *Clarion.* Interesting pose with those apple blossoms in the background. I assure you both had I known of your deep relationship I would never have asked Jane out. Peace."

Waldo offered his hand to Merlin who kept his resting on his knees. "Well, then how may I be of service? Has your grandmother passed, Mr. Tauzin? So many of the elderly do in January, pneumonia carries them off."

"My granny says she'd rather be picked apart by crows than have your cold hands on her body when she goes." Hostility radiated from Merlin in waves.

Jane clutched his hand in case he decided to launch himself over the desk at Waldo. She dove into the conversation quickly. "Miss Olive is in good health, but Brittney is pregnant."

Waldo's pale face became absolutely ghostly in its pallor. "I see. Congratulations to her and the lucky father, a very attractive girl, your sister. But I don't see how this concerns me. I have to pick up a body at the clinic in an hour." He stood, hoping they would do the same.

The couple stayed put. Merlin's accusation came out deep and rough. "She says you are the father—again."

Waldo opened his mouth. They expected a denial to waft out like ectoplasm, but instead the funeral director said, "Same deal as last time, then. You can't say I haven't provided for the boy."

"Nope, that won't do. Last time I wasn't around to stand up for my sister. Considering the circumstances of my own birth, I spent some time reading up on the statute of limitations on statutory rape. Four years ago, Brittney was sixteen. I think we still have a window to prosecute—unless say, you'd want to marry her." Merlin's blue stare caught Waldo like a rabbit about to be carried off by an eagle. Even rabbits scream when trapped.

"Brittney is far too young for me! People would talk. I could be ruined."

"No more ruined than you would be by a jail sentence, and the scandal won't last as long."

Jane made a suggestion. "Why don't you elope before the cause becomes obvious? I think Brittney is the kind of girl who would love a trip to Vegas and a nice diamond ring."

"She would," Merlin agreed, suddenly amiable. "But my sister wouldn't want to live over a funeral parlor. She'd expect a nice house, her own car, private school for the kids. You might have noticed Brittney isn't as dumb as people suppose. In fact, she's fairly clever. She might be an asset to your business if you spruce her up a little."

Standing stiffly, his hands crossed protectively over his crotch, Waldo said, "I doubt she would accept me as a husband. Her motive seemed to be primarily money last time."

"You weren't free to marry last time. You go on and offer her those incentives. See what she has to say. Do it today, maybe right after you pick up that corpse." Merlin stood and offered to shake on it, but the man's hands continued to guard his privates.

He settled for saying, "Welcome to the family, brother. We'll show ourselves out." Merlin helped Jane from her chair, and tucking her arm under his, left Duchamp's Funeral Home a satisfied man.

"Awesome," Jane said. "You really should run for public office. Merlin Tauzin is quite the wheeler-dealer."

"I'd hate to think I inherited that skill from Bernie."

"Who will be running for parish president, leaving his council seat open. You should think about it."

Chapter Thirty-Three

The letter arrived when Merlin was flying offshore. Jane held her breath and opened the fat envelope from the unemployment office. She skimmed through the legalese to the decision. She won her appeal! A check for three-thousand dollars in back payments would be forthcoming and after that a regular stipend for the next six months, providing she continued to seek employment during that time. Ms. Leger noted that Jane Marshall had done no intentional harm to her employer in any way. All other accusations remained unsupported by hard evidence.

Now, she would meet her next car payment with no problem and be able to pay Merlin half the house note. She might take the time to set up an environmental consulting business and contact possible clients. Best of all, she could laugh in Nadia Nixon's broad, brutal face. Call Merlin right now! No, he might be flying. This had to be shared immediately with her mother, though that carried a certain hazard. Kathleen wanted to talk wedding plans every time they connected.

Regardless, Jane called the number in Bozeman and got the greeting, "So, have you decided whether you want a horse and carriage to take you from the service to the reception?"

"No horse and carriage."

"But they are environmentally friendly you have to

admit."

"Yes, they are—but, Mom, I won my appeal against Nadia—I mean the parish government!"

"With my coaching, I knew you would. No surprise there. Can I tell your grandmother we are definitely going with the wedding in the apple orchard when the flowers bloom and not some stuffy, old church? What do you think about a sunrise service and then an English wedding breakfast to follow like the ones in Regency novels?"

"Yes to the orchard, no to sunrise, too early. Maybe a nice brunch. I only want immediate family to attend. You know how I feel about gobs of money being wasted on fancy weddings when it could go to more important causes. In fact, tell people no gifts. They should make a donation to a charity of their choice."

Jane imagined her mother punching the air as Kathleen replied, "Yes, you are truly my daughter. Now, a minister, a justice of the peace, or a Wiccan priestess? I know a woman who does a very meaningful uniting of the male and female elements of nature."

Much as she hated bursting Kathleen's bubble, Jane replied, "Justice of the peace. You know Merlin's people are Catholic. The Wiccan would freak them out."

Her mother sighed. "Yes, you have been raised much more liberally than most. We have to make allowances for more narrow viewpoints."

"Mom, aren't you excited that I won?"

"Of course, dear. But you won't need the money for long. Really, you struck a blow for all working women against the establishment—and I rejoice that you stuck it to that bitch, Nadia, even more. Now when do we get together to go wedding dress shopping?"

"I'll find something down here. Don't worry about it. I do plan to continue working after my marriage, you know. Merlin shouldn't have to support me."

"Naturally. I mean I have every faith that you will find a new job soon. So much to plan if we are going to bring off this wedding by apple blossom time. We'll talk again soon, love." And Kathleen Marshall hung up.

Jane put the phone back in its bracket. It rang immediately. Probably her mother asking if she intended to be married in bare feet, mostly to annoy her grandmother. No, the caller ID indicated the parish council office. Had Nadia phoned to congratulate her, no hard feelings? Unlikely. She imagined with some glee Nadia's big, square teeth gnashing together in anger and frustration.

"Hello?"

"Wofford Langlois here, Jane." The parish president's voice sounded stronger and more sure of itself than at any time since Nadia Nixon had been forced on him as his Chief Administrative Officer. "I wanted to let you know we're opening the bids for the recycling contract in three weeks. We want you to be there in your old capacity of environmental project manager."

"You're offering me my former position?"

"Yes, indeed!"

Jane imagined Woof's hand giving her a genial high five by the tone of his voice. This is what she'd wanted: recycling restored, her old job back—but not so much anymore.

"Thanks for the offer, but I'm in the midst of

setting up a consulting business and planning my wedding. I'm not sure I want to return."

"We heard from the EPA. They are putting that abandoned oil well site on the National Priorities List, thanks to your work. Looks like they will want us to handle it locally since it is a relatively small cleanup. We need you to oversee the project. How about a five-thousand-dollar raise and a corner office?"

"Nadia's office? You may not realize yet that I won my appeal for unemployment payments. Miss Nixon won't take that news well. I really don't think I can work with her anymore, let alone share the same space no matter now roomy. I'll have to say no, but I am so glad you are bringing back recycling."

"Your ardent letter stirred the public and changed some minds on the council. Come back and take credit for your hard work. As for sharing the office, Nadia Nixon is no longer employed here."

Jane's feet wanted to do the happy dance around her desk. She tried to keep the satisfaction out of her voice when she asked, "Really? Did she take another job elsewhere?"

"I fired her. Ever since the council forced that woman on me, I've felt like my balls were in a vise, pardon my French. Always threatening, always saying she'd take matters to the council if I didn't agree with her methods of making the office more efficient. Bernie Freeman forced her on me, but as soon as I announced I wasn't running again, he didn't need her anymore. What she made me do to May—and you. I told the council over and over, all I needed was a competent secretary and a good receptionist, none of this expensive CAO business."

Jane remembered a little too vividly how he'd stood by and let Nadia fire a woman who served him in more than one capacity for forty years. "I'm glad you are back in control, but—"

"No buts. Our parish needs you. May is returning for a month on an hourly basis to train a new young woman to take charge of that front desk, Courtney Plaisance. You might know her since I hear Courtney is sweet on your fiancé's brother. We'll be just one big happy family at the council office if you return."

Woof had hired his own granddaughter, nepotism at its best, alive and well in the Deep South, even if few knew of the relationship. Jane, not really caring but more than willing to change the subject, inquired, "Is Didi LaRoche gone, too?"

"That woman doesn't project the proper image for Ste. Jeanne d'Arc Parish. I put her back in her old position because I have a soft spot for pregnant women and she needs the insurance, but I did make it clear she answers to me and spies for no one else as long as she works here. If I were her, I wouldn't count on, what do they call it now?—her baby daddy for much support."

"Yes, that's what they call it." Bernard the baby daddy. The thought made Jane want to laugh out loud. She contained herself. "I need to talk to Merlin about your offer since we're a team now."

"Outstanding young man with a future. I knew his grandfather well. Congratulations to the both of you on your upcoming marriage. If he needs my help in any way, you let me know."

Her fiancé would get a chuckle out of his public change in status from crazy Merlin Tauzin to outstanding young man. She'd phone him tonight and share all the new developments in the Garbage War.

"Thank you, Mr. Langlois. I'll let you know as soon as possible."

"Call me Woof. We're like family now. I'll be waiting. We need you, Jane. Bye now."

In the evening, she did call Merlin. He laughed out loud—a good deep sound like a bass drum—over their being part of Woof's family.

"Appears we are politically connected now."

"Yes, that might be a good thing in the future. What do you think about my taking the job?"

"Go for it. That's what you wanted."

"You made it possible for me. Everything worked out exactly as you said it would, Merlin the Magician. But now, I'm not so sure I want to go back, office politics and all that dreck."

"Return for now. Get recycling going again and clean up that contaminated site. You'll feel better. Then, quit after our first child is born sometime next year and ask for a say in choosing your successor."

"Sounds like an idea, but about this first child… Merlin, we haven't discussed when or how many or—"

"As soon as possible, as many as you want. I mean who are we saving this earth for if not our kids, right?"

"Right, but, Merlin…you still there?"

His laughter certainly was. "When I get back, I'll use my words—of persuasion, little mama. I love you, Jane. Night."

\*\*\*\*

Slumped down and stretched out to minimize his height, Merlin stayed in the back row of the council chamber three weeks later. A group of proactive recyclers provided an effective screen for a dark Cajun with unusually light eyes. He had no desire to attract his father's attention, but he would not miss Jane's big night. He watched her open and announce the bids after expressing her unhappiness that only two had been submitted, one from Cajuns Care Recycling out of Lafayette and the other from B.O Waste Hauling. Not shy, Burl Oubre sat in the front row wearing his mustard-colored jacket and cleaning his fingernails with a toothpick.

Frowning, Jane addressed the B.O. owner. "Mr. Oubre, when you were awarded the garbage contract against my better judgment, you indicated you had no interest in also providing a recycling program. Yours is the low bid, but in fact you have no equipment or facility to implement this service. Am I correct?"

"I've seen the light about recycling and have taken steps to give this parish the best service possible. Here you go, honey."

Burl leaned over his big belly to hand a large, brown envelope to the nearest councilman. It went hand to hand until it reached Jane sitting next to Woof and clearly under his protective wing for the time being. She opened it.

"It seems Mr. Oubre has purchased Cajuns Care Recycling and now possesses the means to fulfill the contract. We should take his bid under advisement at this time to make sure he can meet all the specifications." From the back of the room, Merlin thought Jane did a fine, professional job of hiding her disgust.

Bernard Freeman, his jaw blue-black and silver, his blue eyes glinting with power, spoke up loud and clear. "We have only the one bid from a local company that will bring more jobs to our parish. I move we accept the offer from B.O. Waste Hauling tonight."

One of his closest cronies on the council jumped to second the motion, which passed with only two dissenting votes. Politics as usual in Ste. Jeanne d'Arc Parish.

"Very well then, the bid is awarded to B.O. Waste Hauling," Jane said tersely. Merlin gave her big points for not rolling her eyes or beating her forehead bloody against the council table in frustration.

Burl Oubre got up and began shaking hands all around the council table. When he reached Jane, he offered a statement instead of his hand. "Now don't you worry, little lady. We are a little short on buggies, but I got some on order. You gonna be first on the list, I guarantee."

The best Jane could manage was a polite "Thank you, I appreciate that" and a worried glance in his direction as Merlin followed Oubre from the room and stopped him by the elevator. They exchanged words, but without heat, clearly reaching an understanding. Her part of the meeting concluded, Jane hurried after the pair. Merlin waited for her, letting Oubre go ahead.

"You didn't threaten him with bodily harm, did you?"

"Nope, my goddess. I told him I intend to run for the council and with my connections I will win. The best bin they have will be on our doorstep tomorrow."

Chapter Thirty-Four

When the apple blossoms bloomed in Montana, the wedding procession made its way along the path the men mowed the day before through knee-high yellow wildflowers to the largest tree in the grove. The bounteous wild mustard covered the disturbed earth and hid the stakes of the condominium layout. Jane had feared the beauty of this shining day would be marred by half-built apartments and large pieces of construction equipment sitting about, but the project failed to gain enough financing and the contractor moved on to more lucrative building for the time being.

Chosen by Kathleen Marshall, the justice of the peace, a tall, conscientious woman who delighted in the great outdoors and performing marriages, led the way without becoming in the least winded. The bridal couple, arm in arm, followed right behind because Kathleen said young women weren't to be given away like chattel. With her silver hair flowing down her back and a wreath of blossoms atop her head, she marched behind them wearing a long, gauzy pink gown she claimed replicated the one she'd worn on her own wedding day. In deference to her mother and daughter, she had agreed to wear a bra and promised to keep the white sandals on her feet this time. Her husband helped her along the rough path. Like all the men in the wedding party, except Doyle still in uniform, he'd forced himself into a black tuxedo not nearly as comfortable as the Nehru suit he'd worn the first time around the apple tree.

Jane had selected her gown from a vintage shop in New Orleans. The full tulle skirt was topped by a tight lace bodice in a floral pattern with long, fingertip sleeves and a high back. Rhinestones winked in the sunlight amid the folds of the skirt and the centers of the lace flowers. She exposed just enough flesh to showcase the solitaire diamond on the gold chain Merlin had given her as a wedding gift. Her dark hair remained styled the same as always, but she'd topped it with a very modest tiara once belonging to her grandmother's grandmother, and a wisp of a veil. Comfortable ballet slipper shoes covered her feet. Not everyone's idea of a wedding ensemble, but she liked its ease and the use of the old rather than the outrageously priced new. Merlin didn't care what she wore. She could come to him naked. In fact, he had suggested that one night when wedding planning got on his nerves.

Harley and Jenny, who had traveled all the way to Montana on his motorcycle, arrived at the tree puffing from the climb. Still, Jenny raised her face to the sun reveling in the beauty of the moment like a small, awestruck child. The apple blossom crown Kathleen provided for her slipped back on her long, streaked hair as she announced to no one in particular that her baby was getting married today and twirled around in her full pink skirt that belled out showing a white petticoat beneath. Jane had taken her along to the vintage store and let her select her own dress. With the gown's scooped, scalloped neckline and little cap sleeves she resembled a Fifties housewife dressed for church, but the outfit gave Jenny such joy that Jane did not mind. Her own mother heartily approved. "Do your own thing," Kathleen always said.

"Really, Mother, try to behave like an adult," Brittney reprimanded Jenny, trying to catch her breath as she clung to Waldo's arm.

Glum-visaged as ever and wearing one of his funeral director suits, her husband did not seem all that miserable with his new, very young wife, though with Waldo it was hard to tell. They had flown in first-class all the way into Bozeman.

Brittney wore her hair pinned up under a small hat with a veil and a large pink silk flower that clung to the side of her head in the latest style of British royalty. Her rose-colored silk maternity dress with its high collar hung straight from the neckline detouring over the mound of her very pregnant belly before falling to her knees. In the soft loam of the orchard, her stylish pumps sunk a little into the earth from supporting all that weight. The spa day and makeover Jane provided earlier showed in the subdued makeup of both mother and daughter. Brittney kept a firm hand on Jayden in his little white shorts and jacket as the child tried to pull away to run and twirl like his grandmother.

"Let them dance," Kathleen commanded and did a few spins herself.

Bringing up the rear, Heath and Doyle pushed their grandmothers along in wheelchairs bedecked with flowers and pink and white ribbons. Both wore pale pink pantsuits with white orchids pinned to their jackets though Ellen's was of tailored linen and Olive's of fuzzy, warm velour. Miss Olive let everyone know neither the altitude nor the temperature of Montana this time of year pleased her.

"Would have been warmer and kinder to old bones in Louisiana," she complained as Doyle put her into place near the wedding tree.

"I do understand," Kathleen said to her. "But isn't this glorious?" She pointed to the blue sky above, the fierce mountains in the distance, the golden meadow, the apple trees embellished with blooms, embracing them all with her wide-spread arms. "Are you upset that they aren't marrying in the Catholic Church, dear?"

Miss Olive considered for a moment. "*Mais*, no. If God ain't here today, he ain't nowhere."

"We could have booked a church," Grandma Ellen said, then relented. "But it is a beautiful day and a lovely spot. Kathleen, I am sorry I refused to come to your wedding all those years ago."

The only outsider to witness the vows was Courtney Plaisance who'd flown in with Doyle and Olive. In the spirit of the day, she wore a white dress sprigged with small pink flowers and accepted an apple blossom crown from Kathleen in good spirit after Brittney rejected it. A modest diamond ring sparkled on her finger, and she brought good wishes from May and Spring.

Squeezing Doyle's arm, she said, "I love your family. They are so—different." Jane sent her a smile.

The brief service began. No way could Merlin be convinced to write his own vows. "I'm no poet, me. I said that to myself the first time I tried to describe your eyes," he'd told Jane.

They agreed on one sentence each at the exchange of the rings. Merlin had chosen a thick gold band for his but refused to let Jane have any say in hers. When she got miffed, he explained that he and Mr. LeClerc had it all worked out. That calmed her down. Jane waited for his words as she held out her finger and saw her wedding band for the first time, a slim gold ring channeled with small chocolate diamonds.

"As your engagement ring represented the sun and the sugarcane fields of Louisiana, this band is brown like its rich soil and made especially for my earth goddess." Merlin Tauzin had dug deep and found his inner poet only for her. Jane blinked the tears from her eyes.

"Well, the priest wouldn't have approved of that," Olive remarked.

"My minister either," said Ellen in solidarity.

Jane ignored them. As she placed Merlin's ring on his long, strong finger, she said, "My falcon, I promise to fly by your side for all eternity."

"Perfect," Kathleen declared.

Epilogue

For the second time in one year, Jane emptied the contents of her desk at the parish council office into a cardboard box. Actually, she needed two for the many photographs and the straggling pothos vine that cluttered its surface. In no hurry, she took a moment to flip through the fat picture album of photos her father took of the wedding, plenty of scenes from the orchard naturally and many more from the champagne brunch at the historic hotel with its dark beams and elegant fixtures in downtown Bozeman.

The wedding party had a room to themselves, but the odd music mix of the Andrews Sisters and Cajun bands did draw some of the curious to the door. Eccentricity not being unusual in Montana, strangers wished them well and accepted a flute of sparkling wine and a piece of the three-layered, white wedding cake festooned with sugar petal apple blossoms if they had some time to stay. Merlin drank only for the toast and spent most of his time dancing, dipping Jane to the tune of *I'll be with You in Apple Blossom Time.* Her dad caught a great snapshot of that and of her new husband whirling the two grandmothers in their wheelchairs to a Cajun beat. Jenny, Kathleen, and Courtney all got their turn to dance with the groom.

Perhaps her favorite photo showed the look of absolute horror on Merlin's face when they left the reception for their honeymoon at the Old Faithful Inn in Yellowstone National Park. They found Big Blue, its tinted windows soaped with the words, "Just Married," trailing a stream of old shoes and flattened beer cans from its trailer hitch. Worst of all, Heath had duct-taped a Barbie doll in a wedding grown to its pristine hood. Jane made Merlin drive some way out of town before she allowed him to pull over and carefully remove both tape and doll, throwing it, the "recycled" cans and shoes into the back of the truck. After all, their families wished them luck in a most appropriate way. Wonderful memories.

Her last day at a job she'd fought to keep and Jane felt a little queasy, not that she minded leaving now. The recycling program rolled along gaining more participants monthly because of her public awareness campaign. The polluted site had been cleaned up. Already new plants and young trees greened its surface and wildlife returned. Her hand-picked successor, an eager young man with Super Fund experience, would move into her space on the second of January.

The new parish president, ready to take office, offered to let her stay on, though most of the department heads had been fired in the usual bloodbath following a change of administration. She pointed out the conflict of interest since her husband would shortly be sworn in as a district councilman. The candidate Bernard Freeman backed for that post lost to Merlin standing tall on a platform of regulated development, consideration of farmers and veterans, and vigorous environmental protection. At the debates, all hints that Merlin Tauzin might be unstable or unable to fulfill his duties because he worked offshore were soundly booed down by a chorus usually directed by Miss Olive and her cohorts from Magnolia Villa. They attended every rally and handed out campaign literature from the baskets on their walkers and wheelchairs. The ordinary people of Ste. Jeanne d'Arc parish, not big business, voted Merlin in as one of their own.

Bernie's bid for parish president failed in the four-way free-for-all that occurred when Woof announced he would not run for office again. While he beat two opponents and made it to the runoffs, word did get out that his light-skinned mistress had presented him with a daughter a few months before the final election. Voters weren't so much shocked at that—a pretty common occurrence among Louisiana politicians, any politician for that matter—but they did get upset with him for dishonoring the upright memory of their beloved Leroy "Lambo" Mouton. Some might have noticed his resemblance to Merlin as well, though the two stayed away from each other's events. Whatever the reason, it showed in a defeat at the polls. Jane knew Bernie would come back in one governmental incarnation or another. Some who sucked the public teat could never wean themselves from it. She felt no pity for him.

Jane had her own future business to build and a part to play in Doyle and Courtney's big Catholic wedding in the spring. Besides her sisters and Jane, Courtney invited Brittney to be among the bridal attendants now that Doyle's sister was a respectable matron, mother of a boy adopted by Waldo Robin, and an adorable girl who thankfully took after the female side of the family. Brittney could be seen in a tasteful black dress with accents of gold jewelry purchased at LeClerc's, not Walmart, as she liked to point out, at every funeral held in Duchamp's Funeral Home. Actually being a great help to Waldo, she dispensed tissues and sympathy, placed floral tributes and made coffee for the mourners. Brittney remained convinced that Jane harbored a jealousy of her new Cadillac with two kiddie seats in the rear and the large house possessing four white columns situated on Main Street, but when Jane thought of Waldo's cold hands on her body, she shuddered and grew nauseous again.

Nausea? Surely not already? She and Merlin had discussed the starting a family issue for several months after the wedding if you could call his hiding her birth control pills a discussion. She retaliated by making him use condoms. Finally, they agreed she'd stop taking the pills six months into their marriage and see what happened next. It could take years to get pregnant, right?

As if conjured by magic, Merlin appeared in her office doorway. "Courtney buzzed me in. Let me carry those boxes for you, cupcake. You might be in a delicate condition."

"I'm only a little bit late, big boy."

Merlin's smile burst forth without restraint from his black stubble. Leave it to a man with a big-ass truck to get the job done.

## A word about the author...

Once a librarian, now a writer of romance, Lynn Shurr grew up in Pennsylvania Dutch country. She attended a state college and earned a very impractical B.A. in English Literature. Her first job out of school really was working as a cashier in a burger joint. Moving from one humble job to another, she traveled to North Carolina, then Germany, then California where she buckled down and studied for an M.A. in Librarianship.

New degree in hand, she found her first reference job in the Heart of Cajun Country, Lafayette, Louisiana. For her, the old saying, "Once you've tasted bayou water, you will always stay here" came true. She raised three children not far from the Bayou Teche and lives there still with her astronomer husband.

When not writing, Lynn likes to paint, cheer for the New Orleans Saints and LSU Tigers, and take long road trips nearly anywhere. Her love of the bayou country, its history and customs, often shows in the background for her books.

You may contact Lynn at www.lynnshurr.com or visit her blog—lynnshurr.blogspot.com.

\*\*\*\*

### Other Books by Lynn Shurr

The Convent Rose

THE SINNERS SERIES:

Goals for a Sinner

Wish for a Sinner

Kicks for a Sinner

Paradise for a Sinner

Love Letter for a Sinner

Thank you for purchasing
this publication of The Wild Rose Press, Inc.
For other wonderful stories of romance,
please visit our on-line bookstore at
www.thewildrosepress.com.

For questions or more information
contact us at
info@thewildrosepress.com.

The Wild Rose Press, Inc.
www.thewildrosepress.com

To visit with authors of
The Wild Rose Press, Inc.
join our yahoo loop at
http://groups.yahoo.com/group/thewildrosepress/

www.ingramcontent.com/pod-product-compliance
Lightning Source LLC
Chambersburg PA
CBHW070531260626
47161CB00002B/333